"Nearly thirteen years ago, a sealed letter was sent to me. It was short and to the point. Your mother sent it. Do you know what it said?"

"No," I said quietly, wondering what was coming next.

"'I've just given birth to a baby boy,' she wrote, 'and he's the seventh son of a seventh son. His name is Thomas J. Ward, and he's my gift to the County. When he's old enough we'll send you word. Train him well. He'll be the best apprentice you've ever had, and he'll also be your last.'"

SEVENTH SON

JOSEPH DELANEY

Books 1 and 2 in the
LAST APPRENTICE
series

GREENWILLOW BOOKS
An Imprint of HarperCollinsPublishers

The Last Apprentice: Seventh Son
Copyright © 2005 by Joseph Delaney

Revenge of the Witch first published in 2004 and *Curse of the Bane* first published in 2005 in Great Britain by The Bodley Head, an imprint of Random House Children's Books, under the titles *The Spook's Apprentice* and *The Spook's Curse*. First published in hardcover in 2005 and 2006 in the United States by Greenwillow Books; first paperback editions 2006 and 2007.

The right of Joseph Delaney to be identified as the author of this work has been asserted by him in accordance with the Copyright, Designs and Patents Act, 1988.

Library of Congress Control Number: 2014952981
ISBN 978-0-06-220970-2 (pbk.)

First Edition
15 16 17 18 LP/RRDH 10 9 8 7 6 5 4 3 2

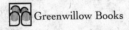 Greenwillow Books

FOR MARIE

❋ BOOK ONE ❋
REVENGE OF THE WITCH
1

❋ BOOK TWO❋
CURSE OF THE BANE
297

❈ BOOK ONE ❈
REVENGE OF THE WITCH

CHAPTER I
A Seventh Son

WHEN the Spook arrived, the light was already beginning to fail. It had been a long, hard day, and I was ready for my supper.

"You're sure he's a seventh son?" he asked. He was looking down at me and shaking his head doubtfully.

Dad nodded.

"And you were a seventh son, too?"

Dad nodded again and started stamping his feet impatiently, splattering my breeches with droplets of brown mud and manure. The rain was dripping from the peak of his cap. It had been raining for most of the month. There were new leaves on the trees, but the spring weather was a long time coming.

My dad was a farmer and his father had been a farmer, too, and the first rule of farming is to keep the farm together. You can't just divide it up among your children; it would get smaller and smaller with each generation until there was nothing left. So a father leaves his farm to his eldest son. Then he finds jobs for the rest. If possible, he tries to find each a trade.

He needs lots of favors for that. The local blacksmith is one option, especially if the farm is big and he's given the blacksmith plenty of work. Then it's odds on that the blacksmith will offer an apprenticeship, but that's still only one son sorted out.

I was his seventh, and by the time it came to me all the favors had been used up. Dad was so desperate that he was trying to get the Spook to take me on as his apprentice. Or at least that's what I thought at the time. I should have guessed that Mam was behind it.

She was behind a lot of things. Long before I was born, it was her money that had bought our farm. How else could a seventh son have afforded it? And Mam wasn't County. She came from a land far across the sea. Most people couldn't tell, but sometimes, if you listened very carefully, there was a slight difference in the way she pronounced certain words.

Still, don't imagine that I was being sold into slavery or something. I was bored with farming anyway, and what they called the town was hardly more than a village in the back of beyond. It was certainly no place that I wanted to spend the rest of my life. So in one way I quite liked the idea of being a spook; it was much more interesting than milking cows and spreading manure.

It made me nervous though, because it was a scary job. I was going to learn how to protect farms and villages from things that go bump in the night. Dealing with ghouls, boggarts, and all manner of wicked beasties would be all in a day's work. That's what the Spook did, and I was going to be his apprentice.

"How old is he?" asked the Spook.

"He'll be thirteen come August."

"Bit small for his age. Can he read and write?"

"Aye," Dad answered. "He can do both, and he also knows Greek. His mam taught him, and he could speak it almost before he could walk."

The Spook nodded and looked back across the muddy path beyond the gate toward the farmhouse, as if he were listening for something. Then he shrugged. "It's a hard enough life for a man, never mind a boy," he said. "Think he's up to it?"

"He's strong and he'll be as big as me when he's full grown," my dad said, straightening his back and drawing himself up to his full height. That done, the top of his head was just about level with the Spook's chin.

Suddenly the Spook smiled. It was the very last thing I'd expected. His face was big and looked as if it had been chiseled from stone. Until then I'd thought him a bit fierce. His long black cloak and hood made him look like a priest, but when he looked at you directly, his grim expression made him appear more like a hangman weighing you up for the rope.

The hair sticking out from under the front of his hood matched his beard, which was gray, but his eyebrows were black and very bushy. There was quite a bit of black hair sprouting out of his nostrils, too, and his eyes were green, the same color as my own.

Then I noticed something else about him. He was carrying a long staff. Of course, I'd seen that as soon as he came within sight, but what I hadn't realized until that moment was that he was carrying it in his left hand.

Did that mean that he was left-handed like me?

It was something that had caused me no end of trouble at the village school. They'd even called in the local priest to look at me, and he'd kept shaking his head and telling me I'd have to fight it before it was too late. I didn't know what he meant. None of my brothers were left-handed and neither was my dad. My mam was cack-handed, though, and it never seemed to bother her much, so when the teacher threatened to beat it out of me and tied the pen to my right hand, she took me away from the school and from that day on taught me at home.

"How much to take him on?" my dad asked, interrupting my thoughts. Now we were getting down to the real business.

"Two guineas for a month's trial. If he's up to it, I'll be back again in the autumn and you'll owe me another ten. If not, you can have him back and it'll be just another guinea for my trouble."

Dad nodded again and the deal was done. We went into the barn and the guineas were paid, but they didn't shake hands. Nobody wanted to touch a spook. My dad was a brave man just to stand within six feet of one.

"I've some business close by," said the Spook, "but I'll be back for the lad at first light. Make sure he's ready. I don't like to be kept waiting."

When he'd gone, Dad tapped me on the shoulder. "It's a new life for you now, son," he told me. "Go and get yourself cleaned up. You're finished with farming."

When I walked into the kitchen, my brother Jack had his arm around his wife, Ellie, and she was smiling up at him.

I like Ellie a lot. She's warm and friendly in a way that makes you feel that she really cares about you. Mam says that marrying Ellie was good for Jack because she helped to make him less agitated.

Jack is the eldest and biggest of us all and, as Dad sometimes jokes, the best looking of an ugly bunch. He is big and strong, all right, but despite his blue eyes and healthy red cheeks, his black bushy eyebrows almost meet in the middle, so I've never agreed with that. One thing I've never argued with is that he managed to attract a kind and pretty wife. Ellie has hair the color of best-quality straw three days after a good harvest and skin that really glows in candlelight.

"I'm leaving tomorrow morning," I blurted out. "The Spook's coming for me at first light."

Ellie's face lit up. "You mean he's agreed to take you on?"

I nodded. "He's given me a month's trial."

"Oh, well done, Tom. I'm really pleased for you," she said.

"I don't believe it!" scoffed Jack. "You, apprentice to a spook! How can you do a job like that when you still can't sleep without a candle?"

I laughed at his joke, but he had a point. I sometimes saw things in the dark, and a candle was the best way to keep them away so that I could get some sleep.

Jack came toward me, and with a roar got me in a headlock and began dragging me round the kitchen table. It was his idea of a joke. I put up just enough resistance to humor him, and after a few seconds he let go of me and patted me on the back.

"Well done, Tom," he said. "You'll make a fortune

doing that job. There's just one problem, though. . . ."

"What's that?" I asked.

"You'll need every penny you earn. Know why?"

I shrugged.

"Because the only friends you'll have are the ones you buy!"

I tried to smile, but there was a lot of truth in Jack's words. A spook worked and lived alone.

"Oh, Jack! Don't be cruel!" Ellie scolded.

"It was only a joke," Jack replied, as if he couldn't understand why Ellie was making so much fuss.

But Ellie was looking at me rather than Jack, and I saw her face suddenly drop. "Oh, Tom!" she said. "This means that you won't be here when the baby's born. . . ."

She looked really disappointed, and it made me feel sad that I wouldn't be at home to see my new niece. Mam had said that Ellie's baby was going to be a girl, and she was never wrong about things like that.

"I'll come back and visit just as soon as I can," I promised.

Ellie tried to smile, and Jack came up and rested

his arm across my shoulders. "You'll always have your family," he said. "We'll always be here if you need us."

An hour later I sat down to supper, knowing that I'd be gone in the morning. Dad said grace as he did every evening and we all muttered "amen" except Mam. She just stared down at her food as usual, waiting politely until it was over. As the prayer ended, Mam gave me a little smile. It was a warm, special smile, and I don't think anyone else noticed. It made me feel better.

The fire was still burning in the grate, filling the kitchen with warmth. At the center of our large wooden table was a brass candlestick, which had been polished until you could see your face in it. The candle was made of beeswax and was expensive, but Mam wouldn't allow tallow in the kitchen because of the smell. Dad made most of the decisions on the farm, but in some things she always got her own way.

As we tucked into our big plates of steaming hot pot, it struck me how old Dad looked tonight—old and tired—and there was an expression that

REVENGE OF THE WITCH

flickered across his face from time to time, a hint of sadness. But he brightened up a bit when he and Jack started discussing the price of pork and whether or not it was the right time to send for the pig butcher.

"Better to wait another month or so," Dad said. "The price is sure to go higher."

Jack shook his head and they began to argue. It was a friendly argument, the kind families often have, and I could tell that Dad was enjoying it. I didn't join in, though. All that was over for me. As Dad had told me, I was finished with farming.

Mam and Ellie were chuckling together softly. I tried to catch what they were saying, but by now Jack was in full flow, his voice getting louder and louder. When Mam glanced across at him, I could tell she'd had enough of his noise.

Oblivious to Mam's glances, and continuing to argue loudly, Jack reached across for the salt cellar and accidentally knocked it over, spilling a small cone of salt on the tabletop. Straightaway he took a pinch and threw it back over his left shoulder. It is an old County superstition. By doing that you were supposed to ward off the bad luck you'd earned by spilling it.

"Jack, you don't need any salt on that anyway," Mam scolded. "It spoils a good hot pot and is an insult to the cook!"

"Sorry, Mam," Jack apologized. "You're right. It's perfect just as it is."

She gave him a smile, then nodded toward me. "Anyway, nobody's taking any notice of Tom. That's no way to treat him on his last night at home."

"I'm all right, Mam," I told her. "I'm happy just to sit here and listen."

Mam nodded. "Well, I've got a few things to say to you. After supper stay down in the kitchen, and we'll have a little talk."

So after Jack, Ellie, and Dad had gone up to bed, I sat in a chair by the fire and waited patiently to hear what Mam had to say.

Mam wasn't a woman who made a lot of fuss; at first she didn't say much, apart from explaining what she was wrapping up for me: a spare pair of trousers, three shirts, and two pairs of good socks that had only been darned once each.

I stared into the embers of the fire, tapping my feet on the flags, while Mam drew up her rocking chair and positioned it so that she was facing directly toward me. Her black hair was streaked with a few strands of gray, but apart from that she looked much the same as she had when I was just a toddler, hardly up to her knees. Her eyes were still bright, and but for her pale skin, she looked a picture of health.

"This is the last time we'll get to talk together for a long while," she said. "It's a big step leaving home and starting out on your own. So if there's anything you need to say, anything you need to ask, now's the time to do it."

I couldn't think of a single question. In fact I couldn't even think. Hearing her say all that had started tears pricking behind my eyes.

The silence went on for quite a while. All that could be heard was my feet tap-tapping on the flags. Finally Mam gave a little sigh. "What's wrong?" she asked. "Has the cat got your tongue?"

I shrugged.

"Stop fidgeting, Tom, and concentrate on what I'm saying," Mam warned. "First of all, are you looking forward to tomorrow and starting your new job?"

"I'm not sure, Mam," I told her, remembering Jack's joke about having to buy friends. "Nobody wants to go anywhere near a spook. I'll have no friends. I'll be lonely all the time."

"It won't be as bad as you think," Mam said. "You'll have your master to talk to. He'll be your teacher, and no doubt he'll eventually become your friend. And you'll be busy all the time. Busy learning new things. You'll have no time to feel lonely. Don't you find the whole thing new and exciting?"

"It's exciting, but the job scares me. I want to do it, but I don't know if I can. One part of me wants to travel and see places, but it'll be hard not to live here anymore. I'll miss you all. I'll miss being at home."

"You can't stay here," Mam said. "Your dad's getting too old to work, and come next winter he's handing the farm over to Jack. Ellie will be having her baby soon, no doubt the first of many; eventually there won't be room for you here. No, you'd better get used to it before that happens. You can't come home."

Her voice seemed cold and a little sharp, and to hear her speak to me like that drove a pain deep into my chest and throat so that I could hardly breathe.

I just wanted to go to bed then, but she had a lot to say. I'd rarely heard her use so many words all in one go.

"You have a job to do and you're going to do it," she said sternly. "And not only do it; you're going to do it well. I married your dad because he was a seventh son. And I bore him six sons so that I could have you. Seven times seven, you are, and you have the gift. Your new master's still strong, but he's some way past his best, and his time is finally coming to an end.

"For nearly sixty years he's walked the County lines doing his duty. Doing what has to be done. Soon it'll be your turn. And if you won't do it, then who will? Who'll look after the ordinary folk? Who'll keep them from harm? Who'll make the farms, villages, and towns safe so that women and children can walk the streets and lanes free from fear?"

I didn't know what to say, and I couldn't look her in the eye. I just fought to hold back the tears.

"I love everyone in this house," she said, her voice softening, "but in the whole wide County, you're the only person who's really like me. As yet, you're just a boy who's still got a lot of growing to do, but you're the seventh son of a seventh son. You've the gift and the strength to do what has to be done. I know you're going to make me proud of you.

"Well, now," Mam said, coming to her feet, "I'm glad that we've got that sorted out. Now off to bed with you. It's a big day tomorrow, and you want to be at your best."

She gave me a hug and a warm smile, and I tried really hard to be cheerful and smile back, but once up in my bedroom I sat on the edge of my bed just staring vacantly and thinking about what Mam had told me.

My mam is well respected in the neighborhood. She knows more about plants and medicines than the local doctor, and when there is a problem with delivering a baby, the midwife always sends for her. Mam is an expert on what she calls breech births. Sometimes a baby tries to get born feet first, but my mother is good at turning them while they are still in the womb. Dozens of women in the County owe their lives to her.

Anyway, that was what my dad always said, but Mam was modest and she never mentioned things like that. She just got on with what had to be done, and I knew that's what she expected of me. So I wanted to make her proud.

But could she really mean that she'd only married

my dad and had my six brothers so she could give birth to me? It didn't seem possible.

After thinking things through, I went across to the window and sat in the old wicker chair for a few minutes, staring through the window, which faced north.

The moon was shining, bathing everything in its silver light. I could see across the farmyard, beyond the two hay fields and the north pasture, right to the boundary of our farm, which ended halfway up Hangman's Hill. I liked the view. I liked Hangman's Hill, from a distance. I liked the way it was the farthest thing you could see.

For years this had been my routine before climbing into bed each night. I used to stare at that hill and imagine what was on the other side. I knew that it was really just more fields and then, two miles farther on, what passed for the local village—half a dozen houses, a small church, and an even smaller school—but my imagination conjured up other things. Sometimes I imagined high cliffs with an ocean beyond, or maybe a forest or a great city with tall towers and twinkling lights.

But now, as I gazed at the hill, I remembered

my fear as well. Yes, it was fine from a distance, but it wasn't a place I'd ever wanted to get close to. Hangman's Hill, as you might have guessed, didn't get its name for nothing.

Three generations earlier, a war had raged over the whole land, and the men of the County had played their part. It had been that worst of all wars, a bitter civil war where families had been divided and where sometimes brother had even fought brother.

In the last winter of the war there'd been a big battle a mile or so to the north, just on the outskirts of the village. When it was finally over, the winning army had brought their prisoners to this hill and hanged them from the trees on its northern slope. They'd hanged some of their own men, too, for what they claimed was cowardice in the face of the enemy, but there was another version of that tale. It was said that some of these men had refused to fight people they considered to be neighbors.

Even Jack never liked working close to that boundary fence, and the dogs wouldn't go more than a few feet into the wood. As for me, because I can sense things that others can't, I couldn't even work in the north pasture. You see, from there I could hear them. I could hear the ropes creaking and the branches groaning under their weight. I could hear the dead, strangling and choking on the other side of the hill.

Mam had said that we were like each other. Well, she was certainly like me in one way: I knew she could also see things that others couldn't. One winter, when I was very young and all my brothers lived at home, the noises from the hill got so bad at night that I could even hear them from my bedroom. My brothers didn't hear a thing, but I did, and I couldn't sleep. Mam came to my room every time I called, even though she had to be up at the crack of dawn to do her chores.

Finally she said she was going to sort it out, and one night she climbed Hangman's Hill alone and went up into the trees. When she came back, everything was quiet, and it stayed like that for months afterward.

So there was one way in which we weren't alike.

Mam was a lot braver than I was.

CHAPTER II
On the Road

I was up an hour before dawn, but Mam was already in the kitchen, cooking my favorite breakfast, bacon and eggs.

Dad came downstairs while I was mopping the plate with my last slice of bread. As we said good-bye, he pulled something from his pocket and placed it in my hands. It was the small tinderbox that had belonged to his own dad and to his granddad before that. One of his favorite possessions.

"I want you to have this, son," he said. "It might come in useful in your new job. And come back and see us soon. Just because you've left home, it doesn't mean that you can't come back and visit."

"It's time to go, son," Mam said, walking across to

give me a final hug. "He's at the gate. Don't keep him waiting."

We were a family that didn't like too much fuss, and as we'd already said our good-byes, I walked out into the yard alone.

The Spook was on the other side of the gate, a dark silhouette against the gray dawn light. His hood was up and he was standing straight and tall, his staff in his left hand. I walked toward him, carrying my small bundle of possessions, feeling very nervous.

To my surprise, the Spook opened the gate and came into the yard. "Well, lad," he said, "follow me! We might as well start the way we mean to go on."

Instead of heading for the road, he led the way north, directly toward Hangman's Hill, and soon we were crossing the north pasture, my heart already starting to thump. When we reached the boundary fence, the Spook climbed over with the ease of a man half his age, but I froze. As I rested my hands against the top edge of the fence, I could already hear the sounds of the trees creaking, their branches bent and bowed under the weight of the hanging men.

"What's the matter, lad?" asked the Spook, turning to look back at me. "If you're frightened of something on your own doorstep, you'll be of little use to me."

I took a deep breath and clambered over the fence. We trudged upward, the dawn light darkening as we moved up into the gloom of the trees. The higher we climbed, the colder it seemed to get, and soon I was shivering. It was the kind of cold that gives you goose pimples and makes the hair on the back of your neck start to rise. It was a warning that something wasn't quite right. I'd felt it before when something had come close that didn't belong in this world.

Once we'd reached the summit of the hill, I could see them below me. There had to be a hundred at least, sometimes two or three hanging from the same tree, wearing soldiers' uniforms with broad leather belts and big boots. Their hands were tied behind their backs and all of them behaved differently. Some struggled desperately so that the branch above them bounced and jerked, while others were just spinning slowly on the end of the rope, pointing first one way, then the other.

As I watched, I suddenly felt a strong wind on my face, a wind so cold and fierce that it couldn't have been natural. The trees bowed low, and their leaves shriveled and began to fall. Within moments, all the branches were bare. When the wind had eased, the Spook put his hand on my shoulder and guided me nearer to the hanging men. We stopped just feet away from the nearest.

"Look at him," said the Spook. "What do you see?"

"A dead soldier," I replied, my voice beginning to wobble.

"How old does he look?"

"Seventeen at the most."

"Good. Well done, lad. Now, tell me, do you still feel scared?"

"A bit. I don't like being so close to him."

"Why? There's nothing to be afraid of. Nothing that can hurt you. Think about what it must have been like for him. Concentrate on him rather than yourself. How must he have felt? What would be the worst thing?"

I tried to put myself in the soldier's place and imagine how it must have been to die like that. The pain and the struggle for breath would have been terrible. But there might have been something even worse. . . .

"He'd have known he was dying and that he'd never be able to go home again. That he'd never see his family again," I told the Spook.

With those words a wave of sadness washed over me. Then, even as that happened, the hanging men slowly began to disappear, until we were alone on the hillside and the leaves were back on the trees.

"How do you feel now? Still afraid?"

I shook my head. "No," I said. "I just feel sad."

"Well done, lad. You're learning. We're the seventh sons of seventh sons, and we have the gift of seeing things that others can't. But that gift can sometimes be a curse. If we're afraid, sometimes there are things that can feed on that fear. Fear makes it worse for us. The trick is to concentrate on what you can see and stop thinking about yourself. It works every time.

"It was a terrible sight, lad, but they're just ghasts," continued the Spook. "There's nothing much we can do about them, and they'll just fade away in their own time. In a hundred years or so there'll be nothing left."

I felt like telling him that Mam did something about them once, but I didn't. To contradict him would have gotten us off to a bad start.

"Now if they were ghosts, that would be different," said the Spook. "You can talk to ghosts and tell them what's what. Just making them realize that they're dead is a great kindness and an important step in getting them to move on. Usually a ghost is a bewildered spirit trapped on this earth but not knowing what's happened. So often they're in torment. Then again, others are here with a definite purpose, and they might have things to tell you. But a ghast is just a fragment of a soul that's gone on to better things. That's what these are, lad. Just ghasts. You saw the trees change?"

"The leaves fell and it was winter."

"Well, the leaves are back now. So you were just looking at something from the past. Just a reminder of the evil things that sometimes happen on this earth. Usually, if you're brave, they can't see you and they don't feel anything. A ghast is just like a reflection in a pond that stays behind when its owner has moved on. Understand what I'm saying?"

I nodded.

"Right, so that's one thing sorted out. We'll be dealing with the dead from time to time, so you might as well get used to them. Anyway, let's get started. We've quite a way to go. Here, from now on you'll be carrying this."

The Spook handed me his big leather bag and, without a backward glance, headed back up the hill. I followed him over its crest, then down through the trees toward the road, which was a distant gray scar meandering its way south through the green and brown patchwork of fields.

"Done much traveling, lad?" the Spook called back over his shoulder. "Seen much of the County?"

I told him I'd never been more than six miles from my dad's farm. Going to the local market was the most traveling I'd ever done.

The Spook muttered something under his breath and shook his head; I could tell that he wasn't best pleased by my answer.

"Well, your travels start today," he said. "We're heading south toward a village called Horshaw. It's just over fifteen miles as the crow flies, and we have to be there before dark."

I'd heard of Horshaw. It was a pit village and had the largest coal yards in the County, holding the output of dozens of surrounding mines. I'd never expected to go there, and I wondered what the Spook's business could be in a place like that.

He walked at a furious pace, taking big, effortless strides. Soon I was struggling to keep up; as well as carrying my own small bundle of clothes and other belongings, I now had his bag, which seemed to be getting heavier by the minute. Then, just to make things worse, it started to rain.

About an hour before noon, the Spook came to a sudden halt. He turned round and stared hard at me. By then I was about ten paces behind. My feet were hurting and I'd already developed a slight limp. The road was little more than a track that was quickly turning to mud. Just as I caught up with him, I stubbed my toe, slipped, and almost lost my balance.

He tutted. "Feeling dizzy, lad?" he asked.

I shook my head. I wanted to give my arm a rest, but it didn't seem right to put his bag down in the mud.

"That's good," said the Spook with a faint smile, the rain dripping from the edge of his hood down onto his beard. "Never trust a man who's dizzy. That's something well worth remembering."

"I'm not dizzy," I protested.

"No?" asked the Spook, raising his bushy

eyebrows. "Then it must be your boots. They won't be much use in this job."

My boots were the same as my dad's and Jack's, sturdy enough and suitable for the mud and muck of the farmyard, but the kind that needed a lot of getting used to. A new pair usually cost you a fortnight's blisters before your feet got bedded in.

I looked down at the Spook's. They were made of strong, good-quality leather, and they had extra-thick soles. They must have cost a fortune, but I suppose that for someone who did a lot of walking, they were worth every penny. They flexed as he walked, and I just knew that they'd been comfortable from the very first moment he pulled them on.

"Good boots are important in this job," said the Spook. "We depend on neither man nor beast to get us where we need to go. If you rely on your own two good legs, then they won't let you down. So if I finally decide to take you on, I'll get you a pair of boots just like mine. Until then, you'll just have to manage as best you can."

At noon we halted for a short break, sheltering from the rain in an abandoned cattle shed. The Spook took a piece of cloth out of his pocket and unwrapped it, revealing a large lump of yellow cheese.

He broke off a bit and handed it to me. I'd seen worse and I was hungry, so I wolfed it down. The Spook only ate a small piece himself before wrapping the rest up again and stuffing it back into his pocket.

Once out of the rain, he'd pulled his hood back, so I now had the chance to look at him properly for the first time. Apart from the full beard and the hangman's eyes, his most noticeable feature was his nose, which was grim and sharp, with a curve to it that suggested a bird's beak. The mouth, when closed, was almost hidden by that mustache and beard. The beard itself had looked gray at first glance, but when I looked closer, trying to be as casual as possible so that he wouldn't notice, I saw that most of the colors of the rainbow seemed to be sprouting there. There were shades of red, black, brown, and, obviously, lots of gray, but as I came to realize later, it all depended on the light.

"Weak jaw, weak character," my dad always used to say, and he also believed that some men wore beards just to hide that fact. Looking at the Spook, though, you could see despite the beard that his jaw was long, and when he opened his mouth he revealed yellow teeth that were very sharp and more suited to gnawing on red meat than nibbling at cheese.

With a shiver, I suddenly realized that he reminded me of a wolf. And it wasn't just the way he looked. He was a kind of predator because he hunted the dark; living merely on nibbles of cheese would make him always hungry and mean. If I completed my apprenticeship, I'd end up just like him.

"You still hungry, lad?" he asked, his green eyes boring hard into my own until I started to feel a bit dizzy.

I was soaked to the skin and my feet were hurting, but most of all I was hungry. So I nodded, thinking he might offer me some more, but he just shook his head and muttered something to himself. Then, once again, he looked at me sharply.

"Hunger's something you're going to have to get used to," he said. "We don't eat much when we're working, and if the job's very difficult, we don't eat anything at all until afterward. Fasting's the safest thing because it makes us less vulnerable to the dark. It makes us stronger. So you might as well start practicing now, because when we get to Horshaw,

I'm going to give you a little test. You're going to spend a night in a haunted house. And you're going to do it alone. That'll show me what you're really made of!"

CHAPTER III
Number Thirteen Watery Lane

WE reached Horshaw as a church bell began to chime in the distance. It was seven o'clock and starting to get dark. A heavy drizzle blew straight into our faces, but there was still enough light for me to judge that this wasn't a place I ever wanted to live in and that even a short visit would be best avoided.

Horshaw was a black smear against the green fields, a grim, ugly little place with about two dozen rows of mean back-to-back houses huddling together mainly on the southern slope of a damp, bleak hillside. The whole area was riddled with mines, and Horshaw was at its center. High above the village was a large slag heap, which marked the entrance to a mine. Behind the slag heap were the coal yards, which stored enough fuel to keep the biggest towns in the County warm through even the longest of winters.

Soon we were walking down through the narrow, cobbled streets, keeping pressed close to the grimy walls to make way for carts heaped with black lumps of coal, wet and gleaming with rain. The huge shire horses that pulled them were straining against their loads, hooves slipping on the shiny cobbles.

There were few people about, but lace curtains twitched as we passed, and once we met a group of dour-faced miners who were trudging up the hill to begin their night shift. They'd been talking in loud voices but suddenly fell silent and moved into a single column to pass us, keeping to the far side of the street. One of them actually made the sign of the cross.

"Get used to it, lad," growled the Spook. "We're needed but rarely welcomed, and some places are worse than others."

Finally we turned a corner into the lowest and meanest street of all. Nobody lived there—you could tell that right away. For one thing, some of the windows were broken and others were boarded up, and although it was almost dark, no lights were showing. At one end of the street was an abandoned corn merchant's warehouse, two huge wooden doors gaping open and hanging from their rusty hinges.

The Spook halted outside the very last house. It was the one on the corner closest to the warehouse, the only house in the street to have a number. That number was crafted out of metal and nailed to the door. It was thirteen, the worst and unluckiest of all numbers, and directly above, there was a street sign high on the wall, hanging from a single rusty rivet and pointing almost vertically toward the cobbles. It said WATERY LANE.

This house did have windowpanes, but the lace curtains were yellow and hung with cobwebs. This must be the haunted house my master had warned me about.

The Spook pulled a key from his pocket, unlocked the door, and led the way into the darkness within. At first I was just glad to be out of the drizzle, but when he lit a candle and positioned it on the floor near the middle of the small front room, I knew that

I'd be more comfortable in an abandoned cowshed. There wasn't a single item of furniture to be seen, just a bare flagged floor and a heap of dirty straw under the window. The room was damp, too, the air very dank and cold, and by the light of the flickering candle I could see my breath steaming.

What I saw was bad enough, but what he said was even worse.

"Well, lad, I've got business to attend to so I'll be off, but I'll be back later. Know what you have to do?"

"No, sir," I replied, watching the flickering candle, worried that it might go out at any second.

"Well, it's what I told you earlier. Weren't you listening? You need to be alert, not dreaming. Anyway, it's nothing very difficult," he explained, scratching at his beard as if there was something crawling about in it. "You just have to spend the night here alone. I bring all my new apprentices to this old house on their first night so I can find out what they're made of. Oh, but there's one thing I haven't told you. At midnight I'll expect you to go down into the cellar and face whatever it is that's lurking there. Cope with that and you're well on your way to being taken on permanently. Any questions?"

I had questions all right, but I was too scared to hear the answers. So I just shook my head and tried to keep my top lip from trembling.

"How will you know when it's midnight?" he asked.

I shrugged. I was pretty good at guessing the time from the position of the sun or the stars, and if I ever woke in the middle of the night, I almost always knew exactly what time it was, but here I wasn't so sure. In some places time seems to move more slowly, and I had a feeling that this old house would be one of them.

Suddenly I remembered the church clock. "It's just gone seven," I said. "I'll listen for twelve chimes."

"Well, at least you're awake now," the Spook said with a little smile. "When the clock strikes twelve, take the stub of the candle and use it to find your way down to the cellar. Until then, sleep if you can manage it. Now listen carefully—there are three important things to remember. Don't open the front door to anyone, no matter how hard they knock, and don't be late going down to the cellar."

He took a step toward the front door.

"What's the third thing?" I called out at the very last moment.

"The candle, lad. Whatever else you do, don't let it go out."

Then he was gone, closing the door behind him, and I was all alone. Cautiously I picked up the candle, walked to the kitchen door, and peered inside. It was empty of everything but a stone sink. The back door was closed, but the wind still wailed beneath it. There were two other doors on the right. One was open, and I could see the bare wooden stairs that led to the bedrooms above. The other one, that closest to me, was closed.

Something about that closed door made me uneasy, but I decided to take a quick look. Nervously I gripped the handle and tugged at the door. It was hard to shift, and for a moment I had a creepy feeling that somebody was holding it closed on the other side. When I tugged even harder, it opened with a jerk, making me lose my balance. I staggered back a couple of steps and almost dropped the candle.

Stone steps led down into the darkness; they were black with coal dust. They curved away to the left so

I couldn't see right down into the cellar, but a cold draft came up them, making the candle flame dance and flicker. I closed the door quickly and went back into the front room, closing the kitchen door, too.

I put the candle down carefully in the corner farthest away from the door and window. Once I was satisfied that it wouldn't fall over, I looked for a place on the floor where I could sleep. There wasn't much choice. I certainly wasn't sleeping on the damp straw, so I settled down in the center of the room.

The flags were hard and cold, but I closed my eyes. Once asleep, I'd be away from that grim old house, and I felt pretty confident that I'd wake just before midnight.

Usually I get to sleep easily, but this was different. I kept shivering with cold, and the wind was beginning to rattle the windowpanes. There were also rustlings and patterings coming from the walls. Just mice, I kept telling myself. We were certainly used to them on the farm. But then, suddenly, there came a disturbing new sound from down below in the depths of the dark cellar.

At first it was faint, making me strain my ears, but gradually it grew until I was in no doubt about what

I could hear. Down in the cellar, something was happening that shouldn't be happening. Someone was digging rhythmically, turning heavy earth with a sharp metal spade. First came the grind of the metal edge striking a stony surface, followed by a soft, squelching, sucking sound as the spade pushed deep into heavy clay and tore it free from the earth.

This went on for several minutes until the noise stopped as suddenly as it had begun. All was quiet. Even the mice stopped their pattering. It was as if the house and everything in it were holding their breath. I know I was.

The silence ended with a resounding thump. Then a whole series of thumps, definite in rhythm. Thumps that were getting louder. And louder. And closer . . .

Someone was climbing the stairs from the cellar.

I snatched up the candle and shrank into the farthest corner. *Thump, thump,* nearer and nearer, came the sound of heavy boots. Who could have been digging down there in the darkness? Who could be climbing the stairs now?

But maybe it wasn't a question of *who* was climbing the stairs. Maybe it was a question of *what*.

I heard the cellar door open and the thump of

boots in the kitchen. I pressed myself back into the corner, trying to make myself small, waiting for the kitchen door to open.

And open it did, very slowly, with a loud creak. Something stepped into the room. I felt coldness then. Real coldness. The kind of coldness that told me something was close that didn't belong on this earth. It was like the coldness of Hangman's Hill, only far, far worse.

I lifted the candle, its flame flickering eerie shadows that danced up the walls and onto the ceiling.

"Who's there?" I asked. "Who's there?" My voice trembled even more than the hand holding the candle.

There was no answer. Even the wind outside had fallen silent.

"Who's there?" I called out again.

Again no reply, but invisible boots grated on the flags as they stepped toward me. Nearer and nearer they came, and now I could hear breathing. Something big was breathing heavily. It sounded like a huge carthorse that had just pulled a heavy load up a steep hill.

At the very last moment the footsteps veered away

from me and halted close to the window. I was holding my breath, and the thing by the window seemed to be breathing for both of us, drawing great gulps of air into its lungs as if it could never get enough.

Just when I could stand it no longer, it gave a huge sigh that sounded weary and sad at the same time, and the invisible boots grated on the flags once more, heavy steps that moved away from the window, back toward the door. When they began to thump their way down the cellar steps, I was finally able to breathe again.

My heart began to slow, my hands stopped shaking, and gradually I calmed down. I had to pull myself together. I'd been scared, but if that was the worst that was going to happen tonight, I'd gotten through it, passed my first test. I was going to be the Spook's apprentice, so I'd have to get used to places like this haunted house. It went with the job.

After about five minutes or so I began to feel better. I even thought about making another attempt to get to sleep, but as my dad sometimes says, "There's no rest for the wicked." Well, I don't know what I'd done wrong, but there was a sudden new sound to disturb me.

It was faint and distant at first—something knocking on a door. There was a pause, and then it happened again. Three distinct raps, but a little nearer this time. Another pause and three more raps.

It didn't take me long to work it out. Something was rapping hard on each door in the street, moving nearer and nearer to number thirteen. When it finally came to the haunted house, the three raps on the front door were loud enough to wake the dead. Would the thing in the cellar climb the steps to answer that summons? I felt trapped between the two: something outside wanting to get in; something below that wanted to be free.

And then, suddenly, it was all right. A voice called to me from the other side of the front door, a voice I recognized.

"Tom! Tom! Open the door! Let me in!"

It was Mam. I was so glad to hear her that I rushed to the front door without thinking. It was raining outside and she'd be getting wet.

"Quickly, Tom, quickly!" Mam called. "Don't keep me waiting."

I was actually lifting the latch to open it when I remembered the Spook's warning: *"Don't open the front door to anyone, no matter how hard they knock."*

But how could I leave Mam out there in the dark?

"Come on, Tom! Let me in!" the voice called again.

Remembering what the Spook had said, I took a deep breath and tried to think. Common sense told me it couldn't be her. Why would she have followed me all this way? How would she have known where we were going? Mam wouldn't have traveled alone either. My dad or Jack would have come with her.

No, it was a something else waiting outside. Something without hands that could still rap on the door. Something without feet that could still stand on the pavement.

The knocking started to get louder.

"Please let me in, Tom," pleaded the voice. "How can you be so hard and cruel? I'm cold, wet, and tired."

Eventually it began to cry, and then I knew for certain that it couldn't possibly be Mam. Mam was strong. Mam never cried no matter how bad things got.

After a few moments the sounds faded and stopped altogether. I lay down on the floor and tried to sleep again. I kept turning over, first one way and then the other, but try as I might, I couldn't get to sleep. The wind began to rattle the windowpanes even louder, and on every hour and half hour the church clock chimed, moving me closer to midnight.

The nearer the time came for me to go down the cellar steps, the more nervous I became. I did want to pass the Spook's test, but, oh, how I longed to be back home in my nice, safe, warm bed.

And then, just after the clock had given a single chime — half past eleven — the digging began again. . . .

Once more I heard the slow *thump, thump* of heavy boots coming up the steps from the cellar; once more the door opened and the invisible boots stepped into the front room. By now the only bit of me that was moving was my heart, which pounded so hard it seemed about to break my ribs. But this time the boots didn't veer away in the direction of the window. They kept coming. *Thump! Thump! Thump!* Coming straight toward me.

I felt myself being lifted roughly by the hair and skin at the nape of my neck, just like a mother cat carries her kittens. Then an invisible arm wrapped itself around my body, pinning my arms to my sides.

I tried to suck in a breath, but it was impossible. My chest was being crushed.

I was being carried toward the cellar door. I couldn't see what was carrying me, but I could hear its wheezing breath and I struggled in a panic, because somehow I knew exactly what was going to happen. Somehow I knew why there'd been the sound of digging from below. I was going to be carried down the cellar steps into the darkness, and I knew that a grave was waiting for me down there. I was going to be buried alive.

I was terrified and tried to cry out, but it was worse than just being held in a tight grip. I was paralyzed and couldn't move a muscle.

Suddenly I was falling. . . .

I found myself on all fours, staring at the open door to the cellar, just inches from the top step. In a panic, my heart thumping too fast to count the beats, I lurched to my feet and slammed the cellar door shut. Still trembling, I went back into the front room to find that one of the Spook's three rules had been broken.

The candle had gone out.

As I walked toward the window, a sudden flash

of light illuminated the room, followed by a loud crash of thunder almost directly overhead. Rain squalled against the house, rattling the windows and making the front door creak and groan as if something were trying to get in.

I stared out miserably for a few minutes, watching the flashes of lightning. It was a bad night, but even though lightning scared me, I would have given anything to be out there walking the streets; anything to have avoided going down into that cellar.

In the distance the church clock began to chime. I counted the chimes, and there were exactly twelve. Now I had to face what was in the cellar.

It was then, as lightning lit the room again, that I noticed the large footprints on the floor. At first I thought they'd been made by the Spook, but they were black, as if the huge boots that made them had been covered with coal dust. They came from the direction of the kitchen door, went almost to the window, and then turned and went back the way they'd come. Back to the cellar. Down into the dark where I had to go!

Forcing myself forward, I searched the floor with my hand for the stub of the candle. Then I scrabbled around for my small bundle of clothes. Wrapped in the center of it was the tinderbox that Dad had given me.

Fumbling in the dark, I shook the small pile of tinder out onto the floor and used the stone and metal to strike up sparks. I kindled that little pile of wood until it burst into flame, just long enough to light the candle. Little had Dad known that his gift would prove so useful so soon.

As I opened the cellar door, there was another flash of lightning and a sudden crash of thunder that shook the whole house and rumbled down the steps ahead of me. I descended into the cellar, my hand trembling and the candle stub dancing till strange shadows flickered against the wall.

I didn't want to go down there, but if I failed the Spook's test, I'd probably be on my way back home as soon as it came light. I imagined my shame at having to tell Mam what had happened.

Eight steps and I was turning the corner so that the cellar was in view. It wasn't a big cellar, but it had dark shadows in the corners that the candlelight couldn't quite reach, and there were spiders' webs hanging from the ceiling in frail, mucky curtains.

Small pieces of coal and large wooden crates were scattered across the earthen floor, and there was an old wooden table next to a big beer barrel. I stepped around the beer barrel and noticed something in the far corner. Something just behind some crates that scared me so much I almost dropped the candle.

It was a dark shape, almost like a bundle of rags, and it was making a noise. A faint, rhythmical sound, like breathing.

I took a step toward the rags; then another, using all my willpower to make my legs move. It was then, as I got so close that I could have touched it, that the thing suddenly grew. From a shadow on the floor it reared up before me until it was three or four times bigger.

I almost ran. It was tall, dark, hooded, and terrifying, with green, glittering eyes.

Only then did I notice the staff that it was holding in its left hand.

"What kept you?" demanded the Spook. "You're nearly five minutes late!"

CHAPTER IV
The Letter

I lived in this house as a child," said the Spook, "and I saw things that would make your big toes curl, but I was the only one who could, and my dad used to beat me for telling lies. Something used to climb up out of the cellar. It would have been the same for you. Am I right?"

I nodded.

"Well, it's nothing to worry about, lad. It's just another ghast, a fragment of a troubled soul that's gone on to better things. Without leaving the bad part of himself behind, he'd have been stuck here forever."

"What did he do?" I asked, my voice echoing back slightly from the ceiling.

The Spook shook his head sadly. "He was a miner whose lungs were so diseased that he couldn't work anymore. He spent his days and nights coughing and struggling for breath, and his poor wife kept them both. She worked in a bakery, but sadly for both of them, she was a very pretty woman, and some pretty women can't be trusted.

"To make it worse, he was a jealous man and his illness made him bitter. One evening she was very late home from work and he kept going to the window, pacing backward and forward, getting more and more angry because he thought she was with another man.

"When she finally came in, he was in such a rage that he broke her head open with a big lump of coal. Then he left her there, dying on the flags, and went down into the cellar to dig a grave. She was still alive when he came back, but she couldn't move and couldn't even cry out. That's the terror that comes to us, because it's how she felt as he picked her up and carried her down into the darkness of the cellar. She'd heard him digging. She knew what he was going to do.

"Later that night he killed himself. It's a sad story,

but although they're at peace now, his ghast's still here and so are her final memories, both strong enough to torment folks like us. We see things that others can't, which is both a blessing and a curse. It's a very useful thing in our trade, though."

I shuddered. I felt sorry for the poor wife who'd been murdered, and I felt sorry for the miner who'd killed her. I even felt sorry for the Spook. Imagine having to spend your childhood in a house like this.

I looked down at the candle, which I'd placed in the middle of the table. It was almost burned down and the flame was starting its last flickering dance, but the Spook didn't show any sign of wanting to go back upstairs. I didn't like the shadows on his face. It looked as if it were gradually changing, as if he were growing a snout or something.

"Do you know how I overcame my fear?" he asked.

"No, sir."

"One night I was so terrified that I screamed out before I could stop myself. I woke everybody up, and in a rage my father lifted me up by the scruff of my neck and carried me down the steps into this cellar. Then he got a hammer and nailed the door shut behind me.

"I wasn't very old. Probably seven at the most. I climbed back up the steps and, screaming fit to burst, scratched and banged at the door. But my father was a hard man, and he left me all alone in the dark and I had to stay there for hours, until long after dawn. After a bit, I calmed down, and do you know what I did then?"

I shook my head, trying not to look at his face. His eyes were glittering very brightly, and he looked more like a wolf than ever.

"I walked down the steps and sat there in this cellar in the darkness. Then I took three deep breaths, and I faced my fear. I faced the darkness itself, which is the most terrifying thing of all, especially for people like us, because things come to us in the dark. They seek us out with whispers and take shapes that only our eyes can see. But I did it, and when I left this cellar the worst was over."

At that moment the candle guttered and then went out, plunging us into absolute darkness.

"This is it, lad," the Spook said. "There's just you, me, and the dark. Can you stand it? Are you fit to be my apprentice?"

His voice sounded different, sort of deeper and

strange. I imagined him on all fours by now, wolf hair covering his face, his teeth growing longer. I was trembling and couldn't speak until I'd taken my third deep breath. Only then did I give him my answer. It was something my dad always said when he had to do something unpleasant or difficult.

"Someone has to do it," I said. "So it might as well be me."

The Spook must have thought that was funny, because his laughter filled the whole cellar before rumbling up the steps to meet the next peal of thunder, which was on its way down.

"Nearly thirteen years ago," said the Spook, "a sealed letter was sent to me. It was short and to the point and it was written in Greek. Your mother sent it. Do you know what it said?"

"No," I said quietly, wondering what was coming next.

"'I've just given birth to a baby boy,' she wrote, 'and he's the seventh son of a seventh son. His name is Thomas J. Ward, and he's my gift to the County. When he's old enough we'll send you word. Train him well. He'll be the best apprentice you've ever had, and he'll also be your last.'

"We don't use magic, lad," the Spook said, his voice hardly more than a whisper in the darkness. "The main tools of our trade are common sense, courage, and the keeping of accurate records, so we can learn from the past. Above all, we don't believe in prophecy. We don't believe that the future is fixed. So if what your mother wrote comes true, then it's because *we* make it come true. Do you understand?"

There was an edge of anger in his voice, but I knew it wasn't directed at me, so I just nodded into the darkness.

"As for being your mother's gift to the County, every single one of my apprentices was the seventh son of a seventh son. So don't you start thinking you're anything special. You've a lot of study and hard work ahead of you.

"Family can be a nuisance," the Spook went on after a pause, his voice softer, the anger gone. "I've only got two brothers left now. One's a locksmith and we get on all right, but the other one hasn't spoken to me for well over forty years, though he still lives here in Horshaw."

By the time we left the house, the storm had blown itself out and the moon was visible. As the Spook closed the front door, I noticed for the first time what had been carved there in the wood.

X

Gregory

The Spook nodded toward it. "I use signs like this to warn others who've the skill to read them or sometimes just to jog my own memory. You'll recognize the Greek letter gamma. It's the sign for either a ghost or a ghast. The cross on the lower right is the Roman numeral for ten, which is the lowest grading of all. Anything above six is just a ghast. There's nothing in that house that can harm you, not if you're brave. Remember, the dark feeds on fear. Be brave and there's nothing much a ghast can do."

If only I'd known that to begin with!

"Buck up, lad," said the Spook. "Your face is nearly down in your boots! Well, maybe this'll cheer you up." He pulled the lump of yellow cheese out of his pocket, broke off a small piece, and handed it to me. "Chew on this," he said, "but don't swallow it all at once."

I followed him down the cobbled street. The air

was damp, but at least it wasn't raining, and to the west the clouds looked like lamb's wool against the sky and were starting to tear and break up into ragged strips.

We left the village and continued south. Right on its edge, where the cobbled street became a muddy lane, there was a small church. It looked neglected — there were slates missing off the roof and paint peeling from the main door. We'd hardly seen anyone since leaving the house, but there was an old man standing in the doorway. His hair was white and it was lank, greasy, and unkempt.

His dark clothes marked him out as a priest, but as we approached him, it was the expression on his face that really drew my attention. He was scowling at us, his face all twisted up. And then, dramatically, he made a huge sign of the cross, actually standing on tiptoe as he began it, stretching the forefinger of his right hand as high into the sky as he could. I'd seen priests make the sign before but never with such a big, exaggerated gesture, filled with so much anger. An anger that seemed directed toward us.

I supposed he'd some grievance against the Spook, or maybe against the work he did. I knew the trade made most people nervous, but I'd never seen a reaction like that.

"What was wrong with him?" I asked when we had passed him and were safely out of earshot.

"Priests!" snapped the Spook, the anger sharp in his voice. "They know everything but see nothing! And that one's worse than most. That's my other brother."

I'd have liked to know more but had the sense not to question him further. It seemed to me that there was a lot to learn about the Spook and his past, but I had a feeling they were things he'd only tell me when he was good and ready.

So I just followed him south, carrying his heavy bag and thinking about what my mam had written in the letter. She was never one to boast or make wild statements. Mam only said what had to be said, so she'd meant every single word. Usually she just got on with things and did what was necessary. The Spook had told me there was nothing much could be done about ghasts, but Mam had once silenced the ghasts on Hangman's Hill.

Being a seventh son of a seventh son was nothing that special in this line of work—you needed that just to be taken on as the Spook's apprentice. But I knew there was something else that made me different.

I was my mam's son, too.

CHAPTER V
Boggarts and Witches

WE were heading for what the Spook called his Winter House.

As we walked, the last of the morning clouds melted away and I suddenly realized that there was something different about the sun. Even in the County, the sun sometimes shines in winter, which is good because it usually means that at least it isn't raining; but there's a time in each new year when you suddenly notice its warmth for the first time. It's just like the return of an old friend.

The Spook must have been thinking almost exactly the same thoughts, because he suddenly halted in his tracks, looked at me sideways, and gave me one of his rare smiles. "This is the first day of spring, lad," he said, "so we'll go to Chipenden."

It seemed an odd thing to say. Did he always go to Chipenden on the first day of the spring, and if so, why? So I asked him.

"Summer quarters. We winter on the edge of Anglezarke Moor and spend the summer in Chipenden."

"I've never heard of Anglezarke. Where's that?" I asked.

"To the far south of the County, lad. It's the place where I was born. We lived there until my father moved us to Horshaw."

Still, at least I'd heard of Chipenden, so that made me feel better. It struck me that, as the Spook's apprentice, I'd be doing a lot of traveling and would have to learn how to find my way about.

Without further delay we changed direction, heading northeast toward the distant hills. I didn't ask any more questions, but that night, as we sheltered in a cold barn once more and supper was just a few more bites of the yellow cheese, my stomach began to think that my throat had been cut. I'd never been so hungry.

I wondered where we'd be staying in Chipenden

REVENGE OF THE WITCH

and if we'd get something proper to eat there. I
didn't know anyone who'd ever been there, but it
was supposed to be a remote, unfriendly place somewhere up in the fells—the distant gray-and-purple
hills that were just visible from my dad's farm. They
always looked to me like huge sleeping beasts, but
that was probably the fault of one of my uncles, who
used to tell me tales like that. At night, he said, they
started to move, and by dawn whole villages had
sometimes disappeared from the face of the earth,
crushed into dust beneath their weight.

The next morning, dark gray clouds were covering the sun once more, and it looked as if we'd wait
some time to see the second day of spring. The wind
was getting up as well, tugging at our clothes as we
gradually began to climb and hurling birds all over
the sky, the clouds racing one another east to hide
the summits of the fells.

Our pace was slow, and I was grateful for that
because I'd developed a bad blister on each heel. So it
was late in the day when we approached Chipenden,
the light already beginning to fail.

By then, although it was still very windy, the sky

had cleared and the purple fells were sharp against the skyline. The Spook hadn't talked much on the journey, but now he sounded almost excited as he called out the names of the fells one by one. There were names such as Parlick Pike, which was the nearest to Chipenden; others — some visible, some hidden and distant — were called Mellor Knoll, Saddle Fell, and Wolf Fell.

When I asked my master if there were any wolves on Wolf Fell, he smiled grimly. "Things change rapidly here, lad," he said, "and we must always be on our guard."

As the first rooftops of the village came into sight, the Spook pointed to a narrow path that led away from the road to twist upward by the side of a small, gurgling stream.

"My house is this way," he said. "It's a slightly longer route, but it means we can avoid going through the village. I like to keep my distance from the folk who live there. They prefer it that way, too."

I remembered what Jack had said about the Spook, and my heart sank. He'd been right. It was a lonely life. You ended up working by yourself.

There were a few stunted trees on each bank,

clinging to the hillside against the force of the wind, but then suddenly, directly ahead was a wood of sycamore and ash; as we entered, the wind died away to a distant sigh. It was just a large collection of trees, a few hundred or so maybe, that offered shelter from the buffeting wind, but after a few moments I realized it was more than that.

I'd noticed before, from time to time, how some trees are noisy, always creaking their branches or rustling their leaves, while others hardly make any sound at all. Far above, I could hear the distant breath of the wind, but within the wood the only sounds to be heard were our boots. Everything was very still, a whole wood full of trees that were so silent it made a shiver run up and down my spine. It almost made me think that they were listening to us.

Then we came out into a clearing, and directly ahead was a house. It was surrounded by a tall hawthorn hedge so that just its upper story and the roof were visible. From the chimney rose a line of white smoke. Straight up into the air it went, undisturbed until, just above the trees, the wind chased it away to the east.

The house and garden, I noticed then, were sitting

in a hollow in the hillside. It was just as if an obliging giant had come along and scooped away the ground with his hand.

I followed the Spook along the hedge until we reached a metal gate. The gate was small, no taller than my waist, and it had been painted a bright green, a job that had been completed so recently that I wondered if the paint had dried properly and whether the Spook would get it on his hand, which was already reaching toward the latch.

Suddenly something happened that made me catch my breath. Before the Spook touched the latch, it lifted up on its own and the gate swung slowly open as if moved by an invisible hand.

"Thank you," I heard the Spook say.

The front door didn't move by itself, because first it had to be unlocked with the large key that the Spook pulled from his pocket. It looked similar to the one he'd used to unlock the door of the house in Watery Lane.

"Is that the same key you used in Horshaw?" I asked.

"Aye, lad," he said, glancing down at me as he pushed open the door. "My brother, the locksmith, gave me this. It opens most locks as long as they're not too complicated. Comes in quite useful in our line of work."

The door yielded with a loud creak and a deep groan, and I followed the Spook into a small, gloomy hallway. There was a steep staircase to the right and a narrow flagged passage on the left.

"Leave everything at the foot of the stairs," said the Spook. "Come on, lad. Don't dawdle. There's no time to waste. I like my food piping hot!"

So leaving his bag and my bundle where he'd said, I followed him down the passage toward the kitchen and the appetizing smell of hot food.

When we got there I wasn't disappointed. It reminded me of my mam's kitchen. Herbs were growing in big pots on the wide window ledge, and the setting sun was dappling the room with leaf-shadows. In the far corner a huge fire was blazing, filling the room with warmth, and right in the middle of the flagged floor was a large oaken table. On it were two enormous empty plates and, at its center, five serving dishes piled high with food next to a jug filled to the brim with hot, steaming gravy.

"Sit down and tuck in, lad," invited the Spook, and I didn't need to be asked twice.

I helped myself to large slices of chicken and beef, hardly leaving enough room on my plate for the mound of roasted potatoes and vegetables that followed. Finally I topped it off with a gravy so tasty that only my mam could have done better.

I wondered where the cook was and how she'd known we'd be arriving just at that exact time to put out the hot food ready on the table. I was full of questions, but I was also tired, so I saved all my energy for eating. When I'd finally swallowed my last mouthful, the Spook had already cleared his own plate.

"Enjoy that?" he asked.

I nodded, almost too full to speak. I felt sleepy.

"After a diet of cheese, it's always good to come home to a hot meal," he said. "We eat well here. It makes up for the times when we're working."

I nodded again and started to yawn.

"There's lots to do tomorrow, so get yourself off to bed. Yours is the room with the green door, at the top of the first flight of stairs," the Spook told me. "Sleep well, but stay in your room and don't go wandering about during the night. You'll hear a bell ring when breakfast's ready. Go down as soon as you hear it — when someone's cooked good food he may get angry if you let it go cold. But don't come down too early either, because that could be just as bad."

I nodded, thanked him for the meal, and went down the passage toward the front of the house. The Spook's bag and my bundle had disappeared. Wondering who could have moved them, I climbed the stairs to bed.

My new room turned out to be much larger than my bedroom at home, which at one time I'd had to share with two of my brothers. This new room had space for a bed, a small table with a candle, a chair, and a dresser, but there was still lots of room to walk about in as well. And there, on top of the dresser, my bundle of belongings was waiting.

Directly opposite the door was a large sash window, divided into eight panes of glass so thick and uneven that I couldn't see much but whorls and swirls of color from outside. The window didn't look as if it had been opened for years. The bed was pushed right up along the wall beneath it, so I pulled off my boots, kneeled up on the quilt, and tried to open the window. Although it was a bit stiff, it proved easier than it had looked. I used the sash cord to raise the bottom half of the window in a series of jerks, just far enough to pop my head out and have a better look around.

I could see a wide lawn below me, divided into two by a path of white pebbles that disappeared into the trees. Above the tree line to the right were the fells, the nearest one so close that I felt I could almost reach out and touch it. I sucked in a deep breath of cool fresh air and smelled the grass before pulling my head back inside and unwrapping my small bundle of belongings. They fitted easily into the dresser's top drawer. As I was closing it, I suddenly noticed the writing on the far wall, in the shadows opposite the foot of the bed.

It was covered in names, all scrawled in black ink on the bare plaster. Some names were larger than others, as if those who'd written them thought a lot of themselves. Many had faded with time, and I wondered if they were the names of other apprentices who'd slept in this very room. Should I add my own name or wait until the end of the first month, when I might be taken on permanently? I didn't have a pen or ink, so it was something to think about later, but I examined the wall more closely, trying to decide which was the most recent name.

I decided it was BILLY BRADLEY—that seemed the clearest and had been squeezed into a small space as the wall filled up. For a few moments I wondered what Billy was doing now, but I was tired and ready for sleep.

The sheets were clean and the bed inviting, so, wasting no more time, I undressed, and the very moment my head touched the pillow I fell asleep.

When I next opened my eyes, the sun was streaming through the window. I'd been dreaming and had been woken suddenly by a noise. I thought it was probably the breakfast bell.

I felt worried then. Had it really been the bell downstairs summoning me to breakfast or a bell in my dream? How could I be sure? What was I supposed to do? It seemed that I'd be in trouble with the cook whether I went down early or late. So, deciding that I probably *had* heard the bell, I dressed and went downstairs right away.

On my way down I heard a clatter of pots and pans coming from the kitchen, but the moment I eased open the door, everything became deathly silent.

I made a mistake then. I should have gone straight back upstairs, because it was obvious that the breakfast wasn't ready. The plates had been cleared away from last night's supper, but the table was still bare and the fireplace was full of cold ashes. In fact, the kitchen was chilly and, worse than that, it seemed to be growing colder by the second.

My mistake was in taking a step toward the table. No sooner had I done that than I heard something make a sound right behind me. It was an angry sound. There was no doubt about that. It was a definite hiss of anger, and it was very close to my left ear. So close that I felt the breath of it.

The Spook had warned me not to come down early, and I suddenly felt that I was in real danger.

As soon as I had entertained that thought, something hit me very hard on the back of the head; I staggered toward the door, almost losing my balance and falling headlong.

I didn't need a second warning. I ran from the room and up the stairs. Then, halfway up, I froze. There was someone standing at the top. Someone tall and menacing, silhouetted against the light from the door of my room.

I halted, unsure which way to go until I was reassured by a familiar voice. It was the Spook.

It was the first time I'd seen him without his long black cloak. He was wearing a black tunic and gray breeches, and I could see that, although he was a tall man with broad shoulders, the rest of his body was thin, probably because some days all he got was a nibble of cheese. He was like the very best farm laborers when they get older. Some, of course, just get fatter, but the majority—like the ones my dad sometimes hires for the harvest now that most of my brothers have left home—are thin, with tough, wiry bodies. "Thinner means fitter," Dad always says, and now, looking at the Spook, I could see why he was able to walk at such a furious pace and for so long without resting.

"I warned you about going down early," he said quietly. "No doubt you got your ears boxed. Let that be a lesson to you, lad. Next time it might be far worse."

"I thought I heard the bell," I said. "But it must have been a bell in my dream."

The Spook laughed softly. "That's one of the first and most important lessons that an apprentice has to learn," he said; "the difference between waking and dreaming. Some never learn that."

He shook his head, took a step toward me, and patted me on the shoulder. "Come, I'll show you round the garden. We've got to start somewhere, and it'll pass the time until breakfast's ready."

When the Spook led me out, using the back door of the house, I saw that the garden was very large, much larger than it had looked from outside the hedge.

We walked east, squinting into the early morning sun, until we reached a wide lawn. The previous evening I'd thought that the garden was completely surrounded by the hedge, but now I realized that I was mistaken. There were gaps in it, and directly ahead was the wood. The path of white pebbles divided the lawn and vanished into the trees.

"There's really more than one garden," said the Spook. "Three, in fact, each reached by a path like this. We'll look at the eastern garden first. It's safe enough when the sun's up, but never walk down this path after dark. Well, not unless you have very good reason and certainly never when you're alone."

Nervously I followed the Spook toward the trees. The grass was longer at the edge of the lawn, and it was dotted with bluebells. I like bluebells because they flower in spring and always remind me that the long, hot days of summer are not too far away, but now I hardly gave them a second glance. The morning sun was hidden by the trees and the air had suddenly gotten much cooler. It reminded me of my visit to the kitchen. There was something strange and dangerous about this part of the woods, and it seemed to be getting steadily colder the farther we advanced into the trees.

There were rooks' nests high above us, and the birds' harsh, angry cries made me shiver even more than the cold. They were about as musical as my dad, who used to start singing as we got to the end of the milking. If the milk ever went sour, my mam used to blame it on him.

The Spook halted and pointed to the ground about five paces ahead. "What's that?" he asked, his voice hardly more than a whisper.

The grass had been cleared, and at the center of the large patch of bare earth was a gravestone. It was vertical but leaning slightly to the left. On the ground before it, six feet of soil was edged with smaller stones, which was unusual. But there was something else even more strange: across the top of the patch of earth, and fastened to the outer stones by bolts, lay thirteen thick iron bars.

I counted them twice just to be sure.

"Well, come on, lad—I asked you a question. What is it?"

My mouth was so dry I could hardly speak, but I managed to stammer out three words: "It's a grave. . . ."

"Good lad. Got it first time. Notice anything unusual?" he asked.

I couldn't speak at all by then. So I just nodded.

He smiled and patted me on the shoulder. "There's nothing to be afraid of. It's just a dead witch, and a pretty feeble one at that. They buried her on unhallowed ground outside a churchyard not too many miles from here. But she kept scratching her way to the surface. I gave her a good talking-to, but she wouldn't listen, so I had her brought here. It makes people feel better. That way they can get on with their lives in peace. They don't want to think about things like this. That's our job."

I nodded again and suddenly realized that I wasn't breathing, so I sucked in a deep lungful of air. My heart was hammering away in my chest, threatening to break out any minute, and I was trembling from head to foot.

"No, she's little trouble now," the Spook continued. "Sometimes, at the full moon, you can hear her stirring, but she lacks the strength to get to the surface and the iron bars would stop her anyway. But there are worse things farther off, there in the trees," he said, gesturing east with his bony finger. "About another twenty paces would bring you to the spot."

Worse? What could be worse? I wondered, but I knew he was going to tell me anyway.

"There are two other witches. One's dead and one's alive. The dead one's buried vertically, head down, but even then, once or twice each year we have to straighten out the bars over her grave. Just keep well away after dark."

"Why bury her head down?" I asked.

"That's a good question, lad," the Spook said. "You see, the spirit of a dead witch is usually what we call 'bone-bound.' They're trapped inside their bones, and some don't even know they're dead.

We try them first head up and that's enough for most. All witches are different, but some are really stubborn. Still bound to her bones, a witch like that tries hard to get back into the world. It's as if they want to be born again, so we have to make things difficult for them and bury them the other way up. Coming out feet first isn't easy. Human babies sometimes have the same trouble. But she's still dangerous, so keep well away.

"Make sure you keep clear of the live one. She'd be more dangerous dead than alive, because a witch that powerful would have no trouble at all getting back into the world. That's why we keep her in a pit. Her name's Mother Malkin, and she talks to herself. Well, it's more of a whisper really. She's just about as evil as you can get, but she's been in her pit for a long time and most of her power's bled away into the earth. She'd love to get her hands on a lad like you. So stay well away. Promise me now that you won't go near. Let me hear you say it."

"I promise not to go near," I whispered, feeling uneasy about the whole thing. It seemed a terrible, cruel thing to keep any living creature — even a witch — in the ground, and I couldn't imagine my mam liking the idea much.

"That's a good lad. We don't want any more accidents like the one this morning. There are worse things than getting your ears boxed. Far worse."

I believed him, but I didn't want to hear about it. Still, he had other things to show me, so I was spared more of his scary words. He led me out of the wood and strode toward another lawn.

"This is the southern garden," the Spook said. "Don't come here after dark either." The sun was quickly hidden by dense branches and the air grew steadily cooler, so I knew we were approaching something bad. He halted about ten paces short of a large stone that lay flat on the ground, close to the roots of an oak tree. It covered an area a bit larger than a grave, and judging by the part that was above ground, the stone was very thick, too.

"What do you think's buried under there?" the Spook asked.

I tried to appear confident. "Another witch?"

"No," said the Spook. "You don't need as much stone as that for a witch. Iron usually does the trick. But the thing under there could slip through iron bars in the twinkling of an eye. Look closely at the stone. Can you see what's carved on it?"

Gregory

I nodded. I recognized the letter, but I didn't know what it meant.

"That's the Greek letter beta," said the Spook. "It's the sign we use for a boggart. The diagonal line means it's been artificially bound under that stone and the name underneath tells you who did it. Bottom right is the Roman numeral for one. That means it's a boggart of the first rank and very dangerous. As I mentioned, we use grades from one to ten. Remember that—one day it might save your life. A grade ten is so weak that most folk wouldn't even notice it was there. A grade one could easily kill you. Cost me a fortune to have that stone brought here, but it was worth every penny. That's a bound boggart now. It's artificially bound and it'll stay there until Gabriel blows his horn.

"There's a lot you need to learn about boggarts, lad, and I'm going to start your training right after breakfast, but there is one important difference between those that are bound and those that are free. A free boggart can often travel miles from its home and, if it's so inclined, do endless mischief. If a boggart's particularly troublesome and won't listen to reason, then it's our job to bind it. Do it well and it's what we call artificially bound. Then it can't move at all. Of course, it's far easier said than done."

The Spook frowned suddenly, as if he'd remembered something unpleasant. "One of my apprentices got into serious trouble trying to bind a boggart," he said, shaking his head sadly, "but as it's only your first day, we won't talk about that yet."

Just then, from the direction of the house, the sound of a bell could be heard in the distance. The Spook smiled. "Are we awake or are we dreaming?" he asked.

"Awake."

"Are you sure?"

I nodded.

"In that case, let's go and eat," he said. "I'll show you the other garden when our bellies are full."

CHAPTER VI
A Girl with Pointy Shoes

THE kitchen had changed since my last visit. A small fire had been made up in the grate and two plates of bacon and eggs were on the table. There was a freshly baked loaf, too, and a large pat of butter.

"Tuck in, lad, before it gets cold," invited the Spook.

I set to immediately, and it didn't take us long to finish off both platefuls and eat half the loaf as well. Then the Spook leaned back in his chair, tugged at his beard, and asked me an important question.

"Don't you think," he asked, his eyes staring straight into mine, "that was the best plate of bacon and eggs you've ever tasted?"

I didn't agree. The breakfast had been well

cooked. It was good, all right, better than cheese, but I'd tasted better. I'd tasted better every single morning when I'd lived at home. My mam was a far better cook, but somehow I didn't think that was the answer the Spook was looking for. So I told a little white lie, the kind of untruth that doesn't really do any harm and tends to make people happier for hearing it.

"Yes," I said, "it was the very best breakfast that I've ever tasted. And I'm sorry for coming down too early and I promise that it won't happen again."

At that, the Spook grinned so much that I thought his face was going to split in two; then he clapped me on the back and led me out into the garden again.

It was only when we were outside that the grin finally faded. "Well done, lad," he said. "There are two things that respond well to flattery: boggarts and some women. Gets them every time."

Well, I hadn't seen any sign of a woman in the kitchen, so it confirmed what I'd suspected—that a boggart cooked our meals. It was a surprise, to say the least. Everyone thought that a spook was a boggart-slayer, or that he fixed them so they couldn't get up to any mischief. Who would have credited that he had one cooking and cleaning for him?

"This is the western garden," the Spook told me as we walked along the third path, the white pebbles crunching under our feet. "It's a safe place to be whether it's day or night. I often come here myself when I've got a problem that needs thinking through."

We passed through another gap in the hedge and were soon walking through the trees. I felt the difference right away. The birds were singing, and the trees were swaying slightly in the morning breeze. It was a happier place.

We kept walking until we came out of the trees onto a hillside with a view of the fells to our right. The sky was so clear that I could see the dry-stone walls that divided the lower slopes into fields and marked out each farmer's territory. In fact, the view extended right to the summits of the nearest fell.

The Spook gestured toward a wooden bench to our left. "Take a pew, lad," he invited.

I did as I was told and sat down. For a few moments the Spook stared down at me, his green eyes locked upon mine. Then he began to pace up and down in front of the bench without speaking.

He was no longer looking at me but stared into space with a vacant expression in his eyes. He thrust back his long black cloak and put his hands in his breeches pockets. Then, very suddenly, he sat down beside me and asked questions.

"How many different types of boggart do you think there are?"

I hadn't a clue. "I know two types already," I said, "the free and the bound. But I couldn't even begin to guess about the others."

"That's good twice over, lad. You've remembered what I taught you and you've shown yourself to be someone who doesn't make wild guesses. You see, there are as many different types of boggart as there are types of people, and each one has a personality of its own. Having said that, though, there are some types that can be recognized and given a name — sometimes on account of the shape they take and sometimes because of their behavior and the tricks they get up to."

He reached into his right pocket and pulled out a small book bound with black leather. Then he handed it to me. "Here, this is yours now," he said. "Take care of it, and whatever you do, don't lose it."

The smell of leather was very strong and the book appeared to be brand new. It was a bit of a disappointment to open it and find it full of blank pages. I suppose I'd expected it to be full of the secrets of the Spook's trade — but no, it seemed that I was expected to write them down, because next the Spook pulled a pen and a small bottle of ink from his pocket.

"Prepare to take notes," he said, standing up and beginning to pace back and forth in front of the bench again. "And be careful not to spill the ink, lad. It doesn't dribble from a cow's udder."

I managed to uncork the bottle. Then, very carefully, I dipped the nib of the pen into it and opened the notebook at the first page.

The Spook had already begun the lesson, and he was talking very fast.

"Firstly, there are hairy boggarts, which take the shape of animals. Most are dogs, but there are almost as many cats and the odd goat or two. But don't forget to include horses as well — they can be very tricky. And whatever their shape, hairy boggarts can be divided up into those that are hostile, friendly, or somewhere between.

"Then there are hall knockers, which sometimes

develop into stone chuckers, which can get very angry when provoked. One of the nastiest types of all is the cattle ripper, because it's just as partial to human blood. But don't run away with the idea that we spooks just deal with boggarts, because the unquiet dead are never very far away. Then, to make things worse, witches are a real problem in the County. We don't have any local witches to worry about now, but to the east, near Pendle Hill, they're a real menace. And remember, not all witches are the same. They fall into four rough categories—the malevolent, the benign, the falsely accused, and the unaware."

By now, as you might have guessed, I was in real trouble. To begin with, he was talking so fast I hadn't managed to write down a single word. Secondly, I didn't even know all the big words he was using. However, just then he paused. I think he must have noticed the dazed expression on my face.

"What's the problem, lad?" he asked. "Come on, spit it out. Don't be afraid to ask questions."

"I didn't understand all that you said about witches," I said. "I don't know what 'malevolent' means. Or 'benign' either."

"Malevolent means evil," he explained. "Benign

means good. And an unaware witch means a witch who doesn't know she's a witch, and because she's a woman that makes her double trouble. Never trust a woman."

"My mother's a woman," I said, suddenly feeling a little angry, "and I trust her."

"Mothers usually are women," said the Spook. "And mothers are usually quite trustworthy, as long as you're their son. Otherwise, look out! I had a mother once and I trusted her, so I remember the feeling well.

"Do you like girls?" he asked suddenly.

"I don't really know any girls," I admitted. "I don't have any sisters."

"Well, in that case you could fall easy victim to their tricks. So watch out for the village girls. Especially any who wear pointy shoes. Jot that down. It's as good a place to start as any."

I wondered what was so terrible about wearing pointy shoes. I knew my mam wouldn't be happy with what the Spook had just said. She believed you should take people as you find them, not just depend on someone else's opinion. Still, what choice did I have? So at the top of the very first page I wrote down *Village Girls with Pointy Shoes*.

He watched me write, then asked for the book and pen. "Look," he said, "you're going to have to take notes faster than that. There's a lot to learn, and you'll have filled a dozen notebooks before long, but for now three or four headings will be enough to get you started."

He then wrote *Hairy Boggarts* at the top of page two. Then *Hall Knockers* at the top of page three; then, finally, *Witches* at the top of page four.

"There," he said. "That's got you started. Just write anything you learn today under one of those four headings. But now for something more urgent. We need provisions. So go down to the village, or we'll go hungry tomorrow. Even the best cook can't cook without provisions. Remember that everything goes inside my sack. The butcher has it, so go there first. Just ask for Mr. Gregory's order.'

He gave me a small silver coin, warning me not to lose my change, then sent me off down the hill on the quickest route to the village.

Soon I was walking through trees again, until at last I reached a stile that brought me onto a steep, narrow lane. A hundred or so paces lower, I turned a corner and the gray slates of Chipenden's rooftops came into view.

The village was larger than I'd expected. There were at least a hundred cottages, then a pub, a schoolhouse, and a big church with a bell tower. There was no sign of a market square, but the cobbled main street, which sloped quite steeply, was full of women with loaded baskets scurrying in and out of shops. Horses and carts were waiting on both sides of the street, so it was clear that the local farmers' wives came here to shop and, no doubt, also folk from hamlets nearby.

I found the butcher's shop without any trouble and joined a queue of boisterous women, all calling out to the butcher, a cheerful, big, red-faced man with a ginger beard. He seemed to know every single one of them by name, and they kept laughing loudly at his jokes, which came thick and fast. I didn't understand most of them, but the women certainly did, and they really seemed to be enjoying themselves.

Nobody paid me much attention, but at last I reached the counter and it was my turn to be served.

"I've called for Mr. Gregory's order," I told the butcher.

As soon as I'd spoken, the shop became quiet and the laughter stopped. The butcher reached behind the counter and pulled out a large sack. I could hear people whispering behind me, but even straining my ears, I couldn't quite catch what they were saying. When I glanced behind, they were looking everywhere but at me. Some were even staring down at the floor.

I gave the butcher the silver coin, checked my change carefully, thanked him, and carried the sack out of the shop, swinging it up onto my shoulder when I reached the street. The visit to the greengrocer's took no time at all. The provisions there were already wrapped, so I put the parcel in the sack, which was now starting to feel a bit heavy.

Until then everything had gone well, but as I went into the baker's, I saw the gang of lads.

There were seven or eight of them sitting on a garden wall. Nothing odd about that, except for the fact that they weren't speaking to one another— they were all busy staring at me with hungry faces, like a pack of wolves, watching every step I took as I approached the baker's.

When I came out of the shop they were still there,

and now, as I began to climb the hill, they started to follow me. Well, although it was too much of a coincidence to think that they'd just decided to go up the same hill, I wasn't that worried. Six brothers had given me plenty of practice at fighting.

I heard the sound of their boots getting closer and closer. They were catching up with me pretty quickly, but maybe that was because I was walking slower and slower. You see, I didn't want them to think I was scared, and in any case, the sack was heavy and the hill I was climbing was very steep.

They caught up with me about a dozen paces before the stile, just at the point where the lane divided a small wood, the trees crowding in on either side to shut out the morning sun.

"Open the sack and let's see what we've got," said a voice behind me.

It was a loud, deep voice accustomed to telling people what to do. There was a hard edge of danger that told me its owner liked to cause pain and was always looking for his next victim.

I turned to face him but gripped the sack even tighter, keeping it firmly on my shoulder. The one who'd spoken was the leader of the gang. There was no doubt about that. The rest of them had thin, pinched faces, as if they were in need of a good meal, but he looked as if he'd been eating for all of them. He was at least a head taller than me, with broad shoulders and a neck like a bull's. His face was broad, too, with red cheeks, but his eyes were very small and he didn't seem to blink at all.

I suppose if he hadn't been there and hadn't tried to bully me, I might have relented. After all, some of the boys looked half starved, and there were a lot of apples and cakes in the sack. On the other hand, they weren't mine to give away.

"This doesn't belong to me," I said. "It belongs to Mr. Gregory."

"His last apprentice didn't let that bother him," said the leader, moving his big face closer to mine. "He used to open the sack for us. If you've any sense, you'll do the same. If you won't do it the easy way, then it'll have to be the hard way. But you won't like that very much and it'll all come down to the same thing in the end."

The gang began to move in closer, and I could feel someone behind me tugging at the sack. Even then, I wouldn't let go, and I stared back into the piggy eyes of the leader, trying hard not to blink.

At that moment something happened that took us all by surprise. There was a movement in the trees somewhere to my right, and we all turned toward it.

There was a dark shape in the shadows, and as my eyes adjusted to the gloom, I saw that it was a girl. She was moving slowly in our direction, but her approach was so silent that you could have heard a pin drop, and so smooth that she seemed to be floating rather than walking. Then she stopped just on the edge of the tree shadows, as if she didn't want to step into the sunlight.

"Why don't you leave him be?" she demanded. It seemed like a question but the tone in her voice told me it was a command.

"What's it to you?" asked the leader of the gang, jutting his chin forward and bunching his fists.

"Ain't me you need to worry about," she answered from the shadows. "Lizzie's back, and if you don't do what I say, it's her you'll answer to."

"Lizzie?" asked the lad, taking a step backward.

"Bony Lizzie. She's my aunt. Don't tell me you ain't heard of her. . . ."

Have you ever felt time slow so much that it

almost appears to stop? Ever listened to a clock when the next tick seems to take forever to follow the last tock? Well, it was just like that until, very suddenly, the girl hissed loudly through her clenched teeth. Then she spoke again.

"Go on," she said. "Be off with you! Be gone, be quick or be dead!"

The effect on the gang was immediate. I glimpsed the expression on some of their faces and saw that they weren't just afraid. They were terrified and close to panic. Their leader turned on his heels and immediately fled down the hill, with the others close behind him.

I didn't know why they were so scared, but I felt like running, too. The girl was staring at me with wide eyes, and I didn't feel able to control my limbs properly. I felt like a mouse paralyzed by the stare of a stoat about to pounce at any moment.

I forced my left foot to move and slowly turned my body toward the trees to follow the direction my nose was pointing, but I was still gripping the Spook's sack. Whoever she was, I still wasn't going to give it up.

"Ain't you going to run as well?" she asked me.

I shook my head, but my mouth was very dry and I couldn't trust myself to try and speak. I knew the words would come out wrong.

She was probably about my own age—if anything, slightly younger. Her face was nice enough, for she had large brown eyes, high cheekbones, and long black hair. She wore a black dress tied tightly at the waist with a piece of white string. But as I took all this in, I suddenly noticed something that troubled me.

The girl was wearing pointy shoes, and immediately I remembered the Spook's warning. But I stood my ground, determined not to run like the others.

"Ain't you going to thank me?" she asked. "Be nice to get some thanks."

"Thanks," I said lamely, just managing to get the word out first time.

"Well, that's a start," she said. "But to thank me properly, you need to give me something, don't you? A cake and an apple will do for now. It ain't much to ask. There's plenty in the sack and Old Gregory won't notice, and if he does, he won't say anything."

I was shocked to hear her call the Spook "Old Gregory." I knew he wouldn't like being called that, and it told me two things. First, the girl had little respect for him, and second, she wasn't the least bit afraid of him. Back where I came from, most people shivered even at the thought that the Spook might be in the neighborhood.

"I'm sorry," I said, "but I can't do that. They're not mine to give."

She glared at me hard then and didn't speak for a long time. I thought at one point that she was going to hiss at me through her teeth. I stared back at her, trying not to blink, until at last a faint smile lit up her face and she spoke again.

"Then I'll have to settle for a promise."

"A promise?" I asked, wondering what she meant.

"A promise to help me just as I helped you. I don't need any help right now, but perhaps one day I might."

"That's fine," I told her. "If you ever need any help in the future, then just ask."

"What's your name?" she asked, giving me a really broad smile.

"Tom Ward."

"Well, my name's Alice and I live yonder," she said, pointing back through the trees. "I'm Bony Lizzie's favorite niece."

Bony Lizzie was a strange name, but it would have been rude to mention it. Whoever she was, her name had been enough to scare the village lads.

That was the end of our conversation. We both turned then to go our separate ways, but as we walked away, Alice called over her shoulder, "Take care now. You don't want to end up like Old Gregory's last apprentice."

"What happened to him?" I asked.

"Better ask Old Gregory!" she shouted as she disappeared back into the trees.

When I got back, the Spook checked the contents of the sack carefully, ticking things off from a list.

"Did you have any trouble down in the village?" he asked when he'd finally finished.

"Some lads followed me up the hill and asked me to open the sack, but I told them no," I said.

"That was very brave of you," said the Spook. "Next time it won't do any harm to let them have a few apples and cakes. Life's hard enough as it is, but some of them come from very poor families. I always order extra in case they ask for some."

I felt annoyed then. If only he'd told me that in

advance! "I didn't like to do it without asking you first," I said.

The Spook raised his eyebrows. "Did you want to give them a few apples and cakes?"

"I don't like being bullied," I said, "but some of them did look really hungry."

"Then next time trust your instincts and use your initiative," said the Spook. "Trust the voice inside you. It's rarely wrong. A spook depends a lot on that because it can sometimes mean the difference between life and death. So that's another thing we need to find out about you. Whether or not your instincts can be relied on."

He paused, staring at me hard, his green eyes searching my face. "Any trouble with girls?" he asked suddenly.

It was because I was still annoyed that I didn't give a straight answer to his question.

"No trouble at all," I answered.

It wasn't a lie because Alice had helped me, which was the opposite of trouble. Still, I knew he really meant had I met any girls, and I knew I should have told him about her. Especially with her wearing pointy shoes.

I made lots of mistakes as an apprentice, and that was my second serious one—not telling the Spook the whole truth.

The first, even more serious one was making the promise to Alice.

CHAPTER VII
Someone Has to Do It

AFTER that my life settled into a busy routine. The Spook taught me fast and made me write until my wrist ached and my eyes stung.

One afternoon he took me to the far end of the village, beyond the last stone cottage to a small circle of willow trees, which are called withy trees in the County. It was a gloomy spot and there, hanging from a branch, was a rope. I looked up and saw a big brass bell.

"When people need help," said the Spook, "they don't come up to the house. Nobody comes unless they're invited. I'm strict about that. They come down here and ring that bell. Then we go to them."

The trouble was that even after weeks had gone

by, nobody came to ring the bell, and I only ever got to go farther than the western garden when it was time to fetch the weekly provisions from the village. I was lonely, too, missing my family, so it was a good job the Spook kept me busy—that meant I didn't have time to dwell on it. I always went to bed tired and fell asleep as soon as my head hit the pillow.

The lessons were the most interesting part of each day, but I didn't learn much about ghasts, ghosts, and witches. The Spook had told me that the main topic in an apprentice's first year was boggarts, together with such subjects as botany, which meant learning all about plants, some of which were really useful as medicines or could be eaten if you had no other food. But my lessons weren't just writing. Some of the work was just as hard and physical as anything I'd done back home on our farm.

It started on a warm, sunny morning, when the Spook told me to put away my notebook and led the way toward his southern garden. He gave me two things to carry: a spade and a long measuring rod.

"Free boggarts travel down leys," he explained. "But sometimes something goes wrong. It can be the result of a storm or maybe even an earthquake. In the County there hasn't been a serious earthquake in living memory, but that doesn't matter, because leys are all interconnected and something happening to one, even a thousand miles away, can disturb all the others. Then boggarts get stuck in the same place for years, and we call them 'naturally bound.' Often they can't move more than a few dozen paces in any direction, and they cause little trouble. Not unless you happen to get too close to one. Sometimes, though, they can be stuck in awkward places, close to a house or even inside one. Then you might need to move the boggart from there and artificially bind it elsewhere."

"What's a ley?" I asked.

"Not everybody agrees, lad," he told me. "Some think they're just ancient paths that crisscross the land, the paths our forefathers walked in ancient times when men were real men and darkness knew its place. Health was better, lives were longer, and everyone was happy and content."

"What happened?"

"Ice moved down from the north and the earth grew cold for thousands of years," the Spook explained. "It was so difficult to survive that men forgot everything they'd learned. The old knowledge was unimportant. Keeping warm and eating was all that mattered. When the ice finally pulled back, the survivors were hunters dressed in animal skins. They'd forgotten how to grow crops and husband animals. Darkness was all-powerful.

"Well, it's better now, although we still have a long way to go. All that's left of those times are the leys, but the truth is they're more than just paths. Leys are really lines of power far beneath the earth. Secret invisible roads that free boggarts can use to travel at great speed. It's these free boggarts that cause the most trouble. When they set up home in a new location, often they're not welcome. Not being welcome makes them angry. They play tricks—sometimes dangerous tricks—and that means work for us. Then they need to be artificially bound in a pit. Just like the one that you're going to dig now. . . .

"This is a good place," he said, pointing at the ground near a big, ancient oak tree. "I think there should be enough space between the roots."

The Spook gave me a measuring rod so that I could make the pit exactly six feet long, six feet deep, and three feet wide. Even in the shade it was too warm to be digging, and it took me hours and hours to get it right because the Spook was a perfectionist.

After digging the pit, I had to prepare a smelly mixture of salt, iron filings, and a special sort of glue made from bones.

"Salt can burn a boggart," said the Spook. "Iron, on the other hand, earths things: Just as lightning finds its way to earth and loses its power, iron can sometimes bleed away the strength and substance of things that haunt the dark. It can end the mischief of troublesome boggarts. Used together, salt and iron form a barrier that a boggart can't cross. In fact, salt and iron can be useful in lots of situations."

After stirring up the mixture in a big metal bucket, I used a large brush to line the inside of the pit. It was like painting but harder work, and the coating had to be perfect in order to stop even the craftiest boggart from escaping.

"Do a thorough job, lad," the Spook told me. "A boggart can escape through a hole no bigger than a pinhead."

Of course, as soon as the pit was completed to the Spook's satisfaction, I had to fill it in and begin again. He had me digging two practice pits a week, which was hard, sweaty work and took up a lot of my time. It was a bit scary, too, because I was working near pits that contained real boggarts, and even in daylight it was a creepy place. I noticed that the Spook never went too far away, though, and he always seemed watchful and alert, telling me you could never take chances with boggarts even when they were bound.

The Spook also told me that I'd need to know every inch of the County—all its towns and villages and the quickest route between any two points. The trouble was that although the Spook said he had lots of maps upstairs in his library, it seemed I always had to do things the hard way, so he started me off by making me draw a map of my own.

At its center was his house and gardens and it had to include the village and the nearest of the fells. The idea was that it would gradually get bigger to include more and more of the surrounding countryside. But drawing wasn't my strong point, and as I said, the Spook was a perfectionist, so the map took a long time to grow. It was only then that he started to show me his own maps, but he made me spend more time carefully folding them up afterward than actually studying them.

I also began to keep a diary. The Spook gave me another notebook for this, telling me for the ump- teenth time that I needed to record the past so that I could learn from it. I didn't write in it every day, though; sometimes I was too tired and sometimes my wrist was aching too much from scribbling at top speed in my other notebook while trying to keep up with what the Spook said.

Then, one morning at breakfast, when I'd been staying with the Spook for just one month, he asked, "What do you think so far, lad?"

I wondered if he were talking about the breakfast. Perhaps there'd be a second course to make up for the bacon, which had been a bit burned that morn- ing. So I just shrugged. I didn't want to offend the boggart, which was probably listening.

"Well, it's a hard job and I wouldn't blame you for deciding to give it up now," he said. "After the first month's passed, I always give each new appren- tice the chance to go home and think very carefully about whether he wants to carry on or not. Would you like to do the same?"

I did my best not to seem too eager, but I couldn't

keep the smile off my face. The trouble was, the more I smiled the more miserable the Spook looked. I got the feeling that he wanted me to stay, but I couldn't wait to be off. The thought of seeing my family again and getting to taste Mam's cooking seemed like a dream.

I left for home within the hour. "You're a brave lad and your wits are sharp," he said to me at the gate. "You've passed your month's trial, so you can tell your dad that, if you want to carry on, I'll be visiting him in the autumn to collect my ten guineas. You've the makings of a good apprentice, but it's up to you, lad. If you don't come back, then I'll know you've decided against it. Otherwise I'll expect you back within the week. Then I'll give you five years' training that'll make you almost as good at the job as I am."

I set off for home with a light heart. You see, I didn't want to tell the Spook, but the moment he'd given me the chance to go home and maybe never come back, I'd already made up my mind to do just that. It was a terrible job. From what the Spook had told me, apart from the loneliness, it was dangerous and terrifying. Nobody really cared whether you lived or died. They just wanted you to get rid of whatever was plaguing them but didn't think for a second about what it might cost you.

The Spook had described how he'd once been half killed by a boggart. It had changed, in the blink of an eye, from a hall knocker to a stone chucker and had nearly brained him with a rock as big as a blacksmith's fist. He said that he hadn't even been paid yet but expected to get the money next spring. Well, next spring was a long time off, so what good was that? As I set off for home, it seemed to me that I'd be better off working on the farm.

The trouble was, it was nearly two days' journey, and walking gave me a lot of time to think. I remembered how bored I'd sometimes been on the farm. Could I really put up with working there for the rest of my life?

Next I started to think about what Mam would say. She'd been really set on me being the Spook's apprentice, and if I stopped I'd really let her down. So the hardest part would be telling her and watching her reaction.

By nightfall on the first day of my journey home, I'd

finished all the cheese the Spook had given me for the trip. So the next day I only stopped once, to bathe my feet in a stream, reaching home just before the evening milking.

As I opened the gate to the yard, Dad was heading for the cowshed. When he saw me, his face lit up with a broad smile. I offered to help with the milking so we could talk, but he told me to go in right away and speak to my mam.

"She's missed you, lad. You'll be a sight for sore eyes."

Patting me on the back, he went off to do his milking, but before I'd taken half a dozen paces Jack came out of the barn and made straight for me.

"What brings you back so soon?" he asked. He seemed a little bit cool. Well, to be honest, he was more cold than cool. His face was sort of twisted up, as if he were trying to scowl and grin at the same time.

"The Spook's sent me home for a few days. I've to make up my mind whether to carry on or not."

"So what will you do?"

"I'm going to talk to Mam about it."

"No doubt you'll get your own way, as usual," Jack said.

By now Jack was definitely scowling, and it made me feel that something had happened while I'd been away. Why else was he suddenly so unfriendly? Was it because he didn't want me coming home?

"And I can't believe you took Dad's tinderbox," he said.

"He gave it to me," I said. "He wanted me to have it."

"He offered it, but that didn't mean you had to take it. The trouble with you is that you only think about yourself. Think of poor Dad. He loved that tinderbox."

I didn't say anything because I didn't want to get into an argument. I knew he was wrong. Dad had wanted me to have the tinderbox, I was sure of it.

"While I'm back, I'll be able to help out," I said, trying to change the subject.

"If you really want to earn your keep, then feed the pigs!" he called as he turned to walk away. It was a job neither of us liked much. They were big, hairy, smelly pigs and always so hungry that it was never safe to turn your back on them.

Despite what Jack had said, I was still glad to be home. As I crossed the yard, I glanced up at the house. Mam's climbing roses covered most of the wall at the back and always did well even though they faced north. Now they were just shooting, but by mid-June they'd be covered in red blossoms.

The back door was always jamming because the house had once been struck by lightning. The door had caught fire and had been replaced, but the frame was still slightly warped, so I had to push hard to force it open. It was worth it, because the first thing I saw was Mam's smiling face.

She was sitting in her old rocking chair in the far corner of the kitchen, a place where the setting sun couldn't reach. If the light was too bright, it hurt her eyes. Mam preferred winter to summer and night to day.

She was glad to see me all right, and at first I tried to delay telling her I'd come home to stay. I put on a brave face and pretended to be happy, but she saw right through me. I could never hide anything from her.

"What's wrong?" she asked.

I shrugged and tried to smile, probably doing

even worse than my brother at disguising my feelings.

"Speak up," she said. "There's no point in keeping it bottled up."

I didn't answer for a long time because I was trying to find a way to put it into words. The rhythm of Mam's rocking chair gradually slowed, until at last it came to a complete halt. That was always a bad sign.

"I've passed my month's trial and Mr. Gregory says it's up to me whether I carry on or not. But I'm lonely, Mam," I confessed at last. "It's just as bad as I expected. I've got no friends. Nobody of my own age to talk to. I feel so alone — I'd like to come back and work here."

I could have said more and told her how happy we used to be on the farm when all my brothers were living at home. I didn't — I knew that she missed them, too. I thought she'd be sympathetic because of that, but I was wrong.

There was a long pause before Mam spoke, and I could hear Ellie sweeping up in the next room, singing softly to herself as she worked.

"Lonely?" Mam asked, her voice full of anger rather than sympathy. "How can you be lonely? You've got yourself, haven't you? If you ever lose yourself, then you'll really be lonely. In the meantime, stop complaining. You're nearly a man now, and a man has to work. Ever since the world began, men have been doing jobs they didn't like. Why should it be any different for you? You're the seventh son of a seventh son, and this is the job you were born to do."

"But Mr. Gregory's trained other apprentices," I blurted out. "One of them could come back and look after the County. Why does it have to be me?"

"He's trained many, but precious few completed their time," Mam said, "and those that did aren't a patch on him. They're flawed or weak or cowardly. They walk a twisted path, taking money for accomplishing little. So there's only you left now, son. You're the last chance. The last hope. Someone has to do it. Someone has to stand against the dark. And you're the only one who can."

The chair began to rock again, slowly picking up speed.

"Well, I'm glad that's settled. Do you want to wait for supper or shall I put you some out as soon as it's ready?" Mam asked.

"I've had nothing to eat all day, Mam. Not even breakfast."

"Well, it's rabbit stew. That ought to cheer you up a bit."

I sat at the kitchen table feeling as low and sad as I could ever remember while Mam bustled about the stove. The rabbit stew smelled delicious, and my mouth began to water. Nobody was a better cook than my mam, and it was worth coming home, even for just a single meal.

With a smile, Mam carried across a big steaming plate of stew and set it down before me. "I'll go and make up your room," she said. "Now you're here, you might as well stay a couple of days."

I mumbled my thanks and wasted no time in starting. As soon as Mam went upstairs, Ellie came into the kitchen.

"Nice to see you back, Tom," she said with a smile. Then she looked down at my generous plate of food. "Would you like some bread with that?"

"Yes, please," I said, and Ellie buttered me three thick slices before sitting at the table opposite me. I finished it all without once coming up for air, finally wiping my plate clean with the last big slice of freshly baked bread.

"Feel better now?"

I nodded and tried to smile, but I knew it hadn't worked properly because Ellie suddenly looked worried. "I couldn't help overhearing what you told your mam," she said. "I'm sure it's not as bad as all that. It's just because the job's all new and strange. You'll soon get used to the work. Anyway, you don't have to go back right away. After a few days at home you'll feel better. And you'll always be welcome here, even when the farm belongs to Jack."

"I don't think Jack's that pleased to see me."

"Why, what makes you say that?" Ellie asked.

"He just didn't seem that friendly, that's all. I don't think he wants me here."

"Don't you worry about your big mean brother. I can sort him out easily enough."

I smiled properly then, because it was true. As my mam once said, Ellie could twist Jack round her little finger.

"What's mainly bothering him is this," Ellie said, smoothing her hand down across her belly. "My mother's sister died in childbirth, and our family still talks of it to this day. It's made Jack nervous, but I'm not bothered at all, because I couldn't be in a better place, with your mam to look after me." She paused. "But there is something else. Your new job worries him."

"He seemed happy enough about it before I went away," I said.

"He was doing that for you because you're his brother and he cares about you. But the work a spook does frightens people. It makes them uneasy. I suppose if you'd left right away it would probably have been all right. But Jack said that on the day you left, you went straight up over the hill into the wood, and that since then the dogs have been uneasy. Now they won't even go into the north pasture.

"Jack thinks you've stirred something up. I suppose it all comes back to this," Ellie went on, patting her belly gently. "He's just being protective, that's all. He's thinking of his family. But don't worry. It'll all sort itself out eventually."

In the end I stayed three days, trying to put on a brave face, but eventually I sensed it was time to go. Mam was the last person I saw before I left. We were alone in the kitchen, and she gave my arm a squeeze and told me that she was proud of me.

"You're more than just seven times seven," she said, smiling at me warmly. "You're my son, too, and you have the strength to do what has to be done."

I nodded in agreement because I wanted her to be happy, but the smile slipped from my face just as soon as I left the yard. I trudged back to the Spook's house with my heart right down in my boots, feeling hurt and disappointed that Mam wouldn't have me back home.

It rained all the way back to Chipenden, and when I arrived, I was cold, wet, and miserable. But as I reached the front gate, to my surprise the latch lifted on its own and the gate swung open without me touching it. It was a sort of welcome, an encouragement to go in, something I'd thought was reserved only for the Spook. I suppose I should have been pleased by that, but I wasn't. It just felt creepy.

I knocked at the door three times before I finally noticed that the key was in the lock. As my knocking had brought no response, I turned the key, then eased the door open.

I checked all the downstairs rooms but one. Then I called up the stairs. There was no answer, so I risked going into the kitchen.

There was a fire blazing in the grate and the table was set for one. At its center was a huge, steaming hot pot. I was so hungry I helped myself and had almost polished off the lot when I saw the note under the salt shaker.

Gone east to Pendle. It's witch trouble, so I'll be away for some time. Make yourself at home, but don't forget to pick up this week's provisions. As usual, the butcher has my sack, so go there first.

Pendle was a big fell, almost a mountain really, far to the east of the County. That whole district was infested with witches and was a risky place to go, especially alone. It reminded me again of how dangerous the Spook's job could be.

But at the same time I couldn't help feeling a bit annoyed. All that time waiting for something to happen, then the moment I'm away the Spook goes off without me!

I slept well that night, but not so deeply that I failed to hear the bell summoning me to breakfast.

I went downstairs on time and was rewarded with the best plate of bacon and eggs I'd eaten in the Spook's house. I was so pleased that, just before leaving the table, I spoke out loud, using the words that my dad said every Sunday after lunch.

"That was really good," I said. "My compliments to the cook."

No sooner had I spoken than the fire flared up in the grate and a cat began to purr. I couldn't see a cat, but the noise it was making was so loud that I'll swear the windowpanes were rattling. It was obvious that I'd said the right thing.

So, feeling right pleased with myself, I set off for the village to pick up the provisions. The sun was shining out of a blue, cloudless sky, the birds were singing, and after the previous day's rain the whole world seemed bright and gleaming and new.

I started at the butcher's, collected the Spook's sack, moved on to the greengrocer's, and finished at the baker's. Some village lads were leaning against the wall nearby. There weren't as many as last time, and their leader, the big lad with the neck like a bull's, wasn't with them.

Remembering what the Spook had said, I walked straight up to them. "I'm sorry about last time," I said, "but I'm new and didn't understand the rules properly. Mr. Gregory said that you can have an apple and a cake each." So saying, I opened the sack and handed each lad just what I'd promised. Their eyes opened so wide that they almost popped out of their sockets and each muttered his thanks.

At the top of the lane someone was waiting for me. It was the girl called Alice, and once again she was standing in the shadow of the trees as if she didn't like the sunlight.

"You can have an apple and a cake," I told her.

To my surprise she shook her head. "I'm not hungry at the moment," she said. "But there's something that I do want. I need you to keep your promise. I need some help."

I shrugged. A promise is a promise and I remembered making it. So what else could I do but keep my word?

"Tell me what you want and I'll do my best," I replied.

Once more her face lit up into a really broad smile. She wore a black dress and had pointy shoes, but that smile somehow made me forget all that. Still, what she said next set me worrying and quite spoiled the rest of the day.

"Ain't going to tell you now," she said. "Tell you

this evening, I will, just as the sun goes down. Come to me when you hear Old Gregory's bell."

I heard the bell just before sunset, and with a heavy heart went down the hill toward the circle of willow trees where the lanes crossed. It didn't seem right, her ringing the bell like that. Not unless she had work for the Spook, but somehow I doubted that.

Far above, the last rays of the sun were bathing the summits of the fells in a faint orange glow, but down below, among the withy trees, it was gray and full of shadows.

I shivered when I saw the girl, because she was pulling the rope with just one hand yet making the clappers of the big bell dance wildly. Despite her slim arms and narrow waist, she had to be very strong.

She stopped ringing as soon as I showed my face, and rested her hands on her hips while the branches continued to dance and shake overhead. We just stared at each other for ages, until my eyes were drawn down toward a basket at her feet. There was something inside it covered with a black cloth.

She lifted the basket and held it out to me.

"What is it?" I asked.

"It's for you, so that you can keep your promise."

I accepted it, but I wasn't feeling very happy. Curious, I reached inside to lift the black cloth.

"No, leave it be," Alice snapped, a sharp edge to her voice. "Don't let the air get to them or they'll spoil."

"What are they?" I asked. It was growing darker by the minute, and I was starting to feel nervous.

"They're just cakes."

"Thank you very much," I said.

"They're not for you," she said, a little smile playing at the corners of her mouth. "Those cakes are for old Mother Malkin."

My mouth became dry, and a chill ran down my spine. Mother Malkin, the live witch the Spook kept in a pit in his garden.

"I don't think Mr. Gregory would like it," I said. "He told me to keep away from her."

"He's a very cruel man, Old Gregory," said Alice. "Poor Mother Malkin's been in that damp, dark hole in the ground for almost thirteen years now. Is it right to treat an old woman so badly?"

I shrugged. I hadn't been happy about it myself. It was hard to defend what he'd done, but he'd said there was a very good reason for it.

"Look," she said, "you won't get into trouble, because Old Gregory need never know. It's just comfort you're bringing to her. Her favorite cakes, made by family. Ain't nothing wrong with that. Just something to keep up her strength against the cold. Gets right into her bones, it does."

Once again I shrugged. All the best arguments seemed to belong to her.

"So just give her a cake each night. Three cakes for three nights. Best do it at midnight, because it's then that she gets most peckish. Give her the first one tonight."

Alice turned to go but stopped and turned to give me a smile. "We could become good friends, you and me," she said with a chuckle.

Then she disappeared into the deepening shadows.

CHAPTER VIII
Old Mother Malkin

BACK at the Spook's cottage, I began to worry, but the more I thought about it, the less clear I was in my own mind. I knew what the Spook would say. He'd throw the cakes away and give me a long lesson on witches and problems with girls wearing pointy shoes.

He wasn't here, so that didn't enter into it. There were two things that made me go into the darkness of the eastern garden, where he kept the witches. The first was my promise to Alice.

"Never make a promise that you're not prepared to keep," my dad always told me. So I had little choice. He'd taught me right from wrong, and just because I was the Spook's apprentice, it didn't mean I'd to change all my ways.

Second I didn't hold with keeping an old woman as a prisoner in a hole in the ground. Doing that to a dead witch seemed reasonable, but not to a live one. I remember wondering what terrible crime she'd committed to deserve that.

What harm could it do just to give her three cakes? A bit of comfort from her family against the cold and damp, that's all it was. The Spook had told me to trust my instincts, and after weighing things in the balance, I felt that I was doing the right thing.

The only problem was that I had to take the cakes myself, at midnight. It gets pretty dark by then, especially if there's no moon visible.

I approached the eastern garden carrying the basket. It was dark, but not quite as dark as I'd expected. For one thing, my eyes have always been pretty sharp at night. My mam's good in the dark, and I think I get it from her side. And for another, it was a cloudless night and the moonlight helped me pick out my way.

As I entered the trees, it suddenly grew colder, and I shivered. By the time I reached the first grave, the one with the stone border and the thirteen bars, I felt even colder. That was where the first witch was buried. She was feeble, with little strength, or so the Spook had said. No need to worry there, I told myself, trying hard to believe it.

Making up my mind to give Mother Malkin the cakes in daylight was one thing, but now, down in the garden close to midnight, I was no longer so sure. The Spook had told me to keep well away after dark. He'd warned me more than once, so it had to be an important rule, and now I was breaking it.

There were all sorts of faint sounds. The rustlings and twitchings were probably nothing, just small creatures I'd disturbed moving out of my path, but they reminded me that I'd no right to be here.

The Spook had told me that the other two witches were about twenty paces farther on, so I counted out my steps carefully. That brought me to a second grave that was just like the first one. I got closer, just to be sure. There were the bars and you could see the earth just beneath them, hard-packed soil without even a single blade of grass. This witch was dead but was still dangerous. She was the one who had been buried head downward. That meant that the soles of her feet were somewhere just below the soil.

As I stared at the grave, I thought I saw something move. It was a sort of twitch; probably just my imagination, or maybe some small animal — a mouse or a shrew or something. I moved on quickly. What if it had been a toe?

Three more paces brought me to the place I was looking for — there was no doubt about it. Again there was a border of stones with thirteen bars. There were three differences, though. First the area under the bars was a square rather than an oblong. Second, it was bigger, probably about four paces by four. Third, there was no packed earth under the bars, just a very black hole in the ground.

I halted in my tracks and listened carefully. There hadn't been much noise so far, just the faint rustlings of night creatures and a gentle breeze. A breeze so light that I'd hardly noticed it. I noticed it when it stopped, though. Suddenly everything was very still and the woods became unnaturally quiet.

You see, I had been listening to try and hear the witch, and now I sensed that she was listening to me.

The silence seemed to go on and on forever, until suddenly I became aware of a faint breathing from the pit. That sound somehow made it possible to move, so I took a few more steps till I was standing very close to its edge, with the toe of my boot actually touching the stone border.

At that moment I remembered something the Spook had told me about Mother Malkin. . . .

"Most of her power's bled away into the earth. She'd love to get her hands on a lad like you."

So I took a step backward—not too far, but the Spook's words had set me thinking. What if a hand came out of the pit and grabbed my ankle?

Wanting to get it over with, I called down gently into the darkness. "Mother Malkin," I said. "I've brought something for you. It's a present from your family. Are you there? Are you listening?"

There was no reply, but the rhythm of the breathing below seemed to quicken. So, wasting no more time and desperate to get back to the warmth of the Spook's house, I reached into the basket and felt under the cloth. My fingers closed upon one of the cakes. It felt sort of soft and squishy and a bit sticky. I pulled it out and held it over the bars.

"It's just a cake," I said softly. "I hope it makes you feel better. I'll bring you another one tomorrow night."

With those words, I let go of the cake and allowed it to fall into the darkness.

I should have gone back to the cottage immediately, but I stayed for a few more seconds to listen. I don't know what I expected to hear, but it was a mistake.

There was a movement in the pit, as if something were dragging itself along the ground. And then I heard the witch begin to eat the cake.

I thought some of my brothers made unpleasant noises at the table, but this was far worse. It sounded even more revolting than our big hairy pigs with their snouts in the swill bucket, a mixture of snuffling, snorting, and chewing mixed with heavy breathing. I didn't know whether or not she was enjoying the cake, but she certainly made enough noise about it.

That night I found it very hard to sleep. I kept thinking about the dark pit and worrying about having to visit it again the following night.

I only just made it down to breakfast on time, and the bacon was burned and the bread a bit on the stale side. I couldn't understand why this was—I'd bought the bread fresh from the baker's only the day before. Not only that, the milk was sour. Could it be because the boggart was angry with me? Did it know what I'd been up to? Had it spoiled the breakfast as some sort of warning?

Working on a farm is hard, and that was what I was used to. The Spook hadn't left me any tasks to do, so I'd nothing to fill my day with. I did walk up to the library, thinking that he probably wouldn't mind if I found myself something useful to read, but to my disappointment the door was locked.

So what could I do but go for a walk? I decided to explore the fells, first climbing Parlick Pike; at the summit I sat on the cairn of stones and admired the view.

It was a clear, bright day and from up there I could see the County spread out below me, with the distant sea an inviting, twinkling blue, way out to the northwest. The fells seemed to go on forever, great hills with names like Calder Fell and Stake House Fell—so many that it seemed it would take a lifetime to explore them.

Nearby was Wolf Fell, and it made me wonder whether there actually were any wolves in the area.

Wolves could be dangerous and it was said that in winter, when the weather was cold, they sometimes hunted in packs. Well, it was spring now, and I certainly didn't see any sign of them, but that didn't mean they weren't there. It made me realize that being up on the fells after nightfall would be quite scary.

Not as scary, I decided, as having to go and feed Mother Malkin another of the cakes, and all too soon the sun began to sink into the west and I was forced to climb down toward Chipenden again.

Once more I found myself carrying the basket through the darkness of the garden. This time I decided to get it over with quickly. Wasting no time, I dropped the second sticky cake through the bars into the black pit.

It was only when it was too late, the very second it left my fingers, that I noticed something that sent a chill straight to my heart.

The bars above the pit had been bent. Last night they'd been perfectly straight, thirteen parallel rods of iron. Now the center ones were almost wide enough to get a head through.

They could have been bent by someone on the

outside, above ground, but I doubted that. The Spook had told me that the gardens and house were guarded and that nobody could get in. He hadn't said how and by what, but I guessed it was by some sort of boggart. Perhaps the same one that made the meals.

So it had to be the witch. She must have climbed up the side of the pit somehow and begun working at the bars. Suddenly the truth of what was happening dawned inside my head.

I'd been so stupid! The cakes were making her stronger.

I heard her below in the darkness, starting to eat the second cake, making the same horrible chewing, snuffling, and snorting noises. I left the trees quickly and went back to the cottage. For all I knew, she might not even need the third one.

After another sleepless night, I'd made up my mind. I decided to go and see Alice, give her back the last cake, and explain to her why I couldn't keep my promise.

First I had to find her. Straight after breakfast I went down to the wood where we'd first met and walked through to its far edge. Alice had said she lived "yonder," but there was no sign of any buildings, just low hills and valleys and more woods in the distance.

Thinking it would be faster to ask directions, I went down into the village. There were surprisingly few people about, but as I'd expected, some of the lads were hanging about near the baker's. It seemed to be their favorite spot. Perhaps they liked the smell. I know I did. Freshly baked bread has one of the best smells in all the world.

They weren't very friendly considering that last time we'd met, I'd given them a cake and an apple each. That was probably because this time the big lad with piggy eyes was with them. Still, they did listen to what I had to say. I didn't go into details — just told them I needed to find the girl we'd met at the edge of the wood.

"I know where she might be," said the big lad, scowling fiercely, "but you'd be stupid to go there."

"Why's that?"

"Didn't you hear what she said?" he asked, raising his eyebrows. "She said Bony Lizzie was her aunt."

"Who's Bony Lizzie?"

They looked at one another and shook their heads

as if I was mad. Why was it that everyone seemed to have heard of her but me?

"Lizzie and her grandmother spent a whole winter here before Gregory sorted them out. My dad's always going on about them. They were just about the scariest witches there've ever been in these parts. They lived with something just as scary, though. It looked like a man but it was really big, with too many teeth to fit into its mouth. That's what my dad told me. He said that back then, during that long winter, people never went out after dark. Some spook you'll be if you've never even heard of Bony Lizzie."

I didn't like the sound of that one little bit. I realized I'd been really stupid. If only I'd told the Spook about my talk with Alice, he'd have realized that Lizzie was back and would have done something about it.

According to the big lad's dad, Bony Lizzie had lived on a farm about three miles southeast of the Spook's place. It had been deserted for years, and nobody ever went there. So that was the most likely place she'd be staying now. That seemed about right to me, because it was in the direction that Alice had pointed.

Just then a group of grim-faced people came out of the church. They turned the corner in a straggly line and headed up the hill toward the fells, the village priest in the lead. They were dressed in warm clothing, and many of them were carrying walking sticks.

"What's all that about?" I asked.

"A child went missing last night," answered one of the lads, spitting onto the cobbles. "A three-year-old. They think he's wandered off up there. Mind you, it's not the first. Two days ago a baby went missing from a farm over on the Long Ridge. It was too young to walk, so it must have been carried off. They think it could be wolves. It was a bad winter, and that sometimes brings them back."

The directions I was given turned out to be pretty good. Even allowing for going back to pick up Alice's basket, it was less than an hour before Lizzie's house came into view.

At that point, in bright sunlight, I lifted the cloth and examined the last of the three cakes. It smelled bad but looked even worse. It seemed to have been made from small pieces of meat and bread, plus other things that I couldn't identify. It was wet and very sticky and almost black. None of the ingredients had been cooked but just sort of pressed together. Then I noticed something even more horrible. There were tiny white things crawling on the cake that looked like maggots.

I shuddered, covered it up with the cloth, and went down the hill to the very neglected farm. Fences were broken, the barn was missing half its roof, and there was no sign of any animals.

One thing *did* worry me, though. Smoke was coming from the farmhouse chimney. It meant that someone was at home, and I began to worry about the thing with too many teeth to fit into its mouth.

What had I expected? It was going to be difficult. How on earth could I manage to talk to Alice without being seen by the other members of her family?

As I halted on the slope, trying to work out what to do next, my problem was solved for me. A slim, dark figure came out of the back door of the farmhouse and began to climb the hill in my direction. It was Alice—but how had she known I was there? There were trees between the farmhouse and me, and the windows were facing in the wrong direction.

Still, she wasn't coming up the hill by chance. She walked straight up toward me and halted about five paces away.

"What do you want?" she asked. "You're stupid coming here. Lucky for you that those inside are asleep."

"I can't do what you asked," I said, holding out the basket toward her.

She folded her arms and frowned. "Why not?" she demanded. "You promised, didn't you?"

"You didn't tell me what would happen," I said. "She's eaten two cakes already and they're making her stronger. She's already bent the bars over the pit. One more cake and she'll be free and I think you know it. Wasn't that the idea all along?" I accused, starting to feel angry. "You tricked me, so the promise doesn't count anymore."

She took a step nearer, but now her own anger had been replaced by something else. Suddenly she looked scared.

"It wasn't my idea. They made me do it," she said, gesturing down toward the farmhouse. "If you don't do as you promised, it'll go hard with both of us. Go on, give her the third cake. What harm can it do? Mother Malkin's paid the price. It's time to let her go. Go on, give her the cake and she'll be gone tonight and never trouble you again."

"I think Mr. Gregory must've had a very good reason for putting her in that pit," I said slowly. "I'm just his new apprentice, so how can I know what's best? When he gets back I'm going to tell him everything that's happened."

Alice gave a little smile—the sort of smile someone gives when they know something that you don't. "He ain't coming back," she said. "Lizzie thought of it all. Got good friends near Pendle, Lizzie has. Do anything for her, they would. They tricked Old Gregory. When he's on the road he'll get what's coming to him. By now he's probably already dead and six feet under. You just wait and see if I'm right. Soon you won't be safe even up there in his house. One night they'll come for you. Unless, of course, you help now. In that case, they might just leave you alone."

As soon as she'd said that, I turned my back and climbed the hill, leaving her standing there. I think she called out to me several times, but I wasn't listening. What she'd said about the Spook was spinning around inside my head.

It was only later that I realized I was still carrying the basket, so I threw it and the last of the cakes into a river; then, back at the Spook's cottage, it didn't take me very long to work out what had happened and decide what to do next.

The whole thing had been planned from the start. They'd lured the Spook away, knowing that, as a new apprentice, I'd still be wet behind the ears and easy to trick.

I didn't believe that the Spook would be so easy to kill or he wouldn't have survived for so many years, but I couldn't rely on him arriving back in time to help me. Somehow I had to stop Mother Malkin from getting out of the pit.

I needed help badly and I thought of going down to the village, but I knew there was a more special kind of help near at hand. So I went into the kitchen and sat at the table.

At any moment I expected to have my ears boxed, so I talked quickly. I explained everything that had happened, leaving nothing out. Then I said that it was my fault and could I please be given some help.

I don't know what I expected. I didn't feel foolish talking to the empty air because I was so upset and frightened, but as the silence lengthened, I gradually realized that I'd been wasting my time. Why should the boggart help me? For all I knew it was a prisoner, bound to the house and garden by the Spook. It might just be a slave, desperate to be free; it might even be happy because I was in trouble.

Just when I was about to give up and leave the kitchen, I remembered something my dad often said before we went off to the local market: "Everyone has his price. It's just a case of making an offer that pleases him but doesn't hurt you too much."

So I made the boggart an offer.

"If you help me now, I won't forget it," I said. "When I become the next Spook, I'll give you every Sunday off. On that day I'll make my own meals so that you can have a rest and please yourself what you do."

Suddenly I felt something brush against my legs under the table. There was a noise, too, a faint purring, and a big ginger cat strolled into view and moved slowly toward the door.

It must have been under the table all the time —
that's what common sense told me. I knew different,
though, so I followed the cat out into the hallway
and then up the stairs, where it halted outside
the locked door of the library. Then it rubbed its
back against it, the way cats do against table legs.
The door slowly swung open to reveal more books
than anyone could ever have read in one lifetime,
arranged neatly on rows of parallel racks of shelves.
I stepped inside, wondering where to begin. And
when I turned around again, the big ginger cat had
vanished.

Each book had its title neatly displayed on the
cover. A lot were written in Latin and quite a few in
Greek. There was no dust or cobwebs. The library
was just as clean and well cared for as the kitchen.

I walked along the first row until something
caught my eye. Near the window there were three
very long shelves full of leather-bound notebooks,
just like the one the Spook had given me, but the
top shelf had larger books with dates on the covers.
Each one seemed to record a period of five years,
so I picked up the one at the end of the shelf and
opened it carefully.

I recognized the Spook's handwriting. Flicking through the pages, I realized that it was a sort of diary. It recorded each job he'd done, the time taken in traveling and the amount he'd been paid. Most importantly, it explained just how each boggart, ghost, and witch had been dealt with.

I put the book back on the shelf and glanced along the other spines. The diaries extended almost up to the present day but went back hundreds of years. Either the Spook was a lot older than he looked or the earlier books had been written by other spooks who'd lived ages ago. I suddenly wondered whether, even if Alice was right and the Spook didn't come back, there was a possibility that I might be able to learn all I needed to know just by studying those diaries. Better still, somewhere in those thousands upon thousands of pages there might be information that would help me now.

How could I find it? Well, it might take time, but the witch had been in the pit for almost thirteen years. There had to be an account of how the Spook had put her there. Then, suddenly, on a lower shelf, I saw something even better.

There were even bigger books, each dedicated

to a particular topic. One was labeled *Dragons and Wormes*. As they were displayed in alphabetical order, it didn't take me long to find just what I was looking for.

Witches.

I opened it with trembling hands to find it was divided into four predictable sections. . . .

The Malevolent, The Benign, The Falsely Accused, and The Unaware.

I quickly turned to the first section. Everything was in the Spook's neat handwriting and, once again, carefully organized into alphabetical order. Within seconds I found a page titled "Mother Malkin."

It was worse than I'd expected. Mother Malkin was just about as evil as you could imagine. She'd lived in lots of places, and in each area she'd stayed, something terrible had happened, the worst thing of all occurring on a moss to the west of the County.

She'd lived on a farm there, offering a place to stay to young women who were expecting babies but had no husbands to support them. That was where she'd gotten the title "Mother." This had gone on for years, but some of the young women had never been seen again.

She'd had a son of her own living with her there, a young man of incredible strength called Tusk. He had big teeth and frightened people so much that nobody ever went near the place. But at last the locals had roused themselves, and Mother Malkin had been forced to flee to Pendle. After she'd gone, they'd found the first of the graves. There was a whole field of bones and rotting flesh, mainly the remains of the children she'd murdered to supply her need for blood. Some of the bodies were those of women; in each case the body had been crushed, the ribs broken or cracked.

The lads in the village had talked about a thing with too many teeth to fit in its mouth. Could that be Tusk, Mother Malkin's son? A son who'd probably killed those women by crushing the life out of them?

That set my hands trembling so much that I could hardly hold the book steady enough to read it. It seemed that some witches used bone magic. They were necromancers who got their power by summoning the dead. But Mother Malkin was even worse. Mother Malkin used blood magic. She got her power by using human blood and was particularly fond of the blood of children.

I thought of the black, sticky cakes and shuddered. A child had gone missing from the Long Ridge. A child too young to walk. Had it been snatched by Bony Lizzie? Had its blood been used to make those cakes? And what about the second child, the one the villagers were searching for? What if Bony Lizzie had snatched that one, too, ready for when Mother Malkin escaped from her pit so that she could use its blood to work her magic? The child might be in Lizzie's house now!

I forced myself to go on reading.

Thirteen years ago, early in the winter, Mother Malkin had come to live in Chipenden, bringing her granddaughter, Bony Lizzie, with her. When the Spook had come back from his winter house in Anglezarke, he'd wasted no time in dealing with her. After driving off Bony Lizzie, he'd bound Mother Malkin with a silver chain and carried her back to the pit in his garden.

The Spook seemed to be arguing with himself in the account. He clearly didn't like burying her alive but explained why it had to be done. He believed that it was too dangerous to kill her: once slain, she had the power to return and would be even stronger and more dangerous than before.

The point was, could she still escape? One cake and she'd been able to bend the bars. Although she wouldn't get the third, two might just be enough. At midnight she might still climb out of the pit. What could I do?

If you could bind a witch with a silver chain, then it might have been worth trying to fasten one across the top of the bent bars to stop her from climbing out of her pit. The trouble was, the Spook's silver chain was in his bag, which always traveled with him.

I saw something else as I left that library. It was beside the door, so I hadn't noticed it as I came in. It was a long list of names on yellow paper, exactly thirty and all written in the Spook's own handwriting. My own name, Thomas J. Ward, was at the very bottom, and directly above it was the name William Bradley, which had been crossed out with a horizontal line; next to it were the letters *RIP*.

I felt cold all over then, because I knew that they meant Rest in Peace and that Billy Bradley had died. More than two thirds of the names on the paper had been crossed off; of those, nine besides Billy were dead.

I supposed that a lot were crossed out simply because they'd failed to make the grade as apprentices, perhaps not even making it to the end of the first month. Those who had died were more worrying. I wondered what had happened to Billy Bradley, and I remembered what Alice had said: *"You don't want to end up like Old Gregory's last apprentice."*

How did Alice know what had happened to Billy? It was probably just that everybody in the locality knew about it, while I was an outsider. Or had her family had something to do with it? I hoped not, but it gave me something else to worry about.

Wasting no more time, I went down to the village. The butcher seemed to have some contact with the Spook. How else had he gotten the sack to put the meat into? So I decided to tell him about my suspicions and try to persuade him to search Lizzie's house for the missing child.

It was late in the afternoon when I arrived at his shop, and it was closed. I knocked on the doors of five cottages before anyone came to answer. They confirmed what I already suspected: The butcher had gone off with the other men to search the fells. They wouldn't be back until noon the following day.

It seemed that after searching the local fells, they were going to cross the valley to the village at the foot of the Long Ridge, where the first child had gone missing. There they'd carry out a wider search and stay overnight.

I had to face it. I was on my own.

Soon, both sad and afraid, I was climbing the lane back toward the Spook's house. I knew that if Mother Malkin got out of her grave, then the child would be dead before morning.

I knew also that I was the only one who might even try to do something about it.

CHAPTER IX
On the Riverbank

BACK at the cottage, I went to the room where the Spook kept his walking clothes. I chose one of his old cloaks. It was too big, of course, and the hem came down almost to my ankles, while the hood kept falling down over my eyes. Still, it would keep out the worst of the cold. I borrowed one of his staffs, too, the one most useful to me as a walking stick: It was shorter than the others and slightly thicker at one end.

When I finally left the cottage, it was close to midnight. The sky was bright and there was a full moon just rising above the trees, but I could smell rain and the wind was freshening from the west.

I walked out into the garden and headed directly for

Mother Malkin's pit. I was afraid, but someone had to do it, and who else was there but me? It was all my fault anyway. If only I'd told the Spook about meeting Alice and what she'd told the lads about Lizzie being back! He could have sorted it all out then. He wouldn't have been lured away to Pendle.

The more I thought about it, the worse it got. The child on the Long Ridge might not have died. I felt guilty, so guilty, and I couldn't stand the thought that another child might die and that would be my fault, too.

I passed the second grave, where the dead witch was buried head down, and moved very slowly forward on my tiptoes until I reached the pit.

A shaft of moonlight fell through the trees to light it up, so there was no doubt about what had happened.

I was too late.

The bars had been bent even farther apart, almost into the shape of a circle. Even the butcher could have eased his massive shoulders through that gap.

I peered down into the blackness of the pit but couldn't see anything. I suppose I had a forlorn hope that she might have exhausted herself bending the bars and was now too tired to climb out.

Fat chance. At that moment a cloud drifted across the moon, making things a lot darker, but I could see the bent ferns. I could see the direction she'd taken. There was enough light to follow her trail.

So I followed her into the gloom. I wasn't moving too quickly, and I was being very, very cautious. What if she was hiding and waiting for me just ahead? I also knew that she probably hadn't gotten very far. For one thing, it wasn't more than five minutes or so after midnight. Whatever was in the cakes she'd eaten, I knew that dark magic would have played some part in getting her strength back. It was a magic that was supposed to be more powerful during the hours of darkness—particularly at midnight. She'd only eaten two cakes, not three, so that was in my favor, but I thought of the terrible strength needed to bend those bars.

Once out of the trees, I found it easy to follow her trail through the grass. She was heading downhill, but in a direction that would take her away from Bony Lizzie's cottage. That puzzled me at first, until I remembered the river in the gully below. A malevolent witch couldn't cross running water—the

Spook had taught me that—so she would have to move along its banks until it curved back upon itself, leaving her way clear.

Once in sight of the river, I paused on the hillside and searched the land below. The moon came out from behind the cloud, but at first, even with its help, I couldn't see anything much down by the river because there were trees on both banks, casting dark shadows.

And then suddenly I noticed something very strange. There was a silver trail on the near bank. It was only visible where the moon touched it, but it looked just like the glistening trail made by a snail. A few seconds later I saw a dark, shadowy thing, all hunched up, shuffling along very close to the riverbank.

I started off down the hill as quickly as I could. My intention was to cut her off before she reached the bend in the river and was able to head directly for Bony Lizzie's place. I managed that and stood there, the river on my right, facing downstream. But next came the difficult part. Now I had to face the witch.

I was trembling and shaking and so out of breath

that you'd have thought I'd spent an hour or so running up and down the fells. It was a mixture of fear and nerves, and my knees felt as if they were going to give way any minute. It was only by leaning heavily on the Spook's staff that I was able to stay on my feet at all.

As rivers went, it wasn't that wide, but it was deep, swollen by the spring rains to a level where it had almost burst its banks. The water was moving fast, too, rushing away from me into the darkness beneath the trees where the witch was. I looked very carefully, but it still took me quite a few moments to find her.

Mother Malkin was moving in my direction. She was a shadow darker than the tree shadows, a sort of blackness that you could fall into, a darkness that would swallow you up forever. I heard her then, even above the noise made by the fast-flowing river. It wasn't just the sound of her bare feet, which were making a sort of slithery noise as they moved toward me through the long grass at the stream's edge. No — there were other sounds that she was making with her mouth and perhaps her nose. The same sort of noises she'd made when I'd fed her the cake. There were snortings and snufflings that once again brought into my mind the memory of our hairy pigs feeding from the swill bucket. Then a different sound, a sucking noise.

When she moved out from under the trees into the open, the moonlight fell on her and I saw her properly for the first time. Her head was bowed low, her face hidden by a tangled mass of white-and-gray hair, so it seemed that she was looking at her feet, which were just visible under the dark gown that came down to her ankles. She wore a black cloak, too, and either it was too long for her or the years she had spent in the damp earth had made her shrink. It hung down to the ground behind her, and it was this, dragging over the grass, that seemed to be making the silver trail.

Her gown was stained and torn, which wasn't really surprising, but some were fresh stains — dark, wet patches. Something was dripping onto the grass at her side, and the drips were coming from what she gripped tightly in her left hand.

It was a rat. She was eating a rat. Eating it raw.

She didn't seem to have noticed me yet. She was very close now, and if nothing happened, she'd bump right into me. I coughed suddenly. It wasn't to warn her. It was a nervous cough, and I hadn't meant it to happen.

She looked up at me then, lifting into the moonlight a face that was something out of a nightmare, a face that didn't belong to a living person. Oh, but she was alive all right. You could tell that by the noises she was making eating that rat.

But there was something else about her that terrified me so much that I almost fainted away on the spot. It was her eyes. They were like two hot coals burning inside their sockets, two red points of fire.

And then she spoke to me, her voice something between a whisper and a croak. It sounded like dry, dead leaves rustling together in a late autumn wind.

"It's a boy," she said. "I like boys. Come here, boy."

I didn't move, of course. I just stood there, rooted to the spot. I felt dizzy and light-headed.

She was still moving toward me and her eyes seemed to be growing larger. Not only her eyes; her whole body seemed to be swelling up. She was expanding into a vast cloud of darkness that within moments would darken my own eyes forever.

Without thinking, I lifted the Spook's staff. My hands and arms did it, not me.

"What's that, boy, a wand?" she croaked. Then she chuckled to herself and dropped the dead rat, lifting both her arms toward me.

It was me she wanted. She wanted my blood. In absolute terror, my body began to sway from side to side. I was like a sapling agitated by the first stirrings of a wind, the first storm wind of a dark winter that would never end.

I could have died then, on the bank of that river. There was nobody to help, and I felt powerless to help myself.

But suddenly it happened. . . .

The Spook's staff wasn't a wand, but there's more than one kind of magic. My arms conjured up something special, moving faster than I could even think.

They lifted the staff and swung it hard, catching the witch a terrible blow on the side of the head.

She gave a sort of grunt and fell sideways into the river. There was a big splash, and she went right under but came up very close to the bank, about five or six paces downstream. At first I thought that that was the end of her, but to my horror, her left arm came out of the water and grabbed a tussock of grass. Then the other arm reached for the bank, and she started to drag herself out of the water.

I knew I had to do something before it was too late. So, using all my willpower, I forced myself to take a step toward her as she heaved more of her body up onto the bank.

When I got close enough, I did something that I can still remember vividly. I still have nightmares about it. But what choice did I have? It was her or me. Only one of us was going to survive.

I jabbed the witch with the end of the staff. I jabbed her hard, and I kept on jabbing her until she finally lost her grip on the bank and was swept away into the darkness.

But it still wasn't over. What if she managed to get out of the water farther downstream? She could still go to Bony Lizzie's house. I had to make sure that didn't happen. I knew it was the wrong thing to kill her and that one day she'd probably come back stronger than ever, but I didn't have a silver chain, so I couldn't bind her. It was now that mattered, not the future. No matter how hard it was, I knew I had to follow the river into the trees.

Very slowly I began to walk along the riverbank, pausing every five or six steps to listen. All
I could hear was the wind sighing faintly through
the branches above. It was very dark, with only the
occasional thin shaft of moonlight managing to pen-
etrate the leaf canopy, each like a long silver spear
embedded in the ground.

The third time I paused, it happened. There was
no warning. I didn't hear a thing. I simply felt it. A
hand slithered up onto my boot, and before I could
move away, it gripped my left ankle hard.

I felt the strength in that grip. It was as if my ankle
were being crushed. When I looked down, all I could
see was a pair of red eyes glaring up at me out of the
darkness. Terrified, I jabbed down blindly toward
the unseen hand that was clutching my ankle.

I was too late. My ankle was jerked violently and
I fell to the ground, the impact driving all the breath
from my body. What was worse, the staff went flying from my hand, leaving me defenseless.

I lay there for a moment or two, trying to catch
my breath, until I felt myself being dragged toward
the riverbank. When I heard the splashing, I knew
what was happening. Mother Malkin was using me

to drag herself out of the river. The witch's legs were thrashing about in the water, and I knew that one of two things would happen: either she'd manage to get out, or I'd end up in the river with her.

Desperate to escape, I rolled over to my left, twisting my ankle away. She held on, so I rolled again and came to a halt with my face pressed against the damp earth. Then I saw the staff, its thicker end lying in a shaft of moonlight. It was out of reach, about three or four paces away.

I rolled toward it. Rolled again and again, digging my fingers into the soft earth, twisting my body like a corkscrew. Mother Malkin had a tight grip on my ankle, but that was all she had. The lower half of her body was still in the water, so despite her great strength, she couldn't stop me from rolling over and twisting her through the water after me.

At last I reached the staff and thrust it hard at the witch. But her own hand moved into the moonlight and gripped the other end.

I thought it was over then. I thought that was the end of me, but to my surprise Mother Malkin suddenly screamed very loudly. Her whole body became rigid, and her eyes rolled up in her head. Then she gave a long, deep sigh and became very still.

We both lay there on the riverbank for what seemed a long time. Only my chest was rising and falling as I gulped in air; Mother Malkin wasn't moving at all. When, finally, she did, it wasn't to take a breath. Very slowly, one hand let go of my ankle and the other released the staff and she slid down the bank into the river, entering the water with hardly a splash. I didn't know what had happened, but she was dead—I was sure of it.

I watched her body being carried away from the bank by the current and swirled right into the middle of the river. Still lit by the moon, her head went under. She was gone. Dead and gone.

CHAPTER X
Poor Billy

I was so weak afterward that I fell to my knees, and within moments I was sick — sicker than I'd ever been before. I kept heaving and heaving even when there was nothing but bile coming out of my mouth, heaving until my insides felt torn and twisted.

At last it ended and I managed to stand. Even then, it was a long time before my breathing slowed down and my body stopped trembling. I just wanted to go back to the Spook's house. I'd done enough for one night, surely?

But I couldn't — the child was in Lizzie's house. That was what my instincts told me. The child was the prisoner of a witch who was capable of murder. So I had no choice. There was nobody else but me, and if I didn't help, then who would? I had to set off for Bony Lizzie's house.

There was a storm surging in from the west, a dark jagged line of cloud that was eating into the stars. Very soon now it would begin to rain, but as I started down the hill toward the house, the moon was still out—a full moon, bigger than I ever remembered it.

It was casting my shadow before me as I went. I watched it grow, and the nearer I got to the house, the bigger it seemed to get. I had my hood up and I was carrying the Spook's staff in my left hand, so that the shadow didn't seem to belong to me any-more. It moved on ahead of me until it fell upon Bony Lizzie's house.

I glanced backward then, half expecting to see the Spook standing behind me. He wasn't there. It was just a trick of the light. So I went on until I'd passed through the open gate into the yard.

I paused before the front door to think. What if I was too late and the child was already dead? Or what if its disappearance was nothing to do with Lizzie and I was just putting myself in danger for nothing? My mind carried on thinking, but, just as it had on the riverbank, my body knew what to do. Before I could stop it, my left hand rapped the staff hard against the wood three times.

For a few moments there was silence, followed by the sound of footsteps and a sudden crack of light under the door.

As the door slowly swung open, I took a step backward. To my relief it was Alice. She was holding a lantern level with her head so that one half of her face was lit while the other was in darkness.

"What do you want?" she asked, her voice filled with anger.

"You know what I want," I replied. "I've come for the child. For the child that you've stolen."

"Don't be a fool," she said. "Go away before it's too late. They've gone off to meet Mother Malkin. They could be back any minute."

Suddenly a child began to cry, a thin wail coming from somewhere inside the house. So I pushed past Alice and went inside.

There was just a single candle flickering in the narrow passageway, but the rooms themselves were in darkness. The candle was unusual. I'd never seen one made of black wax before, but I snatched it up anyway and let my ears guide me to the right room.

I eased open the door. The room was empty of furniture, and the child was lying on the floor on a heap of straw and rags.

"What's your name?" I asked, trying my best to smile. I leaned my staff against the wall and moved closer.

The child stopped crying and tottered to its feet, its eyes very wide. "Don't worry. There's no need to be scared," I said, trying to put as much reassurance into my voice as possible. "I'm going to take you home to your mam."

I put the candle on the floor and picked up the child. It smelled as bad as the rest of the room, and it was cold and wet. I cradled it with my right arm and wrapped my cloak about it as best I could.

Suddenly the child spoke. "I'm Tommy," it said. "I'm Tommy."

"Well, Tommy," I said, "we've got the same name. My name's Tommy, too. You're safe now. You're going home."

With those words, I picked up my staff and went into the passageway and out through the front door. Alice was standing in the yard near the gate. The lantern had gone out, but the moon was still shining, and as I walked nearer, it threw my shadow onto the side of the barn, a giant shadow ten times bigger than I was.

I tried to pass her, but she stepped directly into my path so that I was forced to halt.

"Don't meddle!" she warned, her voice almost a snarl, her teeth gleaming white and sharp in the moonlight. "Ain't none of your business, this."

I was in no mood to waste time arguing with her, and when I moved directly toward her, Alice didn't try to stop me. She stepped back out of my way and called out after me, "You're a fool. Give it back before it's too late. They'll come after you. You'll never get away."

I didn't bother to answer. I never even looked back. I went through the gate and began to climb away from the house.

It started to rain then, hard and heavy, straight into my face. It was the kind of rain that my dad used to call wet rain. All rain is wet, of course, but some kinds do seem to make a better and a faster job of soaking you than others. This was as wet as it got, and I headed back toward the Spook's house as fast as I could.

I wasn't sure if I'd be safe even there. What if the Spook really was dead? Would the boggart still guard his house and garden?

Soon I had more immediate things to worry about. I began to sense that I was being followed. The first time I felt it, I came to a halt and listened, but there was nothing but the howling of the wind and the rain lashing into the trees and drumming onto the earth. I couldn't see much either, because it was very dark now.

So I carried on, taking even bigger strides, just hoping that I was still heading in the right direction. Once I came up against a thick, high hawthorn hedge and had to make a long detour to find a gate, all the time feeling that the danger behind was getting closer. It was just after I'd come through a small wood that I knew for certain that there was someone there. Climbing a hill, I paused for breath close to its summit. The rain had eased for a moment and I looked back down into the darkness, toward the trees. I heard the crack and snap of twigs. Someone was moving very fast through the wood in my direction, not caring where he put his feet.

At the crest of the hill I looked back once more.

The first flash of lightning lit up the sky and the ground below, and I saw two figures come out of the trees and begin to climb the slope. One of them was female, the other shaped like a man, big and burly.

When the thunder crashed again, Tommy began to cry. "Don't like thunder!" he wailed. "Don't like thunder!"

"Storms can't hurt you, Tommy," I told him, knowing it wasn't true. They scared me as well. One of my uncles had been struck by lightning when he'd been out trying to get some cattle in. He'd died later. It wasn't safe being out in the open in weather like this. But although lightning terrified me, it did have its uses. It was showing me the way, each vivid flash lighting up my route back to the Spook's house.

Soon the breath was sobbing in my throat, too, a mixture of fear and exhaustion, as I forced myself to go faster and faster, just hoping that we'd be safe as soon as we entered the Spook's garden. Nobody was allowed on the Spook's property unless invited — I kept telling myself that over and over again, because it was our only chance. If we could just get there first, the boggart would protect us.

I was in sight of the trees, the bench beneath them,

the garden waiting beyond, when I slipped on the wet grass. The fall wasn't hard, but Tommy began to cry even louder. When I'd managed to pick him up, I heard someone running behind me, feet thumping the earth.

I glanced back, struggling for breath. It was a mistake. My pursuer was about five or six paces ahead of Lizzie and catching me fast. Lightning flashed again, and I saw the lower half of his face. It looked as if he had horns growing out of each side of his mouth, and as he ran he moved his head from side to side. I remembered what I'd read in the Spook's library about the dead women who'd been found with their ribs crushed. If Tusk caught me, he'd do the same to me.

For a moment I was rooted to the spot, but he started to make a bellowing sound, just like a bull, and that started me moving again. I was almost running now. I would have sprinted if I could, but I was carrying Tommy and I was too weary, my legs heavy and sluggish, the breath rasping in my throat. At any moment I expected to be grabbed from behind, but I passed the bench where the Spook often gave me lessons and then, at last, I was beneath the first trees of the garden.

But was I safe? If I wasn't, it was all over for both of us, because there was no way I could outrun Tusk to the house. I stopped running, and all I could manage was a few steps before I came to a complete halt, trying to regain my breath.

It was at that moment that something brushed past my legs. I looked down, but it was too dark to see anything. First I felt the pressure, then I heard something purr, a deep throbbing sound that made the ground beneath my feet vibrate. I sensed it move on beyond me, toward the edge of the trees, positioning itself between us and those who'd been following. I couldn't hear any running now, but I heard something else.

Imagine the angry howl of a tomcat multiplied a hundred times. It was a mixture between a throbbing growl and a scream, filling the air with its warning challenge, a sound that could have been heard for miles. It was the most terrifying and threatening sound I'd ever heard, and I knew then why the villagers never came anywhere near the Spook's house. That cry was filled with death.

Cross this line, it said, *and I'll rip out your heart. Cross this line, and I'll gnaw your bones to pulp and gore. Cross this line, and you'll wish you'd never been born.*

So for now we were safe. By now Bony Lizzie and Tusk would be running back down the hill. Nobody would be foolish enough to tangle with the Spook's boggart. No wonder they'd needed me to feed Mother Malkin the blood cakes.

There was hot soup and a blazing fire waiting for us in the kitchen. I wrapped little Tommy in a warm blanket and fed him some soup. Later I brought down a couple of pillows and made up a bed for him close to the fire. He slept like a log while I listened to the wind howling outside and the rain pattering against the windows.

It was a long night, but I was warm and comfortable and I felt at peace in the Spook's house, which was one of the safest places in the whole wide world. I knew now that nothing unwelcome could even enter the garden, never mind cross the threshold. It was safer than a castle with high battlements and a wide moat. I began to think of the boggart as my friend, and a very powerful friend at that.

Just before noon I carried Tommy down to the village. The men were already back from the Long

Ridge, and when I went to the butcher's house, the instant he saw the child, his weary frown turned into a broad smile. I briefly explained what had happened, only going into as much detail as was necessary.

Once I'd finished, he frowned again. "They need sorting out once and for all," he said.

I didn't stay long. After Tommy had been given to his mother and she'd thanked me for the fifteenth time, it became obvious what was going to happen. By then, about thirty or so of the village men had gathered. Some of them were carrying clubs and stout sticks and they were muttering angrily about stoning and burning.

I knew that something had to be done, but I didn't want to be a part of it. Despite all that had happened, I couldn't stand the thought of Alice being hurt, so I went for a walk on the fells for an hour or so to clear my head before walking slowly back toward the Spook's house. I'd decided to sit on the bench for a while and enjoy the afternoon sun, but someone was there already.

It was the Spook. He was safe after all! Until that moment I'd avoided thinking about what I was going to do next. I mean, how long would I have stayed in his house before deciding that he wasn't going to come back? Now it was all sorted out because there he was, staring across the trees to where a plume of brown smoke was rising. They were burning Bony Lizzie's house.

When I got close to the bench, I noticed a big, purple bruise over his left eye. He saw me glance at it and gave me a tired smile.

"We make a lot of enemies in this job," he said, "and sometimes you need eyes in the back of your head. Still, things didn't work out too badly because now we've one less enemy to worry about near Pendle.

"Take a pew," he said, patting the bench at his side. "What have you been up to? Tell me what's been happening here. Start at the beginning and finish at the end, leaving nothing out."

So I did. I told him everything. When I'd finished he stood up and looked down at me, his green eyes staring into mine very hard.

"I wish I'd known Lizzie was back. When I put Mother Malkin into the pit, Lizzie left in a bit of a hurry and I didn't think she'd ever have the nerve to show her face again. You should have told me about meeting the girl. It would have saved everybody a lot of trouble."

I looked down, unable to meet his eyes.

"What was the worst thing that happened?" he asked.

The memory came back, sharp and clear, of the old witch grabbing my boot and trying to drag herself out of the water. I remembered her scream as she gripped the end of the Spook's staff.

When I told him about it, he sighed long and deep.

"Are you sure she was dead?" he asked.

I shrugged. "She wasn't breathing. Then her body was carried to the middle of the river and swept away."

"Well, it was a bad business, all right," he said, "and the memory of it will stay with you for the rest of your life, but you'll just have to live with it. You were lucky in taking the smallest of my staffs with you. That's what saved you in the end. It's made of rowan, the most effective wood of all when dealing with witches. It wouldn't usually have bothered a witch that old and that strong, but she was in running water. So you were lucky, but you did all right for a new apprentice. You showed courage, real courage, and you saved a child's life. But you made two more serious mistakes."

I bowed my head. I thought I'd probably made more than two, but I wasn't going to argue.

"Your most serious mistake was in killing that witch," the Spook said. "She should have been brought back here. Mother Malkin is so strong that she could even break free of her bones. It's very rare, but it can happen. Her spirit could be born into this world again, complete with all her memories. Then she'd come looking for you, lad, and she'd want revenge."

"That would take years though, wouldn't it?" I asked. "A newborn baby can't do much. She'd have to grow up first."

"That's the worst part of it," the Spook said. "It could happen sooner than you think. Her spirit could seize someone else's body and use it as her own. It's called possession, and it's a bad business for everybody concerned. After that, you'll never know when, and from which direction, the danger will come.

"She might possess the body of a young woman, a lass with a dazzling smile, who'll win your heart before she takes your life. Or she might use her beauty to bend some strong man to her will, a knight or a judge, who'll have you thrown into a dungeon where you'll be at her mercy. Then again, time will be on her side. She might attack when I'm not here to help—maybe years from now when you're long past your prime, when your eyesight's failing and your joints are starting to creak.

"But there's another type of possession—one that's more likely in this case. Much more likely. You see, lad, there's a problem with keeping a live witch in a pit like that. Especially one so powerful, who's spent her long life practicing blood magic. She'll have been eating worms and other slithery things, with the wet constantly soaking into her flesh. So in the same way that a tree can slowly be petrified and turned into rock, her body will have been slowly starting to change. Gripping the rowan staff would have stopped her heart, pushing her over the barrier into death, and being washed away by the river might have speeded up the process.

"In this case, she'll still be bound to her bones, like most other malevolent witches, but because of her great strength, she'll be able to move her dead body.

You see, lad, she'll be what we call wick. It's an old County word that you're no doubt familiar with. Just as a head of hair can be wick with lice, her dead body is now wick with her wicked spirit. It'll be heaving like a bowl of maggots and she'll crawl, slither, or drag herself toward her chosen victim. And instead of being hard, like a petrified tree, her dead body will be soft and pliable, able to squeeze into the tiniest space. Able to ooze up someone's nose or into his ear and possess his body.

"There are only two ways to make sure that a witch as powerful as Mother Malkin can't come back. The first is to burn her. But nobody should have to suffer pain like that. The other way is too horrible even to think about. It's a method few have heard about because it was practiced long ago, in a land far away over the sea. According to their ancient books, if you eat the heart of a witch, she can never return. And you have to eat it raw.

"If we practice either method, we're no better than the witch we kill," said the Spook. "Both are barbaric. The only alternative left is the pit. That's cruel as well, but we do it to protect the innocents, those who'd be her future victims. Well, lad, one way or the other, now she's free. There's trouble ahead for sure, but there's little we can do about it now. We'll just have to be on our guard."

"I'll be all right," I said. "I'll manage somehow."

"Well, you'd better start by learning how to manage a boggart," the Spook said, shaking his head sadly.

"That was your other big mistake. A whole Sunday off every week? That's far too generous! Anyway, what should we do about that?" he asked, gesturing toward a thin plume of smoke that was still just visible to the southeast.

I shrugged. "I suppose it'll be all over by now," I said. "There were a lot of angry villagers, and they were talking about stoning."

"All over with? Don't you believe it, lad. A witch like Lizzie has a sense of smell better than any hunting dog. She can sniff out things before they happen and would've been gone long before anyone got near. No, she'll have fled back to Pendle, where most of the brood live. We should follow now, but I've been on the road for days, and I'm too weary and sore and need to gather my strength. But we can't leave Lizzie free for too long, or she'll start to work her mischief again. I'll have to go after her before the end of the week, and you'll be coming with me. It won't be easy, but you might as well get used to the idea. But first things first, so follow me. . . ."

As I followed, I noticed that he had a slight limp and was walking more slowly than usual. So whatever had happened on Pendle, it hadn't been without cost to himself. He led me into the house, up the stairs, and into the library, halting beside the farthest shelves, the ones near the window.

"I like to keep my books in my library," he said, "and I like my library to get bigger rather than smaller. But because of what's happened, I'm going to make an exception."

He reached up and took a book from the very top shelf and handed it to me. "You need this more than I do," he said. "A lot more."

As books went, it wasn't very big. It was even smaller than my notebook. Like most of the Spook's books, it was bound in leather and had its title printed both on the front cover and on the spine. It said *Possession: The Damned, the Dizzy, and the Desperate.*

"What does the title mean?" I asked.

"What it says, lad. Exactly what it says. Read the book and you'll find out."

When I opened the book, I was disappointed. Inside, every word on every page was printed in Latin, a language I couldn't read.

"Study it well and carry it with you at all times," said the Spook. "It's the definitive work."

He must have seen me frowning, because he smiled and jabbed at the book with his finger. "Definitive means that so far it's the best book that's ever been written about possession, but it's a very difficult subject and it was written by a young man who still had a lot to learn. So it's not the last word on the subject, and there's more to discover. Turn to the back of the book."

I did as he told me and found that the last ten or so pages were blank.

"If you find out anything new, then just write it down there. Every little bit helps. And don't worry about the fact that it's in Latin. I'll be starting your lessons as soon as we've eaten."

We went for our afternoon meal, which was cooked almost to perfection. As I swallowed down my last mouthful, something moved under the table and began to rub itself against my legs. Suddenly the sound of purring could be heard. It gradually got louder and louder until all the plates and dishes on the sideboard began to rattle.

"No wonder it's happy," said the Spook, shaking his head. "One day off a year would have been nearer the mark! Still, not to worry, it's business as usual and life goes on. Bring your notebook with you, lad, we've a lot to get through today."

So I followed the Spook down the path to the bench, uncorked the bottle of ink, dipped in my pen, and prepared to take notes.

"Once they've passed the test in Horshaw," said the Spook, starting to limp up and down in front of the bench, "I usually try to ease my apprentices into the job as gently as possible. But now that you've been face-to-face with a witch, you know how difficult and dangerous the job can be, and I think you're ready to find out what happened to my last apprentice. It's linked to boggarts, the topic we've been studying, so you might as well learn from it. Find a clean page and write down this for a heading . . ."

I did as I was told. I wrote down *How to Bind a*

Boggart. Then, as the Spook told the tale, I took notes, struggling to keep up as usual.

As I already knew, binding a boggart involved a lot of hard work which the Spook called "laying." First a pit had to be dug as close as possible to the roots of a large, mature tree. After all the digging the Spook had made me do, I was surprised to learn that a spook rarely dug the pit himself. That was something only done in an absolute emergency. A rigger and his helper usually attended to it.

Next you had to employ a mason to cut a thick slab of stone to fit over the pit like a gravestone. It was very important that the stone be cut to size accurately so as to make a good seal. After you'd coated the lower edge of the stone and the inside of the pit with the mixture of iron, salt, and strong glue, it was time to get the boggart safely inside.

That wasn't too difficult. Blood, milk, or a combination of the two worked every time. The really difficult bit was dropping the stone into position as it fed. Success depended on the quality of the help you hired.

It was best to have a mason standing by and a couple of riggers using chains controlled from a wooden gantry placed above the pit, so as to lower the stone down quickly and safely.

That was the mistake that Billy Bradley made. It was late winter and the weather was foul and Billy was in a rush to get back to his warm bed. So he cut corners.

He used local laborers, who hadn't done that type of work before. The mason had gone off for his supper, promising to return within the hour, but Billy was impatient and couldn't wait. He got the boggart into the pit without too much trouble, but he ran into difficulties with the slab of stone. It was a wet night, and it slipped, trapping his left hand under its edge.

The chain jammed so they couldn't lift the stone, and while the laborers struggled with it and one of them ran back to get the mason, the boggart, in a fury at being trapped under the stone, began to attack Billy's fingers. You see, it was one of the most dangerous boggarts of all: cattle rippers that had got the taste for human blood.

By the time the stone was lifted, almost half an hour had passed, and by then it was too late. The boggart had bitten off Billy's fingers as far down as the second knuckle and had been busily sucking the blood from his body. Billy's screams of pain had faded away to a whimper, and when they got his hand free, only his thumb was left. Soon afterward he died of shock and loss of blood.

"It was a sad business," said the Spook, "and now he's buried under the hedge, just outside the church-yard at Layton—those who follow our trade don't get to rest their bones in hallowed ground. It happened just over a year ago, and if Billy had lived, I wouldn't be talking to you now, because he'd still be my apprentice. Poor Billy, he was a good lad and he didn't deserve that, but it's a dangerous job and if it's not done right . . ."

The Spook looked at me sadly, then shrugged. "Learn from it, lad. We need courage and patience, but above all, we never rush. We use our brains, we think carefully, then we do what has to be done. In the normal course of events I never send an appren-tice out on his own until his first year of training is over. Unless, of course," he added with a faint smile, "he takes matters into his own hands. Then again, I've got to feel sure he's ready for it. Anyway, now it's time for your first Latin lesson. . . ."

CHAPTER XI
The Pit

IT happened just three days later.

The Spook had sent me down into the village to collect the week's groceries. It was very late in the afternoon, and as I left his house carrying the empty sack, the shadows were already beginning to lengthen.

As I approached the stile, I saw someone standing right on the edge of the trees near the top of the narrow lane. When I realized that it was Alice, my heart lurched into a more rapid beat. What was she doing here? Why hadn't she gone off to Pendle? And if she was still here, what about Lizzie?

I slowed down, but I had to pass her to get to the village. I could've gone back and taken a longer route, but I didn't want to give her the satisfaction of thinking I was scared of her. Even so, once I'd climbed over the stile, I stayed on the left-hand side of the lane, keeping close to the high hawthorn hedge, right on the edge of the deep ditch that ran along its length.

Alice was standing in the gloom, with just the toes of her pointy shoes poking out into the sunlight. She beckoned me closer, but I kept my distance, staying a good three paces away. After all that had happened, I didn't trust her one little bit, but I was still glad that she hadn't been burned or stoned.

"I've come to say good-bye," Alice said, "and warn you never to go walking near Pendle. That's where we're going. Lizzie has family living there."

"I'm glad you escaped," I said, coming to a halt and turning to face directly toward her. "I watched the smoke when they burned your house down."

"Lizzie knew they were coming," Alice said, "so we got away with plenty of time to spare. Didn't sniff you out, though, did she? Knows what you did to Mother Malkin, but only found out after it happened. Didn't sniff you out at all, and that worries her. And she said your shadow had a funny smell."

I laughed out loud at that. I mean, it was crazy. How could a shadow have a smell?

"Ain't funny," Alice accused. "Ain't nothing to laugh at. She only smelled your shadow where it had fallen on the barn. I actually saw it, and it was all wrong. The moon showed the truth of you."

Suddenly she took two steps nearer, into the sunlight, then leaned forward a little and sniffed at me. "You do smell funny," she said, wrinkling up her nose. She stepped backward quickly and suddenly looked afraid.

I smiled and put on my friendly voice. "Look," I said, "don't go to Pendle. You're better off without them. They're just bad company."

"Bad company don't matter to me. Won't change me, will it? I'm bad already. Bad inside. You wouldn't believe the things I've been and done. I'm sorry," she said. "I've been bad again. I'm just not strong enough to say no—"

Suddenly, too late, I understood the real reason for the fear on Alice's face. It wasn't me she was scared of. It was what was standing right behind me.

I'd seen nothing and heard nothing. When I did, it was already too late. Without warning, the empty sack was snatched out of my hand and dropped over my head and shoulders, and everything went dark. Strong hands gripped me, pinning my arms to my sides. I struggled for a few moments, but it was useless: I was lifted and carried as easily as a farmhand carries a sack of potatoes. While I was being carried, I heard voices—Alice's voice and then the voice of a woman; I supposed it was Bony Lizzie. The person carrying me just grunted, so it had to be Tusk.

Alice had lured me into a trap. It had all been carefully planned. They must have been hiding in the ditch as I came down the hill from the house.

I was scared, more scared than I'd ever been in my life before. I mean, I'd killed Mother Malkin, and she'd been Lizzie's grandmother. So what were they going to do to me now?

After an hour or so I was dropped onto the ground so hard that all the air was driven from my lungs.

As soon as I could breathe again, I struggled to get free of the sack, but somebody thumped me twice in the back—thumped me so hard that I kept very still. I'd have done anything to avoid being hit like that again, so I lay there, hardly daring to breathe while the pain slowly faded to a dull ache.

They used rope to tie me then, binding it over the sack, around my arms and head and knotting it tightly. Then Lizzie said something that chilled me to the bone.

"There, we've got him safe enough. You can start digging now."

Her face came very close to mine, so that I could smell her foul breath through the sacking. It was like the breath of a dog or a cat. "Well, boy," she said. "How does it feel to know that you'll never see the light of day again?"

When I heard the sound of distant digging, I began to shiver with fright. I remembered the Spook's tale of the miner's wife, especially the worst bit of all when she'd laid there paralyzed, unable to cry out while her husband dug her grave. Now it was going to happen to me. I was going to be buried alive, and I'd have done anything just to see daylight again, even for a moment.

At first, when they cut my ropes and pulled the sack from me, I was relieved. By then the sun had gone down, but I looked up and could see the stars, with the waning moon low over the trees. I felt the wind on my face, and it had never felt so good. My feeling of relief didn't last more than a few moments, though, because I started to wonder exactly what they had in mind for me. I couldn't think of anything worse than being buried alive, but Bony Lizzie probably could.

To be honest, when I saw Tusk close up for the first time, he wasn't quite as bad as I expected. In a way he'd looked worse the night he was chasing me. He wasn't as old as the Spook, but his face was lined and weather-beaten, and a mass of greasy gray hair covered his head. His teeth were too big to fit into his mouth, which meant that he could never close it properly, and two of them curved upward like yellow tusks on either side of his nose. He was big, too, and very hairy, with powerful, muscular arms. I'd felt that grip and had thought it bad enough, but I knew that he had the power in those shoulders to squeeze me so tightly that all the air would be forced from my body and my ribs would shatter.

Tusk had a big curved knife at his belt, with a blade that looked very sharp. But the worst thing about him was his eyes. They were completely dull. It was as if there was nothing alive inside his head;

he was just something that obeyed Bony Lizzie without even a thought. I knew that he'd do anything she told him without question, no matter how terrible it was.

As for Bony Lizzie, she wasn't skinny at all, and I knew, from my reading in the Spook's library, that she was probably called that because she used bone magic. I'd already smelled her breath, but at a glance you'd never have taken her for a witch. She wasn't like Mother Malkin, all shriveled with age, looking like something that was already dead. No, Bony Lizzie was just an older version of Alice. Probably no older than thirty-five, she had pretty brown eyes and hair as black as her niece's. She wore a green shawl and a black dress fastened neatly at her slim waist with a narrow leather belt. There was certainly a family resemblance — except for her mouth. It wasn't the shape of it, it was the way she moved it; the way it twisted and sneered when she talked. One other thing I noticed was that she never looked me in the eye.

Alice wasn't like that. She had a nice mouth, still shaped for smiling, but I realized then that she would eventually become just like Bony Lizzie.

Alice had tricked me. She was the reason I was here rather than safe and sound back in the Spook's house, eating my supper.

At a nod from Bony Lizzie, Tusk grabbed me and tied my hands behind my back. Then he seized me by the arm and dragged me through the trees. First of all I saw the mound of dark soil, then the deep pit beside it, and I smelled the wet, loamy stink of freshly turned earth. It smelled sort of dead and alive at the same time, with things brought to the surface that really belonged deep underground.

The pit was probably more than seven feet deep, but unlike the one the Spook had kept Mother Malkin in, it was irregular in shape, just a great big hole with steep sides. I remember thinking that with all the practice I'd had, I could have dug one far better.

At that moment the moon showed me something else—something I'd have preferred not to see. About three paces away, to the left of the pit, there was an oblong of freshly turned soil. It looked just like a new grave.

Without time even to begin worrying about that, I was dragged right to the edge of the pit, and Tusk

forced my head back. I had a glimpse of Bony
Lizzie's face close to mine, something hard was
jammed into my mouth, and a cold, bitter-tasting
liquid was poured down my throat. It tasted vile and
filled my throat and mouth to the brim, spilling over
and even erupting out of my nose so that I began
to choke, gasping and struggling for breath. I tried
to spit it out, but Bony Lizzie pinched my nostrils
hard with her finger and thumb, so that in order to
breathe I first had to swallow.

That done, Tusk let go of my head and transferred
his grip back to my left arm. I saw then what had
been forced into my mouth—Bony Lizzie held it up
for me to see. It was a small bottle made out of dark
glass. A bottle with a long, narrow neck. She turned
it so that its neck was pointing to the ground and a
few drops fell to the earth. The rest was already in
my stomach.

What had I drunk? Had she poisoned me?

"That'll keep your eyes wide open, boy," she said
with a sneer. "Wouldn't want you dozing off, would
we? Wouldn't want you to miss anything."

Without warning, Tusk swung me around violently toward the pit, and my stomach lurched as I

fell into space. I landed heavily, but the earth at the bottom was soft and although the fall winded me, I was unhurt. So I turned to look up at the stars, thinking that maybe I was going to be buried alive after all. But instead of a shovelful of dirt falling toward me, I saw the outline of Bony Lizzie's head and shoulders peering down, a silhouette against the stars. She started to chant in a strange sort of throaty whisper, though I couldn't catch the actual words.

Next she stretched her arms out above the pit, and I could see that she was holding something in each hand. Giving a strange cry, she opened her hands and two white things dropped toward me, landing in the mud close to my knees.

By the moonlight I saw clearly what they were. They almost seemed to be glowing. She'd dropped two bones into the pit. They were thumb bones—I could see the knuckles.

"Enjoy your last night on this earth, boy," she called down to me. "But don't worry, you won't be lonely because I'll leave you in good company. Dead Billy will be coming to claim his bones. Just next door, he is, so he's not got too far to go. He'll be with you soon, and you two have a lot in common.

He was Old Gregory's last apprentice, and he won't take kindly to you having taken his place. Then, just before dawn, we'll be paying you one last visit. We'll be coming to collect your bones. They're special, your bones are, even better than Billy's, and taken fresh they'll be the most useful I've had for a long time."

Her face drew back, and I heard footsteps walking away.

So that was what was going to happen to me. If Lizzie wanted my bones, it meant that she was going to kill me. I remembered the big curved blade that Tusk wore at his belt, and I began to tremble.

Before that I had Dead Billy to face. When she'd said, "just next door," she must have meant the new grave next to the pit. But the Spook had said that Billy Bradley was buried just outside the churchyard at Layton. Lizzie must have dug up his body, cut off his thumbs, and buried the rest of him here among the trees. Now he'd be coming to get his thumbs back.

Would Billy Bradley want to hurt me? I'd never done him any harm, but he'd probably enjoyed being the Spook's apprentice. Maybe he'd looked forward to finishing his time and becoming a spook himself. Now I'd taken what he once had. Not only that— what about Bony Lizzie's spell? He might think I was the one who'd cut off his thumbs and thrown them into the pit. . . .

I managed to kneel up and spent the next few minutes desperately trying to untie my hands. It was hopeless. My struggles seemed to be making the rope even tighter.

I felt strange, too: light-headed and dry mouthed. When I looked up at the stars, they seemed to be very bright and each star had a twin. If I concen- trated hard, I could make the double stars become single again, but as soon as I relaxed, they drifted apart. My throat was burning and my heart pound- ing three or four times faster than its normal pace.

I kept thinking about what Bony Lizzie had said. Dead Billy would be coming to find his bones. Bones that were lying in the mud less than two paces from where I was kneeling. If my hands had been free, I'd have hurled those bones from the pit.

Suddenly I saw a slight movement to my left. Had I been standing, it would've been just about level with my head. I looked up and watched as a long, plump, white, maggoty head emerged from the side of the pit. It was far, far bigger than any worm I'd ever seen before. Its blind, bloated head moved in a slow circle as it wriggled out the rest of its body. What could this be? Was it poisonous? Could it bite?

And then it came to me. It was a coffin worm! It must be something that had been living in Billy Bradley's coffin, growing fat and sleek. Something white that had never seen the light of day!

I shuddered as the coffin worm wriggled out of the dark earth and plopped into the mud at my feet. I lost sight of it then as it quickly burrowed beneath the surface.

Being so big, the white worm had dislodged quite a bit of soil from the side of the pit, leaving behind a hole like a narrow tunnel. I watched it, horrified but fascinated, because there was something else moving inside it. Something disturbing the earth, which was cascading from the hole to form a growing mound of soil.

Not knowing what it was made it worse. I had to see what was inside, so I struggled to get to my feet. I staggered, feeling light-headed again, the stars starting to spin. I almost fell, but I managed to take a step, lurching forward so that I was close to the narrow tunnel, now just about level with my head.

When I looked inside, I wished I hadn't.

I saw bones. Human bones. Bones that were joined together. Bones that were moving. Two hands without thumbs. One of them without fingers. Bones squelching in the mud, dragging themselves toward me through the soft earth. A grinning skull with gaping teeth.

It was Dead Billy, but instead of eyes, his black sockets stared back at me, cavernous and empty. When a white, fleshless hand emerged into the moonlight and jerked at my face, I stepped away, nearly falling, sobbing with fear.

At that moment, just when I thought I might go out of my mind with terror, the air suddenly became much colder and I sensed something to my right. Someone else had joined me in the pit. Someone who was standing where it was impossible to stand. Half his body was on view; the rest was embedded in the wall of earth.

It was a boy not much older than me. I could only see his left-hand side because the rest of him was somewhere behind, still in the soil. Just as easily as stepping through a door, he swung his right shoulder toward me and the rest of him entered the pit. He smiled at me. A warm, friendly smile.

"The difference between waking and dreaming," he said. "That's one of the hardest lessons to learn. Learn it now, Tom. Learn it now before it's too late. . . ."

For the first time I noticed his boots. They looked very expensive and had been crafted from best-quality leather. They were just like the Spook's.

He lifted his hands up then, so that they were at each side of his head, palms facing outward. The thumbs were missing from each hand. His left hand was also without fingers.

It was the ghost of Billy Bradley.

He crossed his hands over his chest and smiled once more. As Billy faded away, he seemed happy and at peace.

I understood exactly what he'd told me. No, I wasn't asleep, but in a way I'd been dreaming. I'd been dreaming the dark dreams that had come out of the bottle that Lizzie had forced into my mouth.

When I turned back to look at the hole, it was

gone. There never had been a skeleton crawling toward me. Neither had there been a coffin worm.

The potion must have been some kind of poison: something that made it difficult to tell the difference between waking and dreaming. That was what Lizzie had given me. It had made my heart beat faster and made it impossible for me to sleep. It had kept my eyes wide open, but it had also made them see things that weren't really there.

Soon afterward the stars disappeared and it began to rain heavily. It was a long, uncomfortable, cold night and I kept thinking about what would happen to me before dawn. The nearer it got, the worse I felt.

About an hour before sunrise, the rain eased to a light drizzle before fading away altogether. Once more I could see the stars, and by now they no longer seemed double. I was soaked and cold, but my throat had stopped burning.

When a face appeared overhead looking down into the pit, my heart began to race because I thought it was Lizzie come to collect my bones. But, to my relief, it was Alice.

"Lizzie's sent me to see how you're getting on," she called down softly. "Has Billy been yet?"

"He's been and gone," I told her angrily.

"I never meant for this to happen, Tom. If only you hadn't meddled, it would have been all right."

"Been all right?" I said. "By now another child would be dead and the Spook, too, if you'd had your way. And those cakes had the blood of a baby inside. Do you call that being all right? You come from a family of murderers and you're a murderer yourself!"

"Ain't true. It ain't true, that!" Alice protested. "There was no baby. All I did was give you the cakes."

"Even if that were so," I insisted, "you knew what they were going to do afterward. And you would've let it happen."

"I ain't that strong, Tom. How could I stop it? How could I stop Lizzie?"

"I've chosen what I want to do," I told her. "But what will you choose, Alice? Bone magic or blood magic? Which one? Which one will it be?"

"Ain't going to do either. I don't want to be like them. I'll run away. As soon as I get the chance, I'll be off."

"If you mean that, then help me now. Help me get

out of the pit. We could run away together."

"It's too dangerous now," Alice said. "I'll run away later. Maybe weeks from now when they ain't expecting it."

"You mean after I'm dead. When you've got more blood on your hands . . ."

Alice didn't reply. I heard her begin to cry softly, but just when I thought she was on the verge of changing her mind and helping me, she walked away.

I sat there in the pit, dreading what was going to happen to me, remembering the hanging men and now knowing exactly how they must have felt before they died. I knew that I'd never go home. Never see my family again. I'd just about given up all hope when footsteps approached the pit. I came to my feet, terrified, but it was Alice again.

"Oh, Tom, I'm sorry," she said. "They're sharpening their knives. . . ."

The worst moment of all was approaching, and I knew that I only had one chance. The only hope I had was Alice.

"If you're really sorry, then you'll help me," I said softly.

"Ain't nothing I can do," she cried. "Lizzie could

turn on me. She don't trust me. Thinks I'm soft."

"Go and fetch Mr. Gregory," I said. "Bring him here."

"Too late for that, ain't it?" Alice sobbed, shaking her head. "Bones taken in daylight are no use to Lizzie. No use at all. The best time to take bones is just before the sun comes up. So they'll be coming for you in a few minutes. That's all the time you've got."

"Then get me a knife," I said.

"No use, that," she said. "Too strong, they are. Can't fight 'em, can you?"

"No," I said. "I want it to cut the rope. I'm going to run for it."

Suddenly Alice was gone. Had she gone to fetch a knife, or would she be too scared of Lizzie? I waited a few moments, but when she didn't come back I became desperate. I struggled, trying to pull my wrists apart, trying to snap the rope, but it was no use.

When a face peered down at me, my heart jumped with fear, but it was Alice holding something out over the pit. She dropped it, and as it fell, metal gleamed in the moonlight.

Alice hadn't let me down. It was a knife. If I could just cut the rope, I'd be free. . . .

At first, even with my hands tied behind my back, I never had any doubt in my mind that I could do it. The only danger was that I might cut myself a bit, but what did that matter compared to what they'd do to me before the sun came up? It didn't take me long to get a grip on the knife. Positioning it against the rope was more difficult, and it was very hard to move it. When I dropped it for the second time, I began to panic. There couldn't be more than a minute or so before they came for me.

"You'll have to do it for me," I called up to Alice. "Come on, jump down into the pit."

I didn't think she'd really do it, but to my surprise she did. She didn't jump but lowered herself down feet first, facing the side of the pit and hanging on to the edge with her arms. When her body was fully extended, she dropped the final two feet or so.

It didn't take her long to cut the rope. My hands were free, and all we had to do was get out of the pit.

"Let me stand on your shoulders," I said. "Then I'll pull you up."

Alice didn't argue, and at the second attempt

I managed to balance on her shoulders and drag myself up onto the wet grass. Then came the really hard part—pulling Alice out of the pit.

I reached down with my left hand. She gripped it hard with her own and placed her right hand on my wrist for extra support. Then I tried to pull her up.

My first problem was the wet, slippery grass, and I found it hard to keep myself from being dragged over the edge. Then I realized that I didn't have the strength to do it. I'd made a big mistake. Just because she was a girl, that didn't necessarily make her weaker than me. Too late I remembered the way she'd pulled the rope to make the Spook's bell dance. She'd done it almost effortlessly. I should have let her stand on my shoulders. I should have let her get out of the pit first. Alice would have pulled me up without any trouble.

It was then that I heard the sound of voices. Bony Lizzie and Tusk were coming through the trees toward us.

Below me I saw Alice's feet scrabbling against the side of the pit, trying to get a hold. Desperation gave me extra strength. I gave a sudden heave, and she came up over the edge and collapsed beside me.

We got away just in time, running hard with the sound of other feet running behind us. They were quite a long way back at first, but very gradually they began to get closer and closer.

I don't know how long we ran. It felt like a lifetime. I ran until my legs felt like lead and the breath was burning in my throat. We were heading back toward Chipenden—I could tell that from the occasional glimpses I got of the fells through the trees. We were running toward the dawn. The sky was graying now and growing lighter by the minute. Then, just as I felt I couldn't take another step, the tips of the fells were glowing a pale orange. It was sunlight, and I remember thinking that even if we were caught now, at least it was daylight and so my bones would be of no use to Lizzie.

As we came out of the trees onto a grassy slope and began to run up it, my legs finally began to fail. They were turning to jelly, and Alice was starting to pull away from me. She glanced back at me, her face terrified. I could still hear them crashing through the trees behind us.

Then I came to a complete and sudden halt. I stopped because I wanted to stop. I stopped because there was no need to run any farther.

There, standing at the summit of the slope ahead, was a tall figure dressed in black, carrying a long staff. It was the Spook, all right, but somehow he looked different. His hood was thrown back and his hair, lit by the rays of the rising sun, seemed to be streaming back from his head like orange tongues of flame.

Tusk gave a sort of roar and ran up the slope toward him, brandishing his blade, with Bony Lizzie close at his heels. They weren't bothered about us for the moment. They knew who their main enemy was. They could deal with us later.

By now Alice had come to a halt, too, so I took a couple of shaky steps to bring myself level with her. We both watched as Tusk made his final charge, lifting his curved blade and bellowing angrily as he ran.

The Spook had been standing as still as a statue, but then in response he took two big strides down the slope toward him and lifted his staff high. Aiming it like a spear, he drove it hard at Tusk's head. Just before it made contact with his forehead, there was a sort of click and a red flame appeared at the very tip. There was a heavy thud as it struck home. The curved knife went up in the air, and Tusk's body fell like a sack of potatoes. I knew he was dead even before he hit the ground.

Next the Spook cast his staff to one side and reached inside his cloak. When his left hand appeared again, it was clutching something that he cracked high in the air like a whip. It caught the sun, and I knew it was a silver chain.

Bony Lizzie turned and tried to run, but it was too late: The second time he cracked the chain, it was followed almost immediately by a thin, high, metallic sound. The chain began to fall, shaping itself into a spiral of fire to bind itself tightly around Bony Lizzie. She gave one great shriek of anguish, then fell to the ground.

I walked with Alice to the summit of the slope. There we saw that the silver chain was wrapped tightly about the witch from head to toe. It was even tight across her open mouth, hard against her teeth. Her eyes were rolling in her head and her whole body was twitching with effort, but she couldn't cry out.

I glanced across at Tusk. He was lying on his

back with his eyes wide open. He was dead, all right, and there was a red wound in the middle of his forehead. I looked at the staff then, wondering about the flame I'd seen at its tip.

My master looked gaunt, tired, and suddenly very old. He kept shaking his head as if he were weary of life itself. In the shadow of the slope, his hair was back to its usual gray color, and I realized why it had seemed to stream back from his head: It was saturated with sweat and he'd slicked it back with his hand so that it stuck up and out behind his ears. He did it again as I watched. Beads of sweat were dripping from his brow, and he was breathing very rapidly. I realized he'd been running.

"How did you find us?" I asked.

It was a while before he answered, but at last his breathing began to slow and he was able to speak. "There are signs, lad. Trails that can be followed, if you know how. That's something else you'll have to learn."

He turned and looked at Alice. "That's two of them dealt with, but what are we going to do about you?" he asked, staring at her hard.

"She helped me escape," I said.

"Is that so?" asked the Spook. "But what else did she do?"

He looked hard at me then, and I tried to hold his gaze. When I looked down at my boots, he made a clicking noise with his tongue. I couldn't lie to him, and I knew that he'd guessed that she'd played some part in what had happened to me.

He looked at Alice again. "Open your mouth, girl," he said harshly, his voice full of anger. "I want to see your teeth."

Alice obeyed, and the Spook suddenly reached forward, seizing her by the jaw. He brought his face close to her open mouth and sniffed very loudly.

When he turned back to me, his mood seemed to have softened, and he gave a deep sigh. "Her breath is sweet enough," he said. "You've smelled the breath of the other?" he asked, releasing Alice's jaw and pointing down at Bony Lizzie.

I nodded.

"It's caused by her diet," he said. "And it tells you right away what she's been up to. Those who practice bone or blood magic get a taste for blood and raw meat. But the girl seems all right."

Then he moved his face close to Alice's again.

"Look into my eyes, girl," he told her. "Hold my gaze as long as you can."

Alice did as he told her, but she couldn't look at him for long, even though her mouth was twitching with the effort. She dropped her eyes and began to cry softly.

The Spook looked down at her pointy shoes and shook his head sadly. "I don't know," he said, turning at me again. "I just don't know what to do for the best. It's not just her. We've others to think about. Innocents who might suffer in the future. She's seen too much and she knows too much for her own good. It could go either way with her, and I don't know if it's safe to let her go. If she goes east to join the brood at Pendle, then she'll be lost forever and she'll just add to the dark."

"Haven't you anywhere else you could go?" I asked Alice gently. "No other relations?"

"There's a village near the coast. It's called Staumin. I've another aunt lives there. Perhaps she'd take me in . . ."

"Is she like the others?" the Spook asked, staring at Alice again.

"Not so you'd notice," she replied. "Still, it's a

long way and I ain't ever been there before. Could take three days or more to get there."

"I could send the lad with you," said the Spook, his voice suddenly a lot kinder. "He's had a good look at my maps, so I reckon he should be able to find the way. When he gets back, he'll be learning how to fold them up properly. Anyway, it's decided. I'm going to give you a chance, girl. It's up to you whether you take it. If you don't, then one day we'll meet again, and the next time you won't be so lucky."

Then the Spook pulled the usual cloth from his pocket. Inside it was a hunk of cheese for the journey. "Just so you don't go hungry," he said, "but don't eat it all at once."

I hoped we might find something better to eat on the way, but I still mumbled my thanks.

"Don't go straight to Staumin," said the Spook, staring at me hard without blinking. "I want you to go home again first. Take this girl with you, and let your mother talk to her. I've a feeling she might just be able to help. I'll expect you back within two weeks."

That brought a smile to my face. After all that

had happened, a chance to go home for a while was a dream come true. But one thing did puzzle me, because I remembered the letter my mam had sent the Spook. He hadn't seemed that happy with some of the things she'd said. So why should he think my mam would be able to help Alice? I didn't say anything, because I didn't want to risk making the Spook have second thoughts. I was just glad to be away.

Before we left, I told him about Billy. He nodded sadly but said not to worry because he'd do what was necessary.

As we set off, I glanced back and saw the Spook carrying Bony Lizzie over his left shoulder and striding away toward Chipenden. From behind you'd have taken him for a man thirty years younger.

CHAPTER XII
The Desperate and the Dizzy

As we came down the hill toward the farm, warm drizzle was drifting into our faces. Somewhere far off a dog barked twice, but below us everything was quiet and still.

It was late afternoon, and I knew that my dad and Jack would be out in the fields, which would give me a chance to talk to Mam alone. It was easy for the Spook to tell me to take Alice home with me, but the journey had given me time to think, and I didn't know how Mam would take it. I didn't feel she'd be happy having someone like Alice in the house, especially when I told her what she'd been up to. And as for Jack, I'd a pretty good idea what his reaction would be. From what Ellie had told me last time about his attitude to my new job, having the niece of a witch in the house was the last thing he'd want.

As we crossed the yard I pointed to the barn. "Better shelter under there," I said. "I'll go in and explain."

No sooner had I spoken than the loud cry of a hungry baby came from the direction of the farmhouse. Alice's eyes met mine briefly, then she looked down, and I remembered the last time we'd been together when a child had cried.

Without a word, Alice turned and walked into the barn, her silence no more than I expected. You'd think that after all that had happened, there'd have been a lot to talk about on the journey, but we'd hardly spoken. I think she'd been upset by the way the Spook had held her by the jaw and smelled her breath. Maybe it had made her think about all the things she'd been up to in the past. Whatever it was, she'd seemed deep in thought and very sad for most of the time.

I suppose I could have tried harder, but I was too tired and weary, so we'd walked in silence until it had grown into a habit. It was a mistake: I should have made the effort to get to know Alice better then—it might have saved me a lot of trouble later.

As I jerked open the back door, the crying stopped and I heard another sound, the comforting click of Mam's rocking chair.

The chair was by the window, but the curtains weren't fully drawn, and I could see by her face that she'd been peering through the narrow gap between them. She'd watched us enter the yard, and as I came into the room, she began to rock the chair faster and harder, staring at me all the while without blinking, one half of her face in darkness, the other lit by the large candle that was flickering in its big brass holder in the center of the table.

"When you bring a guest with you, it's good manners to invite her into the house," she said, her voice a mixture of annoyance and surprise. "I thought I'd taught you better than that."

"Mr. Gregory told me to bring her here," I said. "Her name's Alice, but she's been keeping bad company. He wants you to talk to her but I thought it was best to tell you what's happened first, just in case you didn't want to invite her in."

So I drew up a chair and told Mam exactly what

had happened. When I'd finished she let out a long sigh, then a faint smile softened her face.

"You've done well, son," she told me. "You're young and new to the job, so your mistakes can be forgiven. Go and bring that poor girl in, then leave us alone to talk. You might want to go upstairs and say hello to your new niece. Ellie will certainly be glad to see you."

So I brought Alice in, left her with my mam, and went upstairs.

Ellie was in the biggest bedroom. It used to belong to my mam and dad, but they'd let her and Jack have it because there was room for another two beds and a cot, which would come in useful as their family grew.

I knocked lightly on the door, which was half open, but only looked into the room when Ellie called out for me to go in. She was sitting on the edge of the big double bed feeding the baby, its head half hidden by her pink shawl. As soon as she saw me, her mouth widened into a smile that made me feel welcome, but she looked tired and her hair lank and greasy. Although I glanced away quickly, Ellie was sharp and I knew she'd seen me staring and read the expression in my eyes, because she quickly smoothed the hair away from her brow.

"Oh, I'm sorry, Tom," she said. "I must look a mess—I've been up all night. I've just grabbed an hour's sleep. You've got to get it while you can with a very hungry baby like this. She cries a lot, especially at night."

"How old is she?" I asked.

"She'll be just six days old tonight. She was born not long after midnight last Saturday."

That was the night I'd killed Mother Malkin. For a moment the memory of it came rushing back and a shiver ran down my spine.

"Here, she's finished feeding now," Ellie said with a smile. "Would you like to hold her?"

That was the last thing I wanted to do. The baby was so small and delicate that I was scared of squeezing it too hard or dropping it, and I didn't like the way its head was so floppy. It was hard to say no, though, because Ellie would have been hurt. As it was, I didn't have to hold the baby for long, because the moment it was in my arms its little face went red and it began to cry.

"I don't think it likes me," I told Ellie.

"She's a *she*, not an *it*," Ellie scolded, making her face all stern and outraged. "Don't worry, it's not you, Tom," she said, her mouth softening into a smile. "I think she's still hungry, that's all."

The baby stopped crying the moment Ellie took her back, and I didn't stay long after that. Then, on my way downstairs, I heard a sound from the kitchen I hadn't expected.

It was laughter, the loud, hearty laughter of two people getting on very well together. The moment I opened the door and walked in, Alice's face became very serious, but Mam carried on laughing aloud for a few moments, and even when she stopped, her face was still lit up with a wide smile. They'd been sharing a joke, a very funny joke, but I didn't like to ask what it was and they didn't tell me. The look in both their eyes made me feel that it was something private.

My dad once told me that women know things that men don't. That sometimes they have a certain look in their eyes, but when you see it, you should never ask them what they're thinking. If you do, they might tell you something you don't want to hear. Well, whatever they'd been laughing at had certainly brought them closer; from that moment on it seemed as if they'd known each other for years. The Spook had been right. If anyone could sort Alice out, it had to be Mam.

I did notice one thing, though. Mam gave Alice the room opposite hers and Dad's. They were the two rooms at the top of the first flight of stairs. Mam had very sharp ears, and it meant that if Alice so much as turned over in her sleep, she would hear it.

So for all that laughter, Mam was still watching Alice.

When he came back from the fields, Jack gave me a really dark scowl and muttered to himself. He seemed angry at something. But Dad was pleased to see me, and to my surprise he shook hands with me. He always shook hands when greeting my other brothers who'd left home, but this was the first time for me. It made me feel sad and proud at the same time. He was treating me as if I were a man, making my own way in the world.

Jack hadn't been in the house five minutes when he came looking for me. "Outside," he said, keeping his voice low so that nobody else could hear. "I want to talk to you."

We walked out into the yard and he led the way around the side of the barn, close to the pigpens, where we couldn't be seen from the house.

"Who's the girl you've brought back with you?"

"Her name's Alice. It's just someone who needs help," I said. "The Spook told me to bring her home so that Mam could talk to her."

"What do you mean, she needs help?"

"She's been keeping bad company, that's all."

"What sort of bad company?"

I knew he wouldn't like it, but I had no choice. I had to tell him. Otherwise he'd only ask Mam.

"Her aunt's a witch, but don't worry—the Spook's sorted it all out and we'll only be staying for a few days."

Jack exploded. I'd never seen him so angry.

"Don't you have the sense you were born with?" he shouted. "Didn't you think? Didn't you think about the baby? There's an innocent child living in this house, and you bring home someone from a family like that! It's beyond belief!"

He raised his fist and I thought he was going to thump me. Instead, he smashed it sideways into the wall of the barn, the sudden thud sending the pigs into a frenzy.

"Mam thinks it's all right," I protested.

"Aye, Mam would," said Jack, his voice suddenly lower but still harsh with anger. "How could she refuse her favorite son anything? And she's just too good-hearted, as well you know. That's why you shouldn't take advantage. Look, it's me you'll answer to if anything happens. I don't like the look of that girl. She looks shifty. I'll be watching her carefully, and if she takes one step out of line, you'll both be on your way before you can blink. And you'll earn your keep while you're here. She can help around the house to make things easier for Mam, and you can pull your weight with the farmwork."

Jack turned and started to walk away, but he still had more to say. "Being so occupied with more important things," he added sarcastically, "you might not have noticed how tired Dad looks. He's finding the job harder and harder."

"Of course I'll help," I called after him, "and so will Alice."

At supper, apart from Mam, everyone was really quiet. I suppose it was having a stranger sitting at the table with us. Although Jack's manners wouldn't let him complain outright, he scowled at Alice almost as much as he did at me. So it was a good job Mam was cheerful and bright enough to light up the whole table.

Ellie had to leave her supper twice to attend to the baby, which kept crying fit to bring the roof down. The second time she fetched it downstairs.

"Never known a baby to cry so much," said Mam with a smile. "At least it's got strong, healthy lungs."

Its tiny face was all red and screwed up again. I would never have said it to Ellie, but it wasn't the best looking of babies. Its face reminded me of an angry little old woman. One moment it was crying fit to burst; then, very suddenly, it became still and quiet. Its eyes were wide open and it was staring toward the center of the table, where Alice was seated close to the big brass candlestick. At first I didn't think anything of it. I thought Ellie's baby was just fascinated by the candle flame. But later Alice helped Mam clear the table, and each time Alice passed by, the baby followed her with its blue eyes, and suddenly, although the kitchen was warm, I shivered.

Later I went up to my old bedroom, and when

I sat down in the wicker chair by the window and gazed out, it was as if I'd never left home.

As I looked northward, toward Hangman's Hill, I thought about the way the baby had seemed so interested in Alice. When I remembered what Ellie had said earlier, I shivered again. Her baby had been born after midnight on the night of the full moon. It was too close to be just a coincidence. Mother Malkin would have been swept away by the river about the time that Ellie's baby had been born. The Spook had warned me that she'd come back. What if she'd come back even earlier than he'd predicted? He expected her to be wick. But what if he was wrong? What if she'd broken free of her bones and her spirit had possessed Ellie's baby at the very moment of its birth?

I didn't sleep a wink that night. There was only one person I could talk to about my fears, and that was Mam. The difficulty was in getting her alone without drawing attention to the fact that I was doing it.

Mam cooked and did other chores that kept her busy most of the day, and usually it would have been no problem to talk to her in the kitchen because I was working close by. Jack had given me the job of repairing the front of the barn, and I must have hammered in hundreds of shiny new nails before sunset.

Alice was the difficulty, though: Mam kept her with her all day, really making the girl work hard. You could see the sweat on her brow and the frowns that kept furrowing her forehead, but despite that, Alice never complained even once.

It was only after supper, when they'd finished the clatter of washing and drying the dishes, that I finally got my chance. That morning Dad had gone off to the big spring market in Topley. He could conduct his business, and it gave him a rare chance to meet up with a few of his old friends, so he'd be away for two or three days. Jack was right. He did look tired, and it would give him a break from the farm.

Mam had sent Alice off to her room to get some rest, Jack had his feet up in the front room, and Ellie was upstairs trying to grab half an hour's sleep before the baby woke again for feeding. So, wasting no time at all, I started to tell Mam what was worrying me. She'd been rocking in her chair, but I'd hardly managed to blurt out my first sentence before the chair came to a halt. She listened carefully as I told her of my fears and reasons to suspect the baby. But her face remained so still and calm that I'd no idea what she was thinking. No sooner had I spat out my last word than she rose to her feet.

"Wait there," she said. "We need to sort this out once and for all."

She left the kitchen and went upstairs. When she came back she was carrying the baby, wrapped in Ellie's shawl. "Bring the candle," she said, moving toward the door.

We went out into the yard, Mam walking fast, as if she knew exactly where she was going and what she was going to do. We ended up at the other side of the cattle midden, standing in the mud on the edge of our pond, which was deep enough and large enough to provide water for our cows even through the driest summer months.

"Keep the candle high so we can see everything," Mam said. "I want there to be no doubt."

Then, to my horror, she stretched out her arms and held the baby over the dark, still water. "If she floats, the witch is inside her," Mam said. "If she sinks, she's innocent. Right, let's see —"

"*No!*" I shouted, my mouth opening all by itself

and the words just tumbling out faster than I could think. "Don't do it, please. It's Ellie's baby."

For a moment I thought she was going to let the baby fall anyway, then she smiled and held it close again and kissed it on the forehead very gently. "Of course it's Ellie's baby, son. Can't you tell that just by looking at her? Anyway, swimming is a test carried out by fools and doesn't work anyway. Usually they tie the poor woman's hands to her feet and throw her into deep, still water. But whether she sinks or floats depends on luck and the kind of body she has. It's nothing to do with witchcraft."

"What about the way the baby kept staring at Alice?" I asked.

Mam smiled and shook her head. "A newborn baby's eyes aren't able to focus properly," she explained. "It was probably just the light of the candle that caught her attention. Remember—Alice was sitting close to it. Later, each time Alice passed by, the baby's eyes would just have been drawn by the change in the light. It's nothing. Nothing to worry about at all."

"But what if Ellie's baby is possessed anyway?" I asked. "What if there's something inside her that we can't see?"

"Look, son, I've delivered both good and evil into this world, and I know evil just by looking at it. This is a good child, and there's nothing inside her to worry about. Nothing at all."

"Isn't it strange, though, that Ellie's baby should be born about the same time that Mother Malkin died?"

"Not really," Mam answered. "It's the way of things. Sometimes, when something bad leaves the world, something good enters in its place. I've seen it happen before."

Of course, I realized then that Mam had never even considered dropping the baby and had just been trying to shock some sense into me, but as we walked back across the yard, my knees were still trembling with the thought of it. It was then, as we reached the kitchen door, that I remembered something.

"Mr. Gregory gave me a little book all about possession," I said. "He told me to read it carefully, but the trouble is, it's written in Latin and I've only had three lessons so far."

"It's not my favorite language," Mam said, pausing by the door. "I'll see what I can do, but it'll have to wait until I get back — I'm expecting to be called away tonight. In the meantime, why don't you ask Alice? She might be able to help."

Mam was right about being called away. A cart came for her just after midnight, the horses all in a sweat. It seemed that a farmer's wife was having a really bad time of it and had already been in labor for more than a day and a night. It was a long way as well, almost twenty miles to the south. That meant that Mam would be away for a couple of days or more.

I didn't really want to ask Alice to help with the Latin. You see, I knew the Spook would have disapproved. After all, it was a book from his library and he wouldn't have liked the idea of Alice even touching it. Still, what choice did I have? Since coming home, I'd been thinking about Mother Malkin more and more, and I just couldn't get her out of my mind. It was just an instinct, just a feeling, but I felt that she was somewhere out there in the dark and she was getting nearer with each night that passed.

So the following night, after Jack and Ellie had gone to bed, I tapped softly on Alice's bedroom door. It wasn't something I could ask her during the day because she was always busy, and if Ellie or Jack overheard, they wouldn't like it. Especially with Jack's dislike of spook's business.

I had to rap twice before Alice opened the door. I'd been worried that she might already be in bed asleep, but she still hadn't undressed and I couldn't stop my eyes from glancing down at her pointy shoes. On the dressing table there was a candle set close to the mirror. It had just been blown out—it was still smoking.

"Can I come in?" I asked, holding my own candle high so that it lit her face from above. "There's something I need to ask you."

Alice nodded me inside and closed the door.

"I've a book that I need to read, but it's written in Latin. Mam said you might be able to help."

"Where is it?" Alice asked.

"In my pocket. It's only a small book. For anyone who knows Latin, reading it shouldn't take that long."

Alice gave a deep, weary sigh. "I'm busy enough as it is," she complained. "What's it about?"

"Possession. Mr. Gregory thinks Mother Malkin could come back to get me and that she'll use possession."

REVENGE OF THE WITCH

"Let's see it then," she asked, holding out her hand. I placed my candle next to hers, then reached into my breeches and pulled out the small book. She skimmed through the pages without a word.

"Can you read it?" I asked.

"Don't see why not. Lizzie taught me, and she knows her Latin backward."

"So you'll help me?"

She didn't reply. Instead she brought the book very close to her face and sniffed it loudly. "You sure this is any good?" she asked. "Written by a priest, this is, and they don't usually know that much."

"Mr. Gregory called it the definitive work," I said, "which means it's the best book ever written on the subject."

She looked up from the book then, and to my surprise her eyes were filled with anger. "I know what definitive means," she said. "Think I'm stupid or something? Studied for years, I have, while you've only just started. Lizzie had lots of books, but they're all burned now. All gone up in flames."

I muttered that I was sorry, and she gave me a smile.

"Trouble is," she said, her voice suddenly soften-ing, "reading this'll take time, and I'm too tired to start now. Tomorrow your mam'll still be away, and I'll be as busy as ever. That sister-in-law of yours has promised to help, but she'll mostly be busy with the baby, and the cooking and cleaning will take me most of the day. But if you were to help . . ."

I didn't know what to say. I'd be helping Jack, so I wouldn't have much free time. The trouble was, men never did any cooking or cleaning, and it wasn't just that way on our farm. It was the same everywhere in the County. Men worked on the farm, outdoors in all weathers, and when they came in, the women had a hot meal waiting on the table. The only time we ever helped in the kitchen was on Christmas Day, when we did the washing up as a special treat for Mam.

It was as if Alice could read my mind, because her smile grew wider. "Won't be too hard, will it?" she asked. "Women feed the chickens and help with the harvest, so why shouldn't men help in the kitchen? Just help me with the washing up, that's all. And some of the pans'll need scouring before I start cooking."

So I agreed to what she wanted. What choice did

I have? I only hoped that Jack wouldn't catch me at it. He'd never understand.

I got up even earlier than usual and managed to scour the pans before Jack came down. Then I took my time over breakfast, eating very slowly, which was unlike me and enough to draw at least one suspicious glance from Jack. After he'd gone off into the fields, I washed the pots as quickly as I could and set to drying them. I might have guessed what would happen, because Jack never had much patience.

He came into the yard cursing and swearing and saw me through the window, his face all screwed up in disbelief. Then he spat into the yard and came around and pulled open the kitchen door with a jerk.

"When you're ready," he said sarcastically, "there's *men's* work to be done. And you can start by checking and repairing the pigpens. Snout's coming tomorrow. There are five to be slaughtered, and we don't want to spend all our time rounding up strays."

Snout was our nickname for the pig butcher, and Jack was right. Pigs sometimes panicked when Snout got to work, and if there was any weakness in the fence they'd find it for sure.

Jack turned to stamp away and then suddenly cursed loudly. I went to the door to see what was the matter. He'd accidentally stepped on a big fat toad, squashing it to a pulp. It was supposed to be bad luck to kill a frog or a toad, and Jack cursed again, frowning so much that his black bushy eyebrows met in the middle. He kicked the dead toad under the drain spout and went off, shaking his head. I couldn't think what had got into him. Jack never used to be so bad tempered.

I stayed behind and dried up every last pot—as he'd caught me at it, I might as well finish the job. Besides, pigs stank and I wasn't much looking forward to the job that Jack had given me.

"Don't forget the book," I reminded Alice as I opened the door to leave, but she just gave me a strange smile.

I didn't get to speak to Alice alone again until late that night, after Jack and Ellie had gone off to bed. I thought I'd have to visit her room again, but instead she came down into the kitchen carrying the book and sat herself down in Mam's rocking chair, close to the embers of the fire.

"Made a good job of those pans, you did. Must be desperate to find out what's in here," Alice said, tapping the spine of the book.

"If she comes back, I want to be ready. I need to know what I can do. The Spook said she'll probably be wick. Do you know about that?"

Alice's eyes widened and she nodded.

"So I need to be ready. If there's anything in that book that can help, I need to know about it."

"This priest ain't like the others," Alice said, holding the book out toward me. "Mostly knows his stuff, he does. Lizzie would love this more than midnight cakes."

I pushed the book into my breeches pocket and drew up a stool on the other side of the hearth, facing what was left of the fire. Then I started to question Alice. At first it was really hard work. She didn't volunteer much, and what I did manage to drag out of her just made me feel a lot worse.

I began with the strange title of the book. *Possession. The Damned, the Dizzy, and the Desperate.* What did it mean? Why call the book that?

"First word is just priest talk," Alice said, turning down the corners of her mouth in disapproval.

"They just use 'damned' for people who do things differently. For people like your mam, who don't go to church and say the right prayers. People who aren't like them. People who are left-handed," she said, giving me a knowing smile.

"Second word's more useful," Alice continued. "A body that's newly possessed has poor balance. It keeps falling over. Takes time, you see, for the possessor that's moved in to fit itself comfortably into its new body. It's like trying to wear in a new pair of shoes. Makes it bad tempered, too. Someone calm and placid can strike out without warning. So that's another way you can tell.

"Then, as for the third word, that's easy. A witch who once had a healthy human body is desperate to get another one. Then, once she succeeds, she's desperate to hold on to it. Ain't going to give it up without a fight. She'll do anything. Anything at all. That's why the possessed are so dangerous."

"If she came here, who would it be?" I asked. "If she were wick, who would she try to possess? Would it be me? Would she try to hurt me that way?"

"Would if she could," Alice said. "Ain't easy though, what with you being what you are. Like to use me, too, but I won't give her the chance. No, she'll go for the weakest. The easiest."

"Ellie's baby?"

"No, that ain't no use to her. She'd have to wait till it's all grown up. Mother Malkin never had much patience, and being trapped in that pit at Old Gregory's would have made her worse. If it's you she's coming to hurt, first she'll get herself a strong, healthy body."

"Ellie then? She'll choose Ellie!"

"Don't you know anything?" Alice said, shaking her head in disbelief. "Ellie's strong. She'd be difficult. No, men are much easier. Especially a man whose heart always rules his head. Someone who can fly into a temper without even thinking."

"Jack?"

"It'll be Jack for sure. Think what it'd be like to have big strong Jack after you. But the book's right about one thing. A body that's newly possessed is easier to deal with. Desperate it is, but dizzy, too."

I got my notebook out and wrote down anything that seemed important. Alice didn't talk as fast as the Spook, but after a bit she got into her stride and it wasn't long before my wrist was aching. When it

came to the really important business—how to deal
with the possessed—there were lots of reminders
that the original soul was still trapped inside the
body. So if you hurt the body, you hurt that innocent soul as well. So just killing the body to get rid
of the possessor was as bad as murder.

In fact that section of the book was disappoint-
ing: There didn't seem to be a lot you could do.
Being a priest, the writer thought that an exorcism,
using candles and holy water, was the best way
to draw out the possessor and release the victim,
but he admitted that not all priests could do it and
that very few could do it really well. It seemed to
me that some of the priests who could do it were
probably seventh sons of seventh sons and that was
what really mattered.

After all that, Alice said she felt tired and went up
to bed. I was feeling sleepy, too. I'd forgotten how
hard farmwork could be and I was aching from head
to foot. Once up in my room, I sank gratefully onto
my bed, anxious to sleep. But down in the yard the
dogs had started to bark.

Thinking that something must have alarmed
them, I opened the window and looked out toward

Hangman's Hill, taking a deep breath of night air to steady myself and clear my head. Gradually the dogs became quieter and eventually stopped barking altogether.

As I was about to close the window, the moon came out from behind a cloud. Moonlight can show the truth of things—Alice had told me that—just as that big shadow of mine had told Bony Lizzie that there was something different about me. This wasn't even a full moon, just a waning moon shrinking down to a crescent, but it showed me something new, something that couldn't be seen without it. By its light, I could see a faint silver trail winding down Hangman's Hill. It crept under the fence and across the north pasture, then crossed the eastern hay field until it vanished from sight somewhere behind the barn. I thought of Mother Malkin then. I'd seen the silver trail the night I'd knocked her into the river. Now here was another trail that looked just the same, and it had found me.

My heart thudding in my chest, I tiptoed downstairs and slipped out through the back door, closing it carefully behind me. The moon had gone behind a cloud, so when I went around to the back of the barn, the silver trail had vanished, but there was still clear evidence that something had moved down the hill toward our farm buildings. The grass was flattened as if a giant snail had slithered across it.

I waited for the moon to reappear so that I could check the flagged area behind the barn. A few moments later the cloud blew away and I saw something that really scared me. The silver trail gleamed in the moonlight, and the direction it had taken was unmistakable. It avoided the pigpen and snaked around the other side of the barn in a wide arc to reach the far edge of the yard. Then it moved toward the house, ending directly under Alice's window, where the old wooden hatch covered the steps that led down to the cellar.

A few generations back, the farmer who'd lived here used to brew ale, which he'd supplied to the local farms and even a couple of inns. Because of that, the locals called our farm Brewer's Farm, although we just called it home. The steps were there so that barrels could be taken in and out without having to go through the house.

The hatch was still in place covering the steps, a big rusty padlock holding its two halves in position, but there was a narrow gap between them, where the two edges of the wood didn't quite meet. It was a gap no wider than my thumb, but the silver trail ended exactly there, and I knew that whatever had slithered toward this point had somehow slipped through that tiny gap. Mother Malkin was back and she was wick, her body soft and pliable enough to slip through the narrowest of gaps.

She was already in the cellar.

We never used the cellar now, but I remembered it well enough. It had a dirt floor, and it was mostly full of old barrels. The walls of the house were thick and hollow, which meant that soon she could be anywhere inside the walls, anywhere in the house.

I glanced up and saw the flicker of a candle flame in the window of Alice's room. She was still up. I went inside, and moments later I was standing outside her bedroom door. The trick was to tap just loud enough to let Alice know I was there without waking anybody else. But as I held my knuckles close to the door, ready to knock, I heard a sound from inside the room.

I could hear Alice's voice. She seemed to be talking to someone.

I didn't like what I was hearing, but I tapped anyway. I waited a moment, but when Alice didn't come to the door, I put my ear against it. Who could she be talking to in her room? I knew that Ellie and Jack were already in bed, and anyway I could hear only one voice, and that was Alice's. It seemed different, though. It reminded me of something I'd heard before. When I suddenly remembered what it was, I moved my ear away from the wood as if it had been burned and took a big step away from the door.

Her voice was rising and falling, just like Bony Lizzie's had when she'd been standing above the pit, holding a small white thumb bone in each hand.

Almost before I realized what I was doing, I seized the door handle, turned it, and opened the door wide.

Alice, her mouth opening and closing, was chanting at the mirror. She was sitting on the edge of a straight-backed chair, staring over the top of a candle flame into the dressing-table mirror. I took a deep breath, then crept nearer so as to get a better look.

It was a County spring and after dark, so the room had a chill to it, but despite that there were big beads of sweat on Alice's brow. Even as I watched, two came together and ran down into her left eye and then beyond it onto her cheek like a tear. She was staring into the mirror, her eyes very wide, but when I called her name she never even blinked.

I moved behind the chair and caught the reflection of the brass candlestick in the mirror, but to my horror the face in the mirror above the flame didn't belong to Alice.

It was an old face, haggard and lined, with coarse gray-and-white hair falling like curtains across each gaunt cheek. It was the face of something that had spent a long time in the damp ground.

The eyes moved then, flicking to the left to meet my gaze. They were red points of fire. Although the face cracked into a smile, the eyes were burning with anger and hate.

There was no doubt. It was the face of Mother Malkin.

What was happening? Was Alice already possessed? Or was she somehow using the mirror to talk to Mother Malkin?

Without thinking, I seized the candlestick

and swung its heavy base into the mirror, which exploded with a loud crack followed by a glittering, tinkling shower of falling glass. As the mirror shattered, Alice screamed, loud and shrill.

It was the worst screech you can possibly imagine. It was filled with torment, and it reminded me of the noise a pig sometimes makes when it's slaughtered. But I didn't feel sorry for Alice, even though now she was crying and pulling at her hair, her eyes wild and filled with terror.

I was aware that the house was quickly filled with other sounds. The first was the cry of Ellie's baby; the second was a man's deep voice cursing and swearing; the third was big boots stamping down the stairs.

Jack burst furiously into the room. He took one look at the broken mirror, then stepped toward me and raised his fist. I suppose he must have thought it was all my fault, because Alice was still screaming, I was holding the candlestick, and there were small cuts on my knuckles caused by flying glass.

Just in time, Ellie came into the room. She had her baby cradled in her right arm and it was still crying fit to burst, but with her free hand she got a grip on Jack and pulled at him until he unclenched his fist and lowered his arm.

"No, Jack," she pleaded. "What good will that do?"

"I can't believe you've done that," Jack said, glaring at me. "Do you know how old that mirror was? What do you think Dad will say now? How will he feel when he sees this?"

No wonder Jack was angry. It had been bad enough waking everybody up, but that dressing table had belonged to Dad's mam. Now that Dad had given me the tinderbox, it was the last thing he owned that once belonged to his family.

Jack took two steps toward me. The candle hadn't gone out when I'd broken the mirror, but when he shouted again it began to flicker.

"Why did you do it? What on earth's got into you?" he roared.

What could I say? So I just shrugged, then stared down at my boots.

"What are you doing in this room anyway?" Jack persisted.

I didn't answer. Anything I said would only make it worse.

"Stay in your own room from now on!" Jack shouted. "I've a good mind to send the pair of you packing now!"

I glanced toward Alice, who was still sitting on the chair, her head in her hands. She'd stopped crying, but her whole body was shaking.

When I looked back, Jack's anger had given way to alarm. He was staring at Ellie, who suddenly seemed to stagger. Before he could move, she lost her balance and fell back against the wall. Jack forgot about the mirror for a few moments while he fussed over Ellie.

"I don't know what came over me," she said, all flustered. "I suddenly felt light-headed. Oh! Jack! Jack! I nearly dropped the baby!"

"You didn't and she's safe. Don't worry yourself. Here, let me take her. . . ."

Once he had the baby in his arms, Jack calmed down. "For now, just clear this mess up," he told me. "We'll talk about it in the morning."

Ellie walked across to the bed and put her hand on Alice's shoulder. "Alice, you come downstairs for a bit while Tom tidies up," she said. "I'll make us all a drink."

Moments later they'd all gone down to the kitchen, leaving me to pick up the pieces of glass. After about ten minutes I went down there myself to get a brush and pan. They were sitting around the kitchen table sipping herb tea, the baby asleep in Ellie's arms. They weren't talking and nobody offered me a drink. Nobody even glanced in my direction.

I went back upstairs and cleared up the mess as best I could, then went back to my own room. I sat on the bed and stared through the window, feeling terrified and alone. Was Alice already possessed? After all, it had been Mother Malkin's face staring back out of the mirror. If she was, then the baby and everyone else were in real danger.

She hadn't tried to do anything then, but Alice was relatively small compared with Jack, so Mother Malkin would have to be sly. She'd wait for everyone to go to sleep. I'd be the main target. Or maybe the baby. A child's blood would increase her strength.

Or had I broken the mirror just in time? Had I broken the spell at the very moment when Mother Malkin was about to possess Alice? Another possibility was that Alice had just been talking to the witch, using the mirror. Even so, that was bad enough. It meant I had two enemies to worry about.

I needed to do something. But what? While I sat there, my head whirling, trying to think things through, there was a tap on my bedroom door. I thought it was Alice, so I didn't go. Then a voice called my name softly. It was Ellie, so I opened the door.

"Can we talk inside?" she asked. "I don't want to risk waking the baby. I've only just gotten her off to sleep again."

I nodded, so Ellie came in and carefully closed the door behind her.

"You all right?" she asked, looking concerned.

I nodded miserably but couldn't meet her eyes.

"Would you like to tell me about it?" she asked. "You're a sensible lad, Tom, and you must have had a very good reason for what you did. Talking it through might make you feel better."

How could I tell her the truth? I mean, Ellie had a baby to care for, so how could I tell her that there was a witch somewhere loose in the house with a taste for children's blood? Then I realized that, for the sake of the baby, I would have to tell her something. She had to know just how bad things were.

She had to get away.

"There is something, Ellie. But I don't know how to tell you."

Ellie smiled. "The beginning would be as good a place as any . . ."

"Something's followed me back here," I said, looking Ellie straight in the eyes. "Something evil that wants to hurt me. That's why I broke the mirror. Alice was talking to it and—"

Ellie's eyes suddenly flashed with anger. "Tell Jack that, and you certainly *would* feel his fist! You mean you've brought something back here, when I've got a new baby to care for? How could you? How could you do that?"

"I didn't know it was going to happen," I protested. "I only found out tonight. That's why I'm telling you now. You need to leave the house and take the baby to safety. Go now, before it's too late."

"What? Right now? In the middle of the night?"

I nodded.

Ellie shook her head firmly. "Jack wouldn't go. He wouldn't be driven out of his own house in the middle of the night. Not by anything. No, I'll wait. I'm going to stay here, and I'm going to say my prayers. My mother taught me that. She said that if you pray really hard, nothing from the dark can ever harm you. And I really do believe that. Anyway, you could be wrong, Tom," she added. "You're young and only just beginning to learn the job, so it may not be quite as bad as you think. And your mam should be back at any time. If not tonight, then certainly tomorrow night. She'll know what to do. In the meantime, just keep out of that girl's room. There's something not right about her."

As I opened my mouth to speak, intending to have one more go at persuading her to leave, an expression of alarm suddenly came over Ellie's face, and she stumbled and put her hand against the wall to save herself from falling.

"Look what you've done now. I feel faint just thinking about what's going on here."

She sat down on my bed and put her head in her hands while I just stared down at her miserably, not knowing what to do or say.

After a few moments she climbed back to her feet again. "We need to talk to your mam as soon as she gets back, but don't forget, stay away from Alice until then. Do you promise?"

I promised, and with a sad smile Ellie went back to her own room.

It was only when she'd gone that it struck me. . . .

Ellie had stumbled for a second time and said she'd felt light-headed. One stumble could be just chance. Just tiredness. But twice! She was dizzy. Ellie was dizzy, and that was the first sign of possession!

I began to pace up and down. Surely I was wrong. Not Ellie! It couldn't be Ellie. Maybe Ellie was just tired. After all, the baby did keep her awake a lot. But Ellie was strong and healthy. She'd been brought up on a farm herself and wasn't one to let things drag her down. And all that talk about saying prayers. She could have said that so I wouldn't suspect her.

But hadn't Alice told me that Ellie would be difficult to possess? She'd also said that it would probably be Jack, but he hadn't shown any sign of dizziness. Still, there was no denying that he had become more and more bad tempered and aggressive, too! If Ellie hadn't held him back, he'd have thumped my head off my shoulders.

But of course, if Alice were in league with Mother Malkin, *everything* she said would be intended to put me off the scent. I couldn't even trust her account of the Spook's book! She could have told me lies all along! I couldn't read Latin, so there was no way to check what she'd said.

I realized that it could be any one of them. An attack could occur at any moment, and I hadn't any way of knowing who it would come from!

With luck, Mam would be back before dawn. She'd know what to do. But dawn was a long time off, so I couldn't afford to sleep. I'd have to keep watch all night long. If Jack or Ellie were possessed, there was nothing I could do about it. I couldn't go into their room, so all I could do was keep an eye on Alice.

I went outside and sat on the stairs between the door to Ellie and Jack's room and my own. From there I could see Alice's door below. If she left her room, at least I'd be able to give a warning.

I decided that if Mam wasn't back, I'd leave at dawn; apart from her, there was just one more chance of help. . . .

It was a long night, and at first I jumped at the slightest sound — a creak of the stairs or a faint movement of the floorboards in one of the rooms. But gradually I calmed down. It was an old house and these were the noises I was used to—the noises you expected as it slowly settled and cooled down during the night. However, as dawn approached, I started to feel uneasy again.

I began to hear faint scratching noises from inside the walls. It sounded like fingernails clawing at stone, and it wasn't always in the same place. Sometimes it was farther up the stairs on the left; sometimes below, close to Alice's room. It was so faint that it was hard to tell whether I was imagining it or not. But I began to feel cold, really cold, and that told me that danger was near.

Next the dogs began to bark, and within a few minutes the other animals were going crazy, too, the hairy pigs squealing so loud you'd have thought the pig butcher had already arrived. If that wasn't enough, the row started the baby crying again.

I was so cold now that my whole body was shaking and trembling. I just had to do something.

On the riverbank, facing the witch, my hands had known what to do. This time it was my legs that acted faster than I could think. I stood up and ran.

Terrified, my heart hammering, I bounded down the stairs, adding to the noise. I just had to get outside and away from the witch. Nothing else mattered. All my courage had gone.

CHAPTER XIII
Hairy Pigs

I ran out of the house and headed north, straight for Hangman's Hill, still in a panic, only slowing down when I'd reached the north pasture. I needed help, and I needed it fast. I was going back to Chipenden. Only the Spook could help me now.

Once I'd reached the boundary fence, the animals suddenly fell silent, and I turned and looked back toward the farm. Beyond it, I could just see the dirt road winding away in the distance, like a dark stain on the patchwork of gray fields.

It was then that I saw a light on the road. There was a cart moving toward the farm. Was it Mam? For a few moments my hopes were high. But as the cart neared the farm gate, I heard a loud hawking cough, the noise of phlegm being gathered in the throat, and then somebody spat. It was just Snout, the pig butcher. He'd five of our biggest hairy pigs to deal with; once dead, each one took a lot of scraping, so he was making an early start.

He'd never done me any harm, but I was always glad when he'd finished his business and left. Mam had never liked him either. She disliked the way he kept hawking up thick phlegm and spitting it out into the yard.

He was a big man, taller even than Jack, with knotted muscles on his forearms. The muscles were necessary for the work he did. Some pigs weighed more than a man and they fought like mad to avoid the knife. However, there was one part of Snout that had gone to seed. His shirts were always short, with the bottom two buttons open, and his fat, white, hairy belly hung down over the brown leather apron he wore to stop his trousers from getting soaked with blood. He couldn't have been much more than thirty, but his hair was thin and lank.

Disappointed that it wasn't Mam, I watched him unhook the lantern from the cart and begin to unload his tools. He set up for business at the front of the barn, right next to the pigpen.

I'd wasted enough time. I had started to climb over the fence into the wood when, out of the corner of my eye, I saw a movement on the slope below. A shadow was heading my way, hurrying toward the stile at the far end of the north pasture.

It was Alice. I didn't want her following me, but it was better to deal with her now than later, so I sat on the boundary fence and waited for her to reach me. I didn't have to wait long because she ran all the way up the hill.

She didn't come that close but stayed about nine or ten paces away, her hands on her hips, trying to catch her breath. I looked her up and down, seeing again the black dress and the pointy shoes. I must have woken her up when I'd run down the stairs; to reach me so soon she must have gotten dressed quickly and followed me straightaway.

"I don't want to talk to you," I called across to her, nervousness making my voice wobbly and higher than usual. "Don't waste your time following me either. You've had your chance, so from now on you'd better keep well away from Chipenden."

"You better had talk to me if you know what's

good for you," Alice said. "Soon it'll be too late, so there's something you'd better know. Mother Malkin's already here."

"I know that," I said. "I saw her."

"Not just in the mirror, though. It ain't just that. She's back there, somewhere inside the house," Alice said, pointing back down the hill.

"I told you, I know that," I said angrily. "The moonlight showed me the trail she made, and when I came upstairs to tell you that, what did I find? You were already talking to her, and probably not for the first time."

I remembered the first night when I went up to Alice's room and gave her the book. As I went inside, the candle had still been smoking in front of the mirror.

"You probably brought her here," I accused. "You told her where I was."

"Ain't true, that," Alice said, an anger in her voice that matched my own. She took about three steps closer to me. "Sniffed her out, I did, and I used the mirror to see where she was. Didn't realize she was so close, did I? She was too strong for me, so I couldn't break away. Lucky you came in when you did. Lucky for me you broke that mirror."

I wanted to believe Alice, but how could I trust her? When she moved a couple of paces nearer, I half turned, ready to jump down onto the grass on the other side of the fence. "I'm going back to Chipenden to fetch Mr. Gregory," I told her. "He'll know what to do."

"Ain't time for that," said Alice. "When you get back it'll be too late. There's the baby to think about. Mother Malkin wants to hurt you, but she'll be hungry for human blood. Young blood's what she likes best. That's what makes her strongest."

My fear had made me forget about Ellie's baby. Alice was right. The witch wouldn't want to possess it, but she'd certainly want its blood. When I brought the Spook back, it would be too late.

"But what can I do?" I asked. "What chance have I got against Mother Malkin?"

Alice shrugged and turned down the corners of her mouth. "That's your business. Surely Old Gregory taught you something that could be useful? If you didn't write it down in that notebook of yours, then maybe it's inside your head. You just have to remember it, that's all."

"He's not said that much about witches," I said, suddenly feeling annoyed with the Spook. Most of my training so far had been about boggarts, with little bits on ghasts and ghosts, while all my problems had been caused by witches.

I still didn't trust Alice, but now, after what she'd just said, I couldn't leave for Chipenden. I'd never get the Spook back here in time. Her warning about the threat to Ellie's baby seemed well intentioned, but if Alice were possessed, or on Mother Malkin's side, they were the very words that gave me no choice but to go back down the hill toward the farm. The very words that would keep me from warning the Spook, yet keep me where the witch could get her hands on me at a time of her own choosing.

On the way down the hill, I kept my distance from Alice, but she was at my side when we walked into the yard and crossed close to the front of the barn.

Snout was there, sharpening his knives; he looked up when he saw me and nodded. I nodded back. After he'd nodded at me, he just stared at Alice without speaking, but he looked her up and down twice. Then, just before we reached the kitchen door, he whistled long and loud. Snout's face had more in common with a pig's than with a wolf's, but it was that kind of whistle, heavy with mockery.

Alice pretended not to hear him. Before making the breakfast, she had another job to do: She went straight into the kitchen and started preparing the chicken we'd be having for our midday meal. It was hanging from a hook by the door, its neck off and its insides already pulled out the evening before. She set to work cleaning it with water and salt, her eyes concentrating hard on what she was doing so that her busy fingers wouldn't miss the tiniest bit.

It was then, as I watched her, that I finally remembered something that might just work against a possessed body.

Salt and iron!

I couldn't be sure, but it was worth a try. It was what the Spook used to bind a boggart into a pit, and it might just work against a witch. If I threw it at someone possessed, it might just drive Mother Malkin out.

I didn't trust Alice and didn't want her to see me helping myself to the salt, so I had to wait until she'd stopped cleaning the chicken and left the kitchen. That done, before going out to start my own chores, I paid a visit to Dad's workshop.

It didn't take me long to find what I needed. From among the large collection of files on the shelf above his workbench I chose the biggest and roughest toothed of them all. Soon I was filing away at the edge of an old iron bucket, the noise setting my teeth on edge. But it wasn't long before an even louder noise split the air.

It was the scream of a dying pig, the first of five.

I knew that Mother Malkin could be anywhere, and if she hadn't already possessed someone, she might choose a victim at any moment. So I had to concentrate and be on my guard at all times. But at least now I had something to defend myself with.

Jack wanted me to help Snout, but I was always ready with an excuse, claiming that I was finishing this or just about to do that. If I got stuck working with Snout, I wouldn't be able to keep an eye on everyone else. As I was just his brother visiting for a few days, not the hired help, Jack wasn't able to insist, but he came very close to it.

In the end, after lunch, his face as black as thunder, he was forced to help Snout himself, which was exactly what I wanted. If he was working in front of the barn, I could keep an eye on him from a distance. I kept using excuses to check on Alice and Ellie, too. Either one of them could be possessed, but if it were Ellie, there'd not be much chance of saving the baby: most of the time it was either in her arms or sleeping in its cot close to her side.

I had the salt and iron, but I wasn't sure whether it would be enough. The best thing would have been a silver chain. Even a short one would have been better than nothing. When I was little, I'd once over-heard Dad and Mam talking about a silver chain that belonged to her. I'd never seen her wearing one, but it might still be in the house somewhere — maybe in the storeroom just below the attic, which Mam always kept locked.

But their bedroom wasn't locked. Normally I'd never have gone into their room without permis-sion, but I was desperate. I searched Mam's jew-elry box. There were brooches and rings in the box, but no silver chain. I searched the whole room. I felt really guilty looking through the drawers, but I did it anyway. I thought there might have been a key to the storeroom, but I didn't find it.

While I was searching, I heard Jack's big boots coming up the stairs. I kept very still, hardly daring to breathe, but he just came up to his bedroom for a few moments and went straight down again. After that, I completed my search but found nothing, so I went down to check on everyone once more.

That day the air had been still and calm, but when I walked by the barn, a breeze had sprung up. The sun was beginning to go down, lighting up everything in a warm, red glow and promising fine weather for the following day. At the front of the barn three dead pigs were now hanging, head down, from big hooks. They were pink and freshly scraped, the last one still dripping blood into a bucket, and Snout was on his knees wrestling with the fourth, which was giving him a hard time of it—it was difficult to tell which of them was grunting the loudest.

Jack, the front of his shirt soaked in blood, glared at me as I passed, but I just smiled and nodded. They were just getting on with the work in hand and there was still quite a bit to do, so they'd be at it long after the sun had set. But so far there wasn't the slightest sign of dizziness, not even a hint of possession.

Within an hour it was dark. Jack and Snout were

still working by the light of the fire that was flickering their shadows across the yard.

The horror began as I went to the shed at the back of the barn to fetch a bag of spuds from the storeroom.

I heard a scream. It was a scream filled with terror. The scream of a woman facing the very worst thing that could possibly happen to her.

I dropped the sack of potatoes and ran around to the front of the barn. There I came to a sudden halt, hardly able to believe what I was seeing.

Ellie was standing about twenty paces away, holding out both her arms, screaming and screaming as if she were being tortured. At her feet lay Jack, blood all over his face. I thought Ellie was screaming because of Jack — but no, it was because of Snout.

He was facing toward me, as if he were waiting for me to arrive. In his left hand he was holding his favorite sharp knife, the long one he always used to cut a pig's throat. I froze in horror, because I knew what I'd heard in Ellie's scream.

With his right arm, he was cradling her baby.

There was thick pig blood on Snout's boots, and

it was still dripping onto them from his apron. He moved the knife closer to the baby.

"Come here, boy," he called in my direction. "Come to me." Then he laughed.

His mouth had opened and closed as he spoke, but it wasn't his voice that came out. It was Mother Malkin's. Neither was it his usual deep belly rumble of laughter. It was the cackle of the witch.

I took a slow step toward Snout. Then another one. I wanted to get closer to him. I wanted to save Ellie's baby. I tried to go faster. But I couldn't. My feet felt as heavy as lead. It was like desperately trying to run in a nightmare. My legs were moving as if they didn't belong to me.

I suddenly realized something that brought me out in a cold sweat. I wasn't just moving toward Snout because I wanted to. It was because Mother Malkin had summoned me. She was drawing me toward him at the pace she wanted, drawing me toward his waiting knife. I wasn't going to the rescue. I was just going to die. I was under some sort of spell. A spell of compulsion.

I'd felt something similar down by the river, but just in time my left hand and arm had acted by themselves to knock Mother Malkin into the water. Now my limbs were as powerless as my mind.

I was moving closer to Snout. Closer and closer to his waiting knife. His eyes were the eyes of Mother Malkin, and his face was bulging horribly. It was as if the witch inside were distorting its shape, swelling the cheeks close to bursting, bulging the eyes close to popping, beetling the brow into craggy overhanging cliffs; below them the bulbous, protruding eyes were centered with fire, casting a red, baleful glow before them.

I took another step and felt my heart thud. Another step and it thudded again. I was much nearer to Snout by now. *Thud, thud* went my heart, a beat for each step.

When I was no more than five paces from the waiting knife, I heard Alice running toward us, screaming my name. I saw her out of the corner of my eye, moving out of the darkness into the glow from the fire. She was heading straight toward Snout, her black hair streaming back from her head as if she were running directly into a gale.

Without even breaking her stride, she kicked toward Snout with all her might. She aimed just above his leather apron, and I watched the toe of her pointy shoe disappear so deeply into his fat belly that only the heel was visible.

Snout gasped, doubled over, and dropped Ellie's baby, but, lithe like a year-old cat, Alice dropped to her knees and caught it just before it hit the ground. Then she spun away, running back toward Ellie.

At the very moment that Alice's pointy shoe touched Snout's belly, the spell was broken. I was free again. Free to move my own limbs. Free to move. Or free to attack.

Snout was almost bent in two, but he straightened back up, and although he'd dropped the baby, he was still holding the knife. I watched as he moved it toward me. He staggered a bit, too—perhaps he was dizzy, or maybe it was just a reaction to Alice's pointy shoe.

Free of the spell, a whole range of feelings surged up inside me. There was sorrow for what had been done to Jack, horror at the danger Ellie's baby had been in, and anger that this could happen to my family. And in that moment I knew that I was born to be a spook. The very best spook who'd ever lived. I could and would make Mam proud of me.

You see, rather than being filled with fear, I was all ice and fire. Deep inside I was raging, full of hot anger that was threatening to explode. While on the outside I was as cold as ice, my mind sharp and clear, my breathing slow.

I thrust my hands into my breeches pockets. Then I brought them out fast, each fist full of what it had found there, and hurled each handful straight at Snout's head, something white from my right hand and something dark from my left. They came together, a white and a black cloud, just as they struck his face and shoulders.

Salt and iron—the same mixture so effective against a boggart. Iron to bleed away its strength; salt to burn it. Iron filings from the edge of the old bucket and salt from Mam's kitchen store. I was just hoping that it would have the same effect on a witch.

I suppose having a mixture like that thrown into your face wouldn't do anybody much good—at the very least it would make you cough and splutter—but the effect on Snout was much worse than that. First he opened his hand and let the knife fall. Then his eyes rolled up into his head and he pitched slowly forward, down onto his knees. Then he hit his forehead very hard on the ground, and his face twisted to one side.

Something thick and slimy began to ooze out of his left nostril. I just stood there watching, unable to move as Mother Malkin slowly bubbled and twisted from his nose into the shape that I remembered. It was her all right, but some of her was the same, while other bits were different.

For one thing, she was less than a third of the size she'd been the last time I saw her. Now her shoulders were hardly past my knees, but she was still wearing the long cloak, which was trailing on the ground, and the gray-and-white hair still fell onto her hunched shoulders like mildewy curtains. It was her skin that was really different. All glistening, strange, and sort of twisted and stretched. However, the red eyes hadn't changed, and they glared at me once before she turned and began to move away toward the corner of the barn. She seemed to be shrinking even more, and I wondered if that was the salt and iron still having an effect. I didn't know what more I could do, so I just stood there watching her go, too exhausted to move.

Alice wasn't having that. By now she'd handed

the baby to Ellie, and she came running across and made straight for the fire. She picked up a piece of wood that was burning at one end, then ran at Mother Malkin, holding it out in front of her.

I knew what she was going to do. One touch, and the witch would go up in flames. Something inside me couldn't let that happen because it was too horrible, so I caught Alice by the arm as she ran past and spun her around so that she dropped the burning log.

She turned on me, her face full of fury, and I thought I was about to feel a pointy shoe. Instead she gripped my forearm so tightly that her fingernails actually bit deep into the flesh.

"Get harder or you won't survive!" she hissed into my face. "Just doing what Old Gregory says won't be enough. You'll die like the others!"

She released my arm, and I looked down at it and saw beads of blood where her nails had cut into me.

"You have to burn a witch," Alice said, the anger in her voice lessening, "to make sure they don't come back. Putting them in the ground ain't no good. It just delays things. Old Gregory knows that, but he's too soft to use burning. Now it's too late. . . ."

Mother Malkin was disappearing around the side of the barn into the shadows, still shrinking with each step, her black cloak trailing on the ground behind her.

It was then that I realized the witch had made a big mistake. She'd taken the wrong route, right across the largest pigpen. By now she was small enough to fit under the lowest plank of wood.

The pigs had had a very bad day. Five of their number had been slaughtered, and it had been a very noisy, messy business that had probably scared them pretty badly. So they weren't best pleased, to say the least, and it probably wasn't a good time to go into their pen. And big hairy pigs will eat any-thing, anything at all. Soon it was Mother Malkin's turn to scream, and it went on for a long time.

"Could be as good as burning, that," said Alice when the sound finally faded away. I could see the relief in her face. I felt the same. We were both glad it was all over. I was tired, so I just shrugged, not sure what to think, but I was already looking back toward Ellie, and I didn't like what I saw.

Ellie was frightened, and she was horrified. She was looking at us as if she couldn't believe what had happened and what we'd done. It was as if she'd seen me properly for the first time. As if she'd suddenly realized what I was.

I understood something, too. For the first time I really felt what it was like to be the Spook's apprentice. I'd seen people move to the other side of the road to avoid passing close to us. I'd watched them shiver or cross themselves just because we'd passed through their village, but I hadn't taken it personally. In my mind it was their reaction to the Spook, not to me.

But I couldn't ignore this, or push it to the side of my mind. It was happening to me directly, and it was happening in my own home.

I suddenly felt more alone than I ever had before.

CHAPTER XIV
The Spook's Advice

BUT not everything turned out badly. Jack wasn't dead after all. I didn't like to ask too many questions because it just got everybody upset, but it seemed that one minute Snout had been about to start scraping the belly of the fifth pig with Jack, and the next he'd suddenly gone berserk and attacked him.

It was just pig's blood on Jack's face. He'd been knocked unconscious with a piece of timber. Snout had then gone into the house and snatched the baby. He'd wanted to use it as bait to get me close so that he could use his knife on me.

Of course, the way I'm telling it now isn't quite right. It wasn't really Snout doing these terrible things. He'd been possessed, and Mother Malkin was just using his body. After a couple of hours Snout recovered and went home puzzled and nursing a very sore belly. He didn't seem to remember anything about what had happened, and none of us wanted to enlighten him.

Nobody slept much that night. After building the fire up high, Ellie stayed down in the kitchen all night and wouldn't let the baby out of her sight. Jack went to bed nursing a sore head, but he kept waking up and having to dash outside to be sick in the yard.

An hour or so before dawn, Mam came home. She didn't seem very happy either. It was as if something had gone wrong.

I lifted her bag to carry it into the house. "Are you all right, Mam?" I asked. "You look tired."

"Never mind me, son. What's happened here? I can tell something's wrong just by looking at your face."

"It's a long story," I said. "We'd better get inside first."

When we walked into the kitchen Ellie was so relieved to see Mam that she started to cry, and that set the baby off crying, too. Jack came down then and everybody tried to tell Mam things at once, but I gave up after a few seconds because Jack started off on one of his rants.

Mam shut him up pretty quickly. "Lower your voice, Jack," she told him. "This is still my house, and I can't abide shouting."

He wasn't happy at being told off in front of Ellie like that, but he knew better than to argue.

She made each one of us tell her exactly what had happened, starting with Jack. I was the last, and when it was my turn, she sent Ellie and Jack up to bed so that we could talk alone. Not that she said much. She just listened quietly, then held my hand.

Finally she went up to Alice's room and spent a long time talking to her alone.

The sun had been up less than an hour when the Spook arrived. Somehow I'd been expecting him. He waited at the gate, and I went out and told the tale again, while he leaned on his staff. When I'd finished, he shook his head.

"I sensed that something was wrong, lad, but I came too late. Still you did all right. You used your initiative and managed to remember some of the things I'd taught you. If all else fails, you can always fall back on salt and iron."

"Should I have let Alice burn Mother Malkin?" I asked.

He sighed and scratched at his beard. "As I told you, it's a cruel thing to burn a witch, and I don't hold with it myself."

"I suppose now I'll have to face Mother Malkin again," I said.

The Spook smiled. "No, lad, you can rest easy, because she won't be coming back to this world. Not after what happened at the end. Remember what I told you about eating the heart of a witch? Well, those pigs of yours did it for us."

"Not just the heart. They ate up every bit," I told him. "So I'm safe? Really safe? She can't come back?"

"Aye, you're safe from Mother Malkin. There are other threats out there just as bad, but you're safe for now."

I felt a big sense of relief, as if a heavy weight had been lifted from my shoulders. I'd been living in a nightmare, and now, with the threat of Mother

Malkin removed, the world seemed a much brighter, happier place. It was over at last, and I could start to look forward to things again.

"Well, you're safe until you make another silly mistake," the Spook added. "And don't say you won't. He who never makes a mistake never makes anything. It's part of learning the job.

"Well, what's to be done now?" he asked, squinting into the rising sun.

"About what?" I asked, wondering what he meant.

"About the girl, lad," he said. "It looks like it's the pit for her. I don't see any way around it."

"But she saved Ellie's baby at the end," I protested. "She saved my life as well."

"She used the mirror, lad. It's a bad sign. Lizzie taught her a lot. Too much. Now she's shown us that she's prepared to use it. What will she do next?"

"But she meant well. She used it to try and find Mother Malkin."

"Maybe, but she knows too much, and she's clever, too. She's just a girl now, but one day she'll be a woman, and some clever women are dangerous."

"My mam's clever," I told him, annoyed at what he'd said. "But she's good, too. Everything she does she does for the best. She uses her brains to help people. One year, when I was really small, the ghasts on Hangman's Hill frightened me so much that I couldn't sleep. Mam went up there after dark and she shut them up. They were quiet for months and months."

I could have added that, on our first morning together, the Spook had told me that there wasn't much to be done about ghasts. And that Mam had proved him wrong. But I didn't. I'd blurted out too much already, and it didn't need to be said.

The Spook didn't say anything. He was staring toward the house.

"Ask my mam what she thinks about Alice," I suggested. "She seems to get on well with her."

"I was going to do that anyway," said the Spook. "It's about time we had a little talk. You wait here until we're finished."

I watched the Spook cross the yard. Even before he reached it, the kitchen door opened and Mam welcomed him over the threshold.

Later, it was possible to work out some of the things that they'd said to each other, but they talked together for almost half an hour, and I never did find out whether ghasts came into the conversation. When the

Spook finally came out into the sunshine, Mam stayed in the doorway. He did something unusual then—something I'd never seen him do before. At first I thought he'd just nodded at Mam as he said good-bye, but there was a bit more to it than that. There was a movement of his shoulders, too. It was slight but very definite, so there was no doubt about it. As he took his leave of Mam, the Spook gave her a little bow.

When he crossed the yard toward me, he seemed to be smiling to himself. "I'll be off on my way back to Chipenden now," he said, "but I think your mother would like you to stay one more night. Anyway, I'm going to leave it up to you," said the Spook. "Either bring the girl back and we'll bind her in the pit, or take her to her aunt in Staumin. The choice is yours. Use your instinct for what's right. You'll know what to do."

Then he was gone, leaving me with my head whirling. I knew what I wanted to do about Alice, but it had to be the right thing.

So I got to eat another of Mam's suppers.

Dad was back by then, but although Mam was happy to see him, there was something not quite right, a sort of atmosphere like an invisible cloud hanging over the table. So it wasn't exactly a celebration party, and nobody had much to say.

The food was good, though, one of Mam's special hot pots, so I didn't mind the lack of conversation—I was too busy filling my belly and getting second helpings before Jack could scrape the dish clean.

Jack had his appetite back, but he was a bit subdued, like everyone else. He'd been through a lot, with a big bump on his forehead to prove it. As for Alice, I hadn't told her what the Spook had said, but I felt she knew anyway. She didn't speak once during dinner. But the quietest one of all was Ellie. Despite the joy of having her baby back, what she'd seen had upset her badly, and I could tell it would take some getting over.

When the others went up to bed, Mam asked me to stay behind. I sat by the fire in the kitchen, just as I had on the night before I went away to begin my apprenticeship. But something in her face told me this conversation was going to be different. Before, she'd been firm with me but hopeful. Confident that things would work out all right. Now she looked sad and uncertain.

"I've been delivering County babies for nearly

twenty-five years," she said, sitting down in her rocking chair, "and I've lost a few. Although it's very sad for the mother and father, it's just something that happens. It happens with farm animals, Tom. You've seen it yourself."

I nodded. Every year a few lambs were born dead. It was something you expected.

"This time it was worse," Mam said. "This time both the mother and the baby died, something that's never happened to me before. I know the right herbs and how to blend them. I know how to cope with severe bleeding. I know just what to do. And this mother was young and strong. She shouldn't have died, but I couldn't save her. I did everything I could, but I couldn't save her. And it's given me a pain here. A pain in my heart."

Mam gave a sort of sob and clutched at her chest. For one awful moment I thought she was going to cry, but then she took a deep breath and the strength came back into her face.

"But sheep die, Mam, and sometimes cows when giving birth," I told her. "A mother was bound to die eventually. It's a miracle that you've gone so long without it happening before."

I did my best, but it was hard to console her. Mam was taking it very badly. It made her look on the gloomy side of things.

"It's getting darker, son," she said to me. "And it's coming sooner than I expected. I'd hoped you'd be a grown man first, with years of experience under your belt. So you're going to have to listen carefully to every-thing your master says. Every little thing will count. You're going to have to get yourself ready as quickly as you can and work hard at your Latin lessons."

She paused then and held out her hand. "Let me see the book."

When I handed it to her, she flicked through the pages, pausing every so often to read a few lines. "Did it help?" she asked.

"Not much," I admitted.

"Your master wrote this himself. Did he tell you that?"

I shook my head. "Alice said it was written by a priest."

Mam smiled. "Your master was a priest once. That's how he started out. No doubt he'll tell you about it one day. But don't ask. Let him tell you in his own good time."

"Was that what you and Mr. Gregory talked about?" I asked.

"That and other things, but mainly about Alice. He asked me what I thought should happen to her. I told him he should leave it to you. So have you made up your mind yet?"

I shrugged. "I'm still not sure what to do, but Mr. Gregory said that I should use my instincts."

"That's good advice, son," Mam said.

"But what do you think, Mam?" I asked. "What did you tell Mr. Gregory about Alice? Is Alice a witch? Tell me that at least."

"No," Mam said slowly, weighing her words carefully. "She's not a witch, but she will be one day. She was born with the heart of a witch, and she's little choice but to follow that path."

"Then she should go into the pit at Chipenden," I said sadly, hanging my head.

"Remember your lessons," Mam said sternly. "Remember what your master taught you. There's more than one kind of witch."

"The benign," I said. "You mean Alice might turn out to be a good witch who helps others?"

"She might. And she might not. Do you know

what I really think? You might not want to hear this."

"I do," I said.

"Alice might end up neither good nor bad. She might end up somewhere in between. That would make her very dangerous to know. That girl could be the bane of your life, a blight, a poison on everything you do. Or she might turn out to be the best and strongest friend you'll ever have. Someone who'll make all the difference in the world. I just don't know which way it will go. I can't see it, no matter how hard I try."

"How could you see it anyway, Mam?" I asked. "Mr. Gregory said he doesn't believe in prophecy. He said the future's not fixed."

Mam put a hand on my shoulder and gave me a little squeeze of reassurance. "There's some choice open to us all," she said. "But maybe one of the most important decisions you'll ever make will be about Alice. Go to bed now, and get a good night's sleep if you can. Make up your mind tomorrow when the sun's shining."

One thing I didn't ask Mam was how she'd managed to silence the ghasts on Hangman's Hill. It was my instincts again. I just knew that it was something she wouldn't want to talk about. In a family, there are some things you don't ask. You know you'll be told when it's the right time.

We left soon after dawn, my heart down in my boots.

Ellie followed me to the gate. I stopped there but waved Alice on, and she sauntered up the hill, swinging her hips, without even once glancing back.

"I need to say something to you, Tom," Ellie said. "It hurts me to do it, but it has to be said."

I could tell by her voice that it was going to be bad. I nodded miserably and forced myself to meet her eyes. I was shocked to see that they were streaming with tears.

"You're still welcome here, Tom," Ellie said, brushing her hair back from her forehead and trying to smile. "That's not changed. But we do have to think of our child. So you'll be welcome here, but not after dark. You see, that's what's made Jack so bad tempered recently. I didn't like to tell you just how strongly he feels, but it has to be said now. He doesn't like the job you're doing at all. Not one little bit. It gives him the creeps. And he's scared for the baby.

"We're frightened, you see. We're frightened that if you're ever here after dark, you might attract something else. You might bring back something bad with you, and we can't risk anything happening to our family. Come and visit us during the day, Tom. Come and see us when the sun's up and the birds are singing."

Ellie hugged me then, and that made it even worse. I knew that something had come between us and that things had changed forever. I felt like crying, but somehow I stopped myself. I don't know how I managed it. There was a big lump in my throat, and I couldn't speak.

I watched Ellie walk back to the farmhouse and turned my attention back to the decision I had to make.

What should I do about Alice?

I'd woken up certain that it was my duty to take her back with me to Chipenden. It seemed the right thing to do. The safe thing to do. It felt like a duty. When I gave Mother Malkin the cakes, I'd let the softness of my heart overrule me. And look where that had gotten me. So it was probably best to deal with Alice now, before it was too late. As the Spook said, you had to think of the innocents who might be harmed in the future.

On the first day of the journey, we didn't speak to each other much. I just told her we were going back to Chipenden to see the Spook. If Alice knew what was going to happen to her, she certainly didn't complain. Then on the second day, as we got closer to the village and were actually on the lower slopes of the fells, no more than a mile or so from the Spook's house, I told Alice what I'd been keeping bottled up inside me; what had been worrying me ever since I'd realized just what the cakes contained.

We were sitting on a grassy bank close to the side of the road. The sun had set and the light was begin-ning to fail.

"Alice, do you ever tell lies?" I asked.

"Everybody tells lies sometimes," she replied. "Wouldn't be human if you didn't. But mostly I tell the truth."

"What about that night when I was trapped in the pit? When I asked you about those cakes. You said there hadn't been another child at Lizzie's house. Was that true?"

"Didn't see one."

"The first one that went missing was no more than a baby. It couldn't have wandered off by itself. Are you sure?"

Alice nodded and then bowed her head, staring down at the grass.

"I suppose it could have been carried off by wolves," I said. "That's what the village lads thought."

"Lizzie said she's seen wolves in these parts. That could be it," Alice agreed.

"So what about the cakes, Alice? What was in them?"

"Suet and pork bits mostly. Bread crumbs, too."

"What about the blood, then? Animal blood wouldn't have been good enough for Mother Malkin. Not when she needed enough strength to bend the bars over the pit. So where did the blood come from, Alice—the blood that was used in the cakes?"

Alice started to cry. I waited patiently for her to finish, then asked the question again.

"Well, where did it come from?"

"Lizzie said I was still a child," Alice said. "They'd used my blood lots of times. So one more time didn't matter. It don't hurt that much. Not when you get used to it. How could I stop Lizzie anyway?"

With that, Alice pushed up her sleeve and showed me her upper arm. There was still enough light to see the scars. And there were a lot of them—some old; some relatively new. The newest one of all hadn't healed properly yet. It was still weeping.

"There's more than that. Lots more. But I can't show 'em all," Alice said.

I didn't know what to say, so I just kept quiet. But I'd already made up my mind, and soon we walked off into the dark, away from Chipenden.

I'd decided to take Alice straight to Staumin, where her aunt lived. I couldn't bear the thought of her ending up in a pit in the Spook's garden. It was just too terrible—and I remembered another pit. I remembered how Alice had helped me from Tusk's pit just before Bony Lizzie had come to collect my bones. But above all, it was what Alice had just told me that had finally changed my mind. Once, she'd been one of the innocents. Alice had been a victim, too.

We climbed Parlick Pike, then moved north onto Blindhurst Fell, always keeping to the high ground.

I liked the idea of going to Staumin. It was near the coast, and I'd never seen the sea before, except from the tops of the fells. The route I chose was more than a bit out of the way, but I fancied exploring and liked being up there close to the sun. Anyway, Alice didn't seem to mind at all.

It was a good journey, and I enjoyed Alice's company, and for the first time we really started to talk. She taught me a lot, too. She knew the names of more stars than I did and was really good at catching rabbits.

As for plants, Alice was an expert on things that the Spook hadn't even mentioned so far, such as deadly nightshade and mandrake. I didn't believe everything she said, but I wrote it down anyway because she'd been taught it by Lizzie and I thought it was useful to learn what a witch believes. Alice was really good at distinguishing mushrooms from poisonous toadstools, some of which were so dangerous that one bite would stop your heart or drive you insane. I had my notebook with me and under the heading called *Botany*, I added three more pages of useful information.

One night, when we were less than a day's walk from Staumin, we stayed in a forest clearing. We'd just cooked two rabbits in the embers of a fire until the meat almost melted in our mouths. After the meal Alice did something really strange. After turning to face me, she reached across and held my hand.

We sat there like that for a long time. She was staring into the embers of the fire, and I was looking up at the stars. I didn't want to break away, but I was all mixed up. My left hand was holding her left hand and I felt guilty. I felt as if I were holding hands with the dark, and I knew the Spook wouldn't like it.

There was no way I could get away from the truth. Alice was going to be a witch one day. It was then that I realized Mam was right. It was nothing to do with prophecy. You could see it in Alice's eyes. She'd always be somewhere in between, neither wholly good nor wholly bad. But wasn't that true of all of us? Not one of us was perfect.

So I didn't pull my hand away. I just sat there, one part of me enjoying holding her hand, which was sort of comforting after all that had happened, while the other part sweated with guilt.

It was Alice who broke away. She took her hand out of mine and then touched my arm where her nails had cut me on the night we destroyed Mother

Malkin. You could see the scars clearly in the glow from the embers.

"Put my brand on you there," she said with a smile. "That won't ever fade away."

I thought that was a strange thing to say, and I wasn't sure what she meant. Back home we put our brand on cattle. We did it to show that they belonged to us and to stop strays getting mixed up with animals from neighboring farms. So how could I belong to Alice?

The following day we came down onto a great flat plain. Some of it was moss land and the worst bits were soggy marsh, but eventually we found our way through to Staumin. I never got to see the aunt because she wouldn't come out to talk to me. Still, she agreed to take Alice in, so I couldn't complain.

There was a big, wide river nearby, and before I left for Chipenden, we walked down its bank as far as the sea. I wasn't really taken with it. It was a gray, windy day, and the water was the same color as the sky and the waves were big and rough.

"You'll be all right here," I said, trying to be cheerful. "It'll be nice when the sun shines."

"Just have to make the best of it," Alice said. "Can't be worse than Pendle."

I suddenly felt sorry for her again. I felt lonely at times, but at least I had the Spook to talk to; Alice didn't even know her aunt properly, and the rough sea made everything seem bleak and cold.

"Look, Alice, I don't expect we'll see each other again, but if you ever need help, try to get word to me," I offered.

I suppose I said that because Alice was the nearest thing to a friend I had. And as a promise, it wasn't quite as daft as the first one I'd made her. I didn't commit myself to actually doing anything. Next time she asked for anything, I'd be talking to the Spook first.

To my surprise, Alice smiled, and she had a strange look in her eyes. It reminded me of what Dad had once said about women sometimes knowing things that men don't—and when you suspect that, you should never ask what they're thinking.

"Oh, we'll meet again," Alice said. "Ain't no doubt about that."

"I'll have to be off now," I said, turning to leave.

"I'll miss you, Tom," Alice said. "Won't be the

same without you."

"I'll miss you, too, Alice," I said, giving her a smile.

As the words came out, I thought that I'd said them out of politeness. But I hadn't been on the road more than ten minutes before I knew I was wrong.

I'd meant every word, and I was feeling lonely already.

I'VE written most of this from memory, but some of it from my notebook and my diary. I'm back at Chipenden now, and the Spook is pleased with me. He thinks I'm making really good progress.

Bony Lizzie's in the pit where the Spook used to keep Mother Malkin. The bars have been straightened out, and she certainly won't be getting any midnight cakes from me. As for Tusk, he's buried in the hole he dug for my grave.

Poor Billy Bradley's back in his grave outside the churchyard at Layton, but at least he's got his thumbs now. None of it's pleasant, but it's something that just goes with the job. You have to like it or lump it, as my dad says.

There's something else I should tell you. The Spook agrees with what Mam said. He thinks that the winters are getting longer and that the dark is growing in power. He's sure that the job's getting harder and harder.

So keeping that in mind, I'll carry on studying and learning—as my mam once told me, you never know just what you can do until you try. So I'm going to try. I'm going to try just as hard as I possibly can because I want her to be really proud of me.

Now I'm just an apprentice, but one day I'll be the Spook.

Thomas J. Ward

❈ BOOK TWO ❈

CURSE OF THE BANE

CHAPTER I
The Horshaw Ripper

WHEN I heard the first scream, I turned away and covered my ears with my hands, pressing hard until my head hurt. At that moment I could do nothing to help. But I could still hear it, the sound of a priest in torment, and it went on for a long time before finally fading away.

So I shivered in the dark barn, listening to rain drumming on the roof, trying to gather my courage. It was a bad night, and it was about to get worse.

Ten minutes later, when the rigger and his mate arrived, I rushed across to meet them in the doorway. Both of them were big men, and I barely came up to their shoulders.

"Well, lad, where's Mr. Gregory?" asked the

rigger, an edge of impatience in his voice. He lifted the lantern he was holding and peered about suspiciously. His eyes were shrewd and intelligent. Neither of the men looked like they would stand any nonsense.

"He's been taken badly," I said, trying to control the nerves that were making my voice sound weak and wobbly. "He's been in bed with a bad fever this past week so he's sent me in his place. I'm Tom Ward. His apprentice."

The rigger looked me up and down quickly, like an undertaker measuring me up for future business. Then he raised one eyebrow so high that it disappeared under the peak of his flat cap, which was still dripping with rain.

"Well, Mr. Ward," he said, an edge of sarcasm sharp in his voice, "we await your instructions."

I put my left hand into my breeches pocket and pulled out the sketch that the stonemason had made. The rigger set the lantern down on the earthen floor and then, with a world-weary shake of his head and a glance at his mate, accepted the sketch and began to examine it.

The mason's instructions gave the dimensions of

the pit that needed to be dug and the measurements of the stone that would be lowered into place.

After a few moments the rigger shook his head again and knelt beside the lantern, holding the paper very close to it. When he came to his feet, he was frowning. "The pit should be nine feet deep," he said. "This only says six."

The rigger knew his job all right. The standard boggart pit is six feet deep, but for a ripper, the most dangerous boggart of all, nine feet is the norm. We were certainly facing a ripper—the priest's screams were proof of that—but there wasn't time to dig nine feet.

"It'll have to do," I said. "It has to be done by morning or it'll be too late and the priest will be dead."

Until that moment they'd both been big men wearing big boots, oozing confidence from every pore. Now, suddenly, they looked nervous. They knew the situation from the note I'd sent summoning them to the barn. I'd used the Spook's name to make sure they came right away.

"Know what you're doing, lad?" asked the rigger. "Are you up to the job?"

I stared straight back into his eyes and tried hard not to blink. "Well, I've made a good start," I said. "I've hired the best rigger and mate in the County."

It was the right thing to say, and the rigger's face cracked into a smile. "When will the stone arrive?" he asked.

"Well before dawn. The mason's bringing it himself. We have to be ready."

The rigger nodded. "Then lead the way, Mr. Ward. Show us where you want it dug."

This time there was no sarcasm in his voice. His tone was businesslike. He wanted the job over and done with. We all wanted the same, and time was short, so I pulled up my hood and, carrying the Spook's staff in my left hand, led the way out into the cold, heavy drizzle.

Their two-wheel cart was outside, the equipment covered with a waterproof sheet, the patient horse between the shafts steaming in the rain.

We crossed the muddy field, then followed the blackthorn hedge to the place where it thinned, beneath the branches of an ancient oak on the boundary of the churchyard. The pit would be close to holy ground, but not too close. The nearest gravestones were just twenty paces away.

"Dig the pit as close as you can get to that," I said, pointing toward the trunk of the tree.

Under the Spook's watchful eye I'd dug lots of practice pits. In an emergency I could have done the job myself, but these men were experts and they'd work fast.

As they went back for their tools, I pushed through the hedge and weaved between the gravestones toward the old church. It was in a bad state of repair: There were slates missing from the roof and it hadn't seen a lick of paint for years. I pushed open the side door, which yielded with a groan and a creak.

The old priest was still in the same position, lying on his back near the altar. The woman was kneeling on the floor close to his head, crying. The only difference now was that the church was flooded with light. She'd raided the vestry for its hoard of candles and lit them all. There were a hundred at least, clustered in groups of five or six. She'd positioned them on benches, on the floor, and on window ledges, but the majority were on the altar.

As I closed the door, a gust of wind blew into the

church and the flames all flickered together. She looked up at me, her face running with tears.

"He's dying," she said, her echoing voice full of anguish. "Why did it take you so long to get here?"

Since the message reached us at Chipenden, it had taken me two days to arrive at the church. It was over thirty miles to Horshaw, and I hadn't set off right away. At first the Spook, still too ill to leave his bed, had refused to let me go.

Usually the Spook never sends apprentices out to work alone until he's been training them for at least a year. I'd just turned thirteen and had been his apprentice for less than six months. It was a difficult, scary trade, which often involved dealing with what we call "the dark." I'd been learning how to cope with witches, ghosts, boggarts, and things that go bump in the night. But was I ready for this?

There was a boggart to bind, which, if done properly, should be pretty straightforward. I'd seen the Spook do it twice. Each time he'd hired good men to help and the job had gone smoothly. But this job was a little different. There were complications.

You see, this priest was the Spook's own brother. I'd seen him just once before, when we'd visited

Horshaw in the spring. He'd glared at us and made a huge sign of the cross in the air, his face twisted with anger. The Spook hadn't even glanced in his direction because there'd been little love lost between them and they hadn't spoken for over forty years. But family was family, and that's why he'd eventually sent me to Horshaw.

"Priests!" the Spook had raved. "Why don't they stick to what they know? Why do they always have to meddle? What was he thinking of, trying to tackle a ripper? Let me get on with my business and other folks get on with theirs."

At last he'd calmed down and spent hours giving me detailed instructions on what had to be done and telling me the names and addresses of the rigger and mason I had to hire. He'd also named a doctor, insisting that only he would do. That was another nuisance because the doctor lived some distance away. I'd had to send word, and I just hoped that he'd set off immediately.

I looked down at the woman, who was dabbing very gently at the priest's forehead with a cloth. His greasy, lank white hair was pulled back from his face and his eyes were rolling feverishly in his head. He hadn't known that the woman was going to send to the Spook for help. If he had, he would have objected, so it was a good job that he couldn't see me now.

Tears were dripping from the woman's eyes and sparkling in the candlelight. She was his house-keeper, not even family, and I remember thinking that he must have been really kind to her to make her get so upset.

"The doctor'll be here soon," I said, "and he'll give him something for the pain."

"He's had pain all his life," she answered. "I've been a big trouble to him, too. It's made him terri-fied of dying. He's a sinner and he knows where he's going."

Whatever he was or had done, the old priest didn't deserve this. Nobody did. He was certainly a brave man. Either brave or very stupid. When the boggart had got up to its tricks, he'd tried to deal with it him-self by using the priest's tools: bell, book, and candle. But that's no way to deal with the dark. In most cases it wouldn't have mattered because the boggart would just have ignored the priest and his exorcism. Eventually it would have moved on and the priest, as often happens, would have taken the credit.

But this was the most dangerous type of boggart we ever have to deal with. Usually, we call them cattle rippers because of their main diet, but when the priest had started meddling, he had become the boggart's victim. Now it was a full-blown ripper with a taste for human blood, and the priest would be lucky to escape with his life.

There was a crack in the flagged floor, a zigzag crack that ran from the foot of the altar to about three paces beyond the priest. At its widest point it was more a chasm and almost half a hand's span wide. After splitting the floor, the boggart had caught the old priest by his foot and dragged his leg down into the ground almost as far as his knee. Now, in the darkness below, it was sucking his blood, drawing the life from him very slowly. It was like a big fat leech, keeping its victim alive as long as possible to extend its own enjoyment.

Whatever I did, it would be touch-and-go whether or not the priest survived. In any case, I had to bind the boggart. Now that it had drunk human blood, it would no longer be content with ripping cattle.

"Save him if you can," the Spook had said as I

prepared to leave. "But whatever else you do, make sure you deal with that boggart. That's your first duty."

I started making my own preparations.

Leaving the rigger's mate to carry on digging the pit, I went back to the barn with the rigger himself. He knew what to do: first of all, he poured water into the large bucket they'd brought with them. That was one advantage of working with people who had experience of the business: They provided the heavy equipment. This was a strong bucket, made of wood, bound with metal hoops and large enough to deal with even a twelve-foot pit.

After filling it about half full with water, the rigger began to shake brown powder into it from the large sack he'd brought in from the cart. He did this a little at a time and then, after each addition, began to stir it with a stout stick.

It soon became hard work as, very gradually, the mixture turned into a thick goo that became more and more difficult to mix. It stank as well, like something that had been dead for weeks, which wasn't really surprising seeing as the bulk of the powder was crushed bone.

The end result would be a very strong glue, and the longer the rigger stirred, the more he began to sweat and gasp. The Spook always mixed his own glue, and he'd made me practice doing the same, but time was very short and the rigger had the muscles for the job. Knowing that, he'd started work without even being asked.

When the glue was ready, I began to add iron filings and salt from the much smaller sacks I'd brought with me, stirring slowly to ensure they were spread evenly right through the mixture. Iron is dangerous to a boggart because it can bleed away its strength, while the salt burns it. Once a boggart is in the pit, it will stay there because the underside of the stone and the sides of the pit are coated with the mixture, forcing it to make itself small and stay within the boundaries of the space inside. Of course, the problem is getting the boggart into the pit in the first place.

For now I wasn't worrying about that. At last the rigger and I were both satisfied. The glue was ready.

As the pit wasn't finished yet, I had nothing to do but wait for the doctor in the narrow, crooked lane that led into Horshaw.

The rain had stopped, and the air seemed very still. It was late September, and the weather was changing for the worse. We were going to have more than just rain soon, and the sudden, first, faint rumble of thunder from the west made me even more nervous. After about twenty minutes I heard the sound of hooves pounding in the distance. Riding as though all the hounds of hell were on his tail, the doctor came around the corner, his horse at full gallop, his cloak flying behind him.

I was holding the Spook's staff, so there was no need for introductions, and in any case the doctor had been riding so fast he was out of breath. So I just nodded at him, and he left his sweating horse munching at the long grass in front of the church and followed me around to the side door. I held it open out of respect so that he could go in first.

My dad's taught me to be respectful to everyone, because that way they'll respect you back. I didn't know this doctor, but the Spook had insisted on him so I knew he'd be good at his job. His name was Sherdley and he was carrying a black leather bag. It looked almost as heavy as the Spook's, which I'd brought with me and left in the barn. The doctor put it down about six feet from his patient and, ignoring the housekeeper, who was still heaving with dry sobs, he began his examination.

I stood just behind him and to one side so that I had the best possible view. Gently he pulled up the priest's black cassock to reveal his legs.

His right leg was thin, white, and almost hairless, but the left, the one gripped by the boggart, was red and swollen, bulging with purple veins that darkened the closer they were to the wide crack in the floor.

The doctor shook his head and let out his breath very slowly. Then he spoke to the housekeeper, his voice so low that I barely caught the words.

"It'll have to come off," he said. "That's his only hope."

At that, the tears started running down her cheeks again and the doctor looked at me and pointed to the door. Once outside, he leaned back against the wall and sighed.

"How long before you're ready?" he asked.

"Less than an hour, Doctor," I replied, "but it depends on the mason. He's bringing the stone himself."

"If it's much longer, we'll lose him. The truth is, I don't really give much for his chances anyway. I can't even give him anything for the pain yet because his body won't stand two doses and I'll have to give him something just before I amputate. Even then, the shock could kill him outright. Having to move him straight afterward makes it even worse."

I shrugged. I didn't even like to think about it.

"You do know exactly what has to be done?" the doctor asked, studying my face carefully.

"Mr. Gregory explained everything," I said, trying to sound confident. In fact, if he'd explained it once, the Spook had explained it a dozen times. Then he'd made me recite it back to him over and over again until he was satisfied.

"About fifteen years ago we dealt with a similar case," the doctor said. "We did what we could, but the man died anyway, and he was a young farmer, fit as a butcher's dog and in the prime of life. Let's just cross our fingers. Sometimes the old ones are a lot tougher than you think."

There was a long silence then, which I broke by checking something I'd been worrying about.

"So you know that I'll need some of his blood."

"Don't tell your grandfather how to suck eggs," the doctor growled, then he gave me a tired smile and pointed down the lane toward Horshaw. "The mason's on his way, so you'd better get off and do your job. You can leave the rest to me."

I listened and heard the distant sound of a cart approaching, so I headed back through the gravestones to see how the riggers were getting on.

The pit was ready, and they'd already assembled the wooden platform under the tree. The rigger's mate had climbed up into the tree and was fixing the block and tackle onto a sturdy branch. It was a device the size of a man's head, made out of iron and hanging with chains and a big hook. We would need it to support the weight of the stone and position it very precisely.

"The mason's here," I said.

Immediately, both men left what they were doing and followed me back toward the church.

Now another horse was waiting in the lane, the stone resting in the back of the cart. No problems so far, but the mason didn't look too happy and he avoided my eyes. Still, wasting no time, we brought the cart around the long way to the gate that led into the field.

Once close to the tree, the mason slipped the hook into the ring in the center of the stone, and it was lifted off the cart. Whether or not it would fit precisely, we'd have to wait and see. The mason had certainly fitted the ring correctly, because the stone hung from the chain balanced horizontally.

It was lowered into a position about two paces from the edge of the pit. Then the mason gave me the bad news.

His youngest daughter was very ill with a fever, the one that had swept right through the County, confining the Spook to his bed. His wife was by her bedside, and he had to get back right away.

"I'm sorry," he said, meeting my eyes properly for the first time. "But the stone's a good 'un and you'll have no problems. I can promise you that."

I believed him. He'd done his best and had worked on the stone at short notice, when he'd rather have been with his daughter. So I paid him and sent him on his way with the Spook's thanks, my thanks, and best wishes for the recovery of his daughter.

Then I turned back to the business in hand. As well as chiseling stone, masons are experts at positioning it, so I'd rather he'd stayed in case anything went wrong. Still, the rigger and mate were good at their job. All I had to do was keep calm and be careful not to make any silly mistakes.

First I had to work fast and coat the sides of the pit with the glue; then, finally, the underside of the stone, just before it was lowered into position.

I climbed down into the pit and, using a brush and working by the light of a lantern held by the rigger's mate, I got to work. It was a careful process. I couldn't afford to miss the tiniest spot because that would be enough to let the boggart escape. And with the pit only being six feet deep rather than the regulation nine, I had to be extra careful.

The mixture keyed itself into the soil as I worked, which was good, because it wouldn't easily crack and flake off as the soil dried out in summer. The bad thing was that it was difficult to judge just how much to apply so that a thick enough outer coat was left on the soil. The Spook had told me that it was something that would come with experience. Up to now he'd been there to check my work and add a few finishing touches. Now, I would have to do the job right myself. First time.

Finally I climbed out of the pit and attended to its upper edge. The top thirteen inches, the thickness of the stone, were longer and broader than the pit itself, so there was a ledge for the stone to rest on without leaving the slightest crack for the boggart to slip through. This needed very careful attention because it was where the stone made its seal with the ground.

As I finished there was a flash of lightning and, seconds later, a heavy rumble of thunder. The storm had moved almost directly overhead.

I went back to the barn to get something important from my bag. It was what the Spook called a bait dish. Made out of metal, it was specially crafted for the job and had three small holes drilled at equal distances from one another, close to its rim. I eased it out, polished it on my sleeve, then ran to the church to tell the doctor that we were ready.

As I opened the door there was a strong smell of tar and, just left of the altar, a small fire was blazing. Over it, on a metal tripod, a pot bubbled and spat. Dr. Sherdley was going to use the tar to stop the bleeding. Painting the stump with it would also prevent the rest of the leg from going bad afterward.

I smiled to myself when I saw where the doctor

had got his wood from. It was wet outside, so he'd gone for the only dry kindling available. He'd chopped up one of the church pews. No doubt the priest wouldn't be too happy, but it might just save his life. In any case he was now unconscious, breathing very deeply, and would stay that way for several hours until the effects of the potion wore off.

From the crack in the floor came the noise of the boggart feeding. It made a nasty gulping, slurping sound as it continued to draw blood from the leg. It was too preoccupied to realize that we were close by and about to bring its meal to an end.

We didn't speak. I just nodded at the doctor and he nodded back. I handed him the deep metal dish to catch the blood I needed, and he took a small metal saw from his bag and laid its cold, shiny teeth against the bone just below the priest's knee.

The housekeeper was still in the same position, but her eyes were squeezed tight shut and she was muttering to herself. She was probably praying, and it was obvious she wouldn't be much help.

So, with a shiver, I knelt down beside the doctor.

He shook his head. "There's no need for you to see this," he said. "No doubt you'll witness worse one day, but it needn't be now. Go on, lad. Back to your own business. I can deal with this. Just send the other two back to give me a hand getting him up onto the cart when I've finished."

I'd been gritting my teeth ready to face it, but I didn't need to be told twice. Full of relief, I went back to the pit. Even before I reached it, a loud scream cut through the air, followed by the sound of anguished weeping. But it wasn't the priest. He was unconscious. It was the housekeeper.

The rigger and his mate had already hoisted the stone aloft again and were busy wiping off the mud. Then, as they went back to the church to help the doctor, I dipped the brush into the last of the mixture and gave the underside of the stone a thorough coating.

I'd hardly time to admire my handiwork before the mate came back at a run. Behind him, moving much more slowly, came the rigger. He was carrying the dish with the blood in it, being careful not to spill a single drop. The bait dish was a very important piece of equipment. The Spook had a store of them back in Chipenden, and they'd been made according to his own specifications.

I lifted a long chain from the Spook's bag. Fastened to a large ring at one end were three shorter chains, each ending in a small metal hook. I slipped the three hooks into the three holes close to the rim of the dish.

When I lifted the chain, the bait dish hung below it in perfect balance, so it didn't need that much skill to lower it into the pit and set it down very gently at its center.

No, the skill was in freeing the three hooks. You had to be very careful to relax the chains so that the hooks dropped away from the dish without tipping it over and spilling the blood.

I'd spent hours practicing this, and despite being very nervous I managed to get the hooks out at my first attempt.

Now it was just a question of waiting.

As I said, rippers are some of the most dangerous boggarts of all because they feed on blood. Their minds are usually quick and very crafty, but while they're feeding they think very slowly and it takes them a long time to work things out.

The amputated leg was still jammed into the crack in the church floor and the boggart was busily slurping blood from it, but sucking very slowly so as to make it last. That's the way with a ripper. It just slurps and sucks, thinking of nothing else until it slowly realizes that less and less blood is reaching its mouth. It wants more blood, but blood comes in lots of different flavors and it likes the taste of what it's been sucking. It likes it very much.

So it wants more of the same, and once it works out that the rest of the body has been separated from the leg, it goes after it. That's why the riggers had to lift the priest up onto the cart. By now the cart would have reached the edge of Horshaw, every clip-clop of the horse's hooves taking it farther from the angry boggart, desperate for more of that same blood.

A ripper's like a bloodhound. It would have a good idea of the direction in which the priest was being taken. It would also realize that he was getting farther and farther away. Then it would be aware of something else. That more of what it needed was very close by.

That's why I'd put the dish into the pit. That was why it was called a bait dish. It was the snare to lure the ripper into the trap. Once it was in there, feeding, we had to work fast, and we couldn't afford to make a single mistake.

I looked up. The mate was standing on the platform, one hand on the short chain, ready to start lowering the stone. The rigger was standing opposite me, his hand on the stone, ready to position it as it came down. Neither of them looked in the least bit afraid, not even nervous, and suddenly it felt good to be working with people like that. People who knew what they were doing. We'd all played our part, all done what had to be done as quickly and efficiently as possible. It made me feel good. It made me feel a part of something.

Quietly we waited for the boggart.

After a few minutes I heard it coming. At first it sounded just like the wind whistling through the trees.

But there was no wind. The air was perfectly

still, and in a narrow band of starlight between the edge of the thundercloud and the horizon, the crescent moon was visible, adding its pale light to that cast by the lanterns.

The rigger and his mate could hear nothing, of course, because they weren't seventh sons of seventh sons like me. So I had to warn them.

"It's on its way," I said. "I'll tell you when."

By now the sound of its approach had become more shrill, almost like a scream, and I could hear something else, too: a sort of low, rumbling growl. It was coming across the graveyard fast, heading straight for the dish of blood inside the pit.

Unlike a normal boggart, a ripper is slightly more than a spirit, especially when it's just been feeding. Even then, most people can't see it, but they can feel it all right, if it ever gets a grip on their flesh.

Even I didn't see much—just something shapeless and a sort of pinky red. Then I felt a movement of the air close to my face and the ripper went down into the pit.

I said "When" to the rigger, who, in turn, nodded to his mate, who tightened his grip upon the short chain. Even before he pulled it, there came a sound from the pit. This time it was loud, and all three of us heard it. I glanced quickly at my companions and saw their eyes widen and mouths tighten with the fear of what was below us.

The sound we heard was the boggart feeding from the dish. It was like the greedy lapping of some monstrous tongue, combined with the ravenous snuffling and snorting of a big carnivorous animal. We had less than a minute or so before it finished it all. Then it would sense our blood. It was rogue now, and we were all on the menu.

The mate began to loosen the chain and the stone came down steadily. I was adjusting one end, the rigger the other. If they'd dug the pit accurately and the stone was exactly the size specified on the sketch, there should be no problem. That's what I told myself—but I kept thinking of the Spook's last apprentice, poor Billy Bradley, who'd died trying to bind a boggart like this. The stone had jammed, trapping his fingers under its edge. Before they could lift it free, the boggart had bitten his fingers off and sucked his blood. Later Billy had died of shock. I couldn't get him out of my mind, no matter how hard I tried.

The important thing was to get the stone into the pit first time—and, of course, to keep my fingers out of the way.

The rigger was in control, doing the job of the mason. At his signal, the chain halted when the stone was just a fraction of an inch clear. He looked at me then, his face very stern, and raised his right eyebrow. I looked down and moved my end of the stone very slightly so that it seemed to be in perfect position. I checked again just to make sure, then nodded to the rigger, who signaled to his mate.

A few turns of the short chain, and the stone eased down into position first time, sealing the boggart into the pit. A scream of anger came from the ripper, and we all heard it. But it didn't matter because it was trapped now and there was nothing more to be scared of.

"Job's a good 'un!" shouted the mate, jumping down from the platform, a grin splitting his face from ear to ear. "It's a perfect fit!"

"Aye," said the rigger, joking drily. "It could've been made for the job."

I felt a huge sense of relief, glad that it was all

over. Then, as the thunder crashed and the lightning flashed directly overhead to illuminate the
stone, I noticed, for the first time, what the mason
had carved there and suddenly felt very proud.

Ward

The large Greek letter beta, crossed with a
diagonal line, was the sign that a boggart had been
laid under it. Below it, to the right, the Roman
numeral for one meant that it was a dangerous
boggart of the first rank. There were ten ranks in
all, and those from one to four could kill. Then,
underneath, was my own name, Ward, which gave
me the credit for what had been done.

I'd just bound my first boggart. And it was a ripper at that!

CHAPTER II
The Spook's Past

TWO days later, back at Chipenden, the Spook made me tell him everything that had happened. When I'd finished, he made me repeat it. That done, he scratched at his beard and gave a great big sigh.

"What did the doctor say about that daft brother of mine?" the Spook asked. "Does he expect him to recover?"

"He said he seemed to be over the worst, but it was too early to tell."

The Spook nodded thoughtfully. "Well, lad, you've done well," he said. "I can't think of one thing you could have done better. So you can have the rest of the day off. But don't let it go to your head. Tomorrow it's business as usual. After all that excitement you need to get back into a steady routine."

The following day he worked me twice as hard as usual. Lessons began soon after dawn and included what he called practicals. Even though I'd now bound a boggart for real, that meant practicing digging pits.

"Do I really have to dig another boggart pit?" I asked wearily.

The Spook gave me a withering look until I dropped my eyes, feeling very uncomfortable.

"Think you're above all that now, lad?" he asked. "Well, you're not, so don't get complacent! You've still a lot to learn. You may have bound your first boggart, but you'd good men helping. One day you might have to dig the pit yourself and do it fast in order to save a life."

After digging the pit and coating it with salt and iron, I had to practice getting the bait dish down into the pit without spilling a single drop of blood. Of course, because it was only part of my training, we used water rather than blood, but the Spook took it very seriously and usually got annoyed if I didn't manage to do it first time. But on this occasion he didn't get the chance. I'd managed it at

Horshaw and I was just as good in practice, succeeding ten times in a row. Despite that, the Spook
didn't give me one word of praise, and I was starting
to feel a bit annoyed.

Next came one practical I really enjoyed—using
the Spook's silver chain. There was a six-foot post
set up in the western garden, and the idea was to
cast the chain over it. The Spook made me stand at
various distances from it and practice for over an
hour at a time, keeping in mind that at some point it
might be a real witch I'd be facing, and if I missed,
I wouldn't get another chance. There was a special
way to use the chain. You coiled it over your left
hand and cast it with a flick of your wrist so that it
spun widdershins, falling in a left-handed spiral to
enclose the post and tighten against it. From a distance of eight feet I could now get the chain over the
post nine times out of ten, but as usual, the Spook
was grudging with his praise.

"Not bad, I suppose," he said. "But don't get
smug, lad. A real witch won't oblige you by standing still while you throw that chain. By the end of
the year I'll expect ten out of ten and nothing less!"

I felt more than a bit annoyed at that. I'd been

working hard and had improved a lot. Not only that, I'd just bound my first boggart and done it without any help from the Spook. It made me wonder if he'd done any better during his own apprenticeship!

In the afternoon the Spook allowed me into his library to work by myself, reading and making notes, but he only let me read certain books. He was very strict about that. I was still in my first year, so boggarts were my main area of study. But sometimes, when he was off doing something else, I couldn't help having a glance at some of his other books, too.

So, after reading my fill of boggarts, I went to the three long shelves near the window and chose one of the large leather-bound notebooks from the very top shelf. They were diaries, some of them written by spooks hundreds of years ago. Each one covered a period of about five years.

This time I knew exactly what I was looking for. I chose one of the Spook's earliest diaries, curious to see how he'd coped with the job as a young man and whether he'd shaped up better than me. Of course, he'd been a priest before training to be a spook, so he'd have been really old for an apprentice.

Anyway, I picked a few pages at random and

started to read. I recognized his handwriting, of course, but a stranger reading an extract for the first time wouldn't have guessed the Spook had written it. When he talks, his voice is typical County, down to earth and without a hint of what my dad calls airs and graces. When he writes, it's different. It's as if all those books he's read have altered his voice, whereas I mostly write the way I talk: If my dad were ever to read my notes, he'd be proud of me and know I was still his son.

At first what I read didn't seem any different from the Spook's more recent writings, apart from the fact that he made more mistakes. As usual, he was very honest, and each time explained just how he'd gone wrong. As he was always telling me, it was important to write everything down and so learn from the past.

He described how, one week, he'd spent hours and hours practicing with the bait dish and his master had gotten angry because he couldn't manage a better average than eight out of ten! That made me feel a lot better. And then I came to something that lifted my spirits even further. The Spook hadn't bound his first boggart until he'd been an apprentice for almost eighteen months. What's more, it had only been a hairy boggart, not a dangerous ripper!

That was the best I could find to cheer me up: Clearly the Spook had been a good, hard-working apprentice. A lot of what I found was routine, so I skipped through the pages quickly until I reached the point when my master became a spook, working on his own. I'd seen all I really needed to see and was just about to close the book when something caught my eye. I flipped back to the start of the entry just to make sure, and this is what I read. It's not exactly word for word, but I have a good memory and it's pretty close. And after reading what he'd written, I certainly wasn't going to forget it.

Late in the autumn I journeyed far to the north of the County, summoned there to deal with an abhuman, a creature who had brought terror to the district for far too long. Many families in the locality had suffered at its cruel hands and there had been many deaths and maimings.

I came down into the forest at dusk. All the leaves had fallen and were rotten and brown on the ground, and the tower was like a black demon finger pointing at the sky. A girl had been seen waving from its solitary window, beckoning frantically for aid. The creature had seized her for its own and now held her as its plaything, imprisoning her within those dank stone walls.

Firstly I made a fire and sat gazing into its flames while gathering my courage. Taking the whetstone from my bag, I sharpened my blade until my fingers could not touch its edge without yielding blood. Finally, at midnight, I went to the tower and hammered out a challenge upon the door with my staff.

The creature came forth brandishing a great club and roared out in anger. It was a foul thing, dressed in the skins of animals, reeking of blood and animal fat, and it attacked me with terrible fury.

At first I retreated, waiting my chance, but the next time it hurled itself at me I released the blade from its recess in my staff and, using all my strength, drove it deep into its head. It fell stone dead at my feet, but I had no regrets at taking its life, for it would have killed again and again and would never have been sated.

It was then that the girl called out to me, her siren voice luring me up the stone steps. There, in the topmost room of the tower, I found her upon a bed of straw, bound fast with a long silver chain. With skin like milk and long fair hair, she was by far the prettiest woman that my eyes had ever seen. Her name was Meg, and she pleaded to be released from the chain. Her voice was so persuasive that my reason fled and the world spun about me.

No sooner had I unbound her from the coils of the chain than she fastened her lips hard upon mine own. And so sweet were her kisses that I almost swooned away in her arms.

I awoke with sunlight streaming through the window and saw her clearly for the first time. She was one of the lamia witches, and the mark of the snake was upon her. Fair of face though she was, her spine was covered with green-and-yellow scales.

Full of anger at her deceit, I bound her again with the chain and carried her at last to the pit at Chipenden. When I released her, she struggled so hard that I barely overcame her, and I was forced to pull her by her long hair through the trees while she ranted and screamed fit to wake the dead. It was raining hard and she slipped on the wet grass, but I carried on dragging her along the ground, though her bare arms and legs were scratched by brambles. It was cruel, but it had to be done.

But when I started to tip her over the edge into the pit, she clutched at my knees and began to sob pitifully. I stood there for a long time, full of anguish, about to topple over the edge myself, until at last I made a decision that I may come to regret.

I helped her to her feet and wrapped my arms about her, and we both wept. How could I put her into the pit, when I realized that I loved her better than my own soul?

I begged her forgiveness, and then we turned together and, hand in hand, walked away from the pit.

From this encounter I have gained a silver chain, an expensive tool that otherwise would have taken many long months of hard work to acquire. What I have lost, or might yet lose, I dare not think about. Beauty is a terrible thing; it binds a man tighter than a silver chain about a witch.

I couldn't believe what I'd just read! The Spook had warned me about pretty women more than once, but here he'd broken his own rule! Meg was a witch, and yet he hadn't put her into the pit!

I quickly leafed through the rest of the notebook, expecting to find another reference to her, but there was nothing—nothing at all! It was as if she'd ceased to exist.

I knew quite a bit about witches, but had never heard of a lamia witch before. So I put the notebook back and searched the next shelf down, where the books were arranged in alphabetical order. I opened the book labeled *Witches*, but there was no reference to a Meg. Why hadn't the Spook written about her? What had happened to her? Was she still alive? Still out there, somewhere in the County?

I was really curious, and I had another idea; I pulled a big book out from the lowest shelf. This was entitled *The Bestiary* and was an alphabetical listing of all sorts of creatures, witches included. At last I found the entry I wanted: *lamia witches*.

It seemed that lamia witches weren't native to the County but came from lands across the sea. They shunned sunlight, but at night they preyed upon men and drank their blood. They were shape-shifters and belonged to two different categories: the feral and the domestic.

The feral were lamia witches in their natural state, dangerous and unpredictable and with little physical resemblance to humans. All had scales rather than skin and claws rather than fingernails. Some scuttled across the ground on all fours, while others had wings and feathers on their upper bodies and could fly short distances.

But a feral lamia could become a domestic lamia by closely associating with humans. Very gradually, it took a woman's form and looked human but for a narrow line of green-and-yellow scales that could still be found on its back, running the length of its spine. Domestic lamias had even been known to grow to share human beliefs. Often they ceased to be malevolent and became benign, working for the good of others.

So had Meg eventually become benign? Had the Spook been right not to bind her in the pit?

Suddenly I realized how late it was, and I ran out of the library to my lesson, my head whirling. A few minutes later my master and I were out on the edge of the western garden, under the trees with a clear view of the fells, the autumn sun dropping toward the horizon. I sat on the bench as usual, busy making notes while the Spook paced back and forth dictating. But I couldn't concentrate.

We started with a Latin lesson. I had a special notebook to write down the grammar and new vocabulary the Spook taught me. There were a lot of lists, and the book was almost full.

I wanted to confront the Spook with what I'd just read, but how could I? I'd broken a rule myself by not keeping to the books he'd specified. I wasn't supposed to have been reading his diaries, and now I wished I hadn't. If I said anything to him about it, I knew he'd be angry.

Because of what I'd read in the library, I found

it harder and harder to keep my mind on what he was saying. I was hungry, too, and couldn't wait until it was supper time. Usually the evenings were mine and I was free to do what I wanted, but today he'd been working me very hard. Still, there was less than an hour before the sun went down and the worst of the lessons were over.

And then I heard a sound that made me groan inside.

It was a bell ringing. Not a church bell. No, this had the higher, thinner note of a much smaller bell — the one that was used by our visitors. Nobody was allowed up to the Spook's house, so people had to go to the crossroads and ring the bell there to let my master know they needed help.

"Go and see to it, lad," the Spook said, nodding in the direction of the bell. Generally we would both have gone, but he was still quite weak from his illness.

I didn't rush. Once out of sight of the house and gardens, I settled down to a stroll. It was too close to dusk to do anything tonight, especially with the Spook still not properly recovered, so nothing would get done until morning anyway. I would bring back an account of the trouble and tell the Spook the details during supper. The later I got back, the less writing there'd be. I'd done enough for one day and my wrist was aching.

Overhung by willow trees, which we in the County call withy trees, the crossroads was a gloomy place even at noon, and it always made me nervous. For one thing, you never knew who might be waiting there; for another, they almost always had bad news because that's why they came. They needed the Spook's help.

This time a lad was waiting there. He wore big miners' boots and his fingernails were dirty. Looking even more nervous than I felt, he dashed off his tale so quickly that my ears couldn't keep up and I had to ask him to repeat it. When he left, I set off back toward the house.

I didn't stroll, I ran.

The Spook was standing by the bench with his head bowed. When I approached, he looked up and his face seemed sad. Somehow I guessed that he knew what I was going to say, but I told him anyway.

"It's bad news from Horshaw," I said, trying to

catch my breath. "I'm sorry, but it's about your brother. The doctor couldn't save him. He died yesterday morning, just before dawn. The funeral's on Friday morning."

The Spook gave a long, deep sigh and didn't speak for several minutes. I didn't know what to say so I just kept silent. It was hard to guess what he was feeling. As they hadn't spoken for more than forty years, they couldn't have been that close, but the priest was still his brother and the Spook must have had some happy memories of him—perhaps from before they'd quarreled or when they were children.

At last the Spook sighed again and then he spoke.

"Come on, lad," he said. "We might as well have an early supper."

We ate in silence. The Spook picked at his food, and I wondered if that was because of the bad news about his brother or because he still hadn't got his appetite back since being ill. He usually spoke a few words, even if they were just to ask me how the meal was. It was almost a ritual because we had to keep praising the Spook's pet boggart, which prepared all the meals, or it got sulky. Praise at supper was very important or the bacon would end up burned the following morning.

"It's a really good hotpot," I said at last. "I can't remember when I last tasted one so good."

The boggart was mostly invisible but sometimes took on the shape of a big ginger cat; if it was really pleased, it would rub itself against my legs under the kitchen table. This time there wasn't even so much as a faint purr. Either I hadn't sounded very convincing or it was keeping quiet because of the bad news.

The Spook suddenly pushed his plate away and scratched at his beard with his left hand. "We're going to Priestown," he said suddenly. "We'll set off first thing tomorrow."

Priestown? I couldn't believe what I was hearing. The Spook shunned the place like the plague and had once told me that he would never set foot within its boundaries. He hadn't explained the reason, and I'd never asked because you could always tell when he didn't want to explain something. But when we'd been within spitting distance of the coast and needed to cross the River Ribble, the Spook's hatred of the town had been a real nuisance. Instead of using the Priestown bridge, we'd had to travel miles inland to the next one so that we could steer clear of it.

"Why?" I asked, my voice hardly more than a whisper, wondering if what I was saying might make him angry. "I thought we might be going to Horshaw, for the funeral."

"We *are* going to the funeral, lad," the Spook said, his voice very calm and patient. "My daft brother only worked in Horshaw, but he was a priest: When a priest dies in the County, they take his body back to Priestown and hold a funeral service in the big cathedral there before laying his bones to rest in the churchyard.

"So we're going there to pay our last respects. But that's not the only reason. I've unfinished business in that godforsaken town. Get out your notebook, lad. Turn to a clean page and make this heading . . ."

I hadn't finished my hotpot, but I did what he asked right away. When he said unfinished business, I knew he meant spook's business, so I pulled the bottle of ink out of my pocket and placed it on the table next to my plate.

Something clicked in my head. "Do you mean that ripper I bound? Do you think it's escaped? There just wasn't time to dig nine feet. Do you think it's gone to Priestown?"

"No, lad, you did fine. There's something far worse than that there. That town is cursed! Cursed with something that I last faced over twenty long years ago. It got the better of me then and put me in bed for almost six months. In fact, I almost died. Since then I've never been back, but as we've a need to visit the place, I might as well attend to that unfinished business. No, it's not some straightforward ripper that plagues that cursed town. It's an ancient evil spirit called the Bane, and it's the only one of its kind. It's getting stronger and stronger, so something needs to be done and I can't put it off any longer."

I wrote *Bane* at the top of a new page, but then, to my disappointment, the Spook suddenly shook his head and followed that with a big yawn.

"Come to think of it, this'll save until tomorrow, lad. You'd better finish up your supper. We'll be making an early start in the morning, so we'd best be off to bed."

CHAPTER III
The Bane

WE set off soon after dawn, with me carrying the Spook's heavy bag as usual. But within an hour I realized the journey would take us two days at least. Usually the Spook walked at a tremendous pace, making me struggle to keep up, but he was still weak and kept getting breathless and stopping to rest.

It was a nice sunny day with just a touch of autumn chill in the air. The sky was blue and the birds were singing, but none of that mattered. I just couldn't stop thinking about the Bane.

What worried me was the fact that the Spook had already nearly been killed once trying to bind it. He was older now and if he didn't get his strength back soon, how could he possibly hope to beat it this time?

So at noon, when we stopped for a long rest, I decided to ask him all about this terrible spirit. I didn't ask him right away because, to my surprise, as we sat down together on the trunk of a fallen tree, he pulled a loaf and a big hunk of ham from his bag and cut us a very generous portion each. Usually, when on the way to a job, we made do with a measly nibble of cheese because you have to fast before facing the dark.

Still, I was hungry, so I didn't complain. I supposed that we'd have time to fast once the funeral was over and that the Spook needed food now to build up his strength again.

At last, when I'd finished eating, I took a deep breath, got out my notebook and finally asked him about the Bane. To my surprise he told me to put the book away.

"You can write this up later when we're on our way back," he said. "Besides, I've a lot to learn about the Bane myself, so there's no point in writing down something that you might need to change later."

I suppose my mouth dropped open at that. I mean, I'd always thought the Spook knew almost everything there was to know about the dark.

"Don't look so surprised, lad," he said. "As you know, I still keep a notebook myself and so will you, if you live to my age. We never stop learning in this job, and the first step toward knowledge is to accept your own ignorance.

"As I said before, the Bane is an ancient, malevolent spirit that has so far got the better of me, I'm ashamed to admit. But hopefully not this time. Our first problem will be to find it," continued the Spook. "It lives in the catacombs down under Priestown cathedral—there are miles and miles of tunnels."

"What are the catacombs for?" I asked, wondering who would build so many tunnels.

"They're full of crypts, lad, underground burial chambers that hold ancient bones. Those tunnels existed long before the cathedral was built. The hill was already a holy site when the first priests came here in ships from the west."

"So who built the catacombs?"

"Some call the builders the Little People on

account of their size, but their true name was the Segantii. Not that much is known about them apart from the fact that the Bane was once their god."

"It's a god?"

"Aye, it was always a powerful force, and the earliest Little People recognized its strength and worshipped it. Reckon the Bane would like to be a god again. You see, it used to roam free in the County. Over the centuries it grew corrupt and evil and terrorized the Little People night and day, turning brother against brother, destroying crops, burning homes, slaughtering innocents. It liked to see people existing in fear and poverty, beaten down until life was hardly worth living. Those were dark, terrible times for the Segantii.

"But it wasn't just the poor people it plagued. The Segantii's king was a good man called Heys. He'd defeated all his enemies in battle and tried to make his people strong and prosperous. But there was one enemy they couldn't beat: the Bane. It suddenly demanded an annual tribute from King Heys. The poor man was ordered to sacrifice his seven sons, starting with the eldest. One son each year until none remained alive. It was more than any father could bear. But somehow Naze, the very last son, managed to bind the Bane to the catacombs. I don't know how he did it—perhaps if I did, it would be easier to defeat this creature. All I know is that its way was blocked by a locked Silver Gate: Like many creatures of the dark it has a vulnerability to silver."

"And so it's still trapped down there after all this time?"

"Yes, lad. It's bound down there until someone opens that gate and sets it free. That's fact and it's something that all the priests know. It's knowledge passed down from generation to generation."

"But isn't there any other way out? How can the Silver Gate keep it in?" I asked.

"I don't know, lad. All I know is that the Bane is bound in the catacombs and is only able to leave through that gate."

I wanted to ask what was wrong with just leaving it there if it was bound and unlikely to escape, but he answered before I could voice the question. The Spook knew me well by now and was good at guessing what I was thinking.

"But we can't just leave things as they are, I'm

afraid, lad. You see, it's growing stronger again now. It wasn't always just a spirit. That only happened after it was bound. Before that, when it was very powerful, it had a physical form."

"What did it look like?" I asked.

"You'll find out tomorrow. Before you enter the cathedral for the funeral service, look up at the stone carving directly above the main doorway. It's as good a representation of the creature as you're likely to see."

"Have you seen the real thing then?"

"Nay, lad. Twenty years ago, when I first tried to kill the Bane, it was still a spirit. But there are rumors that its strength has grown so much that it's now taking the shape of other creatures."

"What do you mean?"

"I mean it's started shape-shifting and it won't be long before it's strong enough to take on its original true form. Then it'll be able to make almost anyone do what it wants. And the real danger is that it might force somebody to unlock the Silver Gate. That's the most worrying thing of all!"

"But where's it getting its strength from?" I wanted to know.

"Blood, mainly."

"Blood?"

"Aye. The blood of animals—and humans. It has a terrible thirst. But fortunately, unlike a ripper, it can't take the blood of a human being unless it's given freely—"

"Why would anyone want to give it their blood?" I asked, astonished at the very idea.

"Because it can get inside people's minds. It tempts them with money, position, and power—you name it. If it can't get what it wants by persuasion, it terrorizes its victims. Sometimes it lures them down to the catacombs and threatens them with what we call the press."

"The press?" I asked.

"Aye, lad. It can make itself so heavy that some of its victims are found squashed flat, their bones broken and their bodies smeared into the ground— you have to scrape them up for burial. They've been pressed, and it's not a pleasant sight. The Bane cannot rip our blood against our will, but remember we're still vulnerable to the press."

"I don't understand how it can make people do these things when it's trapped in the catacombs," I said.

"It can read thoughts, shape dreams, weaken and corrupt the minds of those above ground. Sometimes it even sees through their eyes. Its influence extends up into the cathedral and presbytery, and it terrorizes the priests. It's been working its mischief that way through Priestown for years."

"With the priests?"

"Yes—especially those who are weak-minded. Whenever it can, it gets them to spread its evil. My brother Andrew works as a locksmith in Priestown, and more than once he's sent warnings to me about what's happening. The Bane drains the spirit and the will. It makes people do what it wants, silencing the voices of goodness and reason; they become greedy and cruel, abuse their power, robbing the poor and sick. In Priestown tithes are now collected twice a year."

I knew what a tithe was. A tenth of our farm's income for the year, and we had to pay it as a tax to the local church. It was the law.

"Paying it once is bad enough," the Spook continued, "but twice and it's hard to keep the wolf from the door. Once again, it's beating the people down into fear and poverty, just as it did to the Segantii.

It's one of the purest and most evil manifestations of the dark I've ever met. But the situation can't go on much longer. I've got to put a stop to it once and for all before it's too late."

"How will we do that?" I asked.

"Well, I'm not sure I rightly know just yet. The Bane is a dangerous and clever foe; it may be able to read our minds and know just what we're thinking before we realize it ourselves.

"But apart from silver, it does have one other serious weakness. Women make it very nervous, and it tries to avoid their company. It can't abide being near them. Well, I can understand that easily enough, but how to use it to our advantage needs some thinking about."

The Spook had often warned me to beware of girls and, for some reason, particularly those who wore pointy shoes. So I was used to him saying things like that. But now I knew about him and Meg I wondered if she'd played some part in making him talk the way he did.

Well, my master had certainly given me a lot to think about. And I couldn't help wondering about all those churches in Priestown, and the priests and congregations, all believing in God. Could they all be wrong? If their God was so powerful, why didn't He do something about the Bane? Why did He allow it to corrupt the priests and spread evil out into the town? My dad was a believer, even though he never went to church. None of our family did, because farming didn't stop on Sunday and we were always too busy milking or doing other chores. But it suddenly made me wonder what the Spook believed, especially knowing what Mam had told me—that the Spook had once been a priest himself.

"Do you believe in God?" I asked him.

"I used to believe in God," the Spook replied, his expression very thoughtful. "When I was a child I never doubted the existence of God for a single moment, but eventually I changed. You see, lad, when you've lived as long as I have, there are things that make you wonder. So now I'm not so sure but I still keep an open mind.

"But I'll tell you this," he went on. "Two or three times in my life I've been in situations so bad that I never expected to walk away from them. I've faced the dark and almost, but not quite, resigned myself to death. Then, just when all seemed lost, I've been filled with new strength. Where it came from I can only guess. But with that strength came a new feeling. That someone or something was at my side. That I was no longer alone."

The Spook paused and sighed deeply. "I don't believe in the God they preach about in church," he said. "I don't believe in an old man with a white beard. But there's something watching what we do, and if you live your life right, in your hour of need it'll stand at your side and lend you its strength. That's what I believe. Well, come on, lad. We've dawdled here long enough and had best be on our way."

I picked up his bag and followed him. Soon we left the road and took a shortcut through a wood and across a wide meadow. It was pleasant enough, but we stopped long before the sun set. The Spook was too exhausted to continue and should really have been back at Chipenden, recuperating after his illness.

I had a bad feeling about what lay ahead, a strong sense of danger.

CHAPTER IV
Priestown

PRIESTOWN, built on the banks of the River Ribble, was the biggest town I'd ever visited. As we came down the hill, the river was like a huge snake gleaming orange in the light from the setting sun.

It was a town of churches, with spires and towers rising above the rows of small terraced houses. Set right on the summit of a hill, near the center of the town, was the cathedral. Three of the largest churches I'd seen in my whole life would easily have fitted inside it. And its steeple was something else. Built from limestone, it was almost white, and so high that I guessed on a rainy day the cross at its top would be hidden by clouds.

"Is that the biggest steeple in the world?" I asked, pointing in excitement.

"No, lad," the Spook answered with a rare grin. "But it's the biggest steeple in the County, as well it might be with a town that boasts so many priests. I only wish there were fewer of them, but we'll just have to take our chance."

Suddenly the grin faded from his face. "Talk of the Devil!" he said, clenching his teeth before pulling me through a gap in the hedge into the adjoining field. There he placed his forefinger against his lips for silence and made me crouch down with him while I listened to the sound of approaching footsteps.

It was a good, thick hawthorn hedge and it still had most of its leaves, but through it I could just make out a black cassock above the boots. It was a priest!

We stayed there for quite a while even after the footsteps had faded into the distance. Only then did the Spook lead us back onto the path. I couldn't work out what all the fuss was about. On our travels we'd passed lots of priests. They hadn't been too friendly, but we'd never tried to hide before.

"We need to be on our guard, lad," the Spook explained. "Priests are always trouble, but they represent a real danger in this town. You see, Priestown's bishop is the uncle of the High Quisitor. No doubt you'll have heard of him."

I nodded. "He hunts witches, doesn't he?"

"Aye, lad, he does that. When he catches someone he considers to be a witch or warlock, he puts on his black cap and becomes the judge at the trial—a trial that's usually over very quickly. The following day he puts on a different hat. He becomes the executioner and organizes the burning. He has a reputation for being good at that, and a big crowd usually gathers to watch. They say he positions the stake carefully so that the poor wretch takes a very long time to die. The pain is supposed to make a witch sorry for what she's done, so she'll beg God's forgiveness and, as she dies, her soul will be saved. But that's just an excuse. The Quisitor lacks the knowledge a spook has and wouldn't know a real witch if she reached up from her grave and grabbed his ankle! No, he's just a cruel man who likes to inflict pain. He enjoys his work and he's grown rich from the money he makes selling the homes and property of those he condemns.

"Aye, and that brings me to the problem for us.

You see, the Quisitor counts a spook as a warlock. The Church doesn't like anyone to meddle with the dark, even if they're fighting it. They think only priests should be allowed to do that. The Quisitor has the power of arrest, with armed churchwardens to do his bidding—but cheer up, lad, because that's just the bad news.

"The good news is that the Quisitor lives in a big city way to the south, far beyond the boundaries of the County, and rarely comes north. So if we're spotted and he's summoned, it would take him more than a week to arrive, even on horseback. Also my arrival here should be a surprise. The last thing anyone will expect is that I'll be attending the funeral of a brother I haven't spoken to in forty years."

But his words were of little comfort. As we moved off down the hill, I shivered at what he'd said. Entering the town seemed full of risks. With his cloak and staff he was unmistakably a spook. I was just about to say as much when he gestured left with his thumb and we walked off the road into a small wood. After about thirty paces or so my master came to a halt.

"Right, lad," he said. "Take off your cloak and give it to me."

I didn't argue; from the tone of his voice I realized that he meant business, but I did wonder what he was up to. He took off his own cloak with its attached hood and laid his staff on the ground.

"Right," he said. "Now find me some thin branches and twigs. Nothing too heavy, mind."

A few minutes later I'd done as he asked, and I watched him place his staff among the branches and wrap the whole lot up with our cloaks. Of course, by then I'd already guessed what he was up to. Sticks were poking out of each end of the bundle, and it just looked like we'd been out gathering firewood. It was a disguise.

"There are lots of small inns close to the cathedral," he said, tossing me a silver coin. "It'll be safer for you if we don't stay at the same one, because if they came for me, they'd arrest you, too. Best if you don't know where I am either, lad. The Quisitor uses torture. Capture one of us and he'd soon have the other. I'll set off first. Give me ten minutes, then follow.

"Choose any inn that hasn't got anything to do with churches in its title, so we don't end up in the same one by accident. Don't have any supper, because we'll be working tomorrow. The funeral's at nine in the morning, but try to be early and sit near the back of the cathedral; if I'm there already, keep your distance."

"Working" meant spook's business, and I wondered if we'd be going down into the catacombs to face the Bane. I didn't like the idea of that one little bit.

"Oh, and one more thing," the Spook added as he turned to go. "You'll be looking after my bag, so what should you remember when carrying it in a place like Priestown?"

"To carry it in my right hand," I said.

He nodded in agreement, then lifted the bundle up onto his right shoulder and left me waiting in the wood.

We were both left-handed, something that priests didn't approve of. Left-handers were what they called "sinister," those most easily tempted by the Devil or even in league with him.

I gave him ten minutes or more, just to be sure there was enough distance between us, then, carrying his heavy bag, I set off down the hill, heading for the steeple. Once in the town I started to climb again toward the cathedral, and when I got close, I began my search for an inn.

There were plenty of them, all right; most of the cobbled streets seemed to have one, but the trouble was that all of them seemed to be linked to churches in some way or other. There was the Bishop's Crook, the Steeple Inn, the Jolly Friar, the Miter, and the Book and Candle, to name but a few. The last one reminded me of the reason we'd come to Priestown in the first place. As the Spook's brother had found to his cost, books and candles didn't usually work against the dark. Not even when you used a bell as well.

I soon realized that the Spook had made it easy for himself but very difficult for me, and I spent a long time searching Priestown's maze of narrow streets and the wider roads that linked them. I walked along Fylde Road and then up a wide street called Friargate, where there was no sign of a gate at all. The cobbled streets were full of people, and most of them seemed to be in a rush. The big market near the top of Friargate was closing for the day, but a few customers still jostled and haggled with traders for good prices. The smell of fish was overpowering, and a big flock of hungry seagulls squawked overhead.

Every so often I saw a figure dressed in a black cassock, and I would change direction or cross the road. I found it hard to believe that one town could have so many priests.

Next I walked down Fishergate Hill until I could see the river in the distance, and then all the way back again. Finally I came round in a circle, but without any success. I couldn't just ask somebody to direct me to an inn whose name had nothing to do with churches because they'd have thought me mad. Drawing attention to myself was the last thing I wanted. Even though I was carrying the Spook's heavy black leather bag in my right hand, it still attracted too many curious glances my way.

At last, just as it was getting dark, I found somewhere to stay not too far from the cathedral where I'd first begun my search. It was a small inn called the Black Bull.

Before becoming the Spook's apprentice I'd never stayed at an inn, never having any cause to wander far from my dad's farm. Since then I'd spent the night in maybe half a dozen. It should have been a lot more, for we were often on the road, sometimes for several days at a time, but the Spook liked to save his money, and unless the weather was really bad he thought a tree or an old barn good enough shelter for the night. Still, this was the first inn I'd ever stayed in alone, and as I pushed my way in through the door, I felt a little nervous.

The narrow entrance opened out into a large, gloomy room, lit only by a single lantern. It was full of empty tables and chairs, with a wooden counter at the far end. The counter smelled strongly of vinegar, but I soon realized it was just stale ale that had soaked into the wood. There was a small bell hanging from a rope to the right of the counter, so I rang it.

Presently a door behind the counter opened and a bald man came out, wiping his big hands on a large dirty apron.

"I'd like a room for the night, please," I said, adding quickly, "I might be staying longer."

He looked at me as if I were something he'd just found on the bottom of his shoe, but when I pulled out the silver coin and put it on the counter, his expression became a lot more pleasant.

"Will you be wanting supper, master?" he asked.

I shook my head. I was fasting anyway, but one glance at his stained apron had made me lose my appetite.

Five minutes later I was up in my room with the door locked. The bed looked a mess and the sheets were dirty. I knew the Spook would have complained, but I just wanted to sleep and it was still a lot better than a drafty barn. However, when I looked through the window, I felt homesick for Chipenden.

Instead of the white path leading across the green lawn to the western garden and my usual view of Parlick Pike and the other fells, all I could see was a row of grimy houses opposite, each with a chimney pot sending dark smoke billowing down into the street.

So I lay on top of the bed and, still gripping the handles of the Spook's bag, quickly fell asleep.

Just after eight the next morning, I was heading for the cathedral. I'd left the bag locked inside my room because it would have looked odd carrying it into a funeral service. I was a bit anxious about leaving it at the inn, but the bag had a lock and so did the door, and both keys were safely in my pocket. I also carried a third key.

The Spook had given it to me when I went to Horshaw to deal with the ripper. It had been made by his other brother, Andrew the locksmith, and it opened most locks as long as they weren't too complex. I should have given it back, but I knew the Spook had more than one, and as he hadn't asked, I'd kept it. It was very useful to have, just like the small tinderbox my dad had given me when I started my apprenticeship. I always kept that in my pocket, too. It had belonged to his dad and was a family heirloom—but a very useful one for someone who followed the Spook's trade.

Before long I was climbing the hill, with the steeple to my left. It was a wet morning, a heavy drizzle falling straight into my face, and I'd been right about the steeple. At least the top third of it was hidden by the dark gray clouds that were racing in from the southwest. There was a bad smell of sewers in the air, too, and every house had a smoking chimney, most of the smoke finding its way down to street level.

A lot of people seemed to be rushing up the hill. One woman went by almost running, dragging two children faster than their little legs could manage. "Come on! Hurry up!" she scolded. "We're going to miss it."

For a moment I wondered if they were going to the funeral, too, but it seemed unlikely because their faces were filled with excitement. Right at the top, the hill flattened out and I turned left toward the cathedral. Here an excited crowd was eagerly lining both sides of the road, as if waiting for something. They were blocking the pavement, and I tried to ease my way through as carefully as possible. I kept apologizing, desperate to avoid stepping on anyone's toes, but eventually the people became so thickly packed that I had to come to a halt and wait with them.

I didn't wait long. Sounds of applause and cheers had suddenly erupted to my right. Above them I heard the clip-clop of approaching hooves. A large procession was moving toward the cathedral, the first two riders dressed in black hats and cloaks and wearing swords at their hips. Behind them came more riders, these armed with daggers and huge cudgels, ten, twenty, fifty, until eventually one man appeared riding alone on a gigantic white stallion.

He wore a black cloak, but underneath it expensive chain mail was visible at neck and wrists, and the sword at his hip had a hilt encrusted with rubies. His boots were of the very finest leather, and probably worth more than a farm laborer earned in a year.

The rider's clothes and bearing marked him out as a leader, but even if he'd been dressed in rags, there would have been no doubt about it. He had very blond hair, tumbling from beneath a wide-brimmed red hat, and eyes so blue they put a summer's sky to shame. I was fascinated by his face. It was almost too handsome to be a man's, but it was strong at the same time, with a jutting chin and a determined forehead. Then I looked again at the blue eyes and saw the cruelty glaring from them.

He reminded me of a knight I'd once seen ride past our farm, when I was a young lad. He hadn't so much as glanced our way. To him we didn't exist. Well, that's what my dad said anyway. Dad also said that the man was noble, that he could tell by looking at him that he came from a family that could trace its ancestors back for generations, all of them rich and powerful.

At the word noble, my dad spat into the mud and told me that I was lucky to be a farmer's lad with an honest day's work in front of me.

This man riding through Priestown was also clearly noble and had arrogance and authority written all over his face. To my shock and dismay I realized that I must be looking at the Quisitor, for behind him was a big open cart pulled by two shire horses and there were people standing in the back bound together with chains.

Mostly they were women, but there were a couple of men, too. The majority of them looked as if they hadn't eaten properly for a long time. They wore filthy clothes, and many had clearly been beaten. All were covered in bruises, and one woman had a left eye that looked like a rotten tomato. Some of the women were wailing hopelessly, tears running down their cheeks. One screeched again and again at the top of her voice that she was innocent. But to no avail. They were all captives, soon to be tried and burned.

A young woman suddenly darted toward the cart, reaching up to one of the male prisoners and trying desperately to pass him an apple. Perhaps she was a relative of the prisoner — maybe a daughter.

To my horror, the Quisitor simply turned his horse and rode her down. One moment she was holding out the apple; the next she was on her side on the cobbles, howling in pain. I saw the cruel expression on the Quisitor's face. He'd enjoyed hurting her. As the cart trundled past, followed by an escort of even more armed riders, the crowd's cheers turned to howls of abuse and cries of "Burn them all!"

It was then that I saw the girl chained among the other prisoners. She was no older than me, and her eyes were wide and frightened. Her black hair was streaked across her forehead with the rain, which was dribbling from her nose and the end of her chin like tears. I looked at the black dress she was wearing, then glanced down at her pointy shoes, hardly able to believe what I was seeing.

It was Alice. And she was a prisoner of the Quisitor.

CHAPTER V
The Funeral

MY head was whirling with what I'd witnessed. It was several months since I'd last seen Alice. Her aunt, Bony Lizzie, was a witch the Spook and I had dealt with, but Alice, unlike the rest of her family, wasn't really bad. In fact she was probably the closest I'd ever come to having a friend, and it was thanks to her that a few months back I'd managed to destroy Mother Malkin—the most evil witch in the County.

No, Alice had just been brought up in bad company. I couldn't let her be burned as a witch. Somehow I had to find a way to rescue her, but at that moment I didn't have the slightest clue how it could be done. I decided that as soon as the funeral was over, I'd have to try and persuade the Spook to help.

And then there was the Quisitor. What terrible timing that our visit to Priestown should coincide with his arrival. The Spook and I were in grave danger. Surely now my master wouldn't stay here after the funeral. A huge part of me hoped he'd want to leave right away and not face the Bane. But I couldn't leave Alice behind to die.

When the cart had gone by, the crowd surged forward and began to follow the Quisitor's procession. Jammed in shoulder to shoulder, I'd little choice but to move with them. The cart continued past the cathedral and halted outside a big three-story house with mullioned windows. I assumed that it was the presbytery—the priests' house—and that the prisoners were about to be tried there. They were taken down from the cart and dragged inside, but I was too far away to see Alice properly. There was nothing I could do, but I'd have to think of something quickly, before the burning, which was bound to take place soon.

Sadly, I turned away and pushed through the crowd until I reached the cathedral and Father Gregory's funeral. The building had big buttresses and tall, pointy stained-glass windows. Then, remembering what the Spook had told me, I glanced up at the large stone gargoyle above the main door.

This was a representation of the original form of the Bane, the shape it was slowly trying to return to as it grew stronger down there in the catacombs. The body, covered in scales, was crouching with tense, knotted muscles, long sharp talons gripping the stone lintel. It looked ready to leap down.

I've seen some terrifying things in my time, but I'd never seen anything uglier than that huge head. It had an elongated chin that curved upward almost as far as its long nose, and wicked eyes that seemed to follow me as I walked toward it. Its ears were strange, too, and wouldn't have been out of place on a big dog or even a wolf. Not something to face in the darkness of the catacombs!

Before I went in, I glanced back desperately at the presbytery once more, wondering if there was any real hope of rescuing Alice.

The cathedral was almost empty, so I found a place near the back. Close by, a couple of old ladies were kneeling in prayer with bowed heads and an altar boy was busy lighting candles.

I had plenty of time to look around. The cathedral seemed even bigger on the inside, with a high roof and huge wooden beams; even the slightest cough seemed to echo forever. There were three aisles—the middle one, which led right up to the altar steps, was wide enough to take a horse and cart. This place was grand, all right: Every statue in sight was gilded and even the walls were covered in marble. It was worlds away from the little church in Horshaw where the Spook's brother had gone about his business.

At the front of the central aisle stood Father Gregory's open coffin, with a candle at each corner. I'd never seen such candles in my life. Each one, set in a big brass candlestick, was taller than a man.

People had started to drift into the church. They entered in ones and twos and, like me, selected pews close to the back. I kept looking for the Spook, but there was no sign of him yet.

I couldn't help glancing around for evidence of the Bane. I certainly didn't feel its presence, but perhaps a creature so powerful would be able to feel mine. What if the rumors were true? What if it did have the strength to take on a physical form and was sitting here in the congregation? I looked about nervously, but then relaxed when I remembered what the Spook had told me. The Bane was bound to the catacombs far below, so for now, surely, I was safe.

Or was I? Its mind was very strong, my master had said, and it could reach up into the presbytery or the cathedral to influence and corrupt the priests. Maybe at this very moment it was trying to get inside my head!

I looked up, horrified, and caught the eye of a woman returning to her seat after paying her last respects to Father Gregory. I recognized her instantly as his weeping housekeeper, and she knew me in the same moment. She stopped at the end of my pew.

"Why were you so late?" she demanded in a raised whisper. "If you'd come when I first sent for you, he'd still be alive today."

"I did my best," I said, trying not to attract too much attention to us.

"Sometimes your best ain't good enough then, is it?" she said. "The Quisitor's right about your lot, you're nowt but trouble and deserve all that's coming to you."

At the Quisitor's name I started, but lots of people had begun to stream in, all of them wearing black cassocks and coats. Priests—dozens of them! I'd never thought to see so many in one place at a time. It was as if all the clergymen in the whole world had come together for the funeral of old Father Gregory. But I knew that wasn't true and that they were only the ones who lived in Priestown—and maybe a few from the surrounding villages and towns. The housekeeper said nothing more and hurriedly returned to her pew.

Now I was really afraid. Here I was, sitting in the cathedral, just above the catacombs that were home to the most fearsome creature in the County, at a time when the Quisitor was visiting—and I'd been recognized. I desperately wanted to get as far from that place as possible and looked anxiously around for any sign of my master, but I couldn't see him. I was just deciding that I should probably leave when suddenly the big doors of the church were flung back wide and a long procession entered. There was no escape.

At first I thought the man at the head was the Quisitor, for he had similar features. But he was older, and I remembered the Spook saying that the Quisitor had an uncle who was the bishop of Priestown; I realized it must be him.

The ceremony began. There was a lot of singing and we stood up, sat down, and knelt endlessly. No sooner had we settled in one position than we had to move again. Now if the funeral service had been in Greek I might have understood a bit more of what was going on, because my mam taught me that language when I was little. But most of Father Gregory's funeral was in Latin. I could follow some of it, but it made me realize I'd have to work a lot harder at my lessons.

The bishop spoke of Father Gregory being in heaven, saying that he deserved to be there after all the good work he'd done. I was a little surprised that he made no mention of how Father Gregory had died, but I suppose the priests wanted to keep that quiet. They were probably reluctant to admit that his exorcism had failed.

At last, after almost an hour, the funeral service was over and the procession left the church, this time with six priests carrying the coffin. The four big priests holding the candles had the harder job because they were staggering under their weight. It was only as the last one passed by, walking behind the coffin, that I noticed the triangular base of the big brass candlestick.

On each of its three faces was a vivid representation of the ugly gargoyle that I'd seen above the cathedral door. And although it was probably caused by the flickering of the flame, once again its eyes seemed to follow me as the priest carried the candle slowly by.

All the priests filed out to join the procession and most of the people at the back followed them, but I stayed inside the church for a long time, wanting to keep clear of the housekeeper.

I was wondering what to do. I hadn't seen the Spook, and I had no idea where he was staying or how I was supposed to meet up with him again. I needed to warn him about the Quisitor—and now the housekeeper. I also needed to talk to the Spook about Alice. I hoped he'd know what to do.

Outside, the rain had stopped and the yard at the front of the cathedral was empty. Glancing to my right, I could just see the tail of the procession disappearing round the back of the cathedral, where I supposed the graveyard must be.

I decided to go the other way, through the front gate and out into the street, but I was in for a shock. Across the road two people were having a heated conversation. More precisely, most of the heat was coming from an angry, red-faced priest with a bandaged hand. The other man was the Spook.

They both seemed to notice me at the same time. The Spook gestured with his thumb, signaling me to start walking right away. I did as I was told and my master followed me, keeping to the opposite side of the road.

The priest called out after him, "Think on, John, before it's too late!"

I risked a glance back and saw that the priest hadn't followed us but seemed to be staring at me. It was hard to be sure, but I thought he suddenly seemed far more interested in me than in the Spook.

We walked downhill for several minutes before the ground leveled out. At first there weren't many people around, but the streets soon became narrower and much busier, and after changing direction a couple of times we came to the flagged market. It was a big, bustling square, full of stalls sheltered by wooden frames draped with gray waterproof awnings. I followed the Spook into the crowd, at times not far from his heels. What else could I do? It would have been easy to lose him in a place like that.

There was a large tavern at the northern edge of the market with empty benches outside, and the Spook headed straight for it. At first I thought he was going in and wondered if we were going to buy lunch. If he intended to leave because of the Quisitor, there'd be no need to fast. But instead he turned into a narrow, cobbled blind alley, led me to a low stone wall, and wiped the nearest section with his sleeve. When he'd got most of the beads of water off, he sat himself down and gestured that I should do the same.

I sat down and looked around. The alley was deserted and the walls of warehouses hemmed us in on three sides. There were few windows and they were cracked and smeared with grime, so at least we were out of the way of prying eyes.

The Spook was out of breath with walking, and this gave me a chance to get the first word in.

"The Quisitor's here," I told him.

The Spook nodded. "Aye, lad, he's here all right.

I was standing on the opposite side of the road, but you were too busy gawping at the cart to notice me."

"But didn't you see her? Alice was in the cart—"

"Alice? Alice who?"

"Bony Lizzie's niece. We have to help her. . . ."

As I mentioned before, Bony Lizzie was a witch we'd dealt with in the spring. Now the Spook had her imprisoned in a pit, back in his garden in Chipenden.

"Oh, that Alice. Well, you'd best forget her, lad, because there's nothing to be done. The Quisitor has at least fifty armed men with him."

"But it's not fair," I said, hardly able to believe that he could stay so calm. "Alice isn't a witch."

"Little in this life is fair," the Spook replied. "The truth is, none of them were witches. As you well know, a real witch would have sniffed the Quisitor coming from miles away."

"But Alice is my friend. I can't leave her to die!" I protested, feeling the anger rising inside me.

"This is no time for sentiment. Our job is to protect people from the dark, not to get distracted by pretty girls."

I was furious—especially as I knew the Spook

himself had once been distracted by a pretty girl—
and that one was a witch. "Alice helped save my
family from Mother Malkin, remember!"

"And why was Mother Malkin free in the first
place, lad, answer me that!"

I hung my head in shame.

"Because you got yourself mixed up with that
girl," he continued, "and I don't want it happening again. Especially not here in Priestown, with
the Quisitor breathing down our necks. You'll be
putting your own life in danger—and mine. And
keep your voice down. We don't want to attract any
unwelcome attention."

I looked about me. But for us, the alley was
deserted. A few people could be seen passing the
entrance, but they were some distance away and
didn't so much as glance in our direction. Beyond
them I could see the rooftops at the far side of the
market square and, rising above the chimney pots,
the cathedral steeple. But when I spoke again, I did
lower my voice.

"What's the Quisitor doing here anyway?" I
asked. "Didn't you say that he did his work down
south and only came north when he was sent for?"

"That's mostly true, but sometimes he mounts an expedition up north to the County and even beyond. Turns out that for the last few weeks he's been sweeping the coast, picking up the poor dregs of humanity he had chained up in that cart."

I was angry that he'd said Alice was one of the dregs, because I knew it wasn't true. It wasn't the right time to continue the argument, though, so I kept my peace.

"But we'll be safe enough in Chipenden," continued the Spook. "He's never yet ventured up to the fells."

"Are we going home now, then?" I asked.

"No, lad, not yet. I told you before, I've got unfinished business in this town."

My heart sank, and I looked toward the alley entrance uneasily. People were still scurrying past, going about their business, and I could hear some stallholders calling out the price of their wares. But although there was a lot of noise and bustle, we were thankfully out of sight. Despite that, I still felt uneasy. We were supposed to be keeping our distance from each other. The priest outside the cathedral had known the Spook. The housekeeper knew me. What if someone else walked down the alley and recognized us and we were both arrested? Many priests from County parishes would be in town, and they'd know the Spook by sight. The only good news was that at the moment they were probably all still in the churchyard.

"That priest you were talking to before, who was he? He seemed to know you, so won't he tell the Quisitor you're here?" I asked, wondering if anywhere was really safe. For all I knew that red-faced priest outside the cathedral could even direct the Quisitor to Chipenden. "Oh, and there's something else. Your brother's housekeeper recognized me at the funeral. She was really angry. She might tell somebody that we're here."

It seemed to me that we were taking a serious risk in staying in Priestown while the Quisitor was in the area.

"Calm yourself, lad. The housekeeper won't tell a soul. She and my brother weren't exactly without sin themselves. And as for that priest," said the Spook with a faint smile, "that's Father Cairns. He's family, my cousin. A cousin who meddles and gets a bit excited at times, but he means well all the same.

He's always trying to save me from myself and get me on the path of 'righteousness.' But he's wasting his breath. I've chosen my path—and right or wrong, it's the one I tread."

At that moment I heard footsteps and my heart lurched into my mouth. Someone had turned into the alley and was walking directly toward us!

"Anyway, talking of family," the Spook said, totally unconcerned, "here comes another member. This is my brother Andrew."

A tall man with a thin body and sad, bony face was approaching us across the cobbles. He looked even older than the Spook and reminded me of a well-dressed scarecrow, for although he was wearing good-quality boots and clean clothes, his garments flapped in the wind. He looked more in need of a good breakfast than I did.

Without bothering to brush away the beads of water, he sat on the wall on the other side of the Spook.

"I thought I'd find you here. A sad business, brother," he said gloomily.

"Aye," said the Spook. "There's just the two of us left now. Five brothers dead and gone."

"John, I must tell you, the Quis—"

"Yes, I know," said the Spook, an edge of impatience in his voice.

"Then you must be going. It's not safe for either of you here," said his brother, acknowledging me with a nod.

"No, Andrew, we're not going anywhere until I've done what needs to be done. So I'd like you to make me a special key again," the Spook told him. "For the gate."

Andrew started. "Nay, John, don't be a fool," he said, shaking his head. "I wouldn't have come here if I'd known you wanted that. Have you forgotten the curse?"

"Hush," said the Spook. "Not in front of the boy. Keep your silly superstitious nonsense to yourself."

"Curse?" I asked, suddenly curious.

"See what you've done?" my master hissed angrily to his brother. "It's nothing," he said, turning to me. "I don't believe in such rubbish and neither should you."

"Well, I've buried one brother today," said Andrew. "Get yourself home now, before I find myself burying another. The Quisitor would love to get his hands on the County Spook. Get back to Chipenden while you still can."

"I'm not leaving, Andrew, and that's final. I've got a job to do here, Quisitor or no Quisitor," the Spook said firmly. "So are you going to help or not?"

"That's not the point, and you know it!" Andrew insisted. "I've always helped you before, haven't I? When have I ever let you down? But this is madness. You risk burning just by being here. This isn't the time to meddle with that thing again," he said, gesturing at the alley entrance and raising his eyes toward the steeple. "And think of the boy—you can't drag him into this. Not now. Come back again in the spring when the Quisitor's gone and we'll talk again. You'd be a fool to attempt anything now. You can't take on the Bane and the Quisitor—you're not a young man, nor a well one, by the looks of you."

As they spoke, I looked up at the steeple myself. I suspected that it could be seen from almost anywhere in the town and that the whole town was also visible from the steeple. There were four small windows right near the top, just below the cross. From there you'd be able to see every rooftop in Priestown, most of the streets, and a lot of the people, including us.

The Spook had told me that the Bane could use people, get inside their heads, and peer out through their eyes. I shivered, wondering if one of the priests was up there now, the Bane using him to watch us from the darkness inside the spire.

But the Spook wasn't for changing his mind. "Come on, Andrew, think on! How many times have you told me that the dark's getting stronger in this town? That the priests are becoming more corrupt, that people are afraid? And think about the double tithes and the Quisitor stealing land and burning innocent women and girls. What's turned the priests and corrupted them so much? What terrible force makes good men inflict such atrocities or stand by and let them happen?

"Why, this very day the lad here has seen his friend carted off to certain death. Aye, the Bane is to blame, and the Bane must be stopped now. Do you really think I can let this go on for half a year more? How many more innocent people will have been burned by then, or will perish this winter through poverty, hunger, and cold if I don't do something? The town is rife with rumors of sightings down in the catacombs. If they're true, then the Bane is growing in strength and power, turning from a spirit into a creature clothed in flesh. Soon it could return to its original form, a manifestation of the evil spirit that tyrannized the Little People. And then where will we all be? How easy will it be then for it to terrify or trick someone into opening that gate? No, it's as plain as the nose on your face. I've got to act now to rid Priestown of the dark, before the Bane's power grows any stronger. So I'll ask you again, one more time. Will you make me a key?"

For a moment the Spook's brother buried his face in his hands, just like one of the old women saying her prayers in church. Finally he looked up and nodded. "I still have the mold from last time. I'll have the key ready first thing tomorrow morning. I must be dafter than you," he said.

"Good man," replied the Spook. "I knew you wouldn't let me down. I'll call for it at first light."

"This time I hope you know what you're doing when you get down there!"

The Spook's face reddened with anger. "You do your job, brother, and I'll do mine!" he said.

With that, Andrew stood up, gave a world-weary sigh, and walked off without even a backward glance.

"Right, lad," said the Spook, "you leave first. Go back to your room and stay there till tomorrow. Andrew's shop is down Friargate. I'll have collected the key and will be ready to meet you about twenty minutes after dawn. There shouldn't be many people about that early. Remember where you were standing earlier when the Quisitor rode by?"

I nodded.

"Be on the nearest corner, lad. Don't be late. And remember, we must continue to fast. Oh, and one more thing: Don't forget my bag. I think we might be needing it."

My mind whirled on the way back to the inn. What should I fear most: a powerful man who would hunt me down and burn me at the stake? Or a fearsome creature that had beaten my master in his prime and, through the eyes of a priest, might be watching me at this very moment from the windows high in the steeple?

As I glanced up at the cathedral, my eye caught the blackness of a priest's cassock nearby. I averted my gaze, but not before I'd noted the priest: Father Cairns. Luckily the pavement was busy and he was staring straight ahead and didn't even glance in my direction. I was relieved, for had he seen me here, so close to my inn, it wouldn't have taken much for him to work out where I might be staying. The Spook had said he was harmless, but I couldn't help thinking the fewer people who knew who we were and where we were staying, the better. But my relief was short-lived, for when I got back to my room there was a note pinned to the door.

> *Thomas,*
> *If you would save your master's life, come*
> *to my confessional this evening at seven. After*
> *that it will be too late.*
>
> *Father Cairns*

I felt a sickening unease. How had Father Cairns found out where I was staying? Had someone been following me? Father Gregory's housekeeper? Or the innkeeper? I hadn't liked the look of him at all. Had he sent a message to the cathedral? Or the Bane? Did that creature know my every movement? Had it told Father Cairns where to find me? Whatever had happened, the priests knew where I was staying, and if they told the Quisitor he could come for me at any moment.

I hurriedly opened my bedroom door and locked it behind me. Then I closed the shutters, hoping desperately to keep out the prying eyes of Priestown. I checked that the Spook's bag was where I'd left it, then sat on my bed, not knowing what to do. The Spook had told me to stay in my room until morning. I knew he wouldn't really want me to go and see his cousin. He'd said he was a priest who meddled. Was he just going to meddle again? On the other hand, he'd told me that Father Cairns meant well. But what if the priest really did know something that threatened the Spook? If I stayed, my master might end up in the hands of the Quisitor. Yet if I went to the cathedral, I was walking right into the lair of the Quisitor and the Bane! The funeral had been dangerous enough. Could I push my luck again?

What I really should have done was tell the Spook about the message. But I couldn't. For one thing, he hadn't told me where he was staying.

"Trust your instincts," the Spook had always taught me, so at last I made up my mind. I decided to go and speak to Father Cairns.

CHAPTER VI
A Pact with Hell

GIVING myself plenty of time, I walked slowly through the damp, cobbled streets. My palms were clammy with nerves, and my feet seemed reluctant to move toward the cathedral. It was as if they were wiser than I was, and I had to keep forcing one foot in front of the other. But the evening was chilly, and luckily there weren't many people about. I didn't pass even one priest.

I arrived at the cathedral at about ten minutes to seven, and as I walked through the gate into the big flagged forecourt, I couldn't help glancing up at the gargoyle over the main door. The ugly head seemed bigger than ever and the eyes still seemed wick with life; they followed me as I walked toward the door.

The long chin curved up so much that it almost met the nose, making it unlike any creature I'd ever seen. With its doglike ears and a long tongue protruding from its mouth, and two short horns curving out from its skull, it suddenly reminded me of a goat.

I looked away and entered the cathedral, shivering at the sheer strangeness of the creature. Inside the building it took a few moments for my eyes to adjust to the gloom, and to my relief I saw that the place was almost empty.

I was afraid, though, for two reasons. Firstly, I didn't like being in the cathedral, where priests could appear at any moment. If Father Cairns was tricking me, then I had just walked straight into his trap. Secondly, I was now in the Bane's territory. Soon the day would draw in, and once the sun went down the Bane, like all creatures of the dark, would be at its most dangerous. Perhaps then its mind might reach up from the catacombs and seek me out. I had to get this business over with as quickly as possible.

Where was the confessional? There were just a couple of old ladies at the back of the cathedral, but an old man was kneeling near the front, close to the small door of a wooden box that stood with its back to the stone wall.

That told me what I wanted to know. There was an identical box a bit farther along. The confessional boxes. Each had a candle fixed above it set within a blue glass holder. But only the one near the kneeling man was lit.

I walked down the right-hand aisle and knelt in the pew behind him. After a few moments the door to the confessional box opened and a woman wearing a black veil came out. She crossed the aisle and knelt in a pew while the old man went inside.

After a few moments I could hear him muttering. I'd never been to confession in my life, but I had a pretty good idea of what went on. One of Dad's brothers had become very religious before he'd died. Dad always called him Holy Joe, but his real name was Matthew. He went to confession twice a week, and after hearing his sins the priest gave him a big penance. That meant that afterward he had to say lots of prayers over and over again. I supposed the old man was telling the priest about his sins.

The door stayed closed for what seemed an age, and I started to grow impatient. Another thought struck me: What if it wasn't Father Cairns inside but some other priest? I really would have to make a confession then or it would seem very suspicious. I tried to think of a few sins that might sound convincing. Was greed a sin? Or did you call it gluttony? Well, I certainly liked my food, but I'd had nothing to eat all day and my belly was starting to rumble. Suddenly it seemed madness to be doing this. In moments I could end up a prisoner.

I panicked and stood up to leave. It was only then that I noticed with relief a small card slotted into a holder on the door. A name was written on it: FATHER CAIRNS.

At that moment the door opened and the old man came out, so I took his place in the confessional and closed the door behind me. It was small and gloomy inside, and when I knelt down, my face was very close to a metal grille. Behind the grille was a brown curtain and, somewhere beyond that, a flickering candle. I couldn't see a face through the grille, just the shadowy outline of a head.

"Would you like me to hear your confession?" The priest's voice had a strong County accent, and he breathed loudly.

I just shrugged. Then I realized that he couldn't see me properly through the grille. "No, Father," I said, "but thank you for asking. I'm Tom, Mr. Gregory's apprentice. You wanted to see me."

There was a slight pause before Father Cairns spoke. "Ah, Thomas, I'm glad you came. I asked you here because I need to talk to you. I need to tell you something very important, so I want you to stay here until I've finished. Will you promise me that you won't leave until I've said what I have to say?"

"I'll listen," I replied doubtfully. I was wary of making promises now. In the spring I'd made a promise to Alice, and it had got me in a whole lot of trouble.

"That's a good lad," he said. "We've made a good start to an important task. And do you know what that task is?"

I wondered whether he was talking about the Bane but thought it best not to mention that creature so close to the catacombs, so I said, "No, Father."

"Well, Thomas, we have to put together a plan. We have to work out how we can save your immortal soul. But you know what you have to do to begin the process, don't you? You must walk away from

John Gregory. You must cease practicing that vile trade. Will you do that for me?"

"I thought you wanted to see me about helping Mr. Gregory," I said, starting to feel angry. "I thought he was in danger."

"He is, Thomas. We are here to help John Gregory, but we must begin by helping you. So will you do what I ask?"

"I can't," I said. "My dad paid good money for my apprenticeship, and my mam would be even more disappointed. She says I've a gift and I have to use it to help people. That's what spooks do. We go round helping people when they're in danger from things that come out of the dark."

There was a long silence. All I could hear was the priest's breathing. Then I thought of something else.

"I helped Father Gregory, you know," I blurted out. "He died later, it's true, but I saved him from a worse death. At least he died in bed, in the warmth. He tried to get rid of a boggart," I explained, raising my voice a little. "That's what got him into trouble in the first place. Mr. Gregory could have sorted it out for him. He can do things that a priest can't. Priests can't get rid of boggarts because they don't know how. It takes more than just a few prayers."

I knew that I shouldn't have said that about prayers and I expected him to get very angry. He didn't. He kept calm, and that made it seem a whole lot worse.

"Oh, yes, it takes much more," Father Cairns answered quietly, his voice hardly more than a whisper. "Much, much more. Do you know what John Gregory's secret is, Thomas? Do you know the source of his power?"

"Yes," I said, my own voice suddenly much calmer. "He's studied for years, for the whole of his working life. He's got a whole library full of books and he did an apprenticeship like me and he listened carefully to what his master said and wrote it down in notebooks, just like I do now."

"Don't you think that we do the same? It takes long, long years to train for the priesthood. And priests are clever men being trained by even cleverer men. So how did you accomplish what Father Gregory couldn't, despite the fact that he read from God's holy book? How do you explain the fact that your master routinely does what his brother could not?"

"It's because priests have the wrong kind of training," I said. "And it's because my master and I are both seventh sons of seventh sons."

The priest made a strange noise behind the grille. At first I thought he was choking; then I realized I could hear laughter. He was laughing at me.

I thought that was very rude. My dad always says that you should respect other people's opinions even if they sometimes seem daft.

"That's just superstition, Thomas," Father Cairns said at last. "Being the seventh son of a seventh son means nothing. It's just an old wives' tale. The true explanation for John Gregory's power is something so terrible that it makes me shudder just to think about it. You see, John Gregory has made a pact with hell. He's sold his soul to the Devil."

I couldn't believe what he was saying. When I opened my mouth, no words came out, so I just kept shaking my head.

"It's true, Thomas. All his power comes from the Devil. What you and other County folk call boggarts are just lesser devils who only yield because their master bids them do that. It's worth it to the Devil because, in return, one day he'll get hold of John

Gregory's soul. And a soul is precious to God, a thing of brightness and splendor, and the Devil will do anything to dirty it with sin and drag it down into the eternal flames of Hell."

"What about me?" I said, getting angry again. "I've not sold my soul. But I saved Father Gregory."

"That's easy, Thomas. You're a servant of the Spook, as you call him, who, in turn, is a servant of the Devil. So the power of evil is on loan to you while you serve. But of course, if you were to complete your training in evil and prepare to practice your vile trade as master rather than apprentice, then it would be your turn. You, too, would have to sign away your soul. John Gregory hasn't yet told you this because you're too young, but he would certainly do so one day. And when that day arrived, it would come as no surprise because you'd remember my words to you now. John Gregory has made many serious mistakes in his life and has fallen a long, long way from grace. Do you know that he was once a priest?"

I nodded. "I know that already."

"And do you know how, just fresh from ordination as a priest, he came to leave his calling? Do you know of his shame?"

I didn't reply. I knew that Father Cairns was going to tell me anyway.

"Some theologians have argued that a woman does not have a soul. That debate continues, but of one thing we can be certain — a priest cannot take a wife, because it would distract him from his devotion to God. John Gregory's failing was doubly bad: Not only was he distracted by a woman, but that woman was already betrothed to one of his own brothers. It tore the family apart. Brother turned against brother over a woman called Emily Burns."

By now I didn't like Father Cairns one little bit and knew that if he'd talked to my mam about women not having souls, she'd have flayed him with her tongue to within an inch of his life. But I was curious about the Spook. First I'd heard about Meg and now I was being told that, even earlier, he'd been involved with this Emily Burns. I was astonished and wanted to know more.

"Did Mr. Gregory marry Emily Burns?" I asked, spitting my question right out.

"Never in the eyes of God," answered the priest. "She came from Blackrod, where our family has its roots, and lives there alone to this day. Some say they quarreled, but whatever the case John Gregory eventually took another woman, whom he met in the far north of the County and brought south. Her name was Margery Skelton, a notorious witch. The locals knew her as Meg, and in time she became feared and loathed across the breadth of Anglezarke Moor and the towns and villages to the south of the County."

I said nothing. I know that he expected me to be shocked. I was, at everything he'd said, but reading the Spook's diary back in Chipenden had prepared me for the worst.

Father Cairns gave another deep sniff, then coughed deep in his throat. "Do you know which of his six brothers John Gregory wronged?"

I'd already guessed. "Father Gregory," I answered.

"In devout families such as the Gregorys, it is the tradition that one son takes holy orders. When John threw away his vocation, another brother took his place and began training for the priesthood. Yes, Thomas, it was Father Gregory, the brother we buried today. He lost his betrothed and he lost his brother. What else could he do but turn to God?"

When I'd arrived, the church had been almost

empty, but as we'd talked I'd become aware of sounds outside the confessional box. There'd been footsteps and the increasing murmur of voices. Now, suddenly, a choir began to sing. It would be well after seven by now, and the sun would already have set. I decided to make an excuse and leave, but just as I opened my mouth I heard Father Cairns come to his feet.

"Come with me, Thomas," he said. "I want to show you something."

I heard him open his door and go out into the church, so I followed.

He beckoned me toward the altar where, led by another priest, neatly arranged in three rows of ten, a choir of altar boys was standing on the steps. Each wore a black cassock and white surplice.

Father Cairns halted and put his bandaged hand on my right shoulder.

"Listen to them, Thomas. Don't they sound like holy angels?"

I'd never heard an angel sing so I couldn't answer, but they certainly made a better noise than my dad, who used to start singing as we got near to the end of the milking. His voice was bad enough to turn the milk sour.

"You could have been a member of that choir, Thomas. But you've left it too late. Your voice is already beginning to deepen and a chance to serve has been lost."

He was right about that. Most of the boys were younger than me and their voices were more like girls' than lads'. In any case, my singing wasn't much better than my dad's.

"Still, there are other things you can do. Let me show you . . ."

He led the way past the altar, through a door, and along a corridor. Then we went out into the garden at the rear of the cathedral. Well, it was more the size of a field than a garden, and rather than flowers and roses, vegetables grew there.

It was already beginning to get dark, but there was still enough light to see a hawthorn hedge in the distance with the gravestones of the churchyard just visible beyond it. In the foreground a priest was on his knees, weeding with a trowel. It was a big garden and only a small trowel.

"You come from a family of farmers, Thomas. It's good, honest work. You'd be at home working here," he said, pointing to the kneeling priest.

I shook my head. "I don't want to be a priest," I said firmly.

"Oh, you could never be a priest!" Father Cairns said, his voice filled with shock and indignation. "You've been too close to the Devil for that and now will have to be watched closely for the rest of your life lest you slip back. No, that man is a brother."

"A brother?" I asked, puzzled, thinking he was family or something.

The priest smiled. "At a big cathedral like this, priests have assistants who offer support. We call them brothers because, although they can't administer the sacraments, they do other vital tasks and are part of the family of the Church. Brother Peter is our gardener and very good at it, too. What do you say, Thomas? Would you like to be a brother?"

I knew all about being a brother. Being the youngest of seven, I'd been given all the jobs that nobody else wanted to do. It looked like it was the same here. In any case, I already had a job and I didn't believe what Father Cairns had told me about the Devil and the Spook. It had made me think a bit, but deep down I knew it couldn't be true. Mr. Gregory was a good man.

It was getting darker and chillier by the moment, so I decided it was time to go.

"Thanks for talking to me, Father," I said, "but could you tell me about the danger to Mr. Gregory now, please?"

"All in good time, Thomas," he said, giving me a little smile.

Something in that smile told me that I'd been tricked. That he had no intention at all of helping the Spook.

"I'll think about what you've told me, but I've got to be getting back now or I'll miss my supper," I told him. It seemed a good excuse at the time. He'd no way of knowing that I was fasting because I had to be ready to deal with the Bane.

"We've got supper for you here, Thomas," said Father Cairns. "In fact, we'd like you to stay the night."

Two other priests had come out of the side door and were walking toward us. They were big men, and I didn't like the expressions on their faces.

There was a moment when I could probably have gotten away, but it seemed silly to run when I wasn't really sure what was going to happen.

Then it was too late because the priests stood on each side of me, gripping me firmly by my upper arms and shoulders. I didn't struggle; there was no point. Their hands were big and heavy and I felt that if I stayed in the same spot too long, I'd start to sink into the earth. Then they walked me back into the vestry.

"This is for your own good, Thomas," Father Cairns said as he followed us inside. "The Quisitor will seize John Gregory tonight. He'll have a trial, of course, but the outcome is certain. Found guilty of dealing with the Devil, he will be burned at the stake. That's why I can't let you go back to him. There's still a chance for you. You're just a boy and your soul can still be saved without burning. But if you're with him when he's arrested, then you'll suffer the same fate. So this is for your own good."

"But he's your cousin!" I blurted out. "He's family. How can you do this? Let me go and warn him."

"Warn him?" asked Father Cairns. "Do you think I haven't tried to warn him? I've been warning him for most of his adult life. Now I need to think about his soul more than his body. The flames will cleanse him. By means of pain, his soul can be saved. Don't you see? I'm doing it to help him, Thomas. There are much more important things than our brief existence in this world."

"You've betrayed him! Your own flesh and blood. You've told the Quisitor we're here!"

"Not both of you, just John. So join us, Thomas. Your soul will be cleansed through prayer and your life will no longer be in danger. What do you say?"

There was no point in arguing with someone who was so sure that he was right, so I didn't waste my breath. The only sound to be heard was the echo of our footsteps and the jangle of keys as they led me farther and farther into the gloom of the cathedral.

CHAPTER VII
Escape and Capture

THEY locked me in a small damp room without a window and didn't bring me the supper they'd mentioned. For a bed there was just a small heap of straw. When the door closed I stood there in the dark, listening to the key being turned in the lock and the footsteps echoing away down the corridor.

It was too dark to see my hands before my face, but that didn't worry me much. After nearly six months as the Spook's apprentice, I'd become a lot braver. Being a seventh son of a seventh son, I'd always seen things that others couldn't, but the Spook had taught me that most of them couldn't do you much harm. It was an old cathedral and there was a big graveyard beyond the garden, so that meant there would be things about—unquiet things like ghasts and ghosts—but I wasn't afraid of them.

No, what bothered me was the Bane below in the catacombs! The thought of it reaching into my mind was terrifying. I certainly didn't want to face that, and if it was now as strong as the Spook suspected, it would know exactly what was going on. In fact it had probably corrupted Father Cairns, turning him against his own cousin. It might have worked its evil among the priests and been listening to their conversations. It was bound to know who I was and where I was, and it wouldn't be too friendly, to say the least.

Of course, I didn't plan on staying there all night. You see, I still had the three keys in my pocket, and I intended to use the special one Andrew had made. Father Cairns wasn't the only one with tricks up his sleeve.

The key wouldn't get me beyond the Silver Gate, because you needed something far more subtle and well crafted to open that lock, but I knew it would get me out into the corridor and through any door of the cathedral. I just had to wait awhile until everyone was asleep and then I could sneak out.

If I went too early, I'd probably be caught. On the other hand, if I delayed, I'd be too late to warn the Spook and might get a visit from the Bane, so it was a judgment I couldn't afford to get wrong.

As darkness fell and the noises outside faded, I decided to take my chance. The key turned in the lock without a hint of resistance, but just before I opened the door I heard footsteps. I froze and held my breath as, gradually, they receded into the distance and everything returned to silence.

I waited a long time, listening very carefully. Finally I drew in a slow breath and eased open the door. Fortunately, it opened without a single creak and I stepped out into the corridor, pausing and listening again.

I didn't know for sure that there was anybody left in the cathedral and its side buildings. Perhaps they'd all gone back to the big priests' house? But I couldn't believe they wouldn't have left somebody on guard, so I tiptoed along the dark corridor, afraid to make even the slightest sound.

When I came to the side door of the vestry, I had a shock. I didn't need my key. It was already open.

The sky was clear now and the moon was up, bathing the path in a silver light. I stepped outside and moved cautiously. Only then did I sense somebody behind me, someone standing to the side of the door, hidden in the shadow of one of the big stone buttresses that shored up the sides of the cathedral.

For a moment I froze. Then, my heart pounding so loudly I could hear it, I slowly turned round. The shadowy figure stepped out into the moonlight. I recognized him straightaway. Not a priest, but the brother who'd been on his knees tending the garden earlier. Gaunt of face, Brother Peter was almost totally bald, with just a thin collar of white hair below his ears.

Suddenly he spoke. "Warn your master, Thomas," he said. "Go quickly! Get away from this town while you both can!"

I didn't reply. I just turned and ran down the path as fast as I could. I only stopped running when I reached the streets. I walked so as not to draw too much attention to myself, and I wondered why Brother Peter hadn't tried to stop me. Wasn't that his job? Hadn't he been left on guard?

But I didn't have time to think about that properly.

I had to warn the Spook of his cousin's betrayal before it was too late. I didn't know which inn the Spook was staying at, but perhaps his brother would know. That was a start because I knew where Friargate was: it was one of the roads I'd walked down while searching for an inn, so Andrew's shop wouldn't be too difficult to find. I hurried through the cobbled streets, knowing that I didn't have much time, that the Quisitor and his men would already be on their way.

Friargate was a wide, hilly road with two rows of shops, and I found the locksmith's easily. The name above the shop said ANDREW GREGORY, but the premises were in darkness. I had to knock three times before a light flickered in the upstairs room.

Andrew opened the door and held a candle up to my face. He was wearing a long nightshirt and his face held a mixture of expressions. He looked puzzled, angry, and weary.

"Your brother's in danger," I said, trying to keep my voice as low as possible. "I would have warned him myself, but I don't know where he's staying. . . ."

He beckoned me in without a word and led me through into his workshop. The walls were festooned with keys and locks of every possible shape and size. One large key was as long as my forearm, and I wondered at the size of the lock it belonged to. Quickly I explained what had happened.

"I told him he was a fool to stay here!" he exclaimed, thumping his fist down hard on the top of a workbench. "And damn that treacherous, two-faced cousin of ours! I knew all along he wasn't to be trusted. The Bane must have finally got to him, twisting his mind to get John out of the way—the one person in the whole County who still poses a real threat to it!"

He went upstairs, but it didn't take him long to get dressed. Soon we were heading back through the empty streets, taking a route that led us back in the direction of the cathedral.

"He's staying at the Book and Candle," muttered Andrew Gregory, shaking his head. "Why on earth didn't he tell you that? You could have saved time by going straight there. Let's hope we're not too late!"

But we *were* too late. We heard them from several streets away: men's voices raised in anger and some-one thumping a door loud enough to wake the dead.

We watched from a corner, taking care not to be seen. There was nothing we could do now. The Quisitor was there on his huge horse, and he had about twenty armed men at his command. They had cudgels, and some of them had drawn their swords as if they expected resistance. One of the men hammered on the inn door again with the hilt of his sword.

"Open up! Open up! Be quick about it!" he shouted. "Or we'll break down the door!"

There was the sound of bolts being drawn back, and the innkeeper came to the door in his nightshirt, holding a lantern. He looked bewildered, as if he'd just woken up from a very deep sleep. He saw only the two armed men facing him, not the Quisitor. Perhaps that was why he made a big mistake: He began to protest and bluster.

"What's this?" he cried. "Can't a man get some sleep after a hard day's work? Disturbing the peace at this time of night! I know my rights. There's laws against such things."

"Fool!" shouted the Quisitor angrily, riding closer to the door. "I am the law! A warlock sleeps within your walls. A servant of the Devil! Sheltering a known enemy of the Church carries dire penalties.

Stand aside or pay with your life!"

"Sorry, lord. Sorry!" wailed the innkeeper, holding up his hands in supplication, a look of terror on his face.

In answer the Quisitor simply gestured to his men, who seized the innkeeper roughly. Without ceremony he was dragged into the street and hurled to the ground.

Then, very deliberately, with cruelty etched on his face, the Quisitor rode his white stallion over the innkeeper. A hoof came down hard on his leg and I clearly heard the bone snap. My blood ran cold. The man lay screaming on the ground while four of the guards ran into the house; their boots thumped up the wooden stairs.

When they dragged the Spook outside, he looked old and frail. Perhaps a little afraid, too, but I was too far away to be sure.

"Well, John Gregory, you're mine at last!" cried the Quisitor, in a loud, arrogant voice. "Those dry old bones of yours should burn well!"

The Spook didn't answer. I watched them tie his hands behind his back and lead him away down the street.

"All these years, then it comes to this," muttered Andrew. "He always meant well. He doesn't deserve to burn."

I couldn't believe it was happening. I had a lump in my throat so big that, until the Spook had been taken around the corner and out of sight, I couldn't even speak. "We've got to do something!" I said at last.

Andrew shook his head wearily. "Well, boy, have a think about it and then tell me just what we're supposed to do. Because I haven't a clue. You'd better come back to my place and at first light get as far away from here as possible."

CHAPTER VIII
Brother Peter's Tale

THE kitchen was at the back of the house, overlooking a small flagged yard. As the sky grew lighter, Andrew offered me some breakfast. It wasn't much, just an egg and a slice of toasted bread. I thanked him but had to refuse because I was still fasting. To eat would mean I'd accepted that the Spook was gone and that we wouldn't be facing the Bane together. Anyway, I didn't feel the slightest bit hungry.

I'd done what Andrew had suggested. Since the Spook had been taken, I'd spent every single moment thinking of how we could save him. I thought about Alice, too. If I didn't do something, they were both going to burn.

"Mr. Gregory's bag is still in my room at the Black Bull," I suddenly remembered, turning to the locksmith. "And he must have left his staff and our cloaks in his room at the inn. How will we get them back?"

"Well, that's one thing I can help you with," Andrew said. "It's too risky for either of us to go, but I know someone who could pick them up for you. I'll see to it later."

While I watched Andrew eating, a bell started to ring somewhere in the distance. It had a single dull tone and there was a long pause between each chime. It sounded mournful, like the tolling of a funeral bell.

"Is that from the cathedral?" I asked.

Andrew nodded and carried on chewing his food very slowly. He looked as if he'd as little appetite as I had.

I wondered if it was calling people to an early morning service, but before I could say as much Andrew swallowed his piece of toast and told me, "It means another death at the cathedral or at some other church in the town. Either that or a priest's died somewhere else in the County and the news has only just got here. It's a common sound here these days. I'm afraid any priests who question the darkness and corruption in our town are swiftly dealt with."

I shuddered. "Does everybody in Priestown know it's the Bane that's the cause of the dark times?" I asked. "Or just the priests?"

"The Bane's common enough knowledge. In the area closest to the cathedral, most folk have had the doors to their cellars bricked up, and fear and superstition are rife. Who can blame the townsfolk when they can't even rely on their own priests to protect them? No wonder congregations are dwindling," Andrew said, shaking his head sadly.

"Did you finish the key?" I asked him.

"Aye," he said, "but poor John won't be needing it now."

"We could use it," I said, speaking quickly so that I could finish what I was saying before he stopped me. "The catacombs run right under the cathedral and presbytery, so there could be a way up into them. We could wait until dark, when everyone's asleep, and get up into the house."

"That's just foolishness," Andrew said, shaking

his head. "The presbytery's huge, with a lot of rooms both above and below ground. And we don't even know where the prisoners are being held. Not only that, there are armed men guarding them. Do you want to burn as well? I certainly don't!"

"It's worth a try," I insisted. "They won't expect anyone to come up into the house from below with the Bane down there. We'll have surprise on our side and maybe the guards will be asleep."

"No," Andrew said, shaking his head firmly. "It's madness. It's not worth two more lives."

"Then give me the key and I'll do it."

"You'd never find your way without me. It's a maze of tunnels down there."

"So you do know the way?" I said. "You've been down there before?"

"Aye, I know the way as far as the Silver Gate. But that's as far as I'd ever want to go. And it's twenty years since I went down there with John. That thing down there nearly killed him. It could kill us, too. You heard John: It's changing from a spirit, shape-shifting into God knows what. We could meet anything down there. Folk have spoken of ferocious black dogs with huge, gaping jaws and bared teeth. The Bane can read your mind, remember, take the shape of your worst fears. No, it's too dangerous. I don't know which fate is worse — being burned alive at the stake by the Quisitor or pressed to death by the Bane. They're not choices a young lad should be making."

"Don't worry about that," I said. "You deal with the locks and I'll do my job."

"If my brother couldn't cope, then what hope have you? He was still in his prime then, and you're just a boy."

"I'm not daft enough to try and destroy the Bane," I said. "I'd just do enough to get the Spook to safety."

Andrew shook his head. "How long have you been with him?"

"Nearly six months," I said.

"Well," said Andrew, "that tells us everything, doesn't it? You mean well, I know that, but we'd just be making things worse."

"The Spook told me that burning's a terrible death. The worst death of all. That's why he doesn't hold with burning a witch. Would you let him suffer that? Please, you've got to help. It's his last chance."

This time Andrew didn't say anything. He sat for a long time, deep in thought. When he did get up from his chair, all he said was that I should stay out of sight.

That seemed a good sign. At least he hadn't sent me packing.

I sat in the back, kicking my heels, as the morning slowly wore on. I hadn't slept at all and I was tired, but sleep was the last thing on my mind after the events of the night.

Andrew was working. Most of the time I could hear him in his workshop, but sometimes there was a tinkle from the doorbell as a customer entered or left the shop.

It was almost noon before Andrew came back into the kitchen. There was something different in his face. He looked thoughtful. And walking right behind him was someone else!

I came to my feet, ready to run, but the back door was locked and the two men were between me and the other doorway. Then I recognized the stranger and relaxed. It was Brother Peter, and he was carrying the Spook's bag and staff and our cloaks!

"It's all right, boy," Andrew said, walking up
and laying his hand on my shoulder in reassurance.
"Take that anxious look off your face and sit yourself back down. Brother Peter is a friend. Look, he's
brought you John's things."

He smiled and handed me the bag, staff, and
cloaks. I accepted them with a nod of thanks and put
them in the corner before sitting down. Both men
pulled chairs out from the table and sat facing me.

Brother Peter was a man who'd spent most of
his life working in the open air, and the skin on his
head was weathered by the wind and sun to an even
shade of brown. He was as tall as Andrew but didn't
stand as upright. His back and shoulders were bent,
perhaps with too many years working away at the
earth with a trowel or hoe. His nose was his most
distinctive feature; it was hooked like a crow's beak,
but his eyes were set wide apart and had a kindly
twinkle. My instincts told me that he was a good
man.

"Well," he said, "you were lucky it was me doing
the rounds last night and not one of the others, or
you'd have found yourself back in that cell! As it
was, Father Cairns summoned me just after dawn

and I'd a few awkward questions to answer. He wasn't happy and I'm not sure that he's finished with me yet!"

"I'm sorry," I said.

Brother Peter smiled. "Don't worry, lad. I'm just a gardener with a reputation for being hard of hearing. He won't bother himself for long about me. Not when the Quisitor's got so many others ready for burning!"

"Why did you let me escape?" I asked.

Brother Peter raised his eyebrows. "Not all priests are under the control of the Bane. I know he's your cousin," he said, turning to Andrew, "but I don't trust Father Cairns. I think the Bane may have got to him."

"I've been thinking as much myself," said Andrew. "John was betrayed, and I'm sure the Bane must have been behind it all. It knows John's a threat to it, so it got that weak cousin of ours to get rid of him."

"Aye, I think you're right. Did you notice his hand? He says it's bandaged because he burned himself on a candle, but Father Hendle had an injury in a similar place after the Bane got to him. I think Cairns has given that creature his blood."

I must have looked horrified because Brother Peter came over and put an arm around my shoulders. "Don't worry, son. There are still some good men left in that cathedral, and I may just be a lowly brother, but I count myself one of them and do the Lord's work whenever I can. I'll do everything in my power to help you and your master. The dark hasn't won yet! So let's get down to business. Andrew tells me that you're brave enough to go down into the catacombs. Is that right?" he asked, rubbing the end of his nose thoughtfully.

"Somebody has to do it, so I'm willing to try," I told him.

"And what if you come face-to-face with . . ."

He didn't finish the sentence. It was almost as if he couldn't bring himself to say "the Bane."

"Has anyone told you what you could be facing? About the shape-shifting, and the mind reading and the . . ." He hesitated and looked over his shoulder before whispering, "Pressing?"

"Yes, I've heard," I said, sounding a lot more confident than I felt. "But there are things I could do. It doesn't like silver. . . ."

I unlocked the Spook's bag, reached into it and showed them the silver chain. "I could bind it with this," I said, staring straight into Brother Peter's eyes and trying not to blink.

The two men looked at each other, and Andrew smiled. "Practiced a lot, have you?" he asked.

"For hours and hours," I told him. "There's a post in Mr. Gregory's garden at Chipenden. I can cast this chain at it from eight feet away and drop it clean over it nine times out of ten."

"Well, if you could somehow get past that creature and reach the presbytery tonight, one thing would be on your side. It would certainly be quieter than normal," Brother Peter said. "The death last night was at the cathedral, so the body's already here, rather than out of town. Tonight nearly all the priests will be in there keeping a vigil."

From my Latin lessons I knew that "vigil" meant "awake." It still didn't tell me what they'd be up to.

"They say prayers and watch over the body," Andrew said, smiling at the puzzlement on my face. "Who was it who died, Peter?"

"Poor Father Roberts. Took his own life. Threw himself from the roof. That's five suicides this year already," he said, glancing at Andrew, then staring right back at me. "It gets inside their minds, you see. Makes them do things that are against God and against their conscience. And that's a very hard thing for a priest who's taken holy orders to serve God. So when he can't stand it any longer, he sometimes takes his own life, which is a mortal sin, and the priest knows he can never go to heaven, never be with God. Think how bad it must be to drive them to that! If only we could be rid of this terrible evil before there's nothing good left in the town for it to corrupt."

There was a short silence, as if we were all thinking, but then I saw Brother Peter's mouth moving and I thought that he might be praying for the poor dead priest. When he made the sign of the cross, I was sure of it. Then the two men glanced at each other and they both nodded. Without speaking, they'd reached an agreement.

"I'll go with you as far as the Silver Gate," Andrew said. "After that, Brother Peter here might be able to help . . ."

Was Brother Peter going with us? He must have read the expression on my face because he held up both hands, smiled, and shook his head.

"Oh, no, Tom. I lack the courage to go anywhere near the catacombs. No, what Andrew means is that I can help in another way: by giving you directions. You see, there's a map of the tunnels. It's mounted in a frame just inside the presbytery entrance — the one that leads directly to the garden. I've lost count of the hours I've spent waiting there for one of the priests to come down and give me my duties for the day. Over the years I've gotten to know every inch of that map. Do you want to write this down, or can you remember it?"

"I've got a good memory," I told him.

"Well, just tell me if you want me to repeat anything. As Andrew said, he'll guide you as far as the Silver Gate. Once through it, just keep going until the tunnel forks. Follow the left-hand passage until you reach some steps. They lead up to a door, beyond which is the big wine cellar of the presbytery. It'll be locked, but that should cause no problem at all when you've a friend like Andrew. There's only one other door that leads from the cellar, and it's on the far wall in the right-hand corner."

"But can't the Bane follow me through into the wine cellar and escape?" I asked.

"No—it can only leave the catacombs through the Silver Gate, so you're quite safe from it once you've gone through the door into the wine cellar. Now, before you leave the cellar there's something you should do. There's a trapdoor in the ceiling to the left of the door. It leads up to the path that runs along the north wall of the cathedral—the deliverymen use it to get the wine and ale down there. Unlock it before you go any farther. It should prove a faster escape route than going back to the gate. Is that clear so far?"

"Wouldn't it be a lot easier to use that trapdoor to get down?" I asked. "That way I could avoid the Silver Gate and the Bane!"

"I only wish it were so easy," said Brother Peter. "But it's too risky. The door is visible from the road and from the presbytery. Someone might see you going in."

I nodded thoughtfully.

"Although you can't use it to get in, there's another good reason why you should try to get out that way," Andrew said. "I don't want John to risk coming face-to-face with the Bane again. You see, deep down I think he's afraid—so afraid that he couldn't possibly win—"

"Afraid?" I asked indignantly. "Mr. Gregory's not afraid of anything that belongs to the dark."

"Not so as he'd admit it," continued Andrew. "I'll give you that, all right. He probably wouldn't even admit it to himself. But he was cursed long ago and—"

"Mr. Gregory doesn't believe in curses," I interrupted again. "He told you that."

"If you'll let me get a word in edgeways, I'll explain," insisted Andrew. "This was a dangerous and powerful curse. As big as they ever get. Three whole covens of Pendle witches came together to do it. John had been interfering too much in their business, so they put aside their own quarrels and grievances and cursed him. It was a blood sacrifice, and innocents were slaughtered. It happened on Walpurgis Night, the eve of the first of May, twenty years ago, and afterward they sent it to him on a piece of parchment splattered with blood. He once told me what was written there: *You will die in a dark place, far underground, with no friend at your side!*"

"The catacombs . . ." I said, my voice hardly more than a whisper. If he faced the Bane alone down in the catacombs, then the conditions of the curse would be fulfilled.

"Aye, the catacombs," Andrew said. "As I said, get him away through the hatch. Anyway, Brother Peter, sorry to have interrupted. . . ."

Peter gave a bleak smile and continued. "Once you've unlocked the hatch, go through the door into a corridor. This is the risky part. There's a cell at the far end that they use to hold prisoners. That's where you should find your master. But to get to it, you'll have to pass the guardroom. It's a dangerous business, but it's damp and chilly down there. They'll have a big fire blazing away in the grate and, if God's willing, the door will be closed against the cold. So there you have it! Release Mr. Gregory and get him out through the trapdoor and away from this town. He'll have to come back and deal with that foul creature another time, when the Quisitor's gone."

"Nay!" said Andrew. "After all this I wouldn't have him coming back here."

"But if he doesn't fight the Bane, then who can?"

asked Brother Peter. "I don't believe in curses either. With God's help, John can defeat that evil spirit. You know it's getting worse. No doubt I'll be next."

"Not you, Brother Peter," Andrew said. "I've met few men as strong-minded as you."

"I do my best," he said, shuddering. "When I hear it whispering inside my head, I just pray harder. God gives us the strength we need—that's if we've the sense to ask for it. But something has to be done. I don't know how it's all going to end."

"It'll end when the townsfolk have had enough," said Andrew. "You can only push people so far. I'm surprised they've stood the Quisitor's wickedness for so long. Some of those for burning have relatives and friends here."

"Maybe and maybe not," said Brother Peter. "There are lots of people who love a burning. We can only pray."

CHAPTER IX
The Catacombs

BROTHER Peter went back to his duties at the cathedral while we waited for the sun to go down. Andrew told me that the best way into the catacombs was through the cellar of an abandoned house close to the cathedral; we were less likely to be noticed after dark.

As the hours passed, I began to grow more and more nervous. When talking to Andrew and Brother Peter, I'd tried to sound confident, but the Bane really scared me. I kept rummaging through the Spook's bag, looking for anything that might be of some help.

Of course, I took the long silver chain that he used to bind witches and tied it around my waist, hidden under my shirt. But I knew it was one thing to be able to cast it over a wooden post and quite another to do it to the Bane. Next were salt and iron. After transferring my tinderbox to my jacket pocket, I filled my breeches pockets—the right pocket with salt, the left with iron. The combination worked against most things that haunted the dark. That was how I'd finally dealt with the old witch Mother Malkin.

I couldn't see it being enough to finish off something as powerful as the Bane; if it had been, the Spook would have dealt with it last time, once and for all. However, I was desperate enough to try anything, and just having that and the silver chain made me feel better. After all, I wasn't planning to destroy the Bane this time, but to fend it off long enough to rescue my master.

At last, with the Spook's staff in my left hand and his bag with our cloaks in my right, I was following Andrew through the darkening streets in the direction of the cathedral. Above, the sky was heavy with clouds and it smelled as if rain wasn't very far away. I was learning to hate Priestown, with its narrow cobbled streets and walled backyards. I missed the fells and the wide open spaces. If only I were in Chipenden, back in the routine of my lessons with the Spook! It was hard to accept that my life there might be over.

As we approached the cathedral, Andrew led us into one of the narrow passages that ran between the backs of the terraced houses. He halted at a door, slowly lifted the latch, and nodded me through into the small yard. After closing the yard door carefully, he went up to the back door of the house, which was all in darkness.

A moment later he turned a key in the lock and we were inside. Locking the door behind us, he lit two candles and handed one to me.

"This house has been deserted for well over twenty years," he said, "and it'll stay like this, too, for as you've realized, those like my brother aren't welcome in this town. It's haunted by something pretty nasty, so most people keep well away, and even dogs avoid it."

He was right about there being something nasty in the house. The Spook had carved a sign on the inside of the back door.

It was the Greek letter gamma, which was used for either a ghast or a ghost. The number to the right was a one, meaning it was a ghost of the first rank, dangerous enough to push some people to the edge of insanity.

"His name was Matty Barnes," Andrew said, "and he murdered seven people in this town, maybe more. He had big hands and he used them to choke the life from his victims. They were mainly young women. They say he brought them back here and squeezed the life from them in this very room. Eventually one of the women fought back and stabbed him through the eye with a hat pin. He died slowly of blood poisoning. John was going to talk his ghost into moving on but thought better of it. He always intended to come back here one day and deal with the Bane and wanted to make sure this way down into the catacombs would still be available. Nobody wants to buy a haunted house."

Suddenly I felt the air grow colder, and our candle flames began to flicker. Something was close by and getting nearer by the second. Before I could take another breath, it arrived. I couldn't actually see it, but I sensed something lurking in the shadows in the far corner of the kitchen—something staring at me hard.

That I couldn't actually see it made things worse. The most powerful of ghosts can choose whether or not to make themselves visible. The ghost of Matty Barnes was showing me just how strong it was by keeping hidden, yet letting me know that it was watching me. What's more, I could sense its malevolence. It wished us ill, and the sooner we were out of there the better.

"Am I imagining it, or has it suddenly gotten very chilly in here?" asked Andrew.

"It's cold, all right," I said, not mentioning the presence of the ghost. There was no need to make him more nervous than he already was.

"Then let's move on," Andrew said, leading the way toward the cellar steps.

The house was typical of many terraced houses in the County's towns: a simple two rooms upstairs and two rooms down, with an attic under the eaves. And the cellar door in the kitchen was in exactly the same position as the one in Horshaw, where the Spook had taken me on the first night after I'd become his apprentice. That house had been haunted by a ghast, and to see if I was up to doing the job the Spook had ordered me to go down to the cellar at midnight. It wasn't a night I'd forget; thinking about it now still made me shiver.

Andrew and I followed the steps down into the cellar. The flagged floor was empty but for a pile of old rugs and carpets. It seemed dry enough, but there was a musty smell. Andrew handed me his candle, then quickly dragged the rugs away to reveal a wooden trapdoor.

"There's more than one way into the catacombs," he said, "but this is the easiest and the least risky. You're not likely to get many folk nosing about down here."

He lifted the trapdoor, and I could see stone steps descending into the darkness. There was a smell of damp earth and rot. Andrew took the candle from me and went down first, telling me to wait for a moment. Then he called up, "Down you come, but leave the trap open. We might have to get out of here in a hurry!"

I left the Spook's bag, with the cloaks, in the cellar and followed him, still clutching my master's staff. When I got down, to my surprise I found myself standing on cobbles rather than the mud I'd expected. The catacombs were as well paved as the streets above. Had these been made by the people who'd lived here before the town was built, those who'd worshipped the Bane? If so, the cobbled streets of Priestown had been copied from those of the catacombs.

Andrew set off without another word, and I had a feeling he wanted to get the whole thing over with. I know I did.

At first the tunnel was wide enough for two people to walk side by side, but the cobbled roof was low and Andrew was forced to walk with his head bowed forward. No wonder the Spook had called them the Little People. The builders had certainly been a lot smaller than folk were now.

We'd not gone very far before the tunnel began to narrow; in places it was distorted, as if the weight of the cathedral and the buildings far above were squashing it out of shape. There the cobbles that also lined the roof and walls had fallen away, allowing mud and slime to seep through and ooze down the walls. There was a sound of dripping water in the distance and the echo of our boots on the cobbles.

Soon the passage narrowed even further. I was forced to walk behind Andrew, and our path forked into two even smaller tunnels. After we'd taken the left-hand one, we came to a recess in the wall on our left. Andrew paused and held his candle up so that it lit part of the interior. I stared in horror at what I saw. There were rows of shelves, and they were filled with bones: skulls with eyeless sockets, leg bones, arm bones, finger bones, and bones I didn't recognize, all different sizes, all mixed up. And all human!

"The catacombs are full of crypts like this," Andrew said. "Wouldn't do to get lost down here in the dark."

The bones were small, too, like those of children. They were the remains of the Little People, all right.

We moved on, and soon I could hear fast-flowing water ahead. We turned a corner and there it was, more a small river than a stream.

"This flows under the main street in front of the cathedral," Andrew said, pointing toward the dark water, "and we cross there. . . ."

Stepping-stones, nine in all, broad, smooth, and flat, but each of them only just above the surface of the water.

Once again Andrew led the way, striding effortlessly from stone to stone. At the other side he paused and turned back to watch me complete my crossing.

"It's easy tonight," he said, "but after heavy rain the water level can be well above the stones. Then there's a real danger of being swept away."

We walked on, and the sound of rushing water began to recede into the distance.

Andrew halted suddenly, and I could see over his shoulder that we'd come to a gate. But what a gate! I'd never seen one like it. From floor to ceiling, wall to wall, a grille of metal blocked the tunnel completely, metal that gleamed in the light of Andrew's candle. It seemed to be an alloy that contained a lot of silver, and it had been fashioned by a blacksmith of great skill. Each bar was made up not of solid cylindrical metal, but of several much thinner bars, twisted around to form a spiral. The design was very complex: Patterns and shapes were suggested, but the more I looked the more they seemed to change.

Andrew turned and put his hand on my shoulder. "This is it, the Silver Gate. So listen," he said, "this is important. Is there anything near? Anything from the dark?"

"I don't think so," I said.

"That's not good enough," Andrew snapped, his voice harsh. "You've got to be sure! If we let this creature escape, it'll terrorize the whole County, not just the priests."

Well, I didn't feel the cold, the usual warning that something from the dark was near. So that was one sign that everything was safe. But the Spook had always told me to trust my instincts, so to make doubly sure I took a deep breath and concentrated hard.

Nothing. I sensed nothing at all.

"It's all clear," I told Andrew.

"You sure? You're really sure?"

"I'm sure."

Andrew suddenly dropped to his knees and reached into the pocket of his breeches. There was a small, curved door in the grille, but its tiny lock was very close to the ground, and that was why Andrew was bent so low. Very carefully he was easing the tiniest of keys into the lock. I remembered the huge key displayed on the wall of his workshop.

You would have thought that the bigger the key, the more important it was, but here the opposite was true. What could be more important than the minute key that Andrew now held in his hand? This one had kept the whole County safe from the Bane.

He seemed to struggle and kept positioning and repositioning the key. At last it turned, and Andrew opened the gate and stood up.

"Still want to do this?" he asked.

I nodded, then knelt down, pushed the staff through the open gate, and followed it, crawling on all fours. Immediately Andrew locked the gate behind me and poked the key through the grille. I put it inside my left breeches pocket, pushing it down into the iron filings.

"Good luck," Andrew said. "I'll go back to the cellar and wait for an hour in case you come back this way for some reason. If you don't appear, I'll head home. Wish I could do more to help. You're a brave lad, Tom. I truly wish I'd the courage to go with you."

I thanked him, turned, and carrying the staff in my left hand and the candle in my right, set off into the darkness alone. Within moments the full horror of what I was undertaking descended upon me. Was I mad? I was now in the Bane's lair, and it could appear at any moment. What had I been thinking? It might already know that I was here!

But I took a deep breath and reassured myself with the thought that as it hadn't rushed to the Silver Gate when Andrew unlocked it, it couldn't be all-knowing. And if the catacombs were as extensive as people claimed, then at that very moment the Bane might be miles away. Anyway, what else could I do but keep walking forward? The lives of the Spook and Alice both depended on what I did.

I walked for about a minute before I came to two branching tunnels. Remembering what Brother Peter had told me, I chose the left one. The air around me grew colder, and I sensed that I was no longer alone. In the distance, beyond the light of the candle, there were small, faint, luminous shapes flitting like bats, in and out of crypts along the tunnel walls. As I approached them, they disappeared. They didn't get too near, but I felt certain that they were the ghosts of some of the Little People. The ghosts didn't bother me much; it was the Bane that I couldn't get out of my mind.

I came to the corner and, as I turned, following it to the left, I felt something underfoot and almost tripped. I'd stepped on something soft and sticky.

I moved back and lifted my candle to get a better look. What I saw started my knees shaking and the candle dancing in my trembling hand. It was a dead cat. But it wasn't the fact that it was dead that bothered me; it was the way it had died.

No doubt it had found its way down into the catacombs in search of rats or mice, but it had met with a terrible end. It was lying on its belly, its eyes bulging. The poor animal had been squashed so flat that at no point was its body any thicker than an inch. It had been smeared into the cobbles, but its protruding tongue was still glistening, so it couldn't have been dead very long. I shuddered with horror. It had been pressed, all right. If the Bane found me, that would surely be my fate, too.

I moved on quickly, glad to leave that terrible sight behind, and at last I came to the foot of a flight of stone steps that led up to a wooden door. If Brother Peter was right, behind that was the wine cellar of the priests' house.

I climbed to the top of the steps and used the

Spook's key. A moment later I was easing the door open. Once inside the cellar, I closed it behind me but didn't lock it.

The cellar was very large, with huge barrels of ale and row upon row of dusty wine racks filled with bottles, some of which had clearly been there a long time—they were covered with spiders' webs. It was deadly silent down here, and unless somebody was hiding and watching me, it seemed completely deserted. Of course, the candle only illuminated the small area around me, and beyond the nearest barrels was a darkness that could have hidden anything.

Before he'd left Andrew's house, Brother Peter had told me that the priests only came down into the cellar once a week to collect the wine they needed and that most of them wouldn't dream of going down into the catacombs because of the Bane. But he couldn't promise the same for the Quisitor's men: They weren't local and didn't know enough to be fearful. Not only that, they'd help themselves to the ale and probably wouldn't be content with just one barrel.

I crossed the length of the cellar cautiously, pausing every ten strides or so to listen. At last I could see the door that led to the corridor, and there, in the ceiling to the left, right up against the wall, was a large wooden hatch. We had a similar hatch back home. Our farm had once been called Brewer's Farm because it had supplied ale to neighboring taverns and farms. As Brother Peter had explained, this trapdoor was used to get barrels and crates in and out of the cellar without the bother of going through the presbytery. And he was right in saying that it would be the easiest way of escaping. If I did use it I'd certainly run the risk of being spotted, but going back toward the Silver Gate would mean possibly facing the Bane, and after being locked up the Spook wouldn't be strong enough to deal with it. Not only that, there was the Spook's curse to think about. Whether he believed in it or not, it wasn't worth tempting fate.

There were big barrels of ale standing on end directly under the hatch. Resting the candle on one and setting the staff to one side, I climbed up onto another and was able to reach the lock, which was set into the wooden hatch so that it could be locked or unlocked from either side. It was simple enough

CURSE OF THE BANE

and the Spook's key worked again, but I left the hatch closed for now in case someone spotted it from above.

I unfastened the door to the corridor just as easily, turning the key very slowly so as not to make any noise. It made me realize how lucky the Spook was to have a locksmith for a brother.

Next I eased open the door and stepped through into a long, narrow, flagged corridor. It was deserted, but about twenty steps ahead, on the right, I could see a flickering torch in a wall bracket above a closed door. It had to be the guardroom that Brother Peter had warned me about. Farther down the corridor was a second door, and beyond it stone steps that must lead up to the rooms above.

I walked slowly down the corridor toward the first door, almost on tiptoe and keeping to the shadows. Once close to the guardroom, I could hear sounds coming from within. Somebody coughed, somebody laughed, and there was the murmur of voices.

Suddenly my heart was set racing. I'd heard a deep voice very close to the door, but before I could hide, the door was flung open with some force. It almost hit me, but I stepped back behind it quickly and flattened myself against the rough stones of the wall. Heavy boots stepped out into the corridor.

"I must get back to my work," said a voice that I recognized. It was the Quisitor, and he was talking to someone who was standing just inside the doorway!

"Send someone to collect Brother Peter," he continued, "and have him brought to me when I've finished with the other. Father Cairns may have lost us a prisoner, but he knew who was to blame, I'll say that for him. And at least he had the good sense to report it to me. Bind our good brother's hands tightly behind his back, and don't be gentle. Make the cord cut into his flesh so that he knows exactly what he's facing! It'll be more than a few harsh words, you can be sure of that. Hot irons'll soon loosen his tongue!"

By way of answer there came a burst of loud, cruel laughter from the guards. Then the Quisitor's long black cloak billowed out behind him in the draft as he closed the door and walked quickly toward the steps at the far end of the corridor.

If he turned around, he'd see me right away! For a moment I thought he was going to stop outside the prisoners' cell, but to my relief he continued up the steps and out of sight.

Poor Brother Peter. He was going to be questioned, but there was no way I could warn him. And I'd been the prisoner the Quisitor had referred to. They were going to torture him because he'd let me go free! And not only that—Father Cairns had told the Quisitor about me. Now that he had the Spook, the Quisitor would probably come looking for me, too. I had to rescue my master before it was too late for both of us.

I almost made a big mistake then, intending to approach the cell; however, just in time I realized that the Quisitor's order would be carried out immediately. Sure enough, the guardroom door opened again, and two men came out brandishing clubs and strode away toward the steps.

When the door was again closed from within, I was in full view, but my luck held once more and the guards didn't turn around. After they'd climbed up the steps and out of sight, I waited for a few moments until the echo of their distant boots had faded away and my heart had stopped pounding so loudly. It was then that I heard other voices from the cell ahead. Someone was crying; another chanted in prayer. I rushed in the direction of the sound until I reached a heavy metal door, its top third formed of vertical metal bars.

I held the candle right up close to the bars and peered inside. In the flickering light the cell looked really bad but smelled even worse. There were about twenty people cramped into that small space. Some were lying on the floor and seemed to be asleep. Others were sitting with their backs against the wall. A woman was standing close to the door, and it was her voice that I'd heard. I'd assumed she was praying, but she was chanting gibberish and her eyes were rolling in her head as if what she'd gone through had driven her insane.

I couldn't see the Spook and I couldn't see Alice, but that didn't mean they weren't inside. These were the prisoners, all right. The prisoners of the Quisitor, ready for burning.

Wasting no time, I laid down the staff, unlocked the door, and opened it slowly. I wanted to go in and look for the Spook and Alice, but even before the door was fully open the woman who'd been chanting moved forward and blocked my way.

She shouted something out, spitting her words into my face. I couldn't understand what she said, but it was so loud it made me glance back in the direction of the guardroom. Within seconds, others were at her back, pushing her out into the corridor. There was a girl to her left, no more than a year older than Alice. She had big brown eyes and a kind face, so I appealed to her.

"I'm looking for someone," I said, my voice hardly more than a whisper.

Before I could say anything else, she opened her lips wide as if to speak, revealing two rows of teeth, some broken, others black with decay. Instead of words, loud, wild laughter erupted from her throat, and she immediately set off an uproar from the others around her. These people had been tortured and had spent days or even weeks under the threat of death. It was no good appealing to reason or asking for calm. Fingers jabbed at me, and a big, gangling man with long limbs and wild eyes grabbed my left hand hard and began to pump it up and down in gratitude.

"Thank you! Thank you!" he cried, and his grip became so tight that I thought he would crunch my bones.

I managed to snatch my hand free, pick up the staff, and retreat a few steps. Any moment now the guards would hear the commotion and come out into the corridor to investigate. What if the Spook and Alice weren't in that cell? What if they were being held somewhere else?

It was too late now because, pushed roughly from behind, I was already retreating past the guard-room, and a few seconds more brought me to the door of the wine cellar. I glanced back and saw a line of people following me. At least nobody was shouting now, but there was still too much noise for my liking. I just hoped that the guards had been drinking heavily. They'd probably be used to noise from the prisoners; they wouldn't be expecting a breakout.

Once inside the wine cellar, I climbed onto a barrel and balanced there while I quickly pushed the hatch upward. Through the open hatch I glimpsed a stone buttress of the cathedral's outer wall, and there was a rush of cool air and dampness on my face. It was raining hard.

Other people were clambering up onto the barrels. The man who'd thanked me elbowed me aside roughly and started to pull himself up through the hatch. Moments later he was out, holding a hand down to me, offering to pull me up.

"Come on!" he hissed.

I hesitated. I wanted to see if the Spook and Alice had gotten out of the cell. Then it was too late, because a woman had clambered up onto the barrel beside me and was raising her arms toward the man who, without a moment's hesitation, gripped her wrists, and pulled her up through the open hatch.

After that I'd missed my chance. There were others, some almost fighting among themselves in their desperation to get out. Not everyone was like that, though. Another man pushed a barrel onto its side and rolled it against the upright one to form a step that made it easier to climb. He helped an old woman up and steadied her legs while the man above gripped her wrists and drew her slowly upward.

Prisoners were getting out through the hatch, but others were still coming through the door into the wine cellar and I kept glancing toward them, hoping that one would be the Spook or Alice.

A thought suddenly struck me. What if one of

them was too ill or weak to move and hadn't been able to leave the cell?

I had no choice. I had to go back and see. I jumped down from the barrel, but it was too late: a shout, then angry voices. Boots thundering along the corridor. A big burly guard pushed into the cellar brandishing a cudgel. He looked around and, with a bellow of anger, rushed directly toward me.

CHAPTER X
Girl Spit

WITHOUT a second's hesitation I grabbed the staff and blew out the candle, plunging the cellar into darkness, then moved quickly in the direction of the door that led down into the catacombs.

There was a terrible commotion behind: shouts, screams, and the sounds of a struggle. Glancing back, I saw another of the guards carrying a torch into the cellar, so I slipped behind the wine racks, keeping them between me and the light as I headed for the door in the far wall.

I felt terrible leaving the Spook and Alice behind. To have come this far and still be unable to rescue them left me feeling wretched. I only hoped that somehow in the confusion they'd managed to get out. They could both see well in the dark, and if I could manage to find the door to the catacombs, so could they. I sensed some of the prisoners moving with me, away from the guards into the dark recesses of the cellar. A few seemed to be in front of me. Perhaps among them were my master and Alice, but I couldn't risk calling out and alerting the guards. As I picked my way through the wine racks, ahead of me I thought I saw the door to the catacombs open and close quickly, but it was too dark to be sure.

A few moments later I was through the door. The instant I closed it behind me, I was plunged into a darkness so intense that, for a few seconds, I couldn't see my hand before my face. I stood there at the top of the steps, waiting desperately for my eyes to adjust.

As soon as I could make out the steps, I went down carefully and moved along the tunnel as quickly as I could, aware that, eventually, someone would probably check the door: I hadn't locked it behind me just in case Alice or the Spook were close behind.

I'm usually good at seeing in the dark, but in

those catacombs it seemed to be getting darker and darker, so I came to a halt and tugged the tinderbox out of my jacket pocket. I knelt down and shook a small pile of tinder out onto the stones. Quickly I used the stone and metal to create a spark, and a few seconds later I'd managed to light my candle.

With candlelight to guide me I made better progress, but the air around me grew colder with every step, and not far ahead I could see sinister flickerings on the wall. Again, white luminous shapes were moving in and out of the shadows, but there were now far more than last time. The dead were gathering. My previous walk along the tunnels had disturbed them.

I stopped. What was that? Somewhere in the distance I'd heard the howl of a dog. I came to a halt, my heart pounding. Was it a real dog, or could it be the Bane? Andrew had mentioned a huge black dog with ferocious teeth. A huge dog that was really the Bane. I tried to tell myself it was a real dog I was hearing, one that had somehow found its way down into the catacombs. After all, if a cat could do it, why not a dog?

The howl came again, and it hung in the air for

a long time, echoing and reverberating down the long tunnels. Was it ahead of me or behind? In this tunnel or another one? It was impossible to say. But with the Quisitor and his men behind me, I had no choice but to keep moving toward the gate.

So I walked quickly, shivering with cold, skirting the pressed cat, till I reached the point where the forked tunnels merged. At last I rounded a corner and saw the Silver Gate. There I halted, my knees beginning to shake, my mind afraid to go on. For ahead, in the darkness beyond the candle flame, someone was waiting for me. A shadowy figure was sitting on the floor near the gate, its back against the wall, its head bowed forward. Could it be an escaped prisoner? Someone who'd gotten through the door before me?

I couldn't go back, so I took a few steps toward the gate and held the candle higher. A bearded face turned to me.

"What kept you?" called out a voice I recognized. "I've been waiting here five minutes already!"

It was the Spook, alive and well! I rushed forward, filled with relief that he'd managed to escape. There was an ugly bruise over his left eye and his mouth was swollen. He'd clearly been beaten.

"Are you all right?" I asked anxiously.

"Aye, lad. Give me a few more moments to get my breath back and I'll be right as rain. Just get that gate open and we'll soon be on our way."

"Was Alice with you?" I asked. "Were you in the same cell?"

"No, lad. Best forget all about her. She's no good. Nowt but trouble, and there's nothing we can do to help her now." His voice sounded cruel and hard. "She deserves what's coming to her."

"Burning?" I asked. "You've never held with burning a witch, let alone a young girl, and you told Andrew yourself that she's innocent."

I was shocked. He'd never trusted Alice, but it hurt me to hear him talk that way, especially as he'd faced such a terrible fate himself. And what about Meg? He hadn't always been so cold and heartless. . . .

"For goodness' sake, lad, are you dreaming or awake?" the Spook demanded, his voice full of annoyance and impatience. "Come on, snap out of it! Get the key and open that gate."

When I hesitated, he held out his hand toward me. "Give me my staff, lad. I've been in that damp cell far too long and my old bones are aching tonight. . . ."

I reached out to hand it to him, but as his fingers began to close around it, I suddenly backed away in horror.

It wasn't just the sudden shock of his hot, foul-smelling breath searing up into my face. It was because he was holding out his right hand toward me! His right hand, not his left!

It wasn't the Spook! This wasn't my master!

As I watched, frozen to the spot, his hand dropped back to his side, then, like a snake, began to writhe toward me over the cobbles. Before I could move, his arm slithered and stretched to twice its normal length and his hand closed upon my ankle, holding it in a tight, painful grip. My immediate reaction was to try and drag it away from his dreadful grasp, but I knew that wasn't the way. I kept perfectly still.

I tried to concentrate. I gripped the staff and tried to curb my fear, remembered to breathe. I was terrified, but although my body wasn't moving, my mind was. There was only one explanation and it made me shudder with terror: I was facing the Bane!

Forcing myself to focus, I studied the thing before me carefully, looking hard for anything that might help me in the slightest way. It looked just like the Spook and sounded like him, too. It was impossible to tell the difference, but for the snaking hand.

After watching for a few seconds, I felt a little better. It was a trick the Spook had taught me: when face-to-face with our greatest fears, we should concentrate hard and leave our feelings behind.

"Gets them every time, lad!" he'd once told me. "The dark feeds on fear, and with a calm mind and an empty belly the battle's half won before you even start."

And it was working. My body had stopped shaking and I felt calmer, almost relaxed.

The Bane released my ankle, and the hand slithered back to its side. The creature stood up and took a step toward me. As it did so I heard a curious noise: not the sound of boots I was expecting, more like the scratching of huge claws against the cobbles. The Bane's movement disturbed the air, too, so that the candle flame flickered, distorting the shadow of the Spook cast against the Silver Gate.

Quickly I knelt and placed the candle and the

staff on the floor between us. An instant later I was on my feet, my hands in each of my breeches pockets, grabbing a fistful of salt and one of iron.

"Wasting your time, you are," said the Bane, its voice suddenly nothing like the Spook's at all. Harsh and deep, it reverberated through the very rocks of the catacombs, vibrating up through my boots and setting my teeth on edge. *"Old tricks like that won't get me. Been around too long, I have, to be hurt by that! Your master, Old Bones, tried it once, but it did him no good. No good at all."*

I hesitated, but only for a moment. It might just be lying—anything was worth a try. But then, among the iron filings, my left hand closed upon something hard. It was the small key to the Silver Gate. I couldn't risk losing that.

"Ahhh . . . got what I need, you have," said the Bane with a sly smile.

Had it read my mind? Or perhaps just read the expression on my face, or maybe guessed? Either way, it knew too much.

"Look," it said, a crafty look on its face, *"if Old Bones couldn't fix me, then what chance have you? No chance at all! Down here they'll come, and be searching*

for you soon. Can't you hear the guards now? Burn, you will! Burn with the rest! There's no way out from here but through this gate. No way at all, see. So use the key now before it's too late!"

The Bane stood to one side so that its back was against the tunnel wall. I knew exactly what it wanted: to follow me through the gate, to be free, able to work its mischief anywhere in the County. I knew what the Spook would say; what he'd expect from me. It was my duty to make sure the Bane stayed trapped in the catacombs. That was more important than my own life.

"Don't be a fool!" the Bane hissed, its voice again far louder and harsher than I'd ever heard the Spook's. *"Listen to me and free you'll be! And rewarded as well. A big reward. The same as I offered Old Bones many years ago, but he wouldn't listen. And where has it got him, see? Tell me that! Tomorrow he'll be tried and found guilty. The day after that he'll burn."*

"No!" I said. "I can't do it."

With that the Bane's face filled with anger. It still resembled the Spook, but the features I knew so well were distorted and twisted with evil. It took another step toward me, raising a fist. It might only have been a trick of the candlelight, but the creature seemed to be growing. And I could feel an invisible weight starting to press down on my head and shoulders. As I was forced to my knees, I thought of the cat smeared into the cobbles and realized that the same fate was awaiting me. I tried to suck in a breath, but I couldn't and began to panic. I couldn't breathe! This was it!

The light of the candle was lost in the sudden darkness that covered my eyes. I tried desperately to speak, to beg for mercy, but I knew there would be no mercy unless I unlocked the Silver Gate. What had I been thinking? What a fool I'd been to believe that with a few months' training I could fend off a creature as evil and powerful as the Bane! I was dying—I felt sure of it. Alone in the catacombs. And the worst of it was that I'd failed miserably. I hadn't managed to rescue my master or Alice.

Then I heard something in the distance: the sound of a shoe scuffing against the cobbles. They say that, as you die, the last sense to go is your hearing. And for a moment I thought that the scuffing of that shoe was the last experience I'd have of this life. But then the invisible weight crushing my body slowly eased.

My vision cleared and suddenly I could breathe again. I watched the Bane turn its head and look back toward the bend in the tunnel. The Bane had heard it, too!

The sound came again. This time there was no doubt. Footsteps! Someone was coming!

I looked back toward the Bane and saw that it was changing. I hadn't imagined it before. It was growing. By now its head had almost reached the top of the tunnel, the body curving forward, the face shifting until it was no longer that of the Spook. The chin was elongating, jutting outward and upward to form the beginning of a hook, and the nose was curving downward to meet it. Was it changing into its true form—that of the stone gargoyle above the main door of the cathedral? Had it gained its full strength?

I listened to the approaching footsteps. I would have blown the candle out, only that would have left me in the dark with the Bane. At least it sounded like there was only one person coming rather than a troop of the Quisitor's men. I didn't care who it was. He'd saved me for now.

I saw the feet first, as someone stepped round the

corner and into the candlelight. Pointy shoes, then a slim girl in a black dress and the swing of her hips as she came around the corner.

It was Alice!

She halted, glanced toward me quickly, and her eyes widened. When she looked up at the Bane, her face was angry rather than afraid.

I looked back, and for a moment the Bane's eyes met mine. As well as the anger blazing in them, I could see something else, but before I could work it out Alice ran toward the Bane, hissing like a cat. Then, to my astonishment, she spat up into its face.

What happened next was too quick to see. There was a sudden wind, and the Bane was gone.

We stood motionless for what seemed like a long time. Then Alice turned to face me.

"Didn't like girl spit much, did it?" she said with a faint smile. "Good job I came along when I did."

I didn't reply. I couldn't believe that the Bane had fled so easily, but I was already on my knees, struggling to fit the key into the lock of the Silver Gate. My hands were shaking, and it was just as difficult as it had looked when Andrew did it.

At last I managed to get the key into the right

position and it turned. I pushed the gate open, seized the key and the staff, and crawled through.

"Bring the candle!" I shouted back to Alice, and as soon as she was safely through, I slid the key into the other side of the lock and struggled to turn it. This time it seemed to take an age; at any moment I expected the Bane to come back.

"Can't you go any quicker?" Alice asked.

"It's not as easy as it looks," I told her.

Eventually I managed to lock it and let out a sigh of relief. Then I remembered the Spook.

"Was Mr. Gregory in the cell with you?" I asked.

Alice shook her head. "Not when you let us out. They took him away for questioning about an hour before you came."

I'd been lucky in managing to avoid capture. Lucky in getting the prisoners out of the cell. But luck has a way of balancing itself out. I'd been just an hour too late. Alice was free, but the Spook was still a prisoner, and unless I could do something about it, he was going to burn.

Wasting no more time, I led Alice along the tunnel until we came to the fast-flowing river.

I crossed quickly, but when I turned back, Alice

was still on the far bank, staring down at the water.

"It's deep, Tom," she cried. "It's too deep and the stones are slippery!"

I crossed back to where she was standing. Then, gripping her hand, I led her back across the nine flat stones. We soon reached the open hatch that led up into the empty house and, once inside the cellar, I closed the hatch behind us. To my disappointment, Andrew had already gone. I needed to talk to him, to tell him that the Spook hadn't been in the cell, warn him that Brother Peter was in danger and that the rumors really were true—the Bane's strength was back!

"We'd better stay down here for a while. The Quisitor will start searching the town once he realizes so many of you have escaped. This house is haunted—the last place anybody will want to look is down here in the cellar."

Alice nodded, and for the first time since the spring I looked at her properly. She was as tall as me, which meant that she'd grown at least an inch, too, but she was still dressed as I'd last seen her when I'd taken her to her aunt in Staumin. If it wasn't the same black dress, it was its twin.

Her face was as pretty as ever but thinner, and older, as though it had seen things that had forced it to grow up quickly; things that nobody should have to see. Her black hair was matted and filthy and there were smears of dirt on her face. Alice looked like she hadn't had a wash for at least a month.

"It's good to see you again," I said. "When I saw you in the Quisitor's cart, I thought that would be it."

She didn't reply. Just grabbed my hand and squeezed it. "I'm half starved, Tom. Ain't got anything to eat, have you?"

I shook my head.

"Not even a piece of that moldy old cheese?"

"Sorry," I said. "I've none left."

Alice turned away and seized one edge of the old carpet that was at the top of the heap.

"Help me, Tom," she said. "Need to sit down and I don't fancy the cold stones much."

I put the candle and staff down, and together we pulled the carpet onto the flags. The musty smell was stronger than ever, and I watched the beetles and wood lice that we'd uncovered scurrying away across the cellar floor.

Unconcerned, Alice sat down on the carpet and drew her knees up so that she could rest her chin. "One day I'm going to get even," she said. "Nobody deserves to be treated like that."

I sat down next to her and put my hand on hers. "What happened?" I asked.

She was silent for a while, and just as I'd decided she wasn't going to answer me, she suddenly spoke. "Once she got to know me, my old aunt was good to me. Worked me hard, she did, but always fed me well. I was just getting used to living there at Staumin when the Quisitor came. Took us by surprise and broke down the door. But my aunt weren't no Bony Lizzie. She weren't no witch.

"They swam her down at the pond at midnight while a big crowd watched, all laughing and jeering. Real scared I was, expecting it was my turn next. Tied her feet to her hands and threw her in. Sank like a stone, she did. But it was dark and windy and a big gust came the moment she hit the water; blew a lot of the torches out. Took a long time to find her and drag her out."

Alice buried her face into her hands and gave a sob. I waited quietly until she was able to go on.

When she uncovered her face, her eyes were dry but her lips were trembling.

"When they pulled her out, she was dead. It ain't fair, Tom. She didn't float, she sank, so she must have been innocent, but they'd killed her anyway! After that they left me alone and just put me up in the cart with the rest."

"My mam told me that swimming witches doesn't work anyway," I said. "Only fools use it."

"No, Tom, the Quisitor's no fool. There's a reason for everything he does, you can be sure of that. He's greedy. Greedy for money. He sold my old aunt's cottage and kept the money. We watched him counting it. That's what he does. Calls people witches, gets them out of the way, and takes their houses, land, and money. What's more, he enjoys his work. There's darkness in him. He says he's doing it to rid the County of witches, but he's more cruel than any witch I've ever known—and that's saying something.

"There was a girl called Maggie. Not much older than me, she was. Didn't bother with swimming her. Used a different test and we all had to watch. Quisitor used a long sharp pin. He kept sticking it into her body over and over again. You should have heard her shriek. Poor girl almost went mad with the pain. She kept fainting and they had a bucket of water by the side of the table to bring her round. But at last they found what they were looking for. The Devil's mark! Know what that is, Tom?"

I nodded. The Spook had told me that it was one of the things witchfinders used. But it was another lie, he'd said. There was no such thing as the Devil's mark. Anyone with true knowledge of the dark knew that.

"It's cruel and it ain't just," Alice continued. "After a bit the pain gets too much and your body goes numb, so eventually when the needle goes in you don't feel it. Then they say that's the spot where the Devil touched you, so you're guilty and have to burn. Worst thing was the look on the Quisitor's face. So pleased with himself, he was. I'll get even all right. I'll pay him back for that. Maggie don't deserve to burn."

"The Spook doesn't deserve to burn either!" I said bitterly. "All his life he's worked hard fighting the dark."

"He's a man and he'll get an easier death than

some," said Alice. "The Quisitor gives women a much harder time. Makes sure they take a long time to burn. Says it's harder to save a woman's soul than a man's. That they need a lot of pain to make them feel sorry for their sins."

That brought to mind what the Spook had said about the Bane not being able to abide women. The fact that they made it nervous.

"The creature you spat at was the Bane," I told her. "Have you heard of it? How did you manage to scare it away so easily?"

Alice shrugged. "Ain't too difficult to tell when something ain't comfortable having you around. Some men are like that—I always know when I'm not welcome. I get that feeling near Old Gregory, and it was the same down there. And spit sends most things on their way. Spit three times at a toad and nothing with cold damp skin will bother you for a month or more. Lizzie used to swear by it. Don't think it'll work that way on the Bane, though. Yes, I've heard about that creature. And if it's now able to shape-shift, then we're all in for some serious bother. I took it by surprise, that's all. It'll be ready next time, so I ain't going down there again."

For a while neither of us spoke. I just stared down at the musty old carpet, until suddenly I heard Alice's breathing deepen. When I looked back, her eyes were closed and she'd fallen asleep in the same position, her chin resting on her knees.

I didn't really want to blow the candle out, but I didn't know how long we'd have to stay down in the cellar and it was better to save some light until later.

Once it was out, I tried to get to sleep myself, but it was difficult. For one thing I was cold and kept shivering. For another, I couldn't get the Spook out of my mind. We'd failed to rescue him, and the Quisitor would be really angry at what had happened. It wouldn't be long before he started burning people.

Finally I must have drifted off because I was suddenly woken by the sound of Alice's voice, very close to my left ear.

"Tom," she said, her voice hardly more than a whisper, "there's something over there in the corner of the cellar with us. It's staring at me and I don't like it much."

Alice was right. I could sense something in the corner, and I felt cold. The hair on the back of my neck was beginning to rise. It was probably just Matty Barnes, the strangler, again.

"Don't worry, Alice," I told her. "It's just a ghost. Try and forget about it. As long as you're not afraid, it can't harm you."

"I ain't afraid. At least not now." She paused, then said, "But I was scared in that cell. Didn't sleep a wink, what with all that shouting and screaming. I'll soon be off to sleep again. It's just that I want it to go away. It ain't right, it staring like that."

"I don't know what to do next," I said, thinking about the Spook again.

Alice didn't reply, but her breathing deepened once more. She was asleep. And I must have gone back to sleep myself because a noise woke me up suddenly.

It was the sound of heavy boots. Someone was in the kitchen above us.

CHAPTER XI
The Spook's Trial

THE door creaked open and candlelight filled the room. To my relief it was Andrew.

"Thought I'd find you down here," he said. He was carrying a small parcel. As he put it down and placed the candle next to mine, he nodded toward Alice, who was still sleeping deeply but now lying on her side with her back to us, her face resting on her hands.

"So who's this, then?" he asked.

"She used to live near Chipenden," I told him. "Her name's Alice. Mr. Gregory wasn't there. They'd taken him upstairs for questioning."

Andrew shook his head sadly. "Brother Peter said as much. You couldn't have been more unlucky.

Half an hour later and John would've been back in the cell with the others. As it was, eleven got away, but five were caught again soon afterward. But there's more bad news. The Quisitor's men arrested Brother Peter in the street just after he'd left my shop. I saw it from the upstairs window. So that's me finished in this town. They'll probably come for me next, but I'm not sticking around to answer any questions. I've locked the shop up already. My tools are on the cart and I'm heading south, back toward Adlington, where I used to work."

"I'm sorry, Andrew."

"Well, don't be. Who wouldn't try to help his own brother? Besides, it's not that bad for me. The shop premises were only rented, and I've got a trade at my fingertips. I'll always find work. Here," he said, opening the parcel. "I've brought you some food."

"What time is it?" I asked.

"A couple of hours or so before dawn. I took a risk coming here. After all the commotion, half the town's awake. A lot of people have gone to the big hall down Fishergate. After what happened last night, the Quisitor's holding a quick trial for all the prisoners he's still got."

"Why doesn't he wait till daylight?" I asked.

"Even more people would attend then," Andrew answered. "Wants to get it over and done with before there's any real opposition. Some of the townsfolk are against what he's doing. As for the burning, it'll be tonight, after dark, on the beacon hill at Wortham, south of the river. The Quisitor will have a lot of armed men with him in case there's trouble, so if you've any sense, you'll stay here till nightfall, then be on the road and away."

Even before he managed to unwrap the parcel, Alice rolled toward us and sat up. Maybe she'd smelled the food or had been listening all the time, just pretending to be asleep. There were slices of ham, fresh bread, and two big tomatoes. Without a word of thanks to Andrew, Alice set to work right away, and after just a moment's hesitation I joined her. I was really hungry, and there didn't seem much point in fasting now.

"So I'll be off," said Andrew. "Poor John, but there's nothing we can do now."

"Isn't it worth having one last try to save him?" I asked.

"No, you've done enough. It's too dangerous to go anywhere near the trial. And soon poor John'll be with the rest, under armed guard and on the way to Wortham to be burned alive with all those other poor wretches."

"But what about the curse?" I said. "You said yourself he's cursed to die alone underground, not up on a beacon."

"Oh, the curse. I don't believe in that any more than John does. I was just desperate to stop him going after the Bane with the Quisitor in town. No, I'm afraid my brother's fate is sealed, so you just get yourself away. John once told me that there's a spook operating somewhere near Caster. He covers the County borders to the north. Mention John's name, and he might just take you on. He was once one of John's apprentices."

With a nod, Andrew turned to go. "I'll leave you the candle," he said. "Good luck on the road. And if you ever need a good locksmith, you'll know where to come."

With that he was gone. I listened to him climb the cellar steps and close the back door. A few moments later Alice was licking tomato juice from

her fingers. We'd eaten everything—not a crumb
was left.

"Alice," I said, "I want to go to the trial. There
might be a chance I can do something to help the
Spook. Will you come with me?"

Alice's eyes widened. "Do something? You
heard what he said. Ain't nothing to be done,
Tom! What can you do against armed men? No,
be sensible. Ain't worth the risk, is it? Besides,
why should I try to help? Old Gregory wouldn't
do the same for me. Leave me to burn, he would,
and that's a fact!"

I didn't know what to say to that. In a way it
was true. I'd asked the Spook about helping Alice
and he'd refused. So, with a sigh, I came to my
feet.

"I'm going anyway," I told her.

"No, Tom, don't leave me here. Not with the
ghost . . ."

"I thought you weren't scared."

"I ain't. But last time I fell asleep I felt it starting to squeeze my throat, I did. Might do worse if
you're not here."

"Come with me then. It won't be that dangerous

because it'll still be dark. And the best place to hide is in a big crowd. Come on, please. What do you say?"

"Got a plan?" she asked. "Something you ain't told me about?"

I shook my head.

"Thought as much," she said.

"Look, Alice, I just want to go and see. If I can't help we'll come away. But I'd never forgive myself if I didn't at least try."

Reluctantly, Alice stood up. "I'll come and see what's what," she said. "But you've got to promise me that if it's too dangerous we'll turn back right away. I know the Quisitor better than you do. Trust me, we shouldn't be messing around near him."

"I promise," I told her.

I left the Spook's bag and staff in the cellar and we set off for Fishergate, where the trial was being held.

Andrew had said that half the town was awake. That was an exaggeration, but for so early in the morning there were a lot of candles flickering behind curtains and quite a few people seemed to be hastening through the dark streets in the same direction as we were.

I'd half expected that we wouldn't be able to get anywhere near the building, thinking guards would be lining the road outside, but to my surprise none of the Quisitor's men were anywhere to be seen. The big wooden doors were wide open and a crowd of people filled the doorway, spilling out onto the road outside, as if there wasn't room for them all to fit inside.

I led the way forward cautiously, glad of the darkness. When I reached the back of the crowd, I realized that it wasn't as densely packed as it had first seemed. Inside the hall, the air was tainted with a sweet, sickly scent. It was just one big room with a flagged floor, across which sawdust was scattered unevenly. I couldn't see properly over the backs of the crowd because most of the people were taller than me, but there seemed to be a big space ahead that nobody wanted to move forward into. I grabbed Alice's hand and eased my way into the throng of people, tugging her along behind me.

It was dark toward the back of the hall, but the front was lit by two huge torches at each corner of a wooden platform. The Quisitor was standing at the front of it, looking down. He was saying something, but his voice sounded muffled.

I looked at those about me and saw the range of expressions on their faces: anger, sadness, bitterness, and resignation. Some looked openly hostile. This crowd was probably mainly composed of those who opposed the work of the Quisitor. Some of them might even be relatives and friends of the accused. For a moment that thought gave me hope that some sort of rescue might be attempted.

But then my hopes were dashed: I saw why nobody had moved forward. Below the platform were five long benches of priests with their backs to us, but behind them and facing toward us was a double line of grim-faced armed men. Some had their arms folded; others had hands on the hilts of their swords as if they couldn't wait to draw them from their scabbards. Nobody wanted to get too close to them.

I glanced up toward the ceiling and saw that a high balcony ran along the sides of the hall; faces were peering down, pale white ovals that all looked the same from the ground. That would be the safest place to be, and it would provide a much better view. There were steps to the left and I tugged Alice toward them. Moments later we were moving along the wide balcony.

It wasn't full, and we soon found ourselves a place against the rail about halfway between the doors and the platform. There was still the same sweet stench in the air, much stronger now than it had been when we were standing on the flags below. I suddenly realized what it was. The hall was almost certainly used as a meat market. It was the smell of blood.

The Quisitor wasn't the only person on the platform. Right at the back, in the shadows, a huddle of guards surrounded the prisoners awaiting trial, but immediately behind the Quisitor were two guards gripping a weeping prisoner by the arms. It was a tall girl with long dark hair. She was wearing a tattered dress and had no shoes.

"That's Maggie!" Alice hissed into my ear. "The one they kept sticking pins into. Poor Maggie, it ain't fair. Thought she'd got away . . ."

Up here the sound was much better, and I could hear every word the Quisitor spoke. "By her own lips this woman is condemned!" he called out, his voice loud and arrogant. "She has confessed all and the Devil's mark was found upon her flesh. I sentence her to be bound to the stake and burned alive. And may God have mercy upon her soul."

Maggie began to sob even louder, but one of her captors seized her by the hair and she was dragged away toward a doorway at the back of the platform. No sooner had she disappeared through it than another prisoner wearing a black cassock and with his hands bound behind his back was pulled forward into the torchlight. For a moment I thought I was mistaken, but there was no doubt.

It was Brother Peter. I knew him by the thin collar of white hair that fringed his bald head and by the curve of his back and shoulders. But his face was so badly beaten and streaked with blood that I hardly recognized it. His nose was broken, squashed back against his face, and one eye was closed to a swollen red slit.

Seeing him in that condition made me feel terrible. It was all because of me. To begin with, he'd allowed me to escape; later he'd told me how I could get to the cell to rescue the Spook and Alice. Under torture, he must have told them everything. It was all my fault, and I was racked with guilt.

"Once this was a brother, a faithful servant of the Church!" cried the Quisitor. "But look at him now! Look at this traitor! One who has helped our enemies and allied himself with the forces of darkness. We have his confession, written with his own hand. Here it is!" he shouted, holding up a piece of paper high for all to see.

Nobody got a chance to read it—it could have said anything at all. Even if it was a confession, one look at poor Brother Peter's face told me that it had been beaten out of him. It wasn't fair. There was no justice here. This wasn't a trial at all. The Spook had once told me that when people were tried in the castle at Caster, at least they got a hearing—a judge, a prosecutor, and someone to defend them. But here the Quisitor was doing it all himself!

"He is guilty. Guilty beyond all doubt," he continued. "I therefore sentence him to be taken down to the catacombs and left there. And may God have mercy on his soul!"

There was a sudden gasp of horror from the crowd, but it was loudest of all from the priests seated at the front. They knew exactly what Brother Peter's fate would be. He would be pressed to death by the Bane.

Brother Peter tried to speak, but his lips were too swollen. One of the guards cuffed him about the head while the Quisitor gave a cruel smile. They pulled him away toward the door at the rear of the platform, and no sooner had he been led out of the building than another prisoner was brought forward from the gloom. My heart sank into my boots. It was the Spook.

At first glance, apart from a few bruises on his face, the Spook didn't seem to have had as hard a time as Brother Peter. But then I noticed something more chilling. He was squinting into the torchlight and looked bewildered, with a vacant expression in his green eyes. He seemed lost. It was as if his memory had gone and he didn't even know who he was. I began to wonder just how badly he'd been beaten.

"Before you is John Gregory!" cried the Quisitor, his voice echoing from wall to wall. "A disciple of the Devil, no less, who for many years has plied his evil trade in this county, taking money from poor gullible folk. But does this man recant? Does he accept his sins and beg forgiveness? No, he is stubborn and will not confess. Now only through fire may he be purged and given hope of salvation. But furthermore, not content with the evil he can do, he has trained others and still continues to do so. Father Cairns, I ask you to stand and give testimony!"

From the front row of benches a priest stepped forward into the torchlight closer to the platform. He had his back to me so I couldn't see his face, but I spotted his bandaged hand, and when he spoke it was the same voice that I'd listened to in the confessional box.

"Lord Quisitor, John Gregory brought an apprentice with him on his visit to this town, one whom he has already corrupted. His name is Thomas Ward."

I heard Alice let out a low gasp and my own knees began to tremble. I was suddenly sharply aware of how dangerous it was to be here in the hall, so close to the Quisitor and his armed men.

"By the grace of God the boy fell into my hands," Father Cairns continued, "and, but for the intervention of Brother Peter, who allowed him to escape justice, I would have delivered him to you for questioning. But I did question him myself, lord, and found him to be hardened beyond his years and far beyond persuasion by mere words. Despite my best efforts, he failed to see the error of his ways, and for that we must blame John Gregory, a man not content with practicing his vile trade, one who actively corrupts the young. To my knowledge, over a score of apprentices have passed through his hands and some, in turn, now follow that same trade and have taken on apprentices of their own. By such means does evil spread like a plague through the County."

"Thank you, Father. You may be seated. Your testimony alone is enough to condemn John Gregory!"

As Father Cairns took his seat again, Alice gripped my elbow. "Come on," she whispered into my ear, "it's too dangerous to stay!"

"No, please," I whispered back. "Just a bit longer."

The mention of my name had scared me, but I wanted to stay a few more minutes to see what happened to my master.

"John Gregory, for you there can be only one

punishment!" roared the Quisitor. "You will be bound to a stake and burned alive. I will pray for you. I will pray that pain teaches you the error of your ways. I will pray that you beg God's forgiveness so that, as your body burns, your soul is saved."

The Quisitor stared at the Spook all the while he was ranting, but he might as well have been shouting at a stone wall. There was no understanding behind the Spook's eyes. In a way it was a mercy, because he didn't seem to know what was happening. But it made me realize that, even if I did somehow manage to rescue him, he might never be the same again.

A lump came to my throat. The Spook's house had become my new home, and I remembered the lessons, the conversations with the Spook, and even the scary times when we had to deal with the dark. I was going to miss all that, and the thought of my master being burned alive brought pricking tears to my eyes.

My mam had been right. At first I'd been doubtful about being the Spook's apprentice. I'd feared the loneliness. But she'd told me that I'd have the Spook to talk to; that although he was my teacher, eventually he'd become my friend. Well, I didn't know if that had happened yet, because he was still often stern and fierce, but I was certainly going to miss him.

As the guards dragged him toward the doorway, I nodded to Alice, and keeping my head down and not making eye contact with anybody, I led the way along the balcony and down the steps. Outside I could see that the sky was beginning to grow lighter. Soon we wouldn't have the cover of darkness and someone might recognize one of us. The streets were already busier and the crowd outside the hall had more than doubled since we'd been inside. I pushed through the throng so that I could look down the side of the building, toward the door the prisoners had been taken through.

One glance told me that the situation was hopeless. I couldn't see any prisoners, but that wasn't surprising because there must have been at least twenty guards near the doorway. What chance did we have against so many? With my heart in my boots I turned to Alice. "Let's get back," I said. "There's nothing to be done here."

I was anxious to reach the safety of the cellar, so we walked quickly. Alice followed me without a word.

CHAPTER XII
The Silver Gate

ONCE back in the cellar, Alice turned to me, her eyes blazing with anger.

"It ain't fair, Tom! Poor Maggie. She doesn't deserve to burn. None of 'em do. Something's got to be done."

I shrugged and just stared into space, my mind numb. Soon Alice lay back and fell asleep. I tried to do the same, but I started thinking about the Spook again. Even though it seemed hopeless, should I still go to the burning and see if I could do anything to help? After turning it over in my mind for some time, I finally decided that, at nightfall, I would leave Priestown and go home to talk to my mam.

She'd know what I should do. I was out of my

depth here, and I needed help. I'd be walking all night and would get no sleep then, so it was best to grab what I could now. It took me a while to nod off, but when I did, almost immediately I started to dream, and the next thing I knew I was back in the catacombs.

In most dreams you don't know that you're dreaming. But when you do, one of two things usually happens. Either you wake up right away, or you stay in the dream and do what you want. That's the way it's always been with me, anyway.

But this dream was different. It was as if something was controlling my movements. I was walking down a dark tunnel with the stub of a candle in my left hand, and I was approaching the dark doorway to one of the crypts that held the bones of the Little People. I didn't want to go anywhere near it, but my feet just kept on walking.

I halted at the open doorway, the flickering light of the candle illuminating the bones. Most were on shelves at the rear of the crypt, but a few broken ones were scattered across the cobbled floor and lying in a heap in the corner. I didn't want to go in there, I really didn't, but I seemed to have no choice.

I stepped into the crypt, hearing small fragments of bone crunching beneath my feet, when suddenly I felt very cold.

One winter when I was young, my brother James chased me and filled my ears with snow. I tried to fight back, but he was only one year younger than my eldest brother, Jack, and just as big and strong, so much so that my dad had eventually got him apprenticed to a blacksmith. He shared the same sense of humor as Jack, too. Snow in the ears had been James's daft idea of a joke, but it had really hurt and all my face had gone numb and ached for almost an hour afterward. It was just like that in the dream. Extreme cold. It meant that something from the dark was approaching. The cold began inside my head until it felt frozen and numb, as though it didn't belong to me anymore.

Something spoke from the darkness behind me. Something that was standing close to my back and between me and the doorway. The voice was harsh and deep, and I didn't need to ask who was speaking. Even though I wasn't facing it, I could smell its rank breath.

"I'm got proper," said the Bane. "I'm bound. This is all I have."

I said nothing and there was a long silence. It was a nightmare, and I tried to wake up. I really struggled, but it was useless.

"A pleasant room, this," the Bane continued. "One of my favorite places, it is. Full of old bones. But fresh blood is what I want, and the blood of the young is best of all. But if I can't get blood, then I'll make do with bones. New bones are the best. Give me new bones every time, fresh and sweet and filled with marrow. That's what I like. I love to split young bones and suck out the marrow. But old bones are better than nothing. Old bones like these. They're better than the hunger gnawing away at my insides. Hunger that hurts so much.

"There's no marrow inside old bones. But old bones still have memories, see. I stroke old bones, I do, slowly, so that they give up all their secrets. I see the flesh that once covered them, the hopes and ambitions that ended in this dry, dead brittleness. That fills me up, too. That eases the hunger."

The Bane was very close to my left ear, its voice now hardly more than a whisper. I had a sudden urge to turn round and look at it, but it must have read my mind.

"*Don't turn round, boy,*" it warned. "*Or you won't like what you see. Just answer me this question . . .*"

There was a long pause, and I could feel my heart hammering in my chest. At last the Bane asked its question.

"*After death, what happens?*"

I didn't know the answer. The Spook never spoke about such things. All I knew was that there were ghosts who could still think and talk. And fragments called ghasts that had been left behind when the soul had moved on. But moved on to what? I didn't know. Only God knew. If there was a God.

I shook my head. I didn't speak, and I was too scared to turn around. Behind me I had a sense of something huge and terrifying.

"*There's nothing after death! Nothing! Nothing at all!*" bellowed the Bane close to my ear. "*There's just blackness and emptiness. No thinking. No feeling. Just oblivion. That's all that waits for you on the other side of death. But do my bidding, boy, and I can give you a long, long life! Three score years and ten is the best that most feeble humans can hope for. But ten or twenty times that I could give you! And all you have to do is open the gate and let me go free! Just open the gate and I'll do the rest. Your*" *master could go free, too. I know that's what you want. Go back, you could, to the life you once had."*

A part of me longed to say yes. I faced the Spook being burned and a lonely journey north to Caster with no certainty that I'd be able to continue my apprenticeship. If only things could return to the way they'd been! But although I was tempted to say yes, I knew that it just wasn't possible. Even if the Bane kept its word, I couldn't allow it to roam loose in the County, able to work its evil at will. I knew the Spook would rather die than let that happen.

I opened my mouth to say no, but even before I could get the word out the Bane spoke again.

"The girl would be easy!" it said. *"All she wants is a warm fire. A home to live in. Clean clothes. But think what I offer you! And all I want is your blood. Not a lot, see. And it won't hurt that much. Just enough is all I ask. And then a pact we'll make together. Just let me suck your blood so I can be strong again. Just let me through the gate and give me my freedom. Three times after, I'll do your bidding and you'll live a long, long life. The girl's blood is better than nothing, but you're what I really need. A*

seven times seven, you are. Only once before have I tasted sweet blood like yours. And I still remember it well, I do. The sweet blood of a seven times seven. How strong that would make me! How great would be your reward! Isn't that better than the nothingness of death?

"Ah, death will come to you one day. It will surely come despite all that I do, creeping toward you like the mist on a riverbank on a cold, damp night. But I can delay that moment. Delay it for years and years. It would be a long time before you'd have to face that darkness. That blackness. That nothingness! So what do you say, boy? I'm got proper. I'm bound. But you can help!"

I was scared and tried again to wake up. But suddenly words tumbled out of my mouth, almost as if they'd been spoken by somebody else:

"I don't believe there's nothing after death," I said. "I've a soul and if I live my life right, I'll live on in some way. There'll be something. I don't believe in nothingness. I don't believe in that!"

"No! No!" roared the Bane. *"You don't know what I know! You can't see what I see! I see beyond death. I see the emptiness. The nothingness. I know! I see the horrible state of being nothing. Nothing at all, there is! Nothing at all!"*

My heart began to slow, and I suddenly felt very calm. The Bane was still behind me, but the crypt was starting to get warmer. Now I understood. I knew the Bane's pain. I knew why it needed to feed upon people, upon their blood, upon their hopes and dreams. . . .

"I've a soul and I'll live on," I told the Bane, keeping my voice very calm. "And that's the difference. I have a soul and you don't! For you there is nothing after death! Nothing at all!"

My head was pushed hard against the near wall of the crypt, and there was a hiss of anger behind me. A hiss that changed to a bellow of rage.

"Fool!" shouted the Bane, its voice booming to fill the crypt and echo beyond it down the long, dark tunnels of the catacombs. Violently, it swatted my head sideways, scraping my forehead against the hard, cold stones. Out of the corner of my left eye I could see the size of the huge hand that was gripping my head. Instead of nails, its fingers ended in huge yellow talons.

"You had your chance, but now it's gone forever!" bellowed the Bane. *"But there's someone else who can help me. So if I can't have you, I'll make do with her!"*

I was pushed downward into the heap of bones in the corner. I felt myself falling through them. Down and down I went, deep into a bottomless pit filled with bones. The candle was out, but the bones seemed to glow in the darkness: grinning skulls, rib cages, leg bones and arm bones, fragments of hands, fingers and thumbs, and all the while the dry dust of death covered my face, went up my nose into my mouth and down my throat, until I was choking and could hardly breathe.

"This is what death tastes like!" cried the Bane. *"And this is what death looks like!"*

The bones faded from view and I could see nothing. Nothing at all. I was just falling through blackness. Falling into the dark. I was terrified that the Bane had somehow killed me in my sleep, but I struggled and struggled to wake up. Somehow the Bane had been talking to me while I slept, and I knew who it would now be persuading to do what I'd refused.

Alice!

At last I managed to wake myself up, but it was already too late. A candle was burning close beside me, but it was just a stub. I'd been asleep for hours! The other one had gone, and so had Alice.

I felt in my pocket but only confirmed what I'd guessed already. Alice had taken the key to the Silver Gate.

When I staggered to my feet, I felt dizzy and my head hurt. I touched the back of my hand to my forehead and it came away wet with blood. Somehow the Bane had done that to me in a dream. It could read minds, too. How could you defeat a creature when it knew what you intended before you had a chance to move or even speak? The Spook was right—this creature was the most dangerous thing we'd ever faced.

Alice had left the hatch open and, snatching up the candle, I wasted no time in climbing down the steps into the catacombs. A few minutes later I reached the river, which seemed a bit deeper than before. The water, swirling downstream, was actually covering three of the nine stepping-stones, the ones right in the middle, and I could feel the current tugging at my boots.

I crossed quickly, hoping against hope that I

wouldn't be too late. But when I turned the corner, I saw Alice sitting with her back against the
wall. Her left hand was resting on the cobbles, her
fingers covered in blood.

And the Silver Gate was wide open!

CHAPTER XIII
The Burning

"ALICE!" I cried, staring in disbelief at the open gate. "What have you done?"

She looked up at me, her eyes glistening with tears.

The key was still in the lock. Angrily, I seized it and pushed it back into my breeches pocket, burying it deep within the iron filings.

"Come on!" I snapped, almost too furious to speak. "We've got to get out of here."

I held out my left hand, but she didn't take it. Instead she held her own, the one covered in blood, against her body and looked down at it, wincing with pain.

"What happened to your hand?" I asked.

"Ain't nothing much," she replied. "Soon be right as rain. Everything's going to be all right now."

"No, Alice," I replied, "it's not. The whole County's in danger now, thanks to you."

I pulled gently at her good hand and led her down the tunnel until we came to the river. At the edge of the water she tugged her hand free of mine and I didn't think anything of it. I simply crossed quickly. It was only when I got to the other side that I looked back to see Alice still standing there staring down at the water.

"Come on!" I shouted. "Hurry up!"

"I can't, Tom!" Alice shouted back. "I can't cross!"

I put the candle down and went back for her. She flinched away, but I grabbed hold of her. If she'd struggled I'd have had no chance at all, but the moment my hands touched her, Alice's body became limp and she fell against me. Wasting no time, I bent my knees and lifted her over my shoulder, the way I'd seen the Spook carry a witch.

You see, I had no doubt. If she couldn't cross running water, then Alice had become what the Spook had always feared she would. Her dealings with the Bane had finally made her cross to the dark.

One part of me wanted to leave her there. I knew that's what the Spook would have done. But I couldn't. I was going against him, but I had to do it. She was still Alice, and we'd been through a lot together.

Light as she was, it was still quite difficult to cross the river with her over my shoulder, and I struggled to keep my balance on the stepping-stones. What made it worse was the fact that as soon as I started across, Alice began to wail as if she were in torment.

When we finally reached the other side, I lowered her back onto her feet and picked up the candle.

"Come on!" I said, but she just stood there trembling, and I had to seize her hand and drag her along until we reached the steps that led up to the cellar.

Once back there, I put the candle down and sat on the edge of the old carpet. This time Alice didn't sit. She just folded her arms and leaned back against the wall. Neither of us spoke. There was nothing to say, and I was too busy thinking.

I'd slept for a long time, both before the dream and after it. I went to peer out the door at the top of the cellar steps and saw that the sun was just going down. I'd leave it another half hour and then I'd be on my way. I desperately wanted to help the Spook, but I felt utterly powerless. It hurt me even to think about what was going to happen to him, but what could I possibly do against dozens of armed men? And I wasn't going to the beacon hill just to watch the burning. I couldn't bear that. No, I was going home to see Mam. She'd know what I should do next.

Maybe my life as a spook's apprentice was over. Or she might just suggest that I go to north of Caster and find myself a new master. It was difficult to know what she'd advise me to do.

When I judged it time, I pulled the silver chain from where I'd tied it under my shirt and put it back inside the Spook's bag with his cloak. As my dad always says: "Waste not, want not!" So I also put the salt and iron back into their compartments inside the bag—as much as I could manage to get out of my breeches pockets.

"Come on," I said to Alice. "I'll let you out."

So, wearing my cloak and carrying the bag and the staff, I climbed the steps, then used my other key to unlock the back door. Once we were out in the yard I locked it behind us again.

"Good-bye, Alice," I said, turning to walk away.

"What? Ain't you coming with me, Tom?" Alice demanded.

"Where?"

"To the burning, of course, to find the Quisitor. He's going to get what's coming to him. What he deserves. I'm going to pay him back for what he did to my poor old aunt and Maggie."

"And how are you going to do that?" I asked.

"I gave the Bane my blood, you see," Alice said, her eyes opening very wide. "I put my fingers through the grille, and it sucked it out from under my fingernails. It may not like girls, but it likes their blood. It took what it wanted so the pact's sealed and now it has to do what I say. It has to do my will."

The fingernails of Alice's left hand were black with dried blood. Sickened, I turned away and opened the yard gate, stepping out into the passageway.

"Where you going, Tom? You can't leave now!" Alice shouted.

"I'm going home to talk to Mam," I said, not even turning back to look at her.

"Go home to your mam, then! You're just a mam's lad, a mammy's boy, and you always will be!"

I hadn't taken more than a dozen paces before she came running after me.

"Don't go, Tom! Please don't go!" she cried.

I kept walking. I didn't even turn around.

The next time Alice shouted after me there was real anger in her voice. But more than that, she sounded desperate.

"You can't leave, Tom! I won't let you. You're mine. You belong to me!"

As she ran toward me, I turned around and faced her. "No, Alice," I said. "I don't belong to you. I belong to the light and now you belong to the dark!"

She reached forward and gripped my left forearm very hard. I could feel her nails cutting into my flesh. I flinched with the pain of it but stared back directly into her eyes.

"You don't know what you've done!" I said.

"Oh, yes, I do, Tom. I know exactly what I've done, and one day you're going to thank me for it. You're so worried about your precious Bane, but

CURSE OF THE BANE

believe me, he ain't no worse than the Quisitor,"
said Alice, releasing my arm. "What I've done, I've
done for all our sakes, yours and mine, even Old
Gregory's."

"The Bane will kill him. That's the first thing it
will do now it's free!"

"No, you're wrong, Tom! It ain't the Bane who
wants to kill Old Gregory, it's the Quisitor. Right
now the Bane's his only hope of survival. And that's
all thanks to me."

I felt confused.

"Look, Tom, come with me and I'll show you."

I shook my head.

"Well, whether you come with me or not," she
continued, "I'll do it anyway."

"Do what?"

"I'm going to save the Quisitor's prisoners. All
of 'em! And I'm going to show him what it's like to
burn!"

I looked hard at Alice again, but she didn't flinch
away from my gaze. Anger blazed in her eyes, and at
that moment I felt that she could even have looked
the Spook in the eye, something she wasn't usually
capable of. Alice meant it, all right, and it seemed to

me that the Bane might just obey her and help. After all, they'd made some kind of pact.

If there was any chance of saving the Spook, then I had to be there to help him to safety. I didn't feel at all comfortable about relying on something as evil as the Bane, yet what choice did I have? Alice turned in the direction of the beacon fell and, slowly, I began to follow.

The streets were deserted and we walked quickly, heading south.

"I'd better get rid of this staff," I said to Alice. "It might give us away."

She nodded and pointed to an old broken-down shed. "Leave it behind there," she said. "We can pick it up on our way back."

There was still some light left in the sky to the west and it was reflected in the river, twisting below the heights of Wortham. My eyes were drawn upward to the daunting beacon fell. Its lower slopes were covered in trees, now starting to lose their leaves, but above there was only grass and scrub.

We left the last of the houses behind us and joined a throng of people crossing the narrow stone bridge over the river, moving slowly through the damp, still air. There was a white mist on the riverbank, but we soon rose above it as we climbed up through the trees, trudging through mounds of damp, moldering leaves to emerge near the summit of the hill. A large crowd had already gathered, with more people arriving by the minute. There were three huge piles of branches and twigs ready for lighting, the largest one set between the other two. Rising from these pyres were the thick wooden stakes to which the victims would be tied.

High on the beacon fell, with the lights of the town spread out below us, the air was fresher. The area was lit by torches attached to tall, slender wooden poles, which were swaying gently in the light westerly breeze. But there were patches of darkness where the faces of the crowd were in shadow, and I followed Alice into one of these so that we could watch what was going on without being noticed ourselves.

On guard, with their backs to the pyres, were a dozen big men wearing black hoods, with just slits for eyes and mouths. In their hands they carried cudgels, and they looked eager to use them. These were the assistant executioners, who would help the Quisitor with the burning and, if necessary, keep back the crowd.

I wasn't sure how the crowd would behave. Was it worth hoping that they might do something? Any relatives and friends of the condemned would want to save them, but whether there were enough of them to attempt a rescue was uncertain. Of course, as Brother Peter had said, there were lots of people who loved a burning. Many were here to be entertained.

No sooner had that thought entered my head than, in the distance, I heard the steady beat of drums.

Burn! Burn! Burn, witches, burn! the drums seemed to thunder.

At that sound the crowd began to murmur, their voices swelling to a roar that finally erupted into loud catcalls and hisses. The Quisitor was approaching, riding tall on his big white horse, and behind him trundled the open cart containing the prisoners. Other men on horseback were riding alongside and to the rear of the cart, and they had swords at their hips. Behind them, on foot, were a dozen drummers walking with a swagger, their arms rising and falling theatrically to the beat they were pounding out.

Burn! Burn! Burn, witches, burn!

Suddenly the whole situation seemed hopeless. Some in the front rank of the crowd started to shy rotten fruit at the prisoners, but the guards on the flanks, probably worried about being hit by mistake, drew their swords and rode directly at them, driving them back into the throng, causing the whole mass of people to sway backward.

The cart came nearer and halted, and for the first time I could see the Spook. Some of the prisoners were on their knees, praying. Others were wailing or tearing at their hair, but my master was standing straight and tall, staring ahead. His face looked haggard and tired, and there was the same vague expression in his eyes, as if he still didn't understand what was happening to him. There was a new dark bruise on his forehead above his left eye, and his bottom lip was split and swollen—he'd evidently been given another beating.

A priest stepped forward, a scroll in his right hand, and the rhythm of the drums changed. It became a deep roll that built to a crescendo, then halted suddenly as the priest began to read from the parchment.

"People of Priestown, hear this! We are gathered here to witness the lawful execution by fire of twelve witches and one warlock, the sinful wretches whom you see before you now. Pray for their souls! Pray that through pain they may come to know the error of their ways. Pray that they may beg God's forgiveness and thus redeem their immortal souls."

There was another roll of drums. The priest hadn't finished yet, and in the succeeding silence he continued to read.

"Our Lord Protector, the High Quisitor, wishes this to be a lesson to others who might choose the path of darkness. Watch these sinners burn! Watch their bones crack and their fat melt like candle tallow. Listen to their screams and all the while remember that this is nothing! This is nothing at all compared to the flames of hell! Nothing compared to the eternity of torment that awaits those who do not seek forgiveness!"

The crowd had fallen silent at these words. Perhaps it was the fear of hell that the priest had mentioned, but more likely, I thought, it was something else. It was what I now feared. To stand and watch the horror of what was about to happen. The realization that living flesh and blood was to be put into the flames to endure unspeakable agony.

Two of the hooded men came forward and roughly pulled the first prisoner from the cart—a woman with long gray hair that hung down thickly over her shoulders, almost as far as her waist. As they dragged her toward the nearest pyre, she began to spit and curse, fighting desperately to tear herself free. Some of the crowd laughed and jeered, calling her names, but unexpectedly she managed to break away and began running off into the darkness.

Before the guards could take even a step to follow, the Quisitor galloped his horse past them, its hooves throwing up mud from the soft ground. He seized the woman by the hair, twisting his fingers into her locks before bunching his fist. Then he tugged her upward so violently that her back arched and she was almost lifted from her feet. She gave a high, thin wail as the Quisitor dragged her back to the guards, who seized her again and quickly tied her to one of the stakes on the edge of the largest pyre. Her fate was sealed.

My heart sank as I saw that the Spook was the next prisoner pulled down from the cart. They walked him toward the largest pyre and bound him to the central stake, but not once did he struggle. He still just looked bewildered. I remembered once more how he'd told me that burning was one of the most painful deaths imaginable and he didn't hold with doing that to a witch. To watch him bound there, awaiting his fate, was unbearable. Some of the Quisitor's men were carrying torches, and I imagined them lighting the pyres, the flames leaping up toward the Spook. It was too horrible to think about, and tears began streaming down my face.

I tried to recall what my master had said about something or someone watching what we do. If you lived your life right, he'd told me, in your hour of need it would stand at your side and lend you its strength. Well, he'd lived his life right and had done everything for what he thought was the best. So he deserved something. Surely?

If I'd been part of a family that went to church and prayed more, I'd have prayed then. The habit wasn't in me and I didn't know how, but without realizing it I whispered something to myself. I didn't mean it to be a prayer, but I suppose it was one, really.

"Help him, please," I whispered. "Please help him."

Suddenly the hair on the back of my neck began to move and I instantly felt cold, very cold. Something from the dark was approaching. Something strong and very dangerous. I heard Alice give a sudden gasp and a deep groan, and immediately my vision darkened so that, when I turned and reached toward her, I couldn't even see my hand before my face. The murmur of the crowd receded into the distance and everything grew still and quiet. I felt cut off from the rest of the world, alone in darkness.

I knew that the Bane had arrived. I couldn't see anything, but I could sense it nearby, a vast dark spirit, a great weight that threatened to crush the life from me. I was terrified, for myself and for all the innocent people gathered there, but could do nothing but wait in the darkness for it to end.

When my eyes cleared, I saw Alice start forward. Before I could stop her, she walked out of the shadows and headed directly toward the Spook and the two executioners at the central pyre. The Quisitor was close by, watching. As she approached, I saw him turn his horse toward her and spur it into a canter. For a moment I thought he intended to ride her down, but he brought the animal to a halt, so close that Alice could have reached up and patted its nose.

A cruel smile split his face, and I knew that he recognized her as one of the escaped prisoners. What Alice did next, I'll always remember.

In the sudden silence that had fallen she lifted her hands toward the Quisitor, pointing at him with both forefingers. Then she laughed long and loud and the sound echoed right across the hill, making the hair stand up on the back of my neck again. It was a laugh of triumph and defiance, and I thought how strange it was that the Quisitor was preparing to burn those people, all of them falsely accused, all of them innocents, while free and facing him was a real witch, with real power.

Next, Alice turned on her heels and began to spin, holding her arms stretched out horizontally. As I watched, dark spots began to appear on the nose and head of the Quisitor's white stallion. At first I was puzzled and didn't understand what was happening. But then the horse whinnied in fear and reared up on its hind legs, and I saw that droplets of blood were flying from Alice's left hand. Blood from where the Bane had just fed.

There was a sudden overpowering wind, a blinding flash of lightning, and a clap of thunder so loud that it hurt my ears. I found myself on my knees and could hear people screaming and shouting. I looked back at Alice and saw that she was still spinning, whirling faster and faster. The white horse reared up again, this time unseating the Quisitor, who fell off backward onto the pyre.

Another flash of lightning and suddenly the edge of the pyre was alight, the flames crackling and the Quisitor on his knees with flames all around him. I saw some of the guards rush forward to help him, but the crowd was also moving forward, and one of the guards was dragged from his horse. Within moments a full-scale riot had begun. On all sides people were struggling and fighting. Others were running to escape, and the air was full of shouts and screams.

I dropped the bag and ran to my master, for the flames were traveling fast, threatening to engulf him. Without thinking, I charged straight across the pyre, feeling the heat of the flames, which were already starting to take hold on the larger pieces of wood.

I struggled to untie him, my fingers fumbling at the knots. To my left a man was trying to free the gray-haired woman they'd bound first. I panicked because I was getting nowhere. There were too many knots! They were too tight and the heat was building!

Suddenly there was a shout of triumph to my left. The man had freed the woman and one look told me how: He was holding a knife and had cut through the ropes with ease. He was starting to lead her away from the stake when he glanced toward me. The air was filled with shouts and screams and the crackle of the flames. Even if I'd shouted, he wouldn't have heard me, so I simply held out my left hand toward him. For a moment he seemed to hesitate, staring at my hand, but then he tossed the knife in my direction.

It fell short, into the flames. Without even thinking, I plunged my hand deep into the burning wood and retrieved it. It took just seconds to slash through the ropes.

To have freed the Spook when he had been so close to burning gave me a great feeling of relief. But my happiness was short-lived. We were still far from being safe. The Quisitor's men were all around us, and there was a strong possibility that we'd be spotted and caught. This time we'd both burn!

I had to get him away from the burning pyre to the darkness beyond, to somewhere we couldn't be seen. It seemed to take an age. He leaned on me heavily and took small, unsteady steps. I remembered his bag, so we made for the spot where I'd dropped it. It was only by good fortune that we avoided the Quisitor's men. Of their leader there was no sign, but in the distance I could see mounted men cutting down with their swords anyone within range. At any moment I expected one of them to charge at us. It was getting harder and harder to make progress; the burden of the Spook seemed to increase against my shoulder and I still had the weight of his bag in my right hand. But then someone else was holding his other arm and we were moving toward the darkness of the trees and safety.

It was Alice.

"I did it, Tom! I did it!" she shouted excitedly.

I wasn't sure how to reply. Of course I was pleased, but I couldn't approve of her method. "Where's the Bane now?" I asked.

"Don't you worry about that, Tom. I can tell when it's near, and I don't feel it anywhere now. Must have taken a lot of power to do what it just did, so I reckon it's gone back to the dark for a while to build up its strength."

I didn't like the sound of that. "What about the Quisitor?" I asked. "I didn't see what happened to him. Is he dead?"

Alice shook her head. "Burned his hands when he fell, that's all. But now he knows what it's like to burn!"

As she said that, I became aware of the pain in my own hand, the left one that was supporting the Spook. I looked down and saw that the back of it was raw and blistered. With each step I took the pain seemed to increase.

We crossed the bridge with a jostling crowd of frightened people, all hastening north, eager to be away from the riot and what would follow. Soon the Quisitor's men would regroup, eager to recapture the prisoners and punish anyone who'd played a part in their escape. Anyone in their path would suffer.

Long before dawn we were clear of Priestown and spent the first few hours of daylight in the shelter of a dilapidated cattle shed, afraid that the Quisitor's men might be nearby, searching for escaped prisoners.

The Spook hadn't said a single word when I'd spoken to him, not even after I'd collected his staff and handed it to him. His eyes were still vacant and staring, as though his mind was in an entirely different place. I began to worry that the blow to his head was serious, which gave me little choice.

"We need to get him back to our farm," I told Alice. "My mam will be able to help him."

"Won't take too kindly to seeing me, though, will she?" said Alice. "Not when she finds out what I've done. Neither will that brother of yours."

I nodded, wincing at the pain in my hand. What Alice said was true. It would be better if she didn't come with me, but I needed her to help with the Spook, who was far from steady on his feet.

"What's wrong, Tom?" she asked. She'd noticed my hand and came across to take a look at it.

"Soon fix that," she said. "I won't be long. . . ."

"No, Alice, it's too dangerous!"

But before I could stop her, she slipped out of the shed. Ten minutes later she was back with some small pieces of bark and the leaves of a plant I didn't recognize. She chewed the bark with her teeth until it was in small, fibrous pieces.

"Hold out your hand!" she commanded.

"What's that?" I asked doubtfully, but my hand was really hurting, so I did as I was told.

Gently, she placed the small pieces of bark on the burn and wrapped my hand in the leaves. Then she teased a black thread from her dress and used that to bind them in position.

"Lizzie taught me this," she said. "It'll soon take away the pain."

I was about to protest, but almost immediately the pain began to fade. It was a remedy taught to Alice by a witch. A remedy that worked. The ways of the world were strange. Out of evil good could come. And it wasn't just my hand. Because of Alice and her pact with the Bane, the Spook had been saved.

CHAPTER XIV
Dad's Tale

WE came in sight of the farm about an hour before sunset. I knew that Dad and Jack would just be starting the milking, so it was a good time to arrive. I needed a chance to speak to Mam on my own.

I hadn't been back home since the spring, when the old witch, Mother Malkin, had paid my family a visit. Thanks to Alice's bravery on that occasion, we'd destroyed her, but the incident had upset Jack and his wife, Ellie, and I knew they wouldn't be keen on my staying after dark. Spooks' business scared them, and they were worried that something might happen to their child. So I just wanted to help the Spook and then get back on the road as quickly as possible.

I was also aware that I was risking everyone's lives by bringing the Spook and Alice to the farm. If the Quisitor's men followed us here, they would have no mercy on those harboring a witch and a spook. I didn't want to put my family in any more danger than I had to, so I decided to leave Alice and the Spook just outside the farm boundary. There was an old shepherd's hut belonging to the nearest farm to us. They'd gone over to cattle, so it hadn't been used for years. I helped Alice get the Spook inside and told her to wait there. That done, I crossed the field, heading directly toward the fence that bordered our farmyard.

When I opened the door to the kitchen, Mam was in her usual place in the corner next to the fire, sitting in her rocking chair. The chair was very still, and she just stared at me as I went in. The curtains were already closed, and in the brass candlestick the beeswax candle was alight.

"Sit down, son," she invited, her voice low and soft. "Pull up a chair and tell me all about it." She didn't seem in the least bit surprised to see me.

It was what I was used to. Mam was often in demand when midwives encountered problems with a difficult birth, and eerily, she always knew when someone wanted her help long before the message arrived at the farm. She sensed these things, just as she'd sensed my approach. There was something special about my mam. She had gifts that someone like the Quisitor would want to destroy.

"Something bad's happened, hasn't it?" Mam said. "And what's wrong with your hand?"

"It's nothing, Mam. Just a burn. Alice fixed it. It doesn't hurt at all now."

Mam raised her eyebrows at the mention of Alice. "Tell me all about it, son."

I nodded, feeling a lump come into my throat. I tried three times before I was able to get my first sentence out. When I did manage to speak, it all came out in a rush.

"They almost burned Mr. Gregory, Mam. The Quisitor caught him in Priestown. We've escaped, but they'll be after us, and the Spook's not well. He needs help. We all do."

The tears started to run down my face as I admitted to myself what was now bothering me most of all. The main reason I hadn't wanted to go to the beacon fell was because I'd been scared. I'd been afraid that they'd catch me and that I would burn as well.

"What on earth were you doing in Priestown?" Mam asked.

"Mr. Gregory's brother died and his funeral was there. We had to go."

"You're not telling me everything," Mam said. "How did you escape from the Quisitor?"

I didn't want Mam to know what Alice had done. You see, Mam had once tried to help Alice, and I didn't want her to know how she'd finally ended up, turning to the dark as the Spook had always feared.

But I had no choice. I told her the full story. When I'd finished, Mam sighed deeply. "It's bad, really bad," she said. "The Bane on the loose doesn't bode well for anyone in the County—and a young witch bound to its will—well, I fear for us all. But we'll just have to make the best of it. That's all we can do. I'll get my bag and go and see what I can do for poor Mr. Gregory."

"Thanks, Mam," I told her, suddenly realizing that all I'd talked about had been my own troubles. "But how are things here? How's Ellie's baby doing?" I asked.

Mam smiled, but I detected a hint of sadness in her eyes. "Oh, the baby's doing fine, and Ellie and Jack are happier than they've ever been. But son," she said, touching my arm gently, "I've got some bad news for you, too. It's about your dad. He's been very ill."

I stood up, hardly able to believe what she was saying. The look on her face told me that it was serious.

"Sit down, son," she said, "and listen carefully before you start getting all upset. It's bad, but it could have been a lot worse. It started as a heavy cold, but then it got on his chest and turned to pneumonia and we nearly lost him. He's on the mend now, I hope, but he'll need to wrap up well this winter. I'm afraid he won't be able to do much on the farm anymore. Jack will just have to cope without him."

"I could help out, Mam."

"No, son, you've got your own job to do. With the Bane free and your master weakened, the County needs you more than ever. Look, let me just go up first and tell your dad that you're here. And I wouldn't say anything about the trouble you've had.

We don't want to give him any bad news or nasty shocks. We'll just keep that to ourselves."

I waited in the kitchen, but a couple of minutes later Mam came back downstairs, carrying her bag.

"Well, you go up and see your dad while I go and help your master. He's glad that you're back, but don't keep him talking too long. He's still very weak."

Dad was sitting in bed, propped up on several pillows. He smiled weakly when I came into the room. His face was gaunt and tired, and there was a gray stubble on his chin that made him look much older.

"What a nice surprise, Tom. Sit down," he said, nodding toward the chair at the side of the bed.

"I'm sorry," I said. "If I'd known you were ill, I'd have come home sooner to see you."

Dad held up his hand as if to say it didn't matter. Then he began to cough violently. He was supposed to be getting better, so I wouldn't like to have heard him when he was really ill. The room had a smell of illness. The hint of something you never smelled outdoors. Something that only lingers in sickrooms.

"How's the job going?" he asked when he'd finally

stopped choking.

"Not bad. I'm getting used to it now and I prefer it to farming," I said, pushing all that had happened to the very back of my mind.

"Farming too dull for you, eh?" he asked with a faint smile. "Mind you, I wasn't always a farmer."

I nodded. In his younger days Dad had been a seaman. He'd told lots of tales of the places he'd visited. They'd been rich stories, full of color and excitement. His eyes always shone with a faraway look when he remembered those times. I wanted to see that spark of life return to them.

"Aye, Dad," I said, "tell me one of your stories. The one about that huge whale."

He paused for a moment, then grabbed my hand, pulling me closer. "Reckon there's one story I needs be telling you, son, before it's too late."

"Don't talk daft," I said, shocked by this turn in the conversation.

"Nay, Tom, I'm hoping to see another spring and summer, but I don't think I'm long for this world. I've been thinking a lot lately, and I reckon it's time I told you what I know. I wasn't expecting to see you for a while, but you're here now and who knows when I'll see you next?" He paused and then said, "It's about your mother — how we met and the like."

"You'll see lots of springs, Dad," I said, but I was surprised. For all my father's wonderful stories, there was one he'd never told properly: how he'd met Mam. We could always tell that he never really wanted to talk about it. He either changed the subject or told us to go and ask her. We never did. When you're a child, there are things you don't understand but just don't ask about. You know that your dad and mam don't want to tell you. But today was different.

He shook his head wearily, then bowed it low, as if a great burden was pressing down on his shoulders. When he straightened up again, the faint smile was back on his face.

"I'm not sure she'll thank me for telling you, mind, so let's keep this between ourselves. I'll not be telling your brothers either, and I'd ask you to do the same, son. But I think in your line of work, and you being a seventh son of a seventh son and all, well . . ."

He paused again and shut his eyes. I stared at him and felt a wave of sadness as I realized how old and ill he was looking. He opened his eyes again and began to talk.

"We sailed into a little harbor to take on water," he said, beginning his tale as if he needed to get going quickly before he changed his mind. "It was a lonely place overhung with high, rocky hills, with just the harbormaster's house and a few small fishermen's cottages built of white stone. We'd been at sea for weeks and the captain, being a good man, said that we deserved a break. So he gave us all shore leave. We took it in two shifts and I got the second one, which started well after dark.

"There were a dozen of us, and when we finally made it to the nearest tavern, which was on the edge of a village almost halfway up a mountain, it was almost ready to close. So we drank fast, throwing strong spirits down our throats like there was no tomorrow, and then bought a flagon of red wine each to drink on the way back to the ship.

"I must have drunk too much, because I woke up alone at the side of the steep track that led down to the harbor. The sun was just about to come up, but I wasn't too bothered because we weren't sailing till noon. I climbed to my feet and dusted myself off. It was then that I heard the sound of distant sobbing.

"I listened for almost a minute before I made up

my mind. I mean, it sounded just like a woman, but how could I be sure? There are all sorts of strange tales from those parts about creatures that prey on travelers. I was alone and I don't mind telling you I was scared, but if I hadn't gone to see who was crying I'd never have met your mam and you wouldn't be here now.

"I climbed the steep hill at the side of the track and scrambled down the other side until it brought me right to the edge of a cliff. It was a high cliff, with the waves crashing on the rocks below, and I could see the ship at anchor in the bay and it was so small that it seemed as if it could fit into the palm of my hand.

"A narrow rock jutted up from the cliff like a rat's tooth, and a young woman was sitting with her back to it, facing out to sea. She'd been bound to that rock with a chain. Not only that, but she was as naked as the day she was born."

With those words, Dad blushed so deeply that his face turned almost County-red.

"She started to try and tell me something then. Something that she feared. Something far worse than just being fastened to that rock. But she was

speaking in her own language, and I didn't understand a word of it—I still don't, but she taught you
well enough and, do you know, you were the only
one that she bothered with in that way? She's a
good mother, but none of your brothers heard even
a word of Greek."

I nodded. Some of my brothers hadn't been best
pleased by that, particularly Jack, and it had sometimes made life difficult for me.

"No, she couldn't explain in words what it was,
but there was something out to sea that was terrifying her. I couldn't think what it could be, but then
the tip of the sun came up above the horizon and
she screamed.

"I stared at her, but I couldn't believe what I
was seeing: Tiny blisters began to erupt on her skin
until, within less than a minute, she was a mass of
sores. It was the sun she feared. To this day, as
you've probably noticed, she finds it difficult to be
out even in a County sun, but the sunlight in that
land was fierce and without help she'd have died."

He paused to catch his breath, and I thought about
Mam. I'd always known that she avoided sunlight—
but it was something I'd just taken for granted.

"What could I do?" Dad continued. "I had to think fast, so I took off my shirt and covered her with it. It wasn't big enough, so there was nothing else for it and I had to use my trousers as well. Then I crouched there with my back to the sun, so that my shadow fell over her, protecting her from its fierce light.

"I stayed that way until long after noon, when the sun finally moved out of sight behind the hill. By then my ship had sailed without me and my back was raw with sunburn, but your mam was alive and the blisters had already faded away. I struggled to get her free of the chain, but whoever had tied it knew even more about knots than I did, and I was a seaman. It was only when I finally got it off her that I noticed something so cruel that I could hardly believe it. I mean, she's a good woman, your mam — how could someone have done such a thing, and to a woman, too?"

Dad fell silent and stared down at his hands, and I could see that they were trembling with the memory of what he'd seen. I waited almost a minute, and then I prompted him gently.

"What was it, Dad?" I asked. "What had they done?"

When he looked up, his eyes were full of tears. "They'd nailed her left hand to the rock," he said. "It was a thick nail with a broad head and I couldn't begin to think how I was going to get her hand free without hurting her even more. But she just smiled and tore her hand free, leaving the nail still in the rock. There was blood dripping onto the ground at her feet, but she stood up and walked toward me as if it were nothing.

"I took a step backward and almost fell over the cliff, but she put her right hand on my shoulder to steady me, and then we kissed. Being a seaman who visited dozens of ports each year, I'd kissed a few women before, but usually it was after I'd had a skinful of ale and was numb, sometimes even close to passing out. I'd never kissed a woman when sober and certainly never in broad daylight. I can't explain it, but I knew right away that she was the one for me. The woman I'd spend the rest of my life with."

He started coughing then, and it went on for a long time. When he'd finished, it left him breathless and it was another couple of minutes before I spoke again. I should have let him rest, but I knew I might not get another chance. My mind was racing. Some things in Dad's tale reminded me of what the Spook had written about Meg. She'd also been bound with a chain. When released, she'd kissed the Spook just as Mam had kissed Dad. I wondered if the chain was silver, but I couldn't ask. Part of me didn't want to know the answer. If Dad had wanted me to know, he'd have told me.

"What happened next, Dad? How did you manage to get back home?"

"Your mother had money, son. She lived alone in a big house set in a garden surrounded by a high wall. It wasn't more than a mile or so from where I'd found her, so we went back there and I stayed. Her hand healed quickly, leaving not even the faintest of scars, and I taught her our language. Or, to be honest, she taught me how to teach her. I pointed at objects and said their names aloud. When she'd repeated what I'd said, I'd just nod to say it sounded right. Once was enough for each word. Your mam's sharp, son. Really sharp. She's a clever woman and never forgets a thing.

"Anyway, I stayed at that house for weeks, and I was happy enough but for the odd night or so when her sisters came to visit. There were two of them, tall, fierce-looking women, and they used to build a fire out back behind the house and stay there till dawn, talking to your mam. Sometimes all three of them would dance around the fire; other nights they played dice. But each time they came, there were arguments and they gradually got worse.

"I knew it was something to do with me, because her sisters would glare at me through the window with anger in their eyes and your mam would wave at me to go back into the room. No, they didn't like me much, and that was the main reason, I think, that we left that house and came back to the County.

"I'd set sail as a hired hand, an ordinary seaman, but I came back like a gentleman. Your mam paid for our passage home and we had a cabin all to ourselves. Then she bought this farm and we were married in the little church at Mellor, where my own mam and dad are buried. Your mother doesn't believe what we believe, but she did it for me so that the neighbors wouldn't talk, and before the end of the year your brother Jack was born. I've had a good life, son, and the best part of it started the day I met your mam. But I'm telling you this because I want you to understand. You do realize, don't you, that one day when I'm gone, she'll go back home, back to where she belongs?"

My mouth opened in amazement when Dad said that. "What about her family?" I asked. "Surely she wouldn't leave her grandchildren?"

Dad shook his head sadly. "I don't think she's any choice, son. She once told me she's got what she calls 'unfinished business' back there. I don't know what it is, and she never did tell me why she'd been fastened to the rock to die. She has her own world and her own life, and when the time comes, she'll go back to it, so don't make it hard for her. Look at me, lad. What do you see?"

I didn't know what to say.

"What you see is an old man who's not long for this life. I see the truth of it every time I look in a mirror, so don't try to tell me I'm wrong. As for your mam, she's still in the prime of life. She may not be the girl she once was, but she's still got years of good living left in her. But for what I did that day, your mam wouldn't have looked at me twice. She deserves her freedom, so let her go with a smile. Will you do that, son?"

I nodded and then stayed with him until he calmed down and drifted off to sleep.

CHAPTER XV
The Silver Chain

WHEN I went downstairs, Mam was already back. I was anxious to ask how the Spook was and what she'd done for him, but I didn't get the chance. Through the kitchen window I'd spied Jack crossing the yard with Ellie, their baby cradled in her arms.

"I've done what I can for your master, son," Mam whispered just before Jack opened the door. "We'll talk after supper."

For a moment Jack froze in the doorway, looking at me, a mixture of expressions flickering across his face. At last he smiled and walked forward to rest his arm across my shoulders.

"Good to see you, Tom," he said.

CURSE OF THE BANE

"I was just passing on my way back to Chipenden," I told him. "Thought I'd call in and see how you all were. I'd have visited earlier if I'd known that Dad had been so ill. . . ."

"He's on the mend now," Jack said. "That's the important thing."

"Oh, yes, Tom, he's much better now," Ellie agreed. "He'll be right as rain in a few weeks."

I could see that the sad expression on Mam's face said otherwise. The truth of it was that Dad would be lucky to make it till spring. She knew it, and so did I.

At supper everybody seemed subdued, even Mam. I couldn't work out whether it was my being there or Dad's illness making everyone so quiet, but during the meal Jack could barely more than nod at me, and when he did speak it was to say something sarcastic.

"You're looking pale, Tom," he said. "Must be all that skulking about in the dark. Can't be good for you."

"Don't be cruel, Jack!" Ellie scolded. "Anyway, what do you think about our Mary? Had her christened last month. Grown up quite a bit since you last saw her, hasn't she?"

I smiled and nodded. I was astonished to see how much the baby had grown. Instead of being a tiny thing with a red, wrinkled-up face, she was plump and round, with sturdy limbs and a watchful, alert expression. She looked ready to leave Ellie's knee and start crawling round the kitchen floor.

I hadn't felt very hungry, but the moment Mam heaped a large portion of steaming hot pot onto my plate, I tucked in right away.

No sooner had we finished than she smiled at Jack and Ellie. "I've something to discuss with Tom," she said. "So why don't you two go up and get an early night for once? And don't worry about the washing-up, Ellie. I'll see to it."

There was still some hot pot left in the dish, and I saw Jack's eyes flicker toward it, then back to Mam. But Ellie stood up and Jack followed slowly. I could see he wasn't best pleased.

"I think I'll just take the dogs and walk the boundary fence first," he said. "There was a fox about last night."

As soon as they'd left the room, I blurted out the question I'd been dying to ask.

"How is he, Mam? Is Mr. Gregory going to be all right?"

"I've done what I can for him," Mam said. "But injuries to the head usually sort themselves out one way or the other. Only time will tell. I think the sooner you get him back to Chipenden, the better. He'd be welcome here, but I've got to respect Jack and Ellie's wishes."

I nodded and stared down at the table sadly.

"Can you manage a second helping, Tom?" Mam asked.

I didn't need to be asked twice, and Mam smiled as I tucked in. "I'll just go up and see how your dad is," she said.

She soon came back downstairs. "He's fine," she said. "He's just nodded off to sleep again."

She sat down opposite and watched me eat, her face serious. "The wounds I saw on Alice's fingers — is that where the Bane took blood from her?"

I nodded.

"Do you trust her now, after all that's happened?" she asked suddenly.

I shrugged. "I don't know what to do. She's crossed to the dark, but without her the Spook and lots of other innocent people would have died."

Mam sighed. "It's a nasty business and I'm not

sure the answer's clear yet. I wish I could go with you and help you get your master back to Chipenden, because it won't be an easy journey, but I can't leave your dad. Without careful nursing he could suffer a relapse, and I can't risk that happening."

I cleaned my plate with a piece of bread, then pushed back my chair.

"I think I'd better get going, Mam. The longer I'm here, the more danger I'm putting you all in. There's no way the Quisitor will let us go without a chase. And now the Bane's free and has fed on Alice's blood I can't risk leading him here."

"Don't rush off just yet," Mam said. "I'll slice you some ham and bread to eat on the road."

"Thanks, Mam."

She set to work slicing the bread while I watched, wishing I could stay longer. It would be good to be home again, even if only for one night.

"Tom, in your lessons about witches, did Mr. Gregory tell you about those who use familiars?"

I nodded. Different types of witches gained their power in different ways. Some used bone magic, others blood magic; recently he'd told me about a third and even more dangerous type. They used what was called familiar magic. They gave their blood to some creature—it could be a cat, a toad, or even a bat. In return, it became their eyes and ears and did their will. Sometimes it grew so powerful that they fell completely under its power and had little or no will of their own.

"Well, that's what Alice thinks she's doing now, Tom—using familiar magic. She's made a pact with that creature and is using it to get what she wants. But she's playing a dangerous game, son. If she's not careful, she'll end up belonging to it and you'll never really be able to trust her again. At least, not while the Bane still lives."

"Mr. Gregory said that it was getting stronger, Mam. That soon it would be able to take on the flesh of its original shape. I saw it down in the catacombs—it had shape-shifted into the Spook and tried to trick me. So it's obviously been getting stronger down there."

"That's true enough, but what's just happened will have set it back a bit. You see, the Bane will have used up a lot of energy in flying free of a place it's been bound to for so long. So for now it will be confused and lost, probably a spirit again, not strong enough to clothe itself in flesh at all. It probably won't be able to regain its full strength until the blood pact with Alice is completed."

"Can it see through Alice's eyes?" I asked.

The thought was terrifying. I was about to go off with Alice through the darkness. I remembered the feel of the Bane's weight on my head and shoulders, the expectation that I was about to be pressed and that my last moment had come. Maybe it was safer to wait until daylight. . . .

"No, not yet, son. She gave it her blood and its freedom. In return it will have promised to obey her three times, but each time it'll want more of her blood. After feeding it again at the Wortham burning, she'll be weakened and finding it harder and harder to resist. If she feeds it once more, it will be able to see out of her eyes. Finally, on the last feeding, she'll belong to it and it will have the strength to return to its true form. And there'll be nothing anyone can do to save Alice then," Mam said.

"So wherever it is, it'll be looking for Alice?"

"It will, son, but for a short while, unless she calls it to her, the chances of it finding her will be very slight. Especially when she's on the move. If she stays in one place for any length of time, the Bane will have more chance of finding her. Each night it'll get a little stronger, though, especially if it chances upon some other victim. Any sort of blood would help it, animal or human. Someone alone in the dark would be easy to terrorize. Easy to bend to its will. In a while it'll find Alice, and after that it'll always be somewhere near to her except during daylight hours, when it'll probably stay underground. Creatures of the dark rarely venture abroad when it's light. But with the Bane on the loose, gaining in strength, everyone in the County should be afraid when night falls."

"How did it all start, Mam? Mr. Gregory told me that King Heys of the Little People had to sacrifice his sons to the Bane and that somehow the last son managed to bind it."

"It's a sad and terrible story," Mam said. "What happened to the king's sons doesn't bear thinking about. But I think it's better that you know so you understand just what you're up against. The Bane lived in the long barrows at Heysham, among the bones of the dead. First it took the eldest son there to use him as a plaything, picking the thoughts and dreams from his mind until little remained but misery and darkest despair. And so it went on, with son after son. Think how their father must have felt! He was a king and yet he could do nothing to help."

Mam sighed sadly. "Not one of Heys's sons survived much more than a month of such torment. Three threw themselves from the cliffs nearby to smash themselves to pieces on the rocks below. Two refused to eat and wasted away. The sixth swam out to sea until his strength failed and he drowned—his body was brought back to shore by the spring tides. All six are buried in the stone graves carved from the rock. A further grave holds the body of their father, who died soon after his six sons, of a broken heart. So only Naze, the last of his children, his seventh son, outlived him.

"The king was a seventh son, too, so Naze was like you and had the gift. He was small, even by the standards of his own people, and the old blood ran strongly through his veins. He managed to bind the Bane somehow, but nobody knows how, not even your master. Afterward the creature slew Naze on the spot, pressing him flat against the stones. Then, years later, because they reminded the Bane of how it had been tricked, it broke his bones into tiny pieces and pushed them through the Silver Gate so that at last Naze's people were able to give him a proper burial. His remains are with the others in the stone graves at Heysham, which is named after the ancient king."

We didn't say anything for a few moments. It was a terrible tale.

"Then how can we stop it now it's loose again, Mam?" I asked, breaking the silence. "How can we kill it?"

"Leave that to Mr. Gregory, Tom. Just help him get back to Chipenden and grow fit and well again. He'll work out what to do next. The easiest way would be to bind it again, but even then it would still be able to work its evil as it has more and more in recent years. If it was able to clothe itself in flesh before, down there in the catacombs, then it would do it again, and before long, as its strength grew, it would revert to its natural form, corrupting Priestown and the County beyond. So although we'd be safer with it bound, it's not a final solution. Your master needs to learn how to kill it, for all our sakes."

"But what if he doesn't recover?"

"Let's just hope that he does, for there is more to be done than perhaps you are ready to cope with yet. You see, son, wherever Alice goes, it will use her to hurt others, so your master may have no choice but to put her into a pit."

Mam looked troubled, then suddenly paused and put her hand to her forehead, squeezing her eyes shut as if she had a sudden painful headache.

"Are you all right, Mam?" I asked anxiously.

She nodded and smiled weakly. "Look, son, you sit yourself down for a while. I need to write a letter for you to take."

"A letter? Who for?"

"We'll talk more when I've finished."

I sat in a chair by the fire, staring into the embers while Mam wrote at the table. I kept wondering what she was writing. When she'd finished, she sat down in her rocking chair and handed me the envelope. It was sealed, and on it was written:

To my youngest son, Thomas J. Ward

I was surprised. I'd imagined it must be a letter for the Spook to read when he got better.

"Why are you writing to me, Mam? Why not just tell me what you have to say now?"

"Because every little thing we do changes things, son," Mam said, putting her hand gently on my left forearm. "To see the future is dangerous and to communicate what you see doubly so. Your master must follow his own path. He must find his own way. We each have free will. But there's a darkening ahead, and I have to do everything in my powers to avert the worst that might happen. Only open the letter in a time of great need, when the future looks hopeless. Trust your instincts. You'll know when this moment comes—though I pray for all your sakes that it never does. Till then, keep it safe."

Obediently, I slipped it inside my jacket.

"Now follow me," Mam said. "I've something else for you."

From the tone of her voice and strange manner I guessed where we were heading. And I was right. Carrying the brass candlestick, she led me upstairs to her private storeroom, the locked room just below the attic. Nowadays nobody ever went in that room but Mam. Not even Dad. I'd been in with her a couple of times as a small child, although I could hardly remember it now.

Taking a key from her pocket, she unlocked the door and I followed her inside. The room was full of boxes and chests. I knew she came in here once a month. What she did I couldn't guess.

Mam walked into the room and halted before the large trunk closest to the window. Then she stared at me hard until I felt a bit uneasy. She was my mam and I loved her, but I certainly wouldn't have liked to be her enemy.

"You've been Mr. Gregory's apprentice for nearly six months, so you've had long enough to see things for yourself," she said. "And by now the dark has noticed you and will be trying to hunt you down. So you're in danger, son, and for a while that danger will keep on growing. But remember this. You're growing, too. You're growing up fast. Each breath, each beat of your heart makes you stronger, braver, better. John Gregory's been struggling against the dark for years, preparing the way for you. Because, son, when you're a man, then it'll be the dark's turn to be afraid, because then you'll be the hunter, not the hunted. That's why I gave you life."

She smiled at me for the first time since I'd gone

into the room, but it was a sad smile. Then, lifting the lid of the box, she held the candle up so I could see what lay inside.

A long silver chain with fine links gleamed brightly in the candlelight. "Lift it out," Mam said. "I can't touch it."

I shivered at her words, because something told me that this was the same chain that had bound Mam to the rock. Dad hadn't mentioned it being silver, a vital omission because a silver chain was used to bind a witch. It was an important tool of a spook's trade. Could this mean that Mam was a witch? Perhaps a lamia witch like Meg? The silver chain, the way she'd kissed my dad—it all sounded very familiar.

I lifted out the chain and balanced it in my hands. It was fine and light, of better quality than the Spook's chain, with much more silver in the alloy.

As if she guessed what I'd been thinking, Mam said, "I know your dad told you how we met. But always remember this, son. None of us is either all good or all bad—we're all somewhere in between— but there comes a moment in each life when we take an important step, either toward the light or toward the dark. Sometimes it's a decision we make inside our head. Or maybe it's because of a special person we meet. Because of what your dad did for me, I stepped in the right direction and that's why I'm here today. That chain now belongs to you. So put it away and keep it safe until you need it."

I coiled the chain around my wrist, then slipped it into my inside pocket, next to the letter. That done, Mam closed the lid and I followed her out of the room, waiting while she locked the door.

Downstairs, I picked up the packet of sandwiches and prepared to leave.

"Let's have a look at that hand before you go!"

I held it out and Mam carefully untied the threads and pulled away the leaves. The burn seemed to be healing already.

"That girl knows her stuff," she said. "I'll give her that. Let the air get to it now, and it'll be right as rain in a few days."

Mam hugged me and, after thanking her once more, I opened the back door and stepped out into the night. I was halfway across the field, heading for the boundary fence, when I heard a dog bark and saw a figure heading toward me through the darkness.

It was Jack, and when he got close, I saw by the starlight that his face was twisted with anger.

"Do you think I'm stupid?" he shouted. "Do you? It didn't take five minutes for the dogs to find them!"

I looked at the dogs, which were both cowering behind Jack's legs. They were working dogs and weren't soft, but they knew me and I'd have expected some sort of greeting. Something had scared them badly.

"You might well look," said Jack. "That girl hissed and spat at them and they ran off as if the Devil himself were twisting their tails. When I told her to clear off, she had the cheek to tell me that she was on somebody else's land and it was nothing at all to do with me."

"Mr. Gregory's ill, Jack. I had no choice but to call in and get Mam's help. I kept him and Alice outside the farm boundary. I know how you feel, so I did the best I could."

"I'll bet you did. I'm a grown man, but Mam ordered me to bed like a child. How do you think that makes me feel? And in front of my own wife, too. Sometimes I wonder if the farm will ever really belong to me."

I was angry myself by then, and I felt like telling him that it probably would and a lot sooner than he thought. It would all be his once Dad was dead and Mam had gone back home to her own land. But I bit my lip and said nothing about it.

"I'm sorry, Jack, but I've got to be off," I told him, setting off toward the hut where I'd left Alice and the Spook. After a dozen or so steps I turned, but Jack already had his back to me and was on his way home.

We set off without saying a word. I had a lot to think about, and I think Alice knew that. The Spook just stared into space, but he did seem to be walking better and no longer needed to lean on us.

About an hour before the sun came up, I was the first to break the silence.

"Are you hungry?" I asked. "Mam's made us some breakfast."

Alice nodded and we sat down on a grassy bank and started on the food. I offered some to the Spook, but he pushed my arm away roughly. After a few moments he walked a little way off and sat down on a stile as if he didn't want to be anywhere near us. Or Alice, at least.

"He seems stronger. What did Mam do?" I asked.

"She bathed his forehead and kept looking at his eyes. Then she gave him a potion to drink. I kept my distance, and she didn't even glance in my direction."

"That's because she knows what you've done. I had to tell her. I can't lie to Mam."

"I did what I did for the best. Paid him back, I did, and saved all those people. I did it for you, too, Tom. So you could get Old Gregory back and carry on with your studies. That's what you want, ain't it? Ain't I done the right thing?"

I didn't reply. Alice had stopped the Quisitor burning innocent people. She'd saved a lot of lives, including the Spook's. She'd done all those things and they were all good things. No, it wasn't what she'd done, it was how she'd gone about it. I wanted to help her, but I didn't know how.

Alice belonged to the dark now, and once the Spook was strong enough, he'd want to put her in a pit. She knew that, and so did I.

CHAPTER XVI
A Pit for Alice

AT last, with the sun once more sinking into the west, the fells were directly ahead. Soon we were climbing up through the trees toward the Spook's house, taking the path that avoided Chipenden village.

I halted just short of the front gate. The Spook was about twenty paces farther back, staring up at the house as if he were seeing it for the first time.

I turned to face Alice. "You'd better go," I said.

Alice nodded. There was the Spook's pet boggart to worry about. It guarded the house and grounds. One step inside the gate and she'd be in great danger.

"Where will you stay?" I asked.

"Don't you worry about me none. And don't go

thinking I belong to the Bane either. I ain't stupid. Have to summon him twice more before that happens, don't I? The weather's not that cold yet, so I'll stay close by for a few days. Maybe in what's left of Lizzie's house. Then I'll most likely go east to Pendle. What else can I do?"

Alice still had family in Pendle, but they were witches. Despite what she said, Alice belonged to the dark now. That's where she'd feel most comfortable.

Without another word she turned and walked away into the gloom. Sadly, I watched her until she'd disappeared from sight, then I turned and opened the gate.

I unlocked the front door, and the Spook followed me inside. I led the way to the kitchen, where a fire was blazing in the grate and the table was set for two. The boggart had been expecting us. It was a light supper, just two bowls of pea soup and thick slices of bread. I was hungry after our long walk, so I tucked in straightaway.

For a while the Spook just sat there staring at his bowl of steaming hot soup, but then he picked up a slice of bread and dunked it in.

"It's been hard, lad. And it's good to be home," he said.

I was so astonished that he was speaking again that I almost fell off my chair.

"Are you feeling better?" I asked.

"Aye, lad, better than I did. A good night's sleep and I'll be right as rain. Your mam's a good woman. Nobody in the County knows their potions better."

"I didn't think you'd remember anything," I said. "You seemed distant. Almost like you were sleepwalking."

"That's what it was like, lad. I could see and hear everything, but it didn't seem real. It was just like I was in a nightmare. And I couldn't speak. I couldn't seem to find the words. It was only when I was outside, standing there looking up at this house, that I found myself again. Have you still got the key to the Silver Gate?"

Still surprised, I reached into my left breeches pocket and pulled out the key. I held it out to the Spook.

"Caused a lot of trouble, this," he said, turning it over in his hand. "But you did well, all things considered."

I smiled, feeling happier than I had in days, but when my master spoke again, his voice was harsh.

"Where's the girl?" he snapped.

"Probably not too far away," I admitted.

"Well, we'll deal with her later."

All through supper I thought of Alice. What would she find to eat? Well, she was good at catching rabbits so she wouldn't starve—that was one thing sorted out. However, in the spring, after Bony Lizzie had kidnapped a child, the men from the village had set fire to her house, and the ruin wouldn't provide much shelter on an autumn night. Still, as Alice had said, the weather still hadn't turned cold. No, her biggest threat was from the Spook.

As it turned out, it was the last mild night of the year: The following morning there was a distinct chill in the air. The Spook and I sat on the bench staring toward the fells, the wind getting stronger. The leaves were falling in earnest. The summer was well and truly over.

I'd already got my notebook out, but the Spook seemed in no hurry to start the lesson. He wasn't recovered from his ordeal with the Quisitor. During breakfast he'd said little and spent most of the time staring into space, as if deep in thought.

I was the one who finally broke the silence. "What does the Bane want, now that it's free? What will it do to the County?"

"That's easily answered," said the Spook. "Above all, it wants to grow bigger and more powerful. Then there will be no limit to the terror it will cause. It will cast a shadow of evil over the County. And no living thing will be able to hide from it. It will take blood and read minds until its powers are complete. It will see through the eyes of people who can walk in daylight while it's forced to hide in the dark somewhere underground. Whereas before it just controlled the priests in the cathedral and extended its influence into Priestown, now nowhere in the County will be safe.

"Caster could well be the next to suffer. But first the Bane might just pick on some small hamlet and press everyone to death as a warning, just to show what it can do! That was the way it controlled Heys and the kings who ruled before him. Disobedience meant a whole community would be pressed."

"Mam told me that it'll be looking for Alice," I said miserably.

"That's right, lad! Your foolish friend Alice. It needs her to regain its strength. She's twice given it her blood, so while she remains free she's fast on her way to becoming totally under its control. If nothing happens to stop it, she'll become part of the Bane and have hardly any will left of her own. It could move her, use her just as easily as I can bend my little finger. The Bane knows this—it'll be doing all it can to feed from her again. It'll be searching for her now."

"But she's strong," I protested. "And anyway, I thought the Bane was afraid of women. We both met it in the catacombs when I was trying to rescue you. It had shape-shifted into you in order to trick me."

"So the rumors were true—it had learned to take on a physical form down there."

"Yes, but when Alice spat at it, it ran off. Perhaps she could just keep doing that."

"Yes, the Bane does find it harder to control a woman than a man. Women make it nervous because they're willful creatures and often unpredictable. But once it's drunk the blood of a female, all that changes. It'll be after Alice now and give her no peace. It'll worm its way into her dreams and show her the things she can have—the things that can be hers just for the asking—until finally she'll think there's a need to summon it again. No doubt that cousin of mine was under the Bane's control. Otherwise he'd never have betrayed me like that."

The Spook scratched at his beard. "Aye, the Bane will grow and grow and there'll be little to stop it working its evil through others until everything becomes rotten in the County. That's what happened to the Little People until, finally, desperate measures were called for. We need to find out exactly how the Bane was bound; even better, how it can be killed. That's why we need to go to Heysham. There's a big barrow there, a burial mound, and the bodies of Heys and his sons are in stone graves nearby.

"As soon as I'm strong enough, that's where we're going. As you know, those who suffer violent deaths sometimes have trouble moving on from this world. So we'll visit those graves. If we're lucky, a ghost or two might still linger there. Maybe even the ghost of

Naze, who did the binding. That might well be our only hope because, to be honest, lad, at the moment I haven't a clue how we're going to bring this to an end."

With those words the Spook hung his head and looked really sad and worried. I'd never seen him so low.

"Have you been there before?" I asked, wondering why the ghosts hadn't been given a talking-to and asked to move on.

"Aye, lad, just once. I went there as an apprentice. My master was there to deal with a troublesome sea wraith that had been haunting the shore. That done, on the hill above the cliffs we passed the graves, and I knew there was something there because what had been a warm summer's night suddenly became very cold. When my master kept on walking, I asked him why he wasn't stopping to do something.

"'Leave well enough alone,'" he told me. "'It's a bother to nobody. Besides, some ghosts stay on this earth because they've a task to perform. So it's best to leave 'em to it.' I didn't know what he meant at the time, but as usual he was right."

I tried to imagine the Spook as an apprentice.

He'd have been a lot older than me because he'd trained as a priest first. I wondered what his own master had been like, a man who would take on an apprentice so old.

"Anyway," said the Spook, "we'll be going to Heysham very soon, but before that happens there's something else that has to be done. Know what it is?"

I shivered. I knew what he was going to say.

"We have to deal with the girl, so we need to know where she's hiding. My guess would be in the ruin of Lizzie's house. What do you think?" the Spook demanded.

I was going to tell him that I disagreed, but he stared at me hard until I was forced to drop my gaze to the ground. I couldn't lie to him.

"That's where she'd probably stay," I admitted.

"Well, lad, she can't stay there for much longer. She's a danger to everyone. She'll have to go into a pit. And the sooner the better. So you'd better start digging. . . ."

I looked at him, hardly able to believe what I was hearing.

"Look, lad, it's hard, but it's got to be done. It's

our duty to make the County safe for others, and that girl will always be a threat."

"But that's not fair!" I said. "She saved your life! Back in the spring she saved my life, too. Everything she's done has turned out all right in the end. She means well."

The Spook held up his hand to silence me. "Don't waste your breath!" he commanded, his expression very stern. "I know that she stopped the burning. I know that she saved lives, including my own. But she released the Bane, and I'd rather be dead than have that foul thing loose and free to do its mischief. So follow me and let's get it over with!"

"But if we killed the Bane, Alice would be free! She'd have another chance!"

The Spook's face reddened with anger, and when he spoke there was a sharp edge of menace to his voice. "A witch who uses familiar magic is always dangerous. In time, in her maturity, far more deadly than those who use blood or bone. But usually it's just a bat or a toad—something small and weak that gradually grows in power. But think what that girl's done! The Bane, of all things! And she thinks the Bane is bound to her will!

"She's clever and reckless and there's nothing that she wouldn't dare. And yes, arrogant, too! But even with the Bane dead, it wouldn't be over. If she's allowed to grow into a woman, unchecked, she'll be the most dangerous witch the County has ever seen! We have to deal with her now, before it's too late. I'm the master; you're the apprentice. Follow me and do as you're told!"

With that he turned his back and set off at a furious pace. With my heart down in my boots I followed him back to the house to collect the spade and measuring rod. We went directly to the eastern garden and there, less than fifty paces from the dark pit that held Bony Lizzie, I started to dig a new deep pit, eight feet deep and four feet by four square.

It was after sunset before I'd finished it to the Spook's satisfaction. I climbed out of the pit feeling uneasy, knowing that Bony Lizzie was in her own pit not far away.

"That'll do for now," the Spook said. "Tomorrow morning, go down to the village and fetch the local mason to measure up."

The mason would cement a border of stones around the pit into which thirteen strong iron bars would eventually be set to prevent any chance of escape. The Spook would have to be on watch while he worked to keep him safe from the pet boggart.

As I trudged back toward the house, my master briefly rested his hand on my shoulder. "You've done your duty, lad. That's all that anybody can ask, and I'd just like to tell you that so far you've more than lived up to what your mam promised. . . ."

I looked up at him in astonishment. My mam had once written him a letter saying that I'd be the best apprentice he'd ever had, but he hadn't liked her telling him that.

"Carry on like this," the Spook continued, "and when the day comes for me to retire, I'll be sure I'm leaving the County in very good hands. I hope that makes you feel a little better."

The Spook was always grudging with his praise and to hear him say that was something really special. I suppose he was just trying to cheer me up, but I couldn't get the pit and Alice out of my mind and I'm afraid his praise didn't help at all.

That night I found it hard to sleep, so I was wide awake when it happened.

At first I thought it was a sudden storm. There was a roar and a *whoosh* and the whole house seemed to shake and tremble as if buffeted by a great wind. Something struck my window with terrible force and I clearly heard glass crack. Alarmed, I knelt up on the bed and pulled back the curtains.

The large sash window was divided into eight thick, uneven panes so you couldn't see that much through them at the best of times, but there was a half moon and I could just make out the tops of the trees, bowing and writhing as if their trunks were being shaken by an army of angry giants. And three of my thick windowpanes were cracked. For a moment I was tempted to use the sash cord to raise the bottom half of the window so I could see what was happening. But then I thought better of it. The moon was shining, so it was unlikely to be a natural storm. Something was attacking us. Could it be the Bane? Had it found us?

Next came a loud pounding and ripping noise from somewhere directly above my head. It sounded as if something was beating hard on the roof, thumping it with heavy fists. I heard the slates begin to fly off and crash down onto the flags that bordered the western lawn.

I dressed quickly and rushed downstairs two steps at a time. The back door was wide open and I ran out onto the lawn, straight into the teeth of a wind so powerful that it was hardly possible to breathe, never mind take a step forward. But I did force myself on, one slow step at a time, battling to keep my eyes open as the wind pounded my face.

By the light of the moon I could see the Spook standing halfway between the trees and the house, his black cloak flapping in the fierce wind. He had his staff held high before him as if ready to ward off a blow. It seemed to take an age to reach him.

"What is it? What is it?" I shouted as I finally made it to his side.

My answer came almost immediately, but not from the Spook. A terrible, menacing sound filled the air, a mixture of an angry scream and a throbbing growl that could have been heard for miles. It was the Spook's boggart. I'd heard that sound before, in the spring, when it had prevented Bony Lizzie from chasing me into the western garden. So I knew that down there in the darkness among the trees, it was face-to-face with something that was threatening the house and gardens.

What else could it be but the Bane?

I stood there shivering with fear and cold, my teeth chattering and my body aching from the battering the gale was giving it. But after a few moments the wind subsided and very gradually everything became very still and quiet.

"Back to the house," said the Spook. "There's nothing to be done here until morning."

When we reached the back door, I stood looking at the fragments of tiles that littered the flags.

"Was it the Bane?" I asked.

The Spook nodded. "Didn't take long to find us, did it?" he said, shaking his head. "No doubt the girl's to blame for that. It must have found her first. Either that or she called it."

"She wouldn't do that again," I said, trying to defend Alice. "Did the boggart save us?" I asked, changing the subject.

"Aye, it did for now and at what cost we'll find out in the morning. But I wouldn't bet on it succeeding a second time. I'll stay on watch here," said the Spook. "Go up to your room and get some sleep. Anything could happen tomorrow, so you'll need all your wits about you."

CHAPTER XVII
The Quisitor Arrives

I came downstairs again just before dawn. The clear sky of the night was now overcast, the air perfectly still, and the lawns dusted white with the first real frost of the autumn.

The Spook was near the back door, still standing in almost the same position as when I'd last seen him. He looked tired, and his face was as bleak and gray as the sky.

"Well, lad," he said wearily, "let's go and inspect the damage."

I thought he meant the house, but instead he set off toward the trees in the western garden. Damage there was, certainly, but not as bad as it had sounded last night. There were some big branches down, twigs scattered across the grass, and the bench had been overturned. The Spook gestured and I helped him lift the bench and position it again.

"It's not that bad," I said, trying to cheer him up, for he looked really glum and down in the mouth.

"It's bad enough," he said grimly. "The Bane was always going to get stronger, but this is much faster than I expected. Much faster. It shouldn't have been able to do this so soon. We haven't much time left!"

The Spook led the way back toward the house. We could see slates missing from the roof and one of the chimney pots had been toppled from the stack.

"It'll have to wait until we've time to get it fixed," he said.

Just then there came the sound of a bell from the kitchen. For the first time that morning the Spook gave a faint smile. He looked relieved.

"I wasn't sure we'd be having breakfast this morning," he said. "Perhaps it's not quite as bad as I thought. . . ."

As we entered the kitchen, the first thing I noticed was that the flags between the table and the hearth were spotted with bloodstains. And the kitchen was really chilly. Then I saw why. I'd been the Spook's apprentice for almost six months, but this was the first morning there'd been no fire burning in the grate. And on the table there were no eggs, no bacon, just one thin slice of toast each.

The Spook touched my shoulder in warning. "Say nothing, lad. Eat it up and be grateful for what we've received."

I did as I was told, but when I'd swallowed my last mouthful of toast my belly was still rumbling.

The Spook came to his feet. "That was an excellent breakfast. The bread was toasted to perfection," he said to the empty air. "And thank you for everything you did last night. We're both very grateful."

Mostly, the boggart didn't show itself, but now once again it took the form of the big ginger cat. There was just the faintest of purrs, and it appeared briefly close to the hearth. However, I'd never seen it looking as it did then. Its left ear was torn and bleeding and the fur on its neck was matted with blood. But the worst thing of all was what had been done to its face. It had been blinded in one eye. Where its left eye used to be there was now a raw vertical wound.

"It'll never be quite the same again," said the

Spook sadly when we were outside the back door. "We should be grateful that the Bane's still not regained its full strength or we'd have died last night. That boggart's bought us a little time. Now we've got to use it before it's too late. . . ."

Even as he spoke, the bell began to ring down at the crossroads. Business for the Spook. With all that had happened and the danger from the Bane, I thought he'd ignore it, but I was wrong.

"Well, lad," he said. "Off you go and find out what's wanted."

The bell stopped ringing just before I got there, but the rope was still swaying. Down among the withy trees it was gloomy as usual, but it only took me a second to realize that it wasn't a summons to spook's business. A girl in a black dress was waiting there.

Alice.

"You're taking a big risk!" I told her, shaking my head. "You're lucky that Mr. Gregory didn't come down here with me."

Alice smiled. "Old Gregory couldn't catch me the way he is now. Ain't half the man he was."

"Don't be too sure about that!" I said angrily. "He

made me dig a pit. A pit for you. And that's where you'll end up if you're not careful."

"Old Gregory's strength has gone. No wonder he got you to dig it!" Alice jibed, her voice full of mockery.

"No," I said, "he made me dig it so that I'd accept what has to be done. That it's my duty to put you in there."

Alice's tone suddenly became sad. "Would you really do that to me, Tom?" she asked. "After all we've been through together? I saved you from a pit. Don't you remember that, when Bony Lizzie wanted your bones? When Lizzie was sharpening her knife?"

I remembered it well. But for Alice's help I would have died that night.

"Look, Alice, go to Pendle now before it's too late," I told her. "Get as far away from here as possible!"

"Bane don't agree. Thinks I should stay nearby a while longer, he does."

"The Bane's an it, not a he!" I said, irritated by what Alice was saying.

"No, Tom, he ain't," said Alice. "Sniffed him out, I did, and he's a man-thing for certain!"

"The Bane attacked the Spook's house last night. It could have killed us. Did you send it?"

Alice shook her head in a firm denial. "That ain't nothing to do with me, Tom. I swear it. We talked, that's all, and he told me things."

"I thought you weren't going to have any more dealings with it!" I said, hardly able to believe what she was saying.

"I've tried hard, Tom, I really have. But he comes and whispers things to me. Comes to me in the dark, he does, when I'm trying to sleep. He even talks to me in my dreams. He promises me things."

"What sort of things?"

"It ain't easy, Tom. It's getting colder at nights. The weather's drawing in. Bane said I could have a house with a big fireplace and lots of coal and wood and that I'd never want for anything. He said I could have nice clothes, too, so that people wouldn't look down their noses at me like they do now, thinking I'm something that's just crawled out of a hedge."

"Don't listen to it, Alice. You've got to try harder!"

"Good job I do listen to him sometimes," Alice said, a strange half smile on her face, "otherwise you'd be really sorry. I know something, see. Something that might save Old Gregory's life as well as yours."

"Tell me," I urged.

"Not sure why I should, seeing as you're plotting for me to spend the rest of my days in a pit!"

"That's not fair, Alice."

"I'll help you again, I will. But I wonder if you'd do the same for me . . . ?"

She paused and gave me a sad smile. "You see, the Quisitor's on his way up here to Chipenden. Burned his hands in that fire, that's all, and now he wants revenge. He knows Old Gregory lives somewhere nearby and he's coming with armed men and dogs. Big bloodhounds, they are, with big teeth. He'll be here by noon at the latest. So go and tell Old Gregory what I said. Don't expect he'll say thanks, though."

"I'll go and tell him," I said, and set off right away, running up the hill toward the house. As I ran, I realized that I hadn't thanked Alice, but how could I thank her for using the dark to help us?

The Spook was waiting just inside the back door. "Well, lad," he said, "get your breath back first. I can tell from your face you're bringing bad news."

"The Quisitor's on his way here," I said. "He's found out that we live near Chipenden!"

"And who told you this?" asked the Spook, scratching at his beard.

"Alice. She said he'll be here by noon. The Bane told her . . ."

The Spook sighed deeply. "Well, we'd better get away as soon as possible. First of all, you go down to the village and let the butcher know we're heading north over the fells to Caster and won't be back for some time. Go into the grocer's and tell him the same and say that we won't need any provisions next week."

I ran down into the village and did exactly what he'd told me. When I got back, the Spook was already waiting at the door, ready to set off. He handed me his bag.

"Are we going south?" I asked.

The Spook shook his head. "No, lad, we're heading north as I said. We need to get to Heysham and, if we're lucky, speak to the ghost of Naze."

"But we've told everyone the way we're going. Why didn't I pretend we were heading south?"

"Because I'm hoping the Quisitor will pay a visit

to the village on his way up here. Then, instead of searching for this house, he'll head north and the hounds will pick up our trail. We've got to draw them away from the house. Some of the books in my library are irreplaceable. If he comes here, his men might loot this place and maybe burn it to the ground. No, I can't risk anything happening to my books."

"But what about the boggart? Won't it guard the house and gardens? How can they even get in without the risk of being torn to pieces? Or is it too weak now?"

The Spook sighed and stared down at his boots. "No, it's still got strength enough to deal with the Quisitor and his men, but I don't want unnecessary deaths on my conscience. And even if it killed those who entered, some might get away. What more proof would they need then that I deserve to burn? They'd come back with an army. There'd be no end to it. No peace until the end of my days. I'd have to flee the County."

"But won't they catch us anyway?"

"No, lad. Not if we take the route over the fells. They won't be able to use their horses, and we'll have a good few hours' start. We have the advantage. We know the County well, but the Quisitor's men are outsiders. Anyway, let's get started. We've wasted enough time already!"

Heading for the fells, the Spook set off at a very fast pace. I followed as best I could, carrying his heavy bag as usual.

"Won't some of his men just ride ahead and wait for us at Caster?" I said.

"No doubt they will, lad, and if we were going to Caster, that could just be a problem. No, we're going to pass the town to the east. Then we're going southwest, as I just told you, to Heysham, to visit the stone graves. There's the Bane still to be dealt with and time is running out. Talking to the ghost of Naze is our last chance to find out how to do it."

"And after that? Where will we go? Will we ever be able to come back here?"

"I see no reason why we couldn't in time. Eventually we'll throw the Quisitor off our trail. There are ways to do that. Oh, he'll search for a bit and make a nuisance of himself, no doubt. But before long he'll go back to where he came from. To where he can keep himself warm during the coming winter."

I nodded, but I wasn't entirely happy. I could see all sorts of flaws in the Spook's plan. For one thing, he might have set off strongly, but he still wasn't fully fit, and crossing the fells would be hard work. And they might just catch us before we reached Heysham. Then again, they might search for the Spook's house anyway and burn it out of spite, especially if they lost our trail. And there was next year to worry about. In the spring the Quisitor was bound to come north again. He seemed like a man who'd never give up. I couldn't see any way that life would ever return to normal. And another thought struck me. . . .

What if they caught me? The Quisitor tortured people to make them answer questions. What if they forced me to tell them where I used to live? They confiscated or burned the homes of witches and warlocks. I thought of Dad, Jack, and Ellie with nowhere to live. And what would they do when they saw Mam? She couldn't go out in sunlight. And she often helped the local midwives with difficult deliveries and had a big collection of herbs and other plants. Mam would be in real danger!

I didn't say any of this to the Spook because I could see that he was already weary of my questions.

We were high on the fells within the hour. The weather was calm, and it looked like we'd have a fine day ahead.

If only I could have got out of my mind the reason we were up there, I'd have enjoyed myself because it was good walking weather. We'd only curlews and rabbits for company, and far to the northwest the distant sea was sparkling in the sunshine.

At first the Spook strode out energetically, leading the way. But long before noon he began to flag, and when we stopped and sat ourselves down close to a cairn of stones, he looked utterly weary. As he unwrapped the cheese, I noticed that his hands were trembling.

"Here, lad," he said, handing me a small piece. "Don't eat it all at once."

Doing as he advised, I nibbled on it slowly.

"You do know the girl's following us?" the Spook asked.

I looked at him in astonishment and shook my head.

"She's about a mile or so back there," he told me, gesturing south. "Now we've stopped, she's stopped. What do you suppose she wants?"

"I suppose she's nowhere else to go, apart from east to Pendle, and she doesn't really want to go there. And she'd no choice but to leave Chipenden. It wouldn't be safe when the Quisitor and his men arrived."

"Aye, and maybe it's because she's taken a shine to you and just wants to go where you go. I wish I'd had time to deal with her before we left Chipenden. She's a threat because wherever she is, the Bane won't be too far away. It'll be hiding underground for now, but once it's dark she'll draw it to her like a moth to a candle flame and it'll be hovering about for sure. If she feeds it again, it'll grow stronger and start seeing through her eyes. Before then it may chance upon other victims — people or animals, the effect will be the same. After bloating itself with blood, it'll grow stronger and soon be able to clothe itself in flesh and bones again. Last night was just the start."

"If it hadn't been for Alice, we'd never have left Chipenden," I pointed out. "We'd be prisoners of the Quisitor."

But the Spook chose to ignore me. "Well," he said, "we'd best get on. I'm not getting any younger while I'm sitting here."

But after another hour we rested again. This time the Spook stayed down longer before finally forcing himself to his feet. It went on like that throughout the day, with the periods of rest getting longer and the time we were on our feet getting shorter. Toward sunset the weather began to change. The smell of rain was strong in the air, and soon it began to drizzle.

As darkness fell we began to descend toward a patchwork of drystone wall enclosures. The fell side was steep and the grass was slippery and we both kept losing our footing. What's more, the rain was getting heavier and the wind starting to build from the west.

"We'll rest while I get my breath back," the Spook said.

He led the way to the nearest section of wall, and we clambered over and hunkered down on its eastern edge to shelter from the worst of the rain.

"The damp gets deep into your bones when you're my age," said the Spook. "That's what a lifetime of

County weather does to you. It gets us all eventually. Either your bones or your lungs suffer."

We crouched against the wall miserably. I was tired and weary, and even though we were outside on such a night, it was a struggle to keep awake. Before long I fell into a deep sleep and began to dream. It was one of those long dreams that seem to go on all night. And toward the end it became a nightmare. . . .

CHAPTER XVIII
Nightmare on the Hill

IT was quite definitely the worst nightmare I'd ever had. And in a job like mine I'd had a lot. I was lost and trying to find my way home. I should have been able to manage it easily enough because everything was bathed in the light of the full moon, but every time I turned a corner and thought I recognized some landmark, I was soon proved wrong. At last I came over the top of Hangman's Hill and saw our farm below.

As I walked down the hill, I began to feel very uneasy. Even though it was nighttime, everything was too still and too quiet and nothing was moving below. The fences were in a poor state of repair, something that Dad and Jack would never have allowed to happen, and the barn doors were hanging half off their hinges.

The house looked deserted: Some of the windows were broken and there were slates missing from the roof. I struggled to open the back door, and when it yielded with the usual jerk, I stepped into a kitchen that looked as though it hadn't been lived in for years. There was dust everywhere and cobwebs hung from the ceiling. Mam's rocking chair was right at the center of the room and on it was a piece of folded paper, which I picked up and carried outside to read by the light of the moon.

Your dad's, Jack's, Ellie's, and Mary's graves are up on Hangman's Hill. You'll find your mother in the barn.

My heart aching to bursting point, I ran out into the yard. Then I halted outside the barn, listening carefully. Everything was silent. There wasn't even a breath of wind. I stepped nervously into the gloom, hardly knowing what to expect. Would there be a grave there? Mam's grave?

There was a hole in the roof almost directly above, and within a shaft of moonlight I could see Mam's head. She was looking straight at me. Her body was in darkness, but from the position of her face she seemed to be kneeling on the ground.

Why would she do that? And why did she look so unhappy? Wasn't she pleased to see me?

Suddenly Mam let out a scream of anguish. "Don't look at me, Tom! Don't look at me! Turn away now!" she cried as if in torment.

The moment I looked away, Mam rose up from the floor, and out of the corner of my eye I glimpsed something that turned my bones to jelly. From the neck down, Mam was different. I saw wings and scales and a glint of sharp claws as she flew straight up into the air and smashed her way out through the barn roof, taking half of it with her. I looked up, shielding my face from the pieces of wood and debris that were falling toward me, and saw Mam, a black silhouette against the disk of the full moon as she flew upward from the wreckage of the barn roof.

"No! No!" I shouted. "This isn't true, this isn't happening!"

In reply, a voice spoke inside my head. It was the low hiss of the Bane.

"The moon shows the truth of things, boy. You know that already. All you have seen is true or will come to pass. All it takes is time."

Someone began to shake my shoulder, and I woke up in a cold sweat. The Spook was bending over me.

"Wake up, lad! Wake up!" he called. "It's just a nightmare. It's the Bane trying to get into your mind, trying to weaken us."

I nodded but didn't tell the Spook what had happened in the dream. It was too painful to talk about. I glanced up at the sky. Rain was still falling, but the cloud was patchy and a few stars were visible. It was still dark, but dawn was not far off.

"Have we slept all night?"

"We have that," replied the Spook, "but I didn't plan it that way."

He rose stiffly. "Better move on while we still can," he said anxiously. "Can't you hear 'em?"

I listened and finally, above the noise of the wind and rain, I heard the distant baying of hounds.

"Aye, they're not too far behind," the Spook said.

"Our only hope is to throw them off our scent. We need water to do that, but it needs to be shallow enough for us to walk in. Of course, we'll have to get back on dry land sometime, but the dogs will have to be taken up and down the bank to pick up the scent again. And if there's another stream close by, it makes the job a lot easier."

We scrambled over another wall and walked down a steep slope, moving as fast as we dared across the damp, slippery grass. There was a shepherd's cottage below us, a faint silhouette against the sky, and next to it an ancient blackthorn tree, bent over toward it by the prevailing winds, its bare branches like claws clutching at the eaves. We kept walking toward the cottage for a few moments, but then came to a sudden halt.

There was a wooden pen ahead and to our left. And there was just enough light to see that it contained a small flock of sheep, about twenty or so. And all of them were dead.

"I don't like the look of this one little bit, lad."

I didn't like the look of it either. But then I realized that he didn't mean the dead sheep. He was looking at the cottage beyond.

"We're probably too late," he said, his voice hardly more than a whisper. "But it's our duty to go in and see . . ."

With that he set off toward the cottage, gripping his staff. I followed carrying his bag. As I passed the pen, I glanced sideways at the nearest of the dead sheep. The white wool of its coat was streaked with blood. If that was the work of the Bane, it had fed well. How much stronger would it be now?

The front door was wide open, so without ceremony we went in, the Spook leading the way. He'd just taken one step over the threshold when he halted and sucked in his breath. He was staring to the left. There was a candle somewhere deeper in the room and by its flickering light I could see what, at first glance, I took to be a shadow of the shepherd. But it was too solid to be just a shadow. He had his back to the wall and the crook of his staff was raised above his head as if to threaten us. It took a while for me to understand what I was looking at, but something set my knees a-trembling and my heart fluttering up into my mouth.

On his face was a mixture of anger and terror. His teeth were showing, but some of them were broken and blood was smeared across his mouth. He was upright, but he wasn't standing. He'd been flattened. Pressed back against the wall. Smeared into the stones. It was the work of the Bane.

The Spook took another step into the room. And another. I followed close behind until I could see the whole of the nightmare within. There'd been a baby's crib in the corner, but it had been smashed against the wall and among the debris were blankets and a small sheet streaked with blood. Of the child there was no sign. My master approached the blankets and raised them cautiously. What he saw clearly distressed him, and he motioned at me not to look before replacing the blankets with a sigh.

By now I had spotted the infant's mother. A woman's body was on the floor, partly hidden by a rocking chair. I was grateful that I couldn't see her face. In her right hand she gripped a knitting needle, and a ball of wool had rolled into the hearth close to the embers, which were fading to gray.

The door to the kitchen was open, and I had a sudden sense of dread. I felt certain something was lurking there. No sooner had that thought entered my head than the temperature in the room dropped.

The Bane was still here. I could feel it in my bones. In terror I almost fled from that cottage, but the Spook stood his ground, and while he remained how could I leave him?

At that moment the candle was suddenly extinguished, as if snuffed out by unseen fingers, plunging us into gloom, and a deep voice spoke out of the utter blackness of the kitchen doorway. A voice that resounded through the air and vibrated along the flagged floor of the cottage so that I could feel it in my feet.

"*Hello, Old Bones. At last we meet again. Been looking for you. Knew you were somewhere nearby.*"

"Aye, and now you've found me," said the Spook wearily, resting his staff on the flags and leaning his weight against it.

"*Always were a meddler, weren't you, Old Bones? But you've meddled once too often now. I'll kill the boy first, while you stand and watch. Then it'll be your turn.*"

An invisible hand picked me up and slammed me back against the wall so hard that all the breath was driven from my body. Then the pressure began, a steady force so strong that my ribs felt about to snap. Worst of all was the terrible weight against my

forehead, and I remembered the face of the shepherd, flattened and smeared into the stones. I was
terrified, unable to move or even breathe. A darkness came over my eyes, and the last thing I knew
was a sense that the Spook had rushed toward the
kitchen doorway raising his staff.

Someone was shaking me gently.

I opened my eyes and saw the Spook bending
over me. I was lying on the floor of the cottage. "Are
you all right, lad?" he asked anxiously.

I nodded. My ribs felt sore. With every breath I
took they hurt. But I was breathing. I was still alive.

"Come on, let's see if we can get you to your feet. . . ."

With the Spook supporting me, I managed to
stand.

"Can you walk?"

I nodded and took a step forward. I didn't feel too
steady on my feet, but I could walk.

"Good lad."

"Thanks for saving me," I said.

The Spook shook his head. "I did nothing, lad.
The Bane just disappeared suddenly, as if it had
been called. I saw it moving up the hill. It looked just

like a black cloud blotting out the last of the stars. A terrible thing's been done here," he said, glancing at the horror within the cottage. "But we've got to get away just as fast as we can. First we must save ourselves. We might be able to escape the Quisitor, but with that girl following us the Bane will always be near and growing more powerful all the time. We need to get to Heysham and find out how we can deal with that foul thing once and for all!"

With the Spook leading the way, we left the cottage and continued down the hill. We crossed two more sections of wall, until I could hear the sound of rushing water. My master was moving a lot quicker now, almost as fast as when we'd set out from Chipenden, so I suppose the sleep had done him some good. Whereas I was sore all over and struggling to keep up, his bag heavy in my hand.

We came out onto a steep, narrow path beside a beck, a wide torrent of water rushing headlong downward over rocks.

"About a mile farther down, this empties out into a tarn," said the Spook, striding down the path. "The land levels and two streams flow out of it. It's just what we're looking for."

I followed as best I could. It seemed to be raining harder than ever and the ground was treacherous underfoot. One slip and you'd end up in the water. I wondered if Alice was nearby and if she could walk down a path like this, so close to fast-flowing water. Alice would be in danger, too. The dogs might pick up her scent.

Even above the noise of the beck and the rain, I could hear the bloodhounds; they seemed to be getting closer and closer. Suddenly I heard something that made me catch my breath.

It was a scream!

Alice! I turned and looked back up the path, but the Spook grabbed my arm and pulled me forward. "There's nothing we can do, lad!" he shouted. "Nothing at all! So just keep moving."

I did as I was told, trying to ignore the sounds that were coming from the fell side behind us. There were shouts and yells and more horrifying screams until gradually everything grew quiet and all I could hear was the water rushing by. The sky was much lighter now and below us, in the first dawn light, I could see the pale waters of the tarn spread out among the trees.

My heart ached at the thought of what could have happened to Alice. She didn't deserve this.

"Keep moving, lad," the Spook repeated.

And then we heard something on the path behind us—but moving closer and closer. It sounded like an animal bounding down toward us. A big dog.

It didn't seem fair. We were so close to the tarn and its two streams. Just another ten minutes, and we'd have been able to throw the hounds off our scent. But to my surprise, the Spook wasn't moving any faster. He even seemed to be slowing down. Finally he stopped altogether and pulled me to the side of the path; I wondered if he'd come to the end of his strength. If so, then it was all over for both of us.

I looked to the Spook, hoping he'd produce something from his bag to save us. But he didn't. The dog was now running toward us at full pelt. Yet as it got closer, I noticed something strange about it. For one thing, it was yelping rather than baying like a hound in full cry. And its eyes were fixed ahead rather than upon us. It passed so close that I could have reached out and touched it.

"If I'm not mistaken, it's terrified," said the Spook. "Watch out! Here comes another one!"

The next one passed, yelping like the first, its tail between its legs. Quickly, two more came by. Then, close behind, a fifth hound. All taking no notice of us but running headlong down the muddy path toward the tarn.

"What's happened?" I asked.

"No doubt we'll find out soon enough," said the Spook. "Let's just keep going."

Soon the rain stopped and we reached the tarn. It was big and, for the most part, calm. But near us the beck entered it in a fury of white water, hurtling down a steep slope to agitate the surface. We stood staring at the falling water, where twigs, leaves, and even the occasional log were being swept down into the tarn.

Suddenly something larger hit the water with a tremendous splash. It was thrust deep under the surface but reappeared about thirty or so paces farther on and began to drift toward the western shore of the tarn. It looked like a human body.

I rushed forward to the water's edge. What if it was Alice? But before I could plunge in, the Spook put his hand on my shoulder and gripped it hard.

"It's not Alice," he said softly. "That body's too big. Besides, I think she called the Bane. Why else would it have left so suddenly? With the Bane on her side, she'll have won any argument going on back there. We'd best walk round to the far shore and take a closer look."

We followed the curved shore until, after a few minutes, we were standing on the western bank under the branches of a large sycamore tree, inches deep in fallen leaves. The thing in the water was some distance away but getting closer. I hoped the Spook was right, that the body was too big to be Alice's, but it was still too dark to be sure. And if it wasn't her, whose body was it?

I began to feel afraid, but there was nothing I could do but wait as the sky grew lighter and the body drifted closer toward us.

Slowly the clouds broke up and soon the sky was light enough for us to identify the body beyond all doubt.

It was the Quisitor.

I looked at the floating body. It was on its back and only the face was clear of the water. The mouth was open and so were the eyes. There was terror on the pale dead face. It was as if there wasn't a drop of blood left in his body.

"He's swum a lot of innocents in his time," said the Spook. "The poor, the old, and the lonely. Many who'd worked hard all their lives and just deserved a bit of peace and quiet in their old age, and a bit of respect, too. And now it's his turn. He's got exactly what he deserves."

I knew that swimming a witch was just superstitious nonsense, but I couldn't get out of my head the fact that he was floating. The innocent sank; the guilty floated. Innocents like Alice's aunt, who'd died of shock.

"Alice did this, didn't she?" I said.

The Spook nodded. "Aye, lad. Some would say she did. But it was the Bane, really. Twice she's called him now. Its power over her will be growing, and what she sees, it can see also."

"Shouldn't we be on our way?" I asked nervously, looking back across the lake to where the tarn rushed headlong into it. Beside it was the path. "Won't his men come down here?"

"They might eventually, lad. That's if they've

still got breath in their bodies. But I've a feeling that they won't be in a fit state to do much for a while. No, I'm expecting somebody else, and if I'm not much mistaken, here she comes now. . . ."

I followed the Spook's gaze toward the beck, where a small figure walked down the path and stood for a moment watching the falling water. Then Alice's gaze turned toward us, and she began to walk along the bank in our direction.

"Remember," the Spook warned, "the Bane sees through her eyes now. It's building its strength and power, learning our weaknesses. Be very careful what you say or do."

One part of me wanted to shout out and warn Alice to run away while she still could. There was no knowing what the Spook might do to her. Another part of me was suddenly desperately afraid of her. But what could I do? Deep down, I knew that the Spook was her only hope. Who else could free her from the Bane now?

Alice walked up to stand at the edge of the water, keeping me between her and the Spook. She was staring toward the body of the Quisitor. There was a mixture of terror and triumph on her face.

"You might as well take a good look, girl," said the Spook. "Examine your handiwork close up. Was it worth it?"

Alice nodded. "He got what was coming to him," she said firmly.

"Aye, but at what cost?" asked the Spook. "You belong more and more to the dark. Call the Bane once more and you'll be lost forever."

Alice didn't reply and we stood there for a long time in silence, just staring at the water.

"Well, lad," said the Spook, "we'd best be on our way. Someone else will have to deal with the body because we've got work to do. As for you, girl, you'll come with us if you know what's good for you. And now you'd better listen and you'd better listen carefully because what I'm proposing is your only hope. The only chance you'll ever have to break free of that creature."

Alice looked up, her eyes very wide.

"You do know the danger you're in? You do want to be free?" he asked.

Alice nodded.

"Then come here!" he commanded sternly.

Alice walked obediently to his side.

"Wherever you are, the Bane won't be far behind, so for now you'd better come with me and the lad. I'd rather know roughly where that creature is than have it roaming anywhere it likes through the County, terrorizing decent folks. So listen to me and listen good. For now it's important that you see and hear nothing—that way the Bane will learn nothing from you. But you have to do it willingly, mind. If you cheat in the slightest way, it'll go hard with all of us."

He opened his bag and began to rummage about inside it. "This is a blindfold," he said, holding up a strip of black cloth for Alice to see. "Will you wear it?" he asked.

Alice nodded, and the Spook held out the palm of his left hand toward her. "See these?" he said. "They're plugs of wax for your ears."

Each plug had a small silver stud embedded in it to make it easy to get the wax out afterward.

Alice looked at them doubtfully, but then she tilted her head obediently while the Spook gently inserted the first plug. After pushing in the second plug, he tied the blindfold firmly across her eyes.

We set off, heading northeast, the Spook guiding Alice by her elbow. I hoped we didn't pass anybody on the road. What would they think? We'd certainly attract a lot of unwelcome attention.

CHAPTER XIX
The Stone Graves

IT was daylight, so there was no immediate threat from the Bane. Like most creatures of the dark, it would be hiding underground. And with Alice's eyes covered and her ears plugged, it could no longer look out through her eyes or listen to what we said. It wouldn't know where we were.

I had anticipated another day of hard walking and wondered if we'd get to Heysham before nightfall. But to my surprise, the Spook led us up a track to a large farm and we waited at the gate, the dogs barking fit to wake the dead, while an old farmer limped toward us, leaning on a stick. He had a worried expression on his face.

"I'm sorry," he croaked. "I'm really sorry, but

nothing's changed. If I had it to give, it'd be yours."

It seemed that five years earlier the Spook had rid this man's farm of a troublesome boggart and still hadn't been paid. My master wanted paying now, but not in money.

Within half an hour we were riding in a cart pulled by one of the biggest shire horses I'd ever seen; driving the cart was the farmer's son. At first, before setting off, he'd stared at the blindfolded Alice, a puzzled look on his face.

"Stop gawping at the girl and concentrate on your own business!" the Spook had snapped, and the lad had quickly averted his eyes. He seemed happy enough to take us, glad to be away from his chores for a few hours, and soon we were following the back lanes, passing east of Caster. The Spook made Alice lie down in the cart and covered her with straw so that she couldn't be seen by other travelers.

No doubt the horse was used to pulling a heavy load and with just us three in the back was trotting ahead at a fair old lick. In the distance we could see the city of Caster with its castle. Many a witch had died there after a long trial, but they didn't burn witches in Caster, they hanged them. So, to use one of my dad's seagoing expressions, we gave it a wide berth, and soon we were beyond it and crossing a bridge over the River Lune, before changing our direction to head southwest toward Heysham.

The farmer's lad was told to wait at the end of the lane on the outskirts of the village.

"We'll be back at dawn," said the Spook. "Don't worry. I'll make it well worth your while."

We climbed a narrow track up a hill, with an old church and graveyard on our right. There, on that lee side of the hill, everything was still and quiet and tall ancient trees shrouded the gravestones. But on clambering over a gate onto the cliff top, we were met by a stiff breeze and the tang of the sea. Before us was the ruin of a small stone chapel with just three of its walls standing. We were quite high up, and I could see a bay below, with a sandy beach almost covered by the tide and the sea crashing against the rocks of a small headland in the distance.

"Mostly, shores to the west are flat," said the Spook, "and this is as high as County cliffs ever get. They say this is where the first men landed in the County. They came from a land far to the west and their boat ran aground on the rocks below. Their descendants built that chapel."

He pointed and there, just beyond the ruin, I saw the stone graves. "There's nothing like them anywhere else in the County," said the Spook.

Carved into a huge slab of stone, right on the edge of a steep hill, there was a row of six coffins, each in the shape of a human body and with a stone lid fitting into a groove. They were different sizes and shapes but generally small, as if hewn for children, but these were the graves of six of the Little People. Six of King Heys's sons.

The Spook knelt down beside the nearest of the graves. Above the head of each was a square socket, and he traced the shape of this one with his finger. Then he extended the fingers of his left hand. The span of his hand just covered the socket.

"Now what could those have been used for?" he muttered to himself.

"How big were the Little People?" I asked. The graves were all different sizes, and now that I looked closely I saw that they weren't quite as small as I'd first thought.

By way of answer the Spook opened his bag and pulled out a folded measuring rod. He opened it and measured the grave.

"This is about five foot five long," he announced, "and about thirteen and a half inches wide in the middle. But some belongings would have been buried with the Little People for use in the next world. Few were above five feet tall, and a lot were much smaller. As the years went by, each generation got bigger because there were marriages between them and the invaders from the sea. So they didn't really die out. Their blood still runs through our veins."

The Spook turned to Alice and, to my surprise, untied her blindfold. Next he removed her earplugs, putting everything safely back in his bag. Alice blinked and looked about her. She didn't look happy.

"Don't like it here," she complained. "Something ain't right. It feels bad."

"Does it, girl?" the Spook said. "Well, that's the most interesting thing you've said all day. It's odd, because I find this spot quite pleasant. There's nothing like a bit of bracing sea air!"

It didn't seem bracing to me. The breeze had died

away and now tendrils of mist were snaking in from the sea and it was starting to grow colder. Within an hour it would be dark. I knew what Alice meant. It was a place to be avoided after sunset. I could sense something, and I didn't think it was too friendly.

"There's something lurking nearby," I told the Spook.

"Let's sit over there and give it time to get used to us," said the Spook. "We wouldn't want to frighten it off."

"Is it Naze's ghost?" I asked.

"I hope so, lad! I certainly hope so. But we'll find out soon enough. Just be patient."

We sat on a grassy bank some distance away, while the light slowly failed. I was getting more and more worried.

"What about when it gets dark?" I asked the Spook. "Won't the Bane appear? Now you've taken Alice's blindfold off, it'll know where we are!"

"I think we're safe enough here, lad," said the Spook. "This is possibly the one place in the whole County where it has to keep its distance. Something was done here, and if I'm not mistaken, the Bane won't come within a mile of the place. It might know where we are, but there's not much it can do about it. Am I right, girl?"

Alice shivered and nodded. "Trying to speak to me, he is. But his voice is very faint and distant. He can't even get inside my head."

"That's just what I hoped," said the Spook. "It means our journey here hasn't been wasted."

"He wants me to get right away from here. Wants me to go to him . . ."

"And is that what you want?"

Alice shook her head and shivered.

"Glad to hear it, girl, because after the next time, as I told you, nobody will be able to help you. Where is it now?"

"He's deep under the earth. In a dark, damp cavern. He's found himself some bones, but he's hungry and they aren't enough."

"Right! Now it's time to get down to business," said the Spook. "You two settle yourselves down in the shelter of those walls." He pointed toward the ruin of the chapel. "Try to get some sleep while I keep watch here by the graves."

We didn't argue and settled ourselves down on the grass within the ruins of the chapel. Because of the missing wall, we could still see the Spook and the graves. I thought he might have sat down, but he remained standing, his left hand resting on his staff.

I was tired out and it wasn't long before I fell asleep. But I awoke suddenly. Alice was shaking me by the shoulder.

"What's wrong?" I asked.

"Wasting his time there, he is," Alice said, pointing to where the Spook was now crouched down by the graves. "There's something nearby, but it's back there, close to the hedge."

"Are you sure?"

Alice nodded. "But you go and tell him. Won't take it too kindly coming from me."

I walked over to the Spook and called out, "Mr. Gregory!" He didn't move, and I wondered if he'd gone to sleep crouching down. But slowly he stood up and turned his upper body toward me, keeping his feet in exactly the same position.

There were a few gaps in the cloud, but those patches of starlight weren't enough to let me see the Spook's face. It was just a dark shadow under his hood.

"Alice says there's something back there close to the hedge," I told him.

"Did she now," muttered the Spook. "Then we'd better go and have a look."

We walked back toward the hedge. As we got nearer, it seemed to get even colder so I knew Alice was right. There was some sort of spirit lurking nearby.

The Spook pointed down, then suddenly he was on his knees, pulling at the long grass. I knelt, too, and began to help him. We uncovered two more stone graves. One was about five foot long, but the other was only half that size. It was the smallest grave of all.

"Someone with the old blood running pure in his veins was buried here," said the Spook. "With that would come strength. This is the one we're looking for. This'll be the ghost of Naze, all right! Walk back a little way, lad. Keep your distance."

"Can't I stay and listen?" I asked.

The Spook shook his head.

"Don't you trust me?" I asked.

"Do you trust yourself?" was his reply. "Ask yourself that! For a start, he's more likely to put in an appearance with only one of us here. Anyway, it's better that you don't hear this. The Bane can read minds, remember? Are you strong enough to stop it from reading yours? We can't let it know that we're on to it; that we have a plan; that we know its weaknesses. When it's in your dreams, rummaging through your brain for clues and plans, do you trust yourself not to give anything away?"

I wasn't sure.

"You're a brave lad, the bravest that was ever apprenticed to me. But that's what you are, an apprentice, and we mustn't let ourselves lose sight of that. So get back there with you!" he said, waving me away.

I did as I was told and trudged my way back to the ruined chapel. Alice was asleep so I sat down next to her for a few moments, but I couldn't settle. I was restless because I really wanted to know what the ghost of Naze would have to say for itself. As for the Spook's warning about the Bane rummaging through my mind while I was sleeping, it didn't worry me that much. We were safe from the Bane here, and if the Spook found out what he needed to know, it would all be over for the Bane by tomorrow night.

So I left the ruins again and crept along the wall

nearer to the Spook. It wasn't the first time I'd disobeyed my master, but it was the first time so much had been at stake. I sat down with my back against the wall and waited. But not for long. Even at that distance I began to feel very cold and kept shivering. One of the dead was approaching, but was it the ghost of Naze?

A faint glimmer of light began to form above the smaller of the two graves. It wasn't particularly human in shape, just a luminous column hardly up to the Spook's knees. Immediately I heard him begin to question it. The air was very still, and even though the Spook was keeping his voice low, I could hear every word he said.

"Speak!" said the Spook. "Speak, I command you!"

"Leave me be! Let me rest!" came the reply.

Although Naze had died when he was young and in the prime of life, the voice of the ghost sounded like that of a very old man. It croaked and rasped and was filled with utter weariness. But that didn't necessarily mean this wasn't his ghost. The Spook had told me that ghosts didn't speak as they had in life. They communicated directly to your mind and that was why you could understand one that had lived many ages ago, one that might have spoken a very different language.

"John Gregory's my name and I'm the seventh son of a seventh son," said the Spook, raising his voice. "I'm here to do what should have been done long ago; here to put an end to the evil of the Bane and give you peace at last. But there are things that I need to know. First, you must tell me your name!"

There was a long pause and I thought the ghost wasn't going to answer, but at last it replied.

"I am Naze, the seventh son of Heys. What do you wish to know?"

"It is time to finish this once and for all," said the Spook. "The Bane is free and soon will grow to its full power and threaten the whole land. It must be destroyed. So I've come to you for knowledge. How did you bind it within the catacombs? How can it be slain? Can you tell me that?"

"Are you strong?" the voice of Naze rasped. *"Can you close your mind and prevent the Bane from reading your thoughts?"*

"Aye, I can do that," said the Spook.

"Then maybe there is hope. I will tell you what I did.

How I bound the Bane. Firstly, I made a pact giving it my blood to drink. Three more times after could it drink, and in return three times it must obey my commands. At the deepest point of the catacombs of Priestown is a burial chamber, which contains the urns holding the dust of our ancient dead, the founding fathers of our people. It was to that chamber that I summoned the Bane and gave it my blood to drink. In return I proved myself to be a hard taskmaster.

"The first time I demanded that the Bane should never more return to the barrows and keep well clear of this area where my father and brothers are buried, because I wanted them to rest in peace. The Bane groaned in dismay because the barrows were its favorite dwelling place, where it lay through the daylight hours hugging the bones of the dead and sucking the last of the memories contained within them. But a pact was a pact, and it had no option but to obey. When I summoned it for a second time, I sent it questing to the ends of the earth in search of knowledge, and it was away for a month and a day, giving me all the time that I needed.

"For then I set my people to work, making and fitting the Silver Gate. But even upon its return the Bane knew nothing of this because my mind was strong and I kept my thoughts hidden.

"After giving it my blood for the final time, I told the

Bane what I required, crying out in a loud voice the price that it must pay.

"'You are bound to this place!' I commanded. 'Confined to the inner catacombs with no way out. But because I would wish no being, however foul, to endure without even a glimmer of hope, I have built a Silver Gate. If anyone is ever foolish enough to open that gate in your presence, you may pass through it to freedom. However, following that, if you ever return to this spot, you will be bound here for all eternity!'

"Thus the softness of my heart dictated to me and the binding was not as firm as it might have been. During my lifetime I was filled with compassion for others. Some considered it a weakness, and on this occasion they were proved correct. For I could not doom even the Bane to an eternity of imprisonment without offering it a faint chance of escape."

"You did enough," said the Spook. "And now I'm going to finish the job. If we can only get it back there, it will be bound forever! That is a start. But how can it be slain? Can you tell me that? This creature is so evil now, binding it is no longer enough. I need to destroy it."

"Firstly, it must have taken on the mantle of flesh. Secondly, it must be deep within the catacombs. Thirdly, its

heart must be pierced with silver. Only if all three conditions are met will it finally die. But there is a great risk for he who attempts this. In its death throes the Bane will release so much energy that its slayer will almost certainly die."

The Spook gave a deep sigh. "I thank you for that knowledge," he said to the ghost. "It will be hard, but it must be done, whatever the cost. But your task is now complete. Go in peace. Pass over to the other side."

In reply the ghost of Naze groaned so deeply that the hair began to move on the back of my neck. It was a groan filled with agony.

"There'll be no peace for me," moaned the ghost wearily. *"No peace until the Bane is finally dead . . ."*

And with those words, the small column of light faded away. Wasting no time, I moved back along the wall and into the ruins once more. A few moments later the Spook walked in, lay down on the grass, and closed his eyes.

"I've some serious thinking to do," he whispered.

I didn't say anything. Suddenly I felt guilty for listening to his conversation with Naze's ghost. Now I knew too much. I was afraid that if I told him, he'd send me away and face the Bane alone.

"I'll explain at first light," he whispered. "But for now, get some sleep. It's not safe to leave this spot until the sun comes up!"

To my surprise, I slept quite well. Just before dawn I was awakened by a strange grating sound. It was the Spook, sharpening the retractable blade in his staff with a whetstone that he'd taken from his bag. He worked methodically, occasionally testing it with his finger. At last he was satisfied, and there was a click as the blade snapped back into the staff.

I clambered to my feet and stretched my legs for a few moments while the Spook reached down, unfastened his bag again, and rummaged around inside it.

"I know exactly what to do now," he said. "We can defeat the Bane. It can be done, but it'll be the most difficult task I've ever had to undertake. If I fail, it will go hard with all of us."

"What has to be done?" I asked, feeling bad because I knew already. He didn't answer, and he walked right past me toward Alice, who was sitting up, hugging her knees.

He tied the blindfold in position and inserted the

first of the wax earplugs. "Now for the other one, but before it goes into place, listen well to me, girl, because this is important," he said. "When I take this out tonight, I'll speak to you right away and you must do what I say immediately and without question. Do you understand?"

Alice nodded, and he fitted the second plug. Once again, Alice couldn't see and she couldn't hear. And the Bane wouldn't know what we were up to or where we were going. Unless it somehow managed to read my mind. I began to feel very uneasy about what I'd done. I knew too much.

"Now," said the Spook, turning toward me. "I'll tell you one thing you won't like. We have to go back to Priestown. Back to the catacombs."

Then he turned on his heels and, gripping Alice by her left elbow, walked her back to the horse and cart where the farmer's lad was still waiting.

"We need to get to Priestown as fast as this horse can manage," said the Spook.

"Don't know about that," said the lad. "My old dad expects me back before noon. There's work to be done."

The Spook held out a silver coin. "Here, take this.

Get us there before dark and there'll be another one.
I don't think your dad'll mind too much. He likes to
count his money."

The Spook made Alice lie down at our feet and he
covered her with straw again so that she wouldn't be
visible to anybody we passed, and soon we were on
our way. At first we skirted Caster, but then, instead
of moving back toward the fells, we headed for the
main road that led directly to Priestown.

"Won't it be dangerous to go back in daylight?"
I asked nervously. The road was very busy and we
kept passing other carts and people on foot. "What
if the Quisitor's men spot us?"

"I won't say it's not without risk," said the Spook.
"But those who were searching for us are now probably busy bringing the body down the fellside. No
doubt they'll bring him to Priestown for burial, but
that won't take place till tomorrow; by then it'll all
be over and we'll be on our way. Of course, then
there's the storm to think about. People with any
sense will be indoors, sheltering from the rain."

I looked at the sky. To the south, clouds were
building but didn't look that bad to me. When I said
as much, the Spook smiled.

"You've still a lot to learn, lad," he said. "This will be one of the biggest storms you've ever seen."

"After all that rain I'd have thought we were due a few days of good weather," I complained.

"No doubt we are, lad. But this is far from natural. Unless I'm very much mistaken it's been called up by the Bane, just as it called up the wind to batter my house. It's another sign of just how powerful it's become. It'll wield the storm to show its anger and frustration at not being able to use Alice as it wants. Well, that's good for us: While it's concentrating on that, it's not bothering much about me and you. And it'll help us to get into the town without problems."

"Why do we have to go to the catacombs to kill the Bane?" I asked, hoping that he'd tell me what I already knew. That way I wouldn't have to keep up the pretense any longer.

"It's in case I fail to destroy it, lad. At least once back there, with the Silver Gate locked, the Bane'll be trapped again. This time forever. That's what the ghost of Naze told me. Then, even if I don't succeed in destroying it, at least I'll have returned things to the way they were. And now that's enough of your questions. I need some peace to prepare myself for what I'm going to do. . . ."

We didn't speak again until we reached the outskirts of Priestown. By then the sky was as black as pitch, split with great zigzags of lightning as thunderclaps burst almost directly overhead. The rain was coming straight down and soaking into our clothes, and I was wet and uncomfortable. I felt sorry for Alice because she was still lying on the floor of the cart, which now held almost an inch of water. It must have been really hard not being able to see or hear and not knowing where she was going or when the journey would end.

My own journey ended a lot sooner than I'd expected. On the outskirts of Priestown, when we came to the last crossroads, the Spook called out to the farmer's lad to stop the cart.

"This is where you get out," he said, looking at me sternly.

I gazed at him in astonishment. The rain was dripping from the end of his nose and running into his beard, but he didn't blink as he stared at me with a very fierce expression.

"I want you to go back to Chipenden," he said, pointing toward the narrow road that went roughly

northeast. "Go into the kitchen and tell that boggart
of mine that I might not be coming back. Tell him
that if that's the case he's got to keep the house safe
for when you're ready. Safe and secure until you
complete your apprenticeship and are finally fit to
take over.

"That done, go north of Caster and look for Bill
Arkwright, the local spook. He's a bit of a plodder,
but he's honest enough, and he'll train you for the
next four years or so. In the end you'll need to go
back to Chipenden and do a lot more studying. You
must get your head down in those books to make up
for the fact that I've not been there to train you!"

"Why? What's wrong? Why won't you be coming
back?" I asked. It was another question to which I
already knew the answer.

The Spook shook his head sadly. "Because there's
only one certain way to deal with the Bane, and it's
probably going to cost me my life. The girl's, too,
if I'm not mistaken. It's hard, lad, but it has to be
done. Maybe one day, years from now, you'll be
faced with a task like this yourself. I hope not, but
it sometimes happens. My own master died doing
something similar, and now it's my turn. History

can repeat itself, and if it does, we have to be ready to lay down our lives. It's just something that goes with the job, so you'd better get used to it."

I wondered if the Spook was thinking about the curse. Was he expecting to die because of that? If he died, then there'd be no one to protect Alice down there at the mercy of the Bane.

"But what about Alice?" I protested. "You didn't tell Alice what was going to happen! You tricked her!"

"It had to be done. The girl's probably too far gone to be saved anyway. It's for the best. At least her spirit will be free. It's better than being bound to that filthy creature."

"Please," I begged. "Let me come with you. Let me help."

"The best way you can help is to do what I say!" the Spook said impatiently, and seizing my arm, he pushed me roughly from the cart. I landed awkwardly and fell onto my knees. When I scrambled to my feet, the cart was already moving away, and the Spook wasn't looking back.

CHAPTER XX
Mam's Letter

I waited until the cart was almost out of sight before I began to follow it, my breath sobbing in my throat. I didn't know what I was going to do, but I couldn't bear the thought of what lay ahead. The Spook seemed resigned to his death, and poor Alice didn't even know what was going to happen to her.

There shouldn't have been too much risk of being seen—the rain was teeming straight down and the black clouds above made it almost as dark as midnight. But the Spook's senses were keen, and if I got too close, he'd know right away. So I ran and walked alternately, keeping my distance but still managing to get a glimpse of the cart from time to time. The streets of Priestown were deserted, and despite the rain, even when the cart was far ahead, I could still hear the distant clip-clop of hooves and the trundling of the cart's wheels over the cobbles.

Soon the white limestone spire began to loom up above the rooftops, confirming the Spook's direction and destination. As I'd expected, he was heading for the haunted house with the cellar that led down into the catacombs.

At that moment I felt something very strange. It wasn't the usual numbing sensation of cold that announced the approach of something from the dark. No, this was more like a sudden tiny splinter of ice right inside my head. I'd never experienced anything like it before, but it was all the warning I needed. I guessed what it was and managed to clear my mind just before the Bane spoke.

"Found you at last, I have!"

Instinctively I halted and closed my eyes. When I realized that it wouldn't be able to see out of them, I kept them closed anyway. The Spook had told me that the Bane didn't see the world as we saw it. Even though it might be able to find you, just like a spider linked to its prey by a silken thread, it still wouldn't know where you were. So I had to keep it that way.

Anything my eyes saw would be filtered into my thoughts and soon the Bane would start trying to sift through them. It might be able to pick up clues that I was in Priestown.

"Where are you, boy? Might as well tell me. Sooner or later you'll do it. Easy or hard, it can be. You choose . . ."

The splinter of ice was growing, and the whole of my head was becoming numb. It made me think again of my brother James and the farm. Of how he'd chased me that winter and filled my ears with snow.

"I'm on my way back home," I lied. "Back home for a rest."

As I spoke, I imagined walking into the farmyard with Hangman's Hill just visible on the horizon, through the murk. The dogs were starting to bark and I was approaching the back door, splashing through puddles, the rain driving into my face.

"Where's Old Bones? Tell me that. Where's he going with the girl?"

"Back to Chipenden," I said. "He's going to put Alice in a pit. I tried to talk him out of it, but he wouldn't listen. That's what he always does with a witch."

I imagined myself jerking open the back door and entering the kitchen. The curtains were drawn and the beeswax candle was alight in the brass candlestick on the table. Mam was sitting in her rocking chair. As I came in, she looked up and smiled.

Instantly the Bane was gone and the cold began to fade. I hadn't stopped it from reading my mind, but I'd deceived it. I'd done it! Seconds later my elation faded. Would it pay me another visit? Or worse still, would it pay my family one?

I opened my eyes and began to run as fast as I could toward the haunted house. After a few minutes I heard the sound of the cart again and went back to walking and running alternately.

At last the cart came to a halt, but almost immediately it set off again and I ducked into an alley as it rumbled back toward me. The farmer's lad sat hunched low and flicked the reins, sending the hooves of the big shire horse clattering across the wet cobbles. He was in a rush to get home, and I couldn't say I blamed him.

I waited five minutes or so, to let Alice and the Spook get into the house, before I ran along the street and lifted the latch on the yard door. As I expected, the Spook had locked the back door, but I still had Andrew's key, and a moment later I was standing in the kitchen. I took the candle stub from my pocket, lit it, and after that it didn't take me long to get down into the catacombs.

I heard a scream somewhere ahead and guessed what it was. The Spook was carrying Alice over the river. Even with the blindfold and the earplugs she must have been able to sense the running water.

Soon I was crossing the steps over the river myself, and I reached the Silver Gate just in time. Alice and the Spook were already on the other side, and he was on his knees, just about to close it.

He looked up angrily as I ran toward him. "I might have known it!" he shouted, his voice filled with fury. "Didn't your mam teach you any obedi-ence?"

Looking back, I can see now that the Spook was right, that he just wanted to keep me safe, but I rushed forward, gripped the gate, and started to pull it open. The Spook resisted for a moment, but then he simply let go and came through to my side, carrying his staff.

I didn't know what to say. I wasn't thinking

clearly. I'd no idea what I hoped to achieve by going with them anyway. But suddenly I remembered the curse again.

"I want to help," I said. "Andrew told me about the curse. That you'll die alone in the dark without a friend at your side. Alice isn't your friend, but I am. If I'm there it can't come true."

He lifted the staff above his head as if he was going to hit me with it. He seemed to grow in size until he towered over me. I'd never seen him so angry. Next, to my surprise and dismay, he lowered his staff, took a step toward me, and slapped me across the face. I stumbled backward, hardly able to believe that it had happened.

It wasn't a hard blow, but tears flooded into my eyes and ran down my cheeks. Dad had never slapped me like that. I couldn't believe the Spook had done it, and I felt hurt inside. Hurt much more than by any physical pain.

He stared hard at me for a few moments and shook his head as if I'd been a big disappointment to him. Then he went back through the gate, closing and locking it behind him.

"Do as I say!" he commanded. "You were born

into this world for a reason. Don't throw it away for something you can't change. If you won't do it for me, do it for your mam's sake. Go back to Chipenden. Then go to Caster and do what I've asked. That's what she'd want. Make her proud of you."

With those words the Spook turned on his heels and, guiding Alice by the left elbow, walked her along the tunnel. I watched until they turned the corner and were out of sight.

I must have waited there for half an hour or so, just staring at the locked gate, my mind numb.

At last, all hope gone, I turned and began to retrace my steps. I didn't know what I was going to do. Probably just obey the Spook, I suppose. Go back to Chipenden and then to Caster. What other choice did I have? But I couldn't get out of my mind the fact that the Spook had slapped me. That it was probably the last time we'd ever meet, and we'd parted in anger and disappointment.

I crossed the river, followed the cobble path, and climbed up into the cellar. Once there, I sat on the musty old carpet, trying to decide what to do. Suddenly I remembered another way down into the catacombs that would bring me out beyond the Silver Gate: the hatch that led down to the wine cellar, the one that some of the prisoners had escaped through! Could I get to it without being seen? It was just possible if everybody was in the cathedral.

But even if I could get down into the catacombs, I didn't know what I could do to help. Was it worth disobeying the Spook again and all for nothing? Was I just going to throw my life away when it was my duty to go to Caster and carry on learning my trade? Was the Spook right? Would Mam agree that it was the right thing to do? The thoughts just kept whirling around inside my head but led me to no clear answer.

It was hard to be sure of anything, but the Spook had always told me to trust my instincts, and they seemed to be telling me that I had to try and do something to help. Thinking of that, I suddenly remembered Mam's letter because that's exactly what she'd said.

"Only open the letter in a time of great need. . . . Trust your instincts."

It was a time of great need all right, so, very nervously, I pulled the envelope from my jacket pocket. I stared at it for a few moments, then tore it open and pulled out the letter within. Holding it close to the candle, I began to read.

Dear Tom,

You face a moment of great danger. I had not expected such a crisis to come so soon and now all I can do is prepare you by telling you what you face and indicating the outcomes that depend upon the decision that you must make.

There is much that I cannot see, but one thing is certain. Your master will descend to the burial chamber at the deepest point of the catacombs and there he will confront the Bane in a struggle to the death. Of necessity, he will use Alice to lure it to that spot. He has no choice. But you do have a choice. You can go down to the burial chamber and try to help. But then, of the three who face the Bane, only two will leave the catacombs alive.

If you turn back now, the two down there will surely die. And they'll die in vain.

Sometimes in this life it is necessary to sacrifice oneself for the good of others. I would like to offer you comfort but cannot. Be strong and do what

your conscience tells you. Whatever you choose, I
will always be proud of you.
Mam

I remembered what the Spook had once told me soon after he took me on as his apprentice. He'd spoken it with such conviction that I'd committed it to memory.

"Above all, we don't believe in prophecy. We don't believe that the future is fixed."

I badly wanted to believe what the Spook said because, if Mam was right, one of us—the Spook, Alice, or I—would die below in the dark. But the letter in my hand told me beyond a shadow of all doubt that prophecy was possible. How else could Mam have known that the Spook and Alice would be down in the burial chamber now, about to face the Bane? And how had it happened that I'd read her letter at just the right time?

Instinct? Was that enough to explain it? I shivered and felt more afraid than at any time since I'd started working for the Spook. I felt as if I were walking in a nightmare where everything had been decided in advance and I could do nothing and had no choice at all. How could there be a choice, when to leave Alice and the Spook and walk away would result in their deaths?

And there was another reason why I had to go down into the catacombs again. The curse. Was that why the Spook had slapped me? Was he angry because he secretly believed in it and was afraid? All the more reason to help. Mam had once told me that he'd be my teacher and eventually become my friend. Whether that time had arrived or not, it was hard to say, but I was certainly more of a friend to him than Alice was, and the Spook needed me!

When I left the yard and walked into the alley, it was still raining, but the skies were quiet. I sensed that more thunder was to come and we were in what my dad calls the eye of the storm. It was then, in the relative silence, that I heard the cathedral bell. It wasn't the mournful sound that I'd heard from Andrew's house, tolling for the priest who'd killed himself. It was a bright, hopeful bell summoning the congregation to the evening service.

So I waited in the alley, leaning back against a wall to avoid the worst of the rain. I don't know why I bothered, because I was already soaked to the skin. At last the bell stopped ringing, which I hoped meant that everybody was now inside the cathedral and out of the way. So I began to head slowly toward it, too.

I turned the corner and approached the gate. The light was starting to fail, and the black clouds were still piled up overhead. Then the sky suddenly lit up with a sheet of lightning, and I saw that the area in front of the cathedral was completely deserted. I could see the building's dark exterior with its big buttresses and its tall pointy windows. There was candlelight illuminating the stained glass, and in the window to the left of the door was the image of St. George dressed in armor, holding a sword and a shield with a red cross. On the right was St. Peter, standing in front of a fishing boat. And in the center, over the door, was the malevolent carving of the Bane, the gargoyle head glared at me.

The saint I was named after wasn't there. Thomas the Doubter. Thomas the Disbeliever. I didn't know whether it was my mam or my dad who'd chosen that name, but they'd chosen it well. I didn't believe what the Church believed; one day I'd be buried outside a churchyard, not in it. Once I became a spook, my bones could never rest in holy ground. But it didn't bother me in the slightest. As the Spook often said, priests knew nothing.

I could hear singing from inside the cathedral. Probably the choir I'd heard practicing after I visited Father Cairns in his confessional. For a moment I envied them their religion. They were lucky to have something they could all believe in together. It was easier to be inside the cathedral with all those people than to go down into the damp, cold catacombs alone.

I walked across the flags and onto the wide gravel path that ran parallel to the north wall of the church. Instantly, as I was about to turn the corner, my heart lurched up into my mouth. There was somebody sitting down opposite the hatch with his back against the wall, sheltering from the rain. At his side was a stout wooden club. It was one of the churchwardens.

I almost groaned aloud. I should have expected that. After all those prisoners had escaped, they'd be worried about security—and their cellar full of wine and ale.

I was filled with despair and almost gave up there and then, but just as I turned, about to tiptoe away, I heard a sound and listened again until I was sure. But I hadn't been mistaken. It was the sound of snoring. The warden was asleep! How on earth could he have slept through all that thunder?

Hardly able to believe my luck, I walked toward the hatch very, very slowly, trying not to let my boots crunch on the gravel, worrying that the warden might wake up at any moment and I'd have to run for it.

I felt a lot better when I got closer. There were two empty bottles of wine nearby. He was probably drunk and unlikely to wake up for some time. However, I still couldn't take any chances. I knelt and inserted Andrew's key into the lock very carefully. A moment later I'd pulled the hatch open and lowered myself down onto the barrels below before easing it carefully back into place.

I still had my tinderbox and a stub of candle that I always carried about with me. It didn't take me long to light my candle. Now I could see—but I still didn't know how I was going to find the burial chamber.

CHAPTER XXI
A Sacrifice

I picked my way through the barrels and wine racks until I came to the door that led to the catacombs. By my reckoning, it was less than fifteen minutes or so before nightfall, so I didn't have long. I knew that as soon as the sun went down, my master would make Alice summon the Bane for the final time.

The Spook would try to stab the Bane through the heart with his blade, but he would only get one chance. If he succeeded, the energy released would probably kill him. It was brave of him to be prepared to sacrifice his life, but if he missed, Alice would also suffer. Realizing it had been tricked and was now trapped behind the Silver Gate forever, the Bane would be furious; Alice and my master would certainly both pay with their lives if it wasn't destroyed quickly enough. It would press their bodies into the cobbles.

At the bottom of the steps I paused. Which way should I go? Immediately my question was answered; one of Dad's sayings came into my head.

"*Always put your best foot forward!*"

Well, my best foot was my left foot, so, rather than taking the tunnel directly ahead, the one that led to the Silver Gate and the underground river beyond it, I followed the one to the left. This was narrow, just wide enough to allow one person through, and it curved and sloped steeply downward so that I had a sense of descending a spiral.

The deeper I went, the colder it got, and I knew that the dead were gathering. I kept glimpsing things out of the corner of my eye: the ghosts of the Little People, small shapes hardly more than glimmers of light that kept moving in and out of the tunnel walls. And I had a suspicion that there were more behind me than in front—a feeling that they were following me; that we were all moving down toward the burial chamber.

At last I saw a flicker of candlelight ahead, and I emerged into the burial chamber. It was smaller than I'd expected, a circular room perhaps no more than twenty paces in diameter. There was a high shelf above, recessed into the rock, and on it were the large stone urns that held the remains of the ancient dead. At the center of the ceiling was a roughly circular opening like a chimney, a dark hole into which the candlelight couldn't reach. From that hole dangled chains and a hook.

Water was dripping from the stone ceiling and the walls were covered in green slime. There was a strong stench, too: a mixture of rot and stagnant water.

A stone bench curved around the wall; the Spook was sitting on it, both hands leaning on his staff, while to his right was Alice, still wearing the blindfold and earplugs.

As I approached, he stared at me, but he didn't look angry anymore, just very sad.

"You're even dafter than I thought," he said quietly as I walked up and stood before him. "Go back now while you still can. In a few moments it'll be too late."

I shook my head. "Please, let me stay. I want to help."

The Spook let out a long sigh. "You might make things even worse," he said. "If the Bane gets any warning at all, it'll stay well clear of this place. The girl doesn't know where she is, and I can close my mind against it. Can you? What if it reads your mind?"

"The Bane tried to read my mind a while back. It wanted to know where you were. Where I was, too. But I stood up to it and it failed," I told him.

"How did you stop it?" he asked, his voice suddenly harsh.

"I lied to it. I pretended that I was on my way home and I told it you were on your way to Chipenden."

"And did it believe you?"

"It seemed to," I said, suddenly feeling less certain.

"Well, we'll find out soon enough when it's summoned. Go a little way back up the tunnel then," said the Spook, his voice softer. "You'll be able to watch from there. If things go badly, you might even have half a chance of escaping. Go on, lad! Don't hesitate. It's nearly time!"

I did as I was told, moving back quite some distance into the tunnel. I knew that by now the sun would have dipped below the horizon and dusk would be drawing in. The Bane would leave its hiding place below ground. In its spirit form it could fly freely through the air and pass through solid rock. Once summoned, it would fly straight to Alice, faster than a hawk with folded wings, dropping like a stone toward its prey. If the Spook's plan worked, it wouldn't realize where Alice was waiting. Once it was here, it would be too late. But we'd be here, too, facing its anger when it realized it had been tricked and trapped.

I watched the Spook climb to his feet and stand facing Alice. He bowed his head and stayed perfectly still for a long time. Had he been a priest I'd have thought he was praying. Finally he reached toward Alice, and I saw him draw the wax plug from her left ear.

"Summon the Bane!" he shouted, in a loud voice that filled the chamber and echoed down the tunnel. "Do it now, girl! Don't delay!"

Alice didn't speak. She didn't even move. She didn't need to because she called it from within her mind, willing its presence.

There was no warning of its arrival. One moment there was just silence, the next there was a blast of cold and the Bane appeared in the chamber. From the neck upward, it was the replica of the gargoyle over the main cathedral door: gaping teeth, lolling tongue, huge dog's ears, and wicked horns. From the neck down, it was a vast, black, shapeless boiling cloud.

It had gained the strength to take on its original form! What chance had the Spook against it now?

For one short moment the Bane remained perfectly still while its eyes darted everywhere. Eyes with pupils that were dark green, vertical slits. Pupils shaped like those of a goat.

Then, upon realizing where it was, it let out a groan of anguish and dismay that boomed along the tunnel so that I could feel it vibrate through the very soles of my boots and shiver up into my bones.

"Bound again, I am! Bound fast!" it cried with harsh, hissing coldness that echoed in the chambers and penetrated me like ice.

"Aye," said the Spook. "You're here now and here you'll stay, bound forever to this cursed place!"

"Enjoy what you've done! Suck in your last breath, Old

Bones. Tricked me, you have, but what for? What will you gain but the darkness of death? Nothing, you'll be, but I'll still have my way with the ones above. Still do my bidding, they will. Fresh blood they'll send me down! So all for nothing it was!"

The head of the Bane grew larger, the face becoming even more hideous, the chin lengthening and curving upward to meet the hooked nose. The dark cloud was boiling downward, forming flesh so that now a neck was visible and the beginnings of broad, powerful, muscular shoulders. But instead of skin, they were covered in rough green scales.

I knew what the Spook was waiting for. The moment the chest was clearly defined, he would strike straight for the heart within. Even as I watched, the boiling cloud descended farther to form the body as far down as the waist.

But I was mistaken! The Spook didn't use his blade. As if appearing from nowhere, the silver chain was in his left hand, and he raised his arm to hurl it at the Bane.

I'd seen him do it before. I'd watched him throw it at the witch, Bony Lizzie, so that it formed a perfect spiral and dropped upon her, binding her arms to her sides. She'd fallen to the ground and could do nothing but lie there snarling, the chain enclosing her body and tight against her teeth.

The same would have happened here, I'm sure of it, and it would have been the Bane's turn to lie there helplessly. But at the very moment when the Spook prepared to hurl the silver chain, Alice lurched to her feet and tore off her blindfold.

I know she didn't mean to do it, but somehow she got between the Spook and his target and spoiled his aim. Instead of landing over the Bane's head, the silver chain fell against its shoulder. At its touch, the creature screamed out in agony and the chain fell to the floor.

But it wasn't over yet, and the Spook snatched up his staff. As he held it high, preparing to drive it into the Bane, there was a sudden click, and the retractable blade, made from an alloy containing sil-ver, was now bared, glinting in the candlelight. The blade that I'd watched him sharpening at Heysham. I'd seen him use it once before, when he'd faced Tusk, the son of the old witch, Mother Malkin.

Now the Spook stabbed his staff hard and fast, straight at the Bane, aiming for its heart. It tried to twist away but was too late to avoid the thrust completely. The blade pierced its left shoulder, and it screamed out in agony. Alice backed away, a look of terror on her face, while the Spook pulled back his staff and readied it for a second thrust, his face grim and determined.

But suddenly, both candles were snuffed out, plunging the chamber and tunnel into darkness. Frantically, I used my tinderbox to light my own candle again, but it flickered into life to reveal that the Spook now stood alone in the chamber. The Bane had simply disappeared! And so had Alice!

"Where is she?" I cried, running toward the Spook, who just shook his head sadly.

"Don't move!" he commanded. "It's not finished yet!"

He was staring up at where the chains disappeared into the dark hole in the ceiling. There was a loop and, beside it, a second single length of chain. Affixed to the end of it, and almost touching the floor, was a large hook. It was a sort of block and tackle similar to the ones used by riggers to lower boggart stones into position.

The Spook seemed to be listening for something. "It's somewhere up there," he whispered.

"Is that a chimney?" I asked.

"Aye, lad. Something like that. At least, that was the purpose it sometimes served. Even long after it had been bound and the Little People were dead and gone, weak and foolish men made sacrifices to the Bane on this very spot. The chimney carried the smoke up into its lair above, and they used the chain to send up the burnt offering. Some of them got pressed for their trouble!"

Something was beginning to happen. I felt a draft from the chimney, and there was a sudden chill in the air. I looked up as what looked like smoke began to waft slowly down to fill the upper reaches of the chamber. It was as if all the burnt offerings that had ever been made on this spot were being returned!

But it was far denser than smoke; it looked like water, like a black whirlpool swirling above our heads. Within seconds it became calm and still, resembling the polished surface of a dark mirror. I could even see our reflections in it: me standing next to the Spook, his staff at the ready, blade pointing vertically, ready to jab.

What happened next was too swift to see properly. The surface of the smoke mirror bulged out toward us and something broke through, fast and hard enough to send the Spook sprawling backward. He fell heavily, the staff flying out of his hand and breaking into two unequal pieces with a sharp snapping sound.

At first I stood there stunned, hardly able to think, unable to move a muscle, but at last, my whole body trembling, I went across to see if the Spook was all right.

He was on his back, his eyes closed, a trickle of blood running from his nose down into his open mouth. He was breathing deeply and evenly, so I shook him gently, trying to wake him up. He didn't respond. I walked across to the broken staff and picked up the smaller of the two pieces, the one with the blade attached. It was about the length of my forearm, so I tucked it into my belt. I stood at the side of the chain looking upward.

Somebody had to try to help Alice and destroy this creature once and for all, and I was the only one who could. I couldn't leave her to the Bane. So first I tried to clear my mind. If it was empty, the Bane couldn't read my thoughts. The Spook had probably been practicing that for days, but I would just have to do my best.

I put the end of the candle in my mouth, biting into it with my teeth, then gripped the single chain carefully with both hands, trying to keep it as still as possible. Next I placed my feet above the hook and gripped the chain between my knees. I was good at climbing ropes, and a chain couldn't be that different.

I began to move upward quite fast, the chain cold and biting in my hand. At the bottom of the thick smoke, I took a deep breath, held it, and pushed my head up into the darkness. I couldn't see a thing, and despite not breathing the smoke was getting up my nose and into my open mouth and there was a sharp acrid taste at the back of my throat that reminded me of burned sausages.

Suddenly my head was out of the smoke, and I pulled myself farther up the chain until my shoulders and chest were clear of it. I was in a circular chamber almost identical to the one below except that, rather than a chimney above, there was a shaft below, and the smoke filled the lower half of the chamber.

A tunnel led from the opposite wall into the darkness, and there was another stone bench where Alice was sitting, the smoke almost up to her knees. She was holding out her left hand toward the Bane. That heinous creature was kneeling in the smoke, bending over her, the naked arch of its back reminding me of a large green toad. Even as I watched, it drew her hand into its large mouth, and I heard Alice cry out in pain as it began to suck the blood from beneath her nails. This was the third time the Bane had fed on Alice's blood since she released it. When it had finished, Alice would belong to it!

I was cold, as cold as ice, and my mind was blank. I was thinking about nothing at all. I pulled myself up farther and stepped from the chain onto the stone floor of the upper chamber. The Bane was too preoccupied with what it was doing to be aware of my presence. No doubt in that respect it was like the Horshaw ripper: When it was feeding, hardly anything else mattered.

I stepped closer and pulled the piece of the Spook's staff from my belt. I raised it and held it above my head, the blade pointing at the Bane's scaly green back. All I had to do was bring it down hard and pierce the Bane's heart. It was clothed in flesh, and that would be the end of it. It would be dead. But just as I was tensing my arm, I suddenly became afraid.

I knew what would happen to me. So much energy would be released that I would die, too. I would be a ghost just like poor Billy Bradley, who'd died after having his fingers bitten off by a boggart. He'd been happy once as the Spook's apprentice but now was buried outside the churchyard at Layton. The thought of it was too much to bear.

I was terrified—terrified of death—and I began to tremble again. It started at my knees and traveled right up my body until the hand holding the blade began to shake.

The Bane must have sensed my fear, because it suddenly turned its head, Alice's fingers still in its mouth, blood trickling down its big curved chin. But then, when it was almost too late, my fear simply evaporated away. All at once I realized why I was there facing the Bane. I remembered what Mam had said in her letter.

"Sometimes in this life it is necessary to sacrifice oneself for the good of others."

She'd warned me that of the three who faced the Bane, only two would leave the catacombs alive. I'd somehow thought it was going to be the Spook or Alice who would die, but now I realized that it would be me! I was never going to complete my apprenticeship, never going to become a spook. But by sacrificing my life now, I could save both of them. I was very calm. I simply accepted what had to be done.

I feel sure that at the very last moment the Bane realized what I was going to do, but instead of pressing me dead on the spot, it turned its head back toward Alice, who gave it a strange, mysterious smile.

I struck quickly with all my strength, driving the blade toward its heart. I didn't feel the blade make contact, but a shuddering darkness rose before my eyes; my body quivered from head to foot, so that I had no control over my muscles. The candle dropped out of my mouth and I felt myself falling. I'd missed its heart!

For a moment I thought that I'd died. Everything was dark, but for now the Bane seemed to have vanished. I fumbled around on the floor for my candle and lit it again. Listening carefully, I gestured to Alice to be silent, and heard a sound from the tunnel. The padding of a large dog.

I tucked the piece of staff with the blade back into my belt. Next I eased Mam's silver chain from my jacket pocket and coiled it around my left hand and wrist, ready for throwing. With my other hand I picked up the candle, and without further delay I set off after the Bane.

"No, Tom, no! Leave it be!" Alice called out from behind. "It's over. You can go back to Chipenden!"

She ran toward me, but I pushed her back hard. She staggered and almost fell. When she moved toward me again, I lifted my left hand so that she could see the silver chain.

"Keep back! You belong to the Bane now. Keep your distance or I'll bind you, too!"

The Bane had fed for the final time, and now nothing she said could be trusted. It would have to be dead before she'd be free.

I turned my back on her and moved away quickly. Ahead of me I could hear the Bane; behind me the *click-click* of Alice's pointy shoes as she followed me into the tunnel. Suddenly the padding ahead stopped.

CURSE OF THE BANE

Had the Bane simply vanished and gone to another part of the catacombs? I stopped and listened before moving forward more cautiously. It was then that I saw something ahead. Something on the floor of the tunnel. I halted close to it and my stomach heaved. I was almost sick on the spot.

Brother Peter lay on his back. He'd been pressed. His head was still intact; the wide-open, staring eyes showed the terror he had obviously felt at the time of his death. But from the neck downward his body had been flattened against the stones.

The sight horrified me. During my first few months as an apprentice I'd seen many terrible things and been close to death and the dead more times than I cared to remember. But this was the first time I'd seen the death of someone I cared about—and such a horrible death.

I stood, distracted by the sight of Brother Peter, and the Bane chose that moment to come loping out of the darkness toward me. For a moment it halted and stared at me, the green slits of its eyes glowing in the gloom. Its heavy, muscular body was covered in coarse black hair, and its jaws were wide, revealing the rows of sharp yellow teeth. Something was dripping from that long tongue that lolled forward, beyond the gaping jaws. Instead of saliva, it was blood!

Suddenly the Bane attacked, bounding toward me. I readied my chain and heard Alice scream behind me. Just in time I realized that it had changed its angle of attack. I wasn't the target! Alice was!

I was stunned. I was the threat to the Bane, not Alice. So why her rather than me?

Instinctively I adjusted my aim. Nine times out of ten I could hit the post in the Spook's garden, but this was different. The Bane was moving fast, already beginning to leap. So I cracked the chain and cast it toward the creature, watching it open like a net and drop in the shape of a spiral. All my practice paid off, and it fell over the Bane cleanly and tightened against its body. The Bane rolled over and over, howling, struggling to escape.

In theory it couldn't get itself free, and neither could it vanish or change shape. But I wasn't taking any chances. I had to pierce its heart quickly. I had to finish it now. So I ran forward, pulled the blade from my belt, and prepared to stab into its chest. Its eyes looked up at me as I readied the blade. They were filled with hatred. But there was fear there, too: the absolute terror of death; terror of the nothingness it faced, and it spoke inside my head, begging frantically for its life.

"Mercy! Mercy!" it cried. *"Nothing for us, there is! Just darkness. Is that what you want, boy? You'll die, too!"*

"No, Tom, no! Don't do it!" Alice shouted out behind me, adding her voice to the Bane's. But I didn't listen to either of them. No matter what the cost to myself, it had to die. It was writhing within the coils of the chain, and I stabbed it twice before I found its heart.

The third time I lunged downward the Bane simply vanished, but I heard a loud scream. Whether it was the Bane, Alice, or me who made that sound, I'll never know. Maybe it was all three of us.

I felt a tremendous blow to my chest, followed by a strange sinking feeling. Everything went very quiet, and I felt myself falling into darkness.

The next thing I knew I was standing by a large expanse of water.

Despite its size, it was more like a lake than a sea,

for although a pleasant breeze was blowing toward the shore, the water remained calm, like a mirror, reflecting the perfect blue of the sky.

Small boats were being launched from a beach of golden sand, and beyond them I could see an island quite close to the shore. It was green with trees and rolling meadows and seemed to me more wonderful than anything I'd ever seen before in my whole life. Among the trees on a hilltop was a building like the castle we'd glimpsed from the low fells as we skirted Caster. But instead of being constructed of cold gray stone, it shimmered with light as if built from the beams of a rainbow, and its rays warmed my forehead like a glorious sun.

I wasn't breathing, but I was calm and happy, and I remember thinking that if I was dead then it was nice to be dead and I just had to get to that castle, so I ran toward the nearest of the boats, desperate to get on board. As I drew closer, the people stopped trying to launch the boat and turned their faces toward me. At that moment I knew who they were. They were small, very small, and had dark hair and brown eyes. It was the Little People! The Segantii!

They smiled in welcome, rushed toward me and

began to pull me toward the boat. I'd never felt so happy in my life, so welcomed, so wanted, so accepted. All my loneliness was over. But just as I was about to climb aboard, I felt a cold hand grip my left forearm.

When I turned, there was nobody there, but the pressure on my arm increased until it began to hurt. I could feel fingernails cutting into my skin. I tried to pull away and get into the boat and the Little People tried to help me, but the pressure on my arm was now a burning pain. I cried out and sucked in a huge, painful breath that sobbed in my throat and made my whole body tingle, then grow hotter and hotter as if I were burning inside.

I was lying on my back in the dark. It was raining very hard, and I could feel the raindrops drumming on my eyelids and forehead and even falling into my mouth, which was wide open. I was too weary to open my eyes, but I heard the Spook's voice from some distance away.

"Leave him be!" he said. "Give him peace, girl. That's all we can do for him now!"

I opened my eyes and looked up to see Alice bending over me. Behind her I could see the dark wall of the cathedral. She was gripping my left forearm, her nails very sharp against my skin. She leaned forward and whispered into my ear.

"You don't get away that easily, Tom. You're back now. Back where you belong!"

I sucked in a deep breath and the Spook came forward, his eyes filled with amazement. As he knelt at my side, Alice stood up and drew back.

"How do you feel, lad?" he asked gently, helping me up into a sitting position. "I thought you were dead. When I carried you out of the catacombs, I swear there was no breath left in your body!"

"The Bane?" I asked. "Is it dead?"

"Aye, it is that, lad. You finished it off and nearly did for yourself in the process. But can you walk? We need to get away from here."

Beyond the Spook I could see the guard with the empty bottles of wine by his side. He was still in a drunken sleep, but he could wake up at any moment.

With the Spook's help I managed to get to my feet, and the three of us left the cathedral grounds and made our way through the deserted streets.

At first I was weak and shaky, but as we climbed away from the rows of terraced houses and back up into the countryside, I started to feel stronger. After a while I turned and looked back toward Priestown, which was spread out below us. The clouds had lifted and the moon was out. The cathedral spire seemed to be gleaming.

"It looks better already," I said, stopping to take in the view.

The Spook halted beside me and followed the direction of my gaze. "Most things look better from a distance," he said. "And as a matter of fact, so do most people."

He seemed to be joking, so I smiled.

"Well." He sighed. "It should be a far better place from now on. But, that said, we won't be coming back in a hurry."

After an hour or so on the road we found an old abandoned barn to shelter in. It was drafty, but at least it was dry and there was a bit of the yellow cheese to nibble on. Alice dropped off to sleep right away, but I sat up a long time, thinking about what had happened. The Spook didn't seem tired, either, but just sat in silence, hugging his knees. Eventually he spoke.

"How did you know how to kill the Bane?" he asked.

"I watched you," I answered. "I saw you strike for its heart . . ."

But suddenly I was overcome with shame at my lie and I hung my head low. "No, I'm sorry," I said. "That's not true. I sneaked forward when you talked to the ghost of Naze. I heard everything you said."

"And so you should be sorry, lad. You took a big risk. If the Bane had managed to read your mind—"

"I'm really sorry."

"And you didn't tell me you had a silver chain," he said.

"Mam gave it to me," I answered.

"Well, it's a good job that she did. Anyway, it's in my bag and safe enough for now. Until you need it again . . ." he added ominously.

There was another long silence, as if the Spook were deep in thought.

"When I carried you up from the catacombs, you seemed cold and dead," he said at last. "I've seen death so many times that I know I wasn't mistaken. Then that girl grabbed your arm and you came back. I don't know what to make of it."

"I was with the Little People," I said.

The Spook nodded. "Aye," he said, "they'll all be

at peace now that the Bane's dead. Naze included. But what about you, lad? What was it like? Were you afraid?"

I shook my head. "I was more afraid just after I'd read Mam's letter," I told him. "She knew what was going to happen. I felt that I had no choice. That everything was already decided. But if everything's already decided, then what's the point of living?"

The Spook frowned and held out his hand. "Give me the letter," he demanded.

I took it out of my pocket and passed it to him. He took a long time reading it, but at last he handed it back. He didn't speak for quite a while.

"Your mother is a shrewd and intelligent woman," the Spook said at last. "That accounts for much of what's written there. She'd worked out exactly what I was going to do. She'd more than enough knowledge to do that. It's not prophecy. Life's bad enough as it is without believing in that. You chose to go down the steps. But you had another choice. You could have walked away, and then everything would have been different."

"But once I'd chosen, she was right. Three of us faced the Bane and only two survived. I was dead.

You carried me back to the surface. How can we explain that?"

The Spook didn't reply, and the silence between us grew longer and longer. After a while I lay down and fell into a dreamless sleep. I didn't mention the curse. I knew it was something he wouldn't want to talk about.

CHAPTER XXII
A Bargain's a Bargain

IT was almost midnight, and a horned moon was rising above the trees. Rather than approaching his house by the most direct route, the Spook brought us toward it from the east. I thought of the eastern garden ahead and the pit that lay in wait for Alice. The pit that I'd dug.

Surely he wasn't going to put her in the pit now? Not after all she'd done to help put things right? She'd allowed him to blindfold her and seal her ears with wax. And then she'd sat there for hours in silence and darkness without complaining even once.

But then I saw the stream ahead and was filled with new hope. It was narrow but fast flowing, the water sparkling silver in the moonlight, and there was a single stepping-stone at its center.

He was going to test Alice.

"Right, girl," he said, his expression stern. "You lead the way. Over you go!"

When I looked at Alice's face, my heart sank. She looked terrified, and I remembered how I'd had to carry her across the river near the Silver Gate. The Bane was dead now, its power over Alice broken, but was the damage already done beyond all hope of repair? Had Alice moved too close to the dark? Could she never be free? Never be able to cross running water? Was she a fully fledged malevolent witch?

Alice hesitated at the water's edge and began to tremble. Twice she lifted her foot to make the simple step to the flat stone at the center of the stream. Twice she put it down again. Beads of sweat gathered on her forehead and began to roll down toward her nose and eyes.

"Go on, Alice, you can do it!" I called, trying to encourage her. For my trouble I got a withering stare from the Spook.

With a sudden, terrible effort Alice stepped

onto the stone and swung her left leg forward almost immediately to carry herself over to the far bank. Once there, she hurriedly sat down and buried her face in her hands.

The Spook made a clicking noise with his tongue, crossed the stream, and strode quickly up the hill toward the trees on the edge of the garden. I waited behind while Alice got to her feet, then together we walked up to where the Spook was waiting, his arms folded.

When we reached him, the Spook suddenly stepped forward and seized Alice. Gripping her by the legs, he threw her back over his shoulder. She began to wail and struggle, but without another word he clutched her more firmly, then turned and strode into the garden.

I followed behind desperately. He was heading deep into the eastern garden, moving directly toward the graves where the witches were kept, toward the empty pit. It didn't seem fair! Alice had passed the test, hadn't she?

"Help me, Tom! Help me, please!" Alice cried.

"Can't she have one more chance?" I pleaded. "Just one more chance? She crossed. She's not a witch."

"She just about got away with it this time," snarled the Spook over his shoulder. "But there's badness inside her, just waiting its chance."

"How can you say that? After all she's done—"

"This is the safest way. It's the best thing for everyone!"

I knew then that it was time for what my dad calls "a few home truths." I had to tell him what I knew about Meg, even though he might hate me for it and not want me as his apprentice anymore. But perhaps a reminder of his past might make him change his mind. The thought of Alice going into the pit was unbearable, and the fact that I'd been made to dig it made it a hundred times worse.

The Spook reached the pit and halted at its very edge. As he moved to lower Alice into the darkness, I shouted out, "You didn't do it to Meg!"

He turned toward me with a look of utter astonishment on his face.

"You didn't put Meg in the pit, did you?" I cried out. "And she was a witch! You didn't do it because you cared too much about her! So please don't do it to Alice! It isn't right!"

The Spook's expression of astonishment changed to one of fury and he stood there, tottering on the edge of the pit; for a moment I didn't know whether he was going to throw Alice down or fall into it himself. He stood there for what seemed like a very long time, but then, to my relief, his fury seemed to give way to something else and he turned and walked away, still carrying Alice.

He walked beyond the new, empty pit, passed the one where Bony Lizzie was imprisoned, strode away from the graves where the two dead witches were buried, and stepped onto the path of white stones that led toward the house.

Despite his recent illness, all that he'd been through, and the weight of Alice over his shoulder, the Spook was walking so fast that I was struggling to keep up. He pulled the key from the left pocket of his breeches, opened the back door of the house, and was inside before my foot even touched the step.

He walked straight into the kitchen and halted close to the fireplace, where flames were flickering sparks up the chimney. The kitchen was warm, the candles lit, with cutlery and plates set for two on the table.

Slowly the Spook eased Alice from his shoulder and set her down. The moment her pointy shoes touched the flags, the fire died right down, the candle flickered and almost went out, and the air grew distinctly chilly.

The next moment there was a growl of anger that rattled the crockery and vibrated right through the floor. It was the Spook's pet boggart. Had Alice walked into the garden, even with the Spook close by, she would have been torn to pieces. But because the Spook had been carrying her, it wasn't until her feet touched the ground that the boggart became aware of Alice's presence. And now it wasn't best pleased.

The Spook placed his left hand on top of Alice's head. Next, with his left foot he stamped hard three times against the flags.

The air grew very still, and the Spook called out in a loud voice, "Hear me now! Listen well to what I say!"

There was no answer, but the fire recovered a little and the air didn't seem quite so cold.

"While this child is in my house, harm not a hair of her head!" ordered the Spook. "But watch everything that she does and ensure that she does all that I command."

With that, he stamped three more times against the flags. In answer, the fire flared up in the grate and the kitchen suddenly seemed warm and welcoming.

"And now prepare supper for three!" the Spook commanded. Then he beckoned and we followed him out of the kitchen and up the stairs. He paused outside the locked door of the library.

"While you're here, girl, you'll earn your keep," the Spook growled. "There are books in there that can't be replaced. You'll never be allowed inside, but I'll give you one book at a time and you can make a copy of it. Is that understood?"

Alice nodded.

"Your second job will be to tell my lad everything that Bony Lizzie taught you. And I mean everything. He'll write it all down. A lot of it'll be nonsense, of course, but that doesn't matter because it'll still add to our store of knowledge. Are you prepared to do that?"

Again Alice nodded, her expression very serious.

"Right, so that's settled," said the Spook. "You'll sleep in the room above Tom's, the one right at the top of the house. And now, think well on what I'm saying. That boggart down in the kitchen knows what you are and what you almost became. So don't take even one little step out of line, because it'll be watching everything that you do. And it would like nothing better than to . . ."

The Spook sighed long and hard. "It doesn't bear thinking about," he said. "So don't give it the chance. Will you do what I ask, girl? Can you be trusted?"

Alice nodded, and her mouth widened into a big smile.

At supper the Spook was unusually quiet. It was like the calm before a storm. Nobody said much, but Alice's eyes were everywhere and they returned again and again to the huge, blazing log fire that was filling the room with warmth.

At last, the Spook pushed back his plate and sighed. "Right, girl," he said, "off you get to bed. I've a few things that need to be said to the lad."

When Alice had gone, the Spook pushed back his chair and strode toward the fire. He bent and warmed his hands over the flames before turning to face me. "Well, lad," he growled, "spit it out. Where did you find out about Meg?"

"I read it in one of your diaries," I said sheepishly, bowing my head.

"I thought as much. Didn't I warn you about that? You've disobeyed me again! There are things in my library that you're not meant to read yet," the Spook said sternly. "Things you're not quite ready for. I'll be the judge of what's fit for you to read. Is that understood?"

"Yes, sir," I said, addressing him by that title for the first time in months. "But I'd have found out about Meg anyway. Father Cairns mentioned her, and he told me about Emily Burns, too, and how you took her away from your brother and it split your family."

"Can't keep much from you, can I, lad?"

I shrugged, feeling relieved to have gotten it all off my chest.

"Well," he said, coming back toward the table, "I've lived to a good age and I'm not proud of everything I've done, but there's always more than one side to every story. None of us is perfect, lad, and one day you'll find out all you need to know and then you can make up your own mind about me. There's little point in picking through the bones now, but as for Meg, you'll be meeting her when we get to Anglezarke. That'll be sooner than you think because, depending on the weather, we'll be setting off for my winter house in a month or so. What else did Father Cairns have to say for himself?"

"He said that you'd sold your soul to the Devil. . . ."

The Spook smiled. "What do priests know? No, lad, my soul still belongs to me. I've fought long, long years to hold on to it, and against all the odds it's still mine. And as for the Devil, well, I used to think that evil was more likely to be inside each one of us, like a bit of tinder just waiting for the spark to set it alight. But more recently I've begun to wonder if, after all, there is something behind all that we face, something hidden deep within the dark. Something that grows stronger as the dark grows stronger. Something that a priest would call the Devil. . . ."

The Spook looked at me hard, his green eyes boring into my own. "What if there were such a thing as the Devil, lad? What would we do about it?"

I thought for a few moments before I answered. "We'd need to dig a really big pit," I said. "A bigger pit than any spook has ever dug before. Then we'd need bags and bags of salt and iron and a really big stone."

The Spook smiled. "We would that, lad. There'd be work for half the masons, riggers, and mates in the County! Anyway, get off to bed with you now. It's back to your lessons tomorrow, so you'll need a good night's sleep."

As I opened the door to my room, Alice emerged from the shadows on the stairs.

"I really like it here, Tom," she said, giving me a wide smile. "Nice big warm house, it is. A good place to be now that winter's drawing in."

I smiled back. I could have told her that we'd be off to Anglezarke soon, to the Spook's winter houe, but she was happy and I didn't want to spoil her first night.

"One day this house will belong to us, Tom. Don't you feel it?" she asked.

I shrugged. "Nobody knows what's going to happen in the future," I said, putting Mam's letter to the back of my mind.

"Old Gregory tell you that, did he? Well, there are lots of things he doesn't know. You'll be a better spook than he ever was. Ain't nothing more certain than that!"

Alice turned and went up the stairs swinging her hips. Suddenly she looked back.

"Desperate for my blood, the Bane was," she said. "So I made the bargain even before he drank. I just wanted to make everything all right again, so I asked that you and Old Gregory could go free. Bane agreed. A bargain's a bargain, so he couldn't kill Old Gregory and he couldn't hurt you. You killed the Bane, but I made it possible. At the end that's why it attacked me. It couldn't touch you. Don't tell Old Gregory though. He wouldn't understand."

Alice left me standing on the stairs while what she'd done slowly became clear in my mind. In a way she'd sacrificed herself. It would have killed her just as it had killed Naze. But she'd saved me and the Spook. Saved our lives. And I would never forget it.

Stunned by what she'd said, I went into my room and closed the door. It took me a long time to get to sleep.

ONCE again I've written most of this from memory, just using my notebook when necessary.

Alice has been good and the Spook's really pleased with the work she's been doing. She writes very quickly, but her hand is still clear and neat. She's also doing as she promised, telling me the things that Bony Lizzie taught her so that I can write them all down.

Of course, although Alice doesn't know it yet, she won't be staying with us for that long. The Spook told me that she'll start to distract me too much and I won't be able to concentrate on my studies. He's not happy about having a girl with pointy shoes living in his house, especially one who's been so close to the dark.

It's late October now, and soon we'll be setting off for the Spook's winter house on Anglezarke Moor. Nearby there's a farm run by some people whom the Spook trusts. He thinks that they'll let Alice stay with them. Of course, he's made me promise not to tell Alice yet. Anyway, I'll be sad to see her go.

And of course I'll meet Meg, the lamia witch. Maybe I'll meet the Spook's other woman, too. Blackrod is close to the moor, and that's where Emily Burns is still supposed to live. I have a feeling that there are lots of other things in the Spook's past that I still don't know about.

I'd rather stay here in Chipenden, but he's the Spook and I'm only the apprentice. And I've come to realize that there's a very good reason for everything that he does.

THOMAS J. WARD